ALCHEMY
&
ASHES

ALSO BY AMY YORKE

The Wilderise Tales

The Good and the Green
The Bright and the Blue
The Ancient and the Amber
The Silent and the Silver

The Shadowbound Duet

Alchemy & Ashes

ALCHEMY & ASHES

THE SHADOWBOUND DUET
BOOK ONE

AMY YORKE

GLASSLOOK
PRESS

*For the people who have been waiting
in the shadows for a better world to arrive.*

It's time to step into the light and claim it.

Map of the Kingdom of
SELARA
during the reign of
GOD-KING RONAN III
Phoenix Cypress Grove
KALLA
LAKE MERVAL
PALADOR MOUNTAINS
RIVER MARA
SERAT
Irai Oasis
Lost Marshes
MINAR

ITHYRIA
(former borders)
PYKA
Avaris
Machair Wastes
Red
Cliffs
enval
FAROS
SERT
QUEEN'S
BAY
GREEN SEA
THE ENEZ
ISLANDS
PORT LIMIN
BLUE SEA

The City of
FAROS
during the reign of
God-King Ronan III
NORTH ROAD
Temple of Sai
Temple of Aynar
Temple of Vahlo
Calian Theatre
Alchemists' Guild
Nor Do
Great Library
RIVER MARA
Palace Market
Temple of Kevensa
Temple of Vayla
Arena
QUEE BA
VAYLANIAN PALACE
MINAR ROAD
SOUTH ROAD
Sou Doc

The Schools of
MAGIC & ALCHEMY
IN ORDER DESCENDING

LIGHT

FIRE

WIND

WATER

NATURE

EARTH

SHADOW

Translator's Note

This book has been adapted into narrative format from the personal diaries of individuals (*see* Reference Guide *for complete list*) who lived during the Second Age of Selara and translated into English from Old Selaran. For a direct translation of the diaries, refer to the excellent work of Selaran scholar Marielle Lopez, *Selaran Accounts from the Second Age*[1]. For a cleaner (but less authentic) treatment of these events, refer to *Selara during the Nithyrian Crisis: A History*[2] by Thomas Reynolds.

Old Selaran is a colorful language; the speakers of the time period had a particular fondness for the vulgar word *oiwej*, which has no direct translation into English. The words that have been chosen as substitutes are also considered vulgar in English, and there are many of them.

---

[1] Marielle Lopez, *Selaran Accounts from the Second Age*. 2nd ed. (Bravo Press, 2019).

[2] Thomas Reynolds, *Selara during the Nithyrian Crisis: A History*. (Decatur University, 2007).

This narrative edition, like the source material, covers topics that may be sensitive to some readers, including graphic violence, blood, murder, death, war, poisoning, kidnapping/abduction, torture, racism/xenophobia, explicit sexual content, and a mention of previous SA.

References to "earth" should not be interpreted as indicating that the events took place on our planet; similarities to modern Earth cultures have been included to enhance relatability.

Reference Guide

CHARACTERS

*House Verran of the Nithyrian Province
(formerly the Kingdom of Nithyria)*

SYLVARA *(sill-VAH-rah)*, prefers SYLVIE *(SILL-vee)*
LADY ADRIA *(AY-dree-ah)*, her sister and head of House Verran
SETH, her brother
DIANA (of House Sergia), her mother. Deceased.
LYSANDER, her father. Deceased.

Royal House Alta of Selara

GOD-KING RONAN III *(ROH-nan)*, head of House Alta
NONA, his aunt and heir of House Alta
GOD-KING AURELIAN IV, his father. Deceased.
QUEEN CALIA, his mother. Deceased.

House Horatio

LORD CYRUS *(SYE-rus)*, head of House Horatio and God-King Ronan's Grand Vizier
TYPHON *(TYE-fun)*, his oldest son and an emissary to Nithyria
QUINN, his youngest daughter

House Juni

QUEEN CLAUDIA, Dowager Queen and God-King Ronan's grandmother

House Faber

TITUS, heir of House Faber

The Alchemists' Guild

ZARA OF EKI, Guild Mistress
HERMES MAGNUS, Alchemist of House Verran

Enez Islands

LARUS ADAMA *(LAIR-us ah-DAH-mah)*, Guardian of House Verran
FELIX MARCH, Leader of the Third Navy

Orsa

TARAN ORINSEN *(TAIR-ahn OR-ihn-sehn)*, leader of God-King Ronan's Royal Guard

PLACES

THE KINGDOM OF SELARA *(sell-AH-rah)*
- Faros, the southeastern capital at the delta of the River Mara. Home of Houses Alta and Horatio
- Minar, a port city on the southern coast. Home of House Juni

THE PROVINCE OF NITHYRIA *(nye-THEE-ree-ah)*
- Kalla, a city in the Palador Mountains. Home of House Verran
- Pyka, a port city occupied by the Orsa
- Avaris, a ruined city of the Machair Plains

THE ENEZ *(EH-nehz)* ISLANDS

THE GODS

VAYLA *(VAY-lah)*, Goddess of the Sun, Light, and Life
VAHLO *(VAH-loh)*, God of the Moon, Shadow, and Death
ARNAN *(AR-nan)*, God of the Sea, the Harvest, and the Feast
KERENSA *(keh-REHN-sah)*, Goddess of Beauty, Love, and Voyages
SAI *(SYE)*, God of War, the Hunt, and the Forge

Chapter One

The knife at my throat needs sharpening.

Its jagged edge bites into my skin as a man closes in behind me. This is the desperate blade of a man who owns no better weapon. This is the blade of a man who has no better option.

This is the blade of a man who will kill me.

Footsteps crunch on dry dirt as other attackers approach my sister and our Guardian. They're arguing about what broke the carriage wheel. They don't hear them coming.

I don't cry out to warn them. I don't need to.

The man reeks of blood and sweat and death. This isn't his first ambush. This may not even be his first ambush today.

But it will be his last.

"Scream, and I'll kill you," he whispers, his voice as harsh as the desert that surrounds us. He kicks at the bend behind my knees, intending me to walk forward but nearly knocking me off my balance. My throat stings as the knife, dull though it may be, draws blood.

The man is forcing me into the shadow of our carriage, and I suppose I ought to be afraid of what he intends to do to me there. Nothing good happens in the shadows. Not for most people.

I, however, am not most people.

The second I leave the light, I draw on the power within me and deepen the shadow to the black of a moonless night. The sun is strong overhead in this blighted land, but it holds no power in the impenetrable darkness I've created.

The man lowers his knife in confusion.

I spin back towards the carriage, putting distance between us. I can see him clearly, even in the darkness. It's the gift of the shadow-born, those whose magic settled into the lowest elemental school. We're reviled by some and feared by most, all because we know what lurks in the dark while others can only wonder.

What lurks in the dark is always men, men like this one.

He's tall and bone thin, so thin that I can barely see his eyes in their deep hollows even with my gift. But it's the state of his arms that draws my attention. They're covered in twisted scars, jagged lines that reach to the knife in his hand.

I know those scars. This man is an ash-harvester. All of them end up with scars like this eventually.

This man is one of our people.

These lands were once ours as well. The Machair Wastes were once the Machair Plains, a flat and fertile land east of the mountains House Verran calls home. They were the pride of old Nithyria. I remember watching waves of wind travel through fields of grain from up on the hilltop of Avaris as a child, an ocean of gold.

Five years ago, those same fields ran red with blood. And then, just before the war was over, God-King Aurelian destroyed them. Stripped them and scoured them with magic, tainted them with poison. They say it will take one hundred years for the rain to wash it from the soil. But it won't matter even if it does. With the fields laid bare, the dunes of the great Serath Desert blew in on the wind, and the land was lost forever.

Even the vultures don't come here.

The road we're on was built on a dry riverbed. It's the shortest path through the Wastes, and the only one that's even remotely safe. It's patrolled in the north by our people and in the south by the Selarans, but with the Great Festival of the Gods on the horizon, God-King Ronan's patrols must have been too preoccupied to clear out the few people desperate or depraved enough to remain here.

My sister Adria will have some choice words about that, no doubt, once she finishes barbecuing our other attackers. Judging by the smell of smoke and burning flesh, they're already medium well.

Silently, I draw my sword. My blade is deadly sharp, of course, and nearly as long as I am tall. It's not a sword for the battlefield. It's the sword of a lady, a sword meant for dueling in the defense of honor.

It's more than my honor that I'm defending.

"Where are you, bitch?" the man spits at me. He's close, and I really ought to end this. It won't take much, just a quick thrust of my blade. There are several places on his body that would do. Larus made me drill on the dummies in the castle courtyard until my blisters had blisters. Heart. Kidney. Lung. And yes, throat. An especially good spot to strike an armored opponent.

This man wears no armor, and I'd be better served to thrust at his abdomen, but there's a kind of poetry in stabbing him in the throat after he scratched mine.

I should do it. Just lean forward a little and pierce an artery. He'll be dead in seconds.

He's literally right here. I'm so close, I barely need to lean.

Here's the thing though: I've never killed someone.

I've never even hurt someone, not on purpose. Not with a real weapon. The war was over before my magic settled, and so I spent an entire lifetime training for nothing. I've barely set foot beyond our lands. I've never fought a bandit or a highwayman or an Orsan raider.

I've never even gotten into a tavern brawl.

"Don't worry," Larus would say as he'd take the dull point of my training blade to the gut. "The killing blow will come to you. When you're on the battlefield, your survival instinct won't let you fail."

This was a battlefield once. I feel the moves I've practiced a thousand times in my muscles, feel the twitch of anticipation before the strike.

But my survival instinct seems to be somewhere else.

On the other side of the carriage, Adria cries out. For a moment, I worry, but I can hear frustration in the grunts that follow, not pain. She'll win, of course. She always does.

I'm just glad she isn't here to see me hesitate.

I'm going to stab him. I'm just going to do it before he turns behind the carriage and makes things tougher for Adria and Larus. I don't need to think about it anymore. His back is to me now, and he won't even see it coming.

I step forward, and the road falls out underneath me.

Earth magic, the second-lowest school. The man must have it. It must be how they managed the ambush. They waited until the other carriages in our caravan had crossed over the hill and then sent the ground up into our carriage's wheels.

It won't be long before the other carriages return for us. They're our escort, accompanying Adria, the head of House Verran, and me, the second in line for the title after our brother, on our trip to the capital. Our attackers are lucky that our brother Seth stayed behind in Kalla. Though a year younger than Adria, he's just as formidable as she is.

And about a million times more formidable than me. I'm about to fall on my own sword.

I cry out, fighting for my balance, and the blade-wielder spins towards my voice. He deftly navigates the crumbling sand and dirt beneath us as he makes his way to me.

I thrust my sword forward to counter my fall, and he blindly runs right into it.

Oh, *shit*.

The brutal steel cuts through him like butter. The handle reverberates in my hand as the blade passes through layer after layer of flesh and muscle.

It's exactly what needed to happen. What I should have done of my own accord.

And it makes me feel *sick*.

I need to focus. I'm not going to throw up. This is fine. It's just a training exercise, and this man is a particularly juicy dummy. He's not a person with feelings and hopes and dreams. He's not someone's child, someone's lover, someone's friend. His life isn't draining through the gaping wound I'm about to leave in his chest. I need to focus and withdraw the sword or risk it getting stuck.

It's harder to remove the blade than I thought it would be, but I manage it. He surprises me by grabbing at it, lunging around blindly in the dark as he chokes and gasps, the blood filling his punctured lung. I should probably stab him again. But he's getting further from me, pulled away by the sinking ground, and I have another problem to deal with: there's a screaming woman running around the carriage.

She crouches into the shadows, unaware of my presence. Her hair and tattered dress are smoldering from Adria's flames. "Please!" she shouts. "I surrender. I surrender!"

It could be a trick. She could be trying to ambush Adria and Larus when they come to find her.

I should kill her. Before she has the chance to kill them, I should kill her.

She's young, I realize as she turns towards me, sensing something off about the shadow. My same age: twenty-one, maybe a few years older at most.

What is she doing out here?

She's scared. I see it in the shake of her leg, the way she curls her shoulder away from my unnatural darkness. I see it in the prayer she whispers to Vayla. *Help me, lady of light. Protect me.* She's terrified, just like I am.

"Step forward," I tell her, the point of my blade inches from her back, hidden by shadow. I'm glad she can't see it shaking. "Hands up."

She jumps out of her skin at my voice, but she does as I command, stepping back into the light. "Please," she says again. "We were told to. They paid us. We had no choice. We hadn't eaten in a week."

"Who paid you?" I lift the shadows. The effort of the magic is weighing on me, draining me in the way only magic can do. And with the man on the ground dying—*he's dying. Oh, gods. I've killed him*—and this woman willing to talk, it's a waste of energy.

The woman's eyes flash with fear as she sees me and then terror as she sees the man on the ground. She backs away from my sword. "I don't know," she says. "I never saw them. I told Marcus it wasn't the right carriage. Too nice, I said. Please."

I shouldn't listen to her. She's probably lying, probably just trying to save herself. I should just take her out like Larus and Adria have taken out all the others.

Why can't I do this?

Gods, and they think I'm going to be an assassin. I can't kill a couple of nameless bandits in the Machair Wastes, let alone God-King Ronan III, ruler of Selara.

Thankfully, I'm just Plan B. Plan A has finished the barbecue and has moved on to the dessert: helping me.

The woman cowers against the carriage as my sister, a fiery blonde champion of death and destruction, arrives.

Adria doesn't panic. She doesn't even lose her footing on the churned-up patch of road. Adria is everything I am not, and I don't just mean the hair. (Mine is brown like our mother's was.) No matter how hard I train, I can never seem to put muscle on my small frame, but Adria is seemingly made of muscle alone. She's wearing the same leather armor that I am, but where it hangs awkwardly over my curves, it seems to fit her like a glove. Adria was trained by Larus just as I was, but no matter how many times I've practiced with my sword, my moves are clumsy and easy to read. Adria is the embodiment of Kerensa's grace and Sai's fury.

Adria doesn't hesitate. Adria doesn't second-guess herself. She approaches the gasping man, the man I stabbed. *A man named Marcus.* And she puts him out of his misery with a clean, powerful thrust of her sword to his neck.

I gag as I watch his blood pour out into the sand beyond the road, turning my head and hoping she doesn't notice.

I'm ashamed that I left him in that state. I should have finished him. What she did to him was a mercy.

Then she turns to face the woman who surrendered.

"Please," says the woman.

There's a glint in Adria's eyes. A flame appears at the end of the index finger of her sword hand. Tiny, precise, no larger than a candle's. Her fire isn't the wild wind of the forest fire, the fires that burn the trees to make the ash that harvesters like the dead man—*Marcus*—sweep up to give to Selara. No, her flame is like an arrow. I've seen it before, once. Not long after the war, when the Orsa thought they'd take what little we had left.

The black, smoldering holes between their dead eyes.

I shudder at the memory. I can't let her do this.

"She surrendered," I say as I lower my sword, trying to conceal my shaking hand. "She knows something about the ambush."

Adria pauses, frowning. Something unreadable flickers across her face. There's a chance here. She's curious. "Go on," she says.

The woman stammers now, far more frightened than when it was just the two of us. "It's—it's like I said. There was a man who paid us. Marcus met him."

"So you've never seen this man?" asks Adria.

"N-no," says the woman. "But I could find him, maybe. He said to take out the carriages. Said there would be food in it, and coin for us if we did it—"

"Kill her," says Adria.

"What? Me?" I expected Adria to ignore me. I expected my plea for the woman's life to fail. But I didn't think she'd make me do it.

"No, Sylvie. I was talking to her," she says, glaring at me. "I mean, I might as well have been. She could have killed you ten times over by now."

She could have, but she didn't. How could I kill her? This woman is our prisoner. It's one thing to kill the man who attacked me. I was defending myself, and Adria killing him was a mercy I was too weak to grant him. But this woman is innocent. She may have been involved in the attack, but she didn't hurt us. "She said she could find the man who hired them."

"We don't need her to know who sent them. It's Ronan, Sylvie. It's always Ronan."

The God-King of Selara. The man who invited us, the children of the failed rebellion, to the Great Festival. The man who killed our father.

The man we're going to kill.

"If you let her live, she's going to run right back to him. Kill her."

Adria is right. I know she's right. I knew it the moment I saw her.

If Ronan hired her, if he hired these people to kill us, we can't let them live. We can't take the chance that they'll come for us again. We can't take the chance that they'll come for our people.

"I'm sorry," I say.

She's young, like me. She's frightened, like me.

The woman cowers back as I lift my sword.

Chapter Two

Ten years earlier, I stood at the gates of Castle Pyka, watching as my family rode off for war.

My father, tall as a mountain on his destrier, his golden hair flowing behind him. My uncle, his general, younger and darker, but no less deadly. My brother and my sister, seventeen and eighteen, each the spitting image of my father, each as powerful with their fire magic, each as devastating with the blade. Our blue and green banners blowing in the cool sea air.

My mother had left weeks earlier. She was shadow-born like me and from a lower house, but my father loved her anyway. Her mission was different. Secret. There was no parade for her parting. No banners, no trumpets. She left without a word in the dead of night.

In the castle courtyard, only Larus remained with me. The Guardian of our house, a man with dark skin and long locks of coiled hair who would never be mistaken for our kin. And yet he was as loyal to our house as any of them. More loyal, even.

I cried silently, my tears burning hot tracks down my freckled cheeks. I didn't scream or yell or beg for them to come back. I knew at eleven that they wouldn't, no matter how much I wanted them to. I knew by then that there were things that mattered to them more than me.

Larus pulled me to him, wrapping his arm around my narrow shoulders. "You'll see them all again soon," he said. "You'll see."

Larus was the best person I knew. He ran my father's house, one of the Great Houses of Nithyria. He managed the castle and the port. He trained the children in the art of combat, in magic, in manners. He would have served as a general in his army if my father had let him. When my father asked him to stay behind to care for me, to care for his house and his legacy, he didn't complain.

I trusted Larus more than anyone in the world. When he told me I'd see my family again soon, I took him at his word. I dried my eyes and went back into the castle, practicing all day and night, preparing to join the fight as soon as my magic settled. As soon as I could, I would see them again. At home, if the war ended quickly, or on the battlefield if it didn't.

Larus said I would see them all again.

Larus was wrong.

"What are you waiting for?" asks Adria.

The woman is frozen against the carriage, her teeth chattering from fear despite the harsh desert heat. My sword is inches from her chest. She should be running, hiding, doing anything but just standing there.

This is a test. I know what Adria thinks of me. I know that she still sees me as her baby sister, the girl who stayed behind while she led my father's armies after he fell. She doesn't believe I can do it. Not just that I can't kill this woman. She believes I won't kill Ronan.

There's a part of me that wants to do what she asks simply because she's the one asking. A part of me that longs for her approval, that wants to show her that she's wrong about me.

But killing this woman isn't the same as killing Ronan. To kill Ronan is vengeance. It's the vengeance that I've dreamt of every night for the last six years. Every night since the night the letter arrived. The black mark on the page. My father's death, a stain on the paper and my memory.

This isn't vengeance.

This is murder.

Maybe this woman *was* hired by Ronan to kill us. Maybe he invited us to the festival just to lure us out onto this road, to take us out before we could do the same to him.

Or maybe, as she said, she didn't intend to hurt us at all. Maybe she was hired by a merchant to take out a rival. Maybe she was starving and did only what she had to do to survive.

I understand why Adria wants her dead. She sees everything as a battle and everyone who isn't us as an enemy. It's the safest choice. It's what has kept her alive.

But I'm not like her. We have only one enemy, and his name is Ronan.

I lower my weapon and turn to face Adria, to plead with her to spare this woman's life.

But before I can do so, there's a deep, guttural yell from behind the carriage, and the sound of a man slumping to the ground. Then Larus sheathes his blade.

"Is everyone alright?" he asks as he rounds the carriage. Larus has been the Guardian of House Verran since before I was born, but he barely looks different now than he did when I was a child. There's more white in his beard and eyebrows, and his locks are so long now they nearly reach his waist, but his skin is still smooth, and his eyes are still bright.

And he's every bit the fighter he always was. He's breathing heavily, and there's a burn mark on one of his leather pauldrons, but he looks otherwise unharmed.

He stops next to the cowering woman, glancing at my outstretched blade. "Who's this?"

"One of our attackers. My sister seems to think we should let her live." Adria's voice is mocking as she walks over to me and places a finger to the small cut on my throat. She doesn't cauterize it, thankfully. Gods, it hurts when she does that, although it does stop the bleeding quickly. Instead, she holds her bloodied finger in front of my face for emphasis. "She nearly thought herself to death, by the looks of it."

"Sylvie?" Larus gestures for me to approach him. "Are you hurt?"

I lower my sword, grateful for this distraction. The poor woman doesn't even move. I walk to Larus and lift my head, revealing what I imagine to be a nasty little cut, judging by its persistent sting.

"You'll need an elixir for that," he says.

"She surrendered, Larus," I say, gesturing to the woman. If I can get him on my side, maybe I can save her. "She said they were paid to attack someone. Maybe not us. She said it wasn't the right carriage."

He turns to Adria. "Probably one of Ronan's men that paid her."

"Agreed," says Adria.

The woman has sunk to the ground. She's crying softly. Defeated. She's helping my argument by looking so helpless.

"Larus, we can't just kill her after she surrendered. It isn't honorable."

This is the right thing to say, and I know it. Larus is nothing if not a man of honor, and though I doubt he'd show her the same mercy if we were at war, he knows that we aren't at war. Not yet. He wipes the sweat from his brow, looking between Adria and me.

"Fine. Let her go. She's clearly no threat to us. Let Vahlo decide if she deserves to live."

"Thank you," I say to him, ignoring Adria's scowl.

The woman, who has surely been listening to our every word, doesn't move.

"Go," I say to her, helping her up. She takes a few cautious steps away, looking over her shoulder as if she's worried we intend to shoot her in the back. Even Adria wouldn't do something that dishonorable.

I don't think she would, at least.

Then, with one last grateful look in my direction, the woman flees out into the wastes, vanishing behind the sand-covered rocks that must have concealed them when the attack began.

"Earth-born," says Larus once she's gone, glancing at the damage to the road. He spits at the ground. "Dull and dirty blades, all of them. Shameful with an earth-born among them." Many of the earth-born have a command of metal in addition to the rocks and dirt, but perhaps this one didn't. Though magic is divided into schools, and though those schools are largely determined by your personality when your magic settles near adulthood, there's a great deal of variation in specific abilities. Larus is earth-born himself, and he has an affinity for steel: crafting it, honing it, wielding it. "What did I tell you about keeping your blade sharp?"

"I know, I know. Blades sharp, wits sharper," I say.

"Although I can't say I'm truly upset. If they'd kept their blades sharper, you might not be here."

I swallow and look down. Larus, to his credit, doesn't push any further. He'll save the lecture for when we're alone.

By the time the other carriages arrive and we get underway again, it's nearly nightfall. For once, I'm grateful to be shadow-born as I watch the landscape shift from desert sands to the fertile river valley through the carriage window, something no one else can see in the dark.

They've all seen it before, anyway, though not since the war. No one from House Verran has returned to the capital since Adria's surrender except Typhon, the king's emissary who has reported our every breath to the Grand Vizier since the war ended. And I've never been. It wouldn't have been safe for me to go, even before the war. I was the future of House Verran. The backup plan, in case the others failed.

I guess some things never change.

When we arrive in Fenval, we've missed the ferry we'd planned to take down the River Mara, forcing us to stay a night at an inn. It's a rough place, far from the wealth and opulence of Faros. I doubt they've hosted one of the Great Houses in quite some time, maybe ever. But the host is gracious, the beer is strong, and I'm grateful for a night in a real bed after three days on the road.

It's late when we arrive, but it doesn't stop Adria from going hard at the bar. It's difficult to say whether she's more likely to find someone to fuck or to fight tonight. Knowing the fire-born, it'll probably be both. Either way, I don't want to be around for it, so I find a quiet spot in the shadows where I can see but not be seen.

Larus finds me there anyway. He knows me too well for me to hide from him.

I sigh as he takes the seat across from me.

"Sylvie," he says, his voice low. "What happened out there?"

Chapter Three

Neither Adria nor Larus saw what happened with the man who held the knife to my throat. It would be easy enough to lie to Larus, to tell him I'd stabbed the man on purpose and that I was going to finish the job before Adria arrived.

It would be better for me if I did lie to him. My power as a shadow-born is fueled by secrets and lies. The more I deceive others, the darker my shadows become. It doesn't matter much under ordinary circumstances, but in a fight against the fire-born or the light-born, light-born like God-King Ronan, it could be the difference between life and death.

There are shadow-born who go through the world lying to everyone they meet. But my mother wasn't like that. She kept her secrets, but she knew who to trust.

I'll lie to my sister if she asks me about it. But I won't lie to Larus.

"I'd forgotten how good the beer is here," he says as he takes a deep gulp from a clay mug. "I never got a taste for Nithyrian wine."

I can't help but snort at that. "Really?" I had seen Larus at the bottom of a bottle more than once.

"There's a difference between drinking something and liking it."

"I suppose," I say, though I don't really know what he means.

There's a long pause while Larus drinks his beer. He's waiting for me to say something, but I just stare at him in silence, thinking of the fight.

He took out three of the bandits while Adria dealt with their fire-born. They'd gone over the entire thing in painstaking detail on our way to the inn, with Adria constantly trying to bring up my ridiculous act of mercy and Larus stopping her short every time she tried. I appreciated that. Though he loved all of the Verran children, we all knew Larus had a soft spot for me.

I wish I had remembered any of the things he taught me when it mattered.

"I choked," I admit when Larus sets down his empty glass. "I got lucky. He ran into my sword." He opens his mouth to speak, but I cut him off. "I know what you're going to say."

He looks around the bar. Adria is chatting with a redheaded man somewhat amiably; she doesn't seem to be in any trouble, although that could change at any moment. He must decide that she can handle herself in any case because he stands and gestures for me to follow him.

"Let's take a walk."

I follow Larus through a back door onto a deck overlooking the river. It's a dark night with only a crescent moon to help him see, so I take the lead and guide us down the steps and along a path on the riverbank.

The river is wide and slow, its banks shrouded in reeds and rushes that reach my waist. This thin strip of land is the lifeblood of Selara. It's surrounded on both sides by hundreds of miles of desert, much of it as treacherous as the desert we crossed to reach Fenval. The land we're walking on now will flood just after the harvest in a couple of months. When the waters recede in the new year, they'll leave behind everything the plants need to grow. This is how Selara survives.

And it's how Nithyria survives too now. Almost all of our arable land was destroyed in the war, leaving us nearly completely reliant on Selara for food. They're only too happy to feed us in exchange for the most precious resource in the world: the ash of the phoenix cypress, a tree that only grows one place in the world.

The forests of Nithyria.

"Tell me what you thought I would say," says Larus finally as we pass into a copse of low-growing palms.

"I don't know. Something about how I should have fallen back on my training like you've told me a thousand times. That I got stuck in my head again, and that I can't count on every person I fight to kill themselves for me. That it was a good thing Adria was there to save me. But you'd also say that you know I don't really need saving, not if I'm at my best, and you know I won't let you down again."

"How diplomatic of me," says Larus. His face is solemn, but there's a hint of a smile in his voice. "Did the version of me in your head offer any sort of comfort?"

"A pat on the shoulder," I say.

"Like this?"

I laugh as Larus awkwardly pats my right shoulder three times in quick succession.

"And did it work? Do you feel comforted but also gently reminded of your duty?"

"I do," I say, but the words don't feel quite right. "I—"

The face of the dead man on the road flashes into my mind. *Marcus.* He had been one of our men once. One of the people we're trying to save.

There would be no saving him. He died there today.

I swallow a sob. "I know I'm just the backup plan, but how in the fuck am I supposed to…?"

I stop short of saying it. We can't discuss our plans to kill Ronan now that we've left Nithyria, but I know Larus gets my meaning.

My desire for vengeance runs bone deep, but after today, I'm worried if it's enough. What will happen if I choke when it really matters?

Larus hesitates a moment, stroking his beard and looking around. Then he sighs. "I told her just to tell you. But you know how she is."

That gets my attention. There *is* more to this than they'd told me. "Told Adria to tell me what?"

"If I tell you this, it stays between us. Let the secret strengthen you."

I nod, urging him to continue.

"You're not the backup plan," he says. "Adria knew you would assume you were, and she wanted you to do so. You're used to living in her shadow. You're comfortable there. But you aren't the backup in case Adria fails. You *are* the plan."

I'm sorry, *what*?

Is Larus going senile? Did he somehow miss what happened today or the conversation we had not even five minutes ago about how big of a fuck-up I am?

"Think about it, Sylvie. Did you think one of you would face him in single combat? Did you think you were going there to challenge him to a duel or to fight him on the battlefield? Did you forget who he is and what he can do?"

Ronan, like most of House Alta, is light-born. The light-born are the top in the alchemical chain of magic and the rarest of all magic wielders. According to the Codex, our most sacred text, they wield the sun goddess Vayla's powers as their own.

The full knowledge of what they're capable of is a secret. But Ronan has a power that's unique even for the light-born, and that one everyone knows about: he can read people. Not their thoughts, but their feelings. He can sense what anyone feels when they're near him.

He can even sense when someone has murderous intent. It has saved him from assassins before. It will save him from us if we aren't careful.

We need to keep Ronan from finding out our plans until Seth can raise our armies and Larus can prepare one of the navies of the Enez Islands to lay siege to Faros, using the cover of the Great Festival to hide their movements.

But until now, I'd imagined that when the time was right, Adria would strike. Then I'd use my magic to hide us and get us out of there. And if something happened to Adria, a dagger in the dark would work as well as her dart of flame.

I would be the backup plan. Like always.

"I know we can't attack him outright, at least not in the beginning. But I don't get how I'm meant to be the plan."

"It could be months before we're ready to strike. It could take the entire festival and maybe even sometime after it. We need to maintain access to him. From what we've learned of him, he allows few into his confidence. What do you think the chances are that Adria can stay on his good side for longer than a day?"

I smirk. Adria is many things, but I've known her to toss out friends more often than she changes her toothbrush. If she manages to get through a single conversation without losing her head and giving everything away, it will be a miracle. "Slim to none."

Alright, sure, I'm less likely to immediately piss Ronan off, but then what? "The plan is for me to befriend him?"

Larus grimaces in the way that he does when he's about to have to talk to me about something uncomfortable. "Befriending would be good. But Adria thinks—and, well, I agree with her—there's a chance he'll see you as more than a friend."

Are they fucking serious?

I clench my fist. Ronan? They want me to *seduce* the one man in the world that I truly hate? My one and only enemy?

I drop my voice low. My eyebrow twitches with barely contained rage. "He killed my father, Larus. His father killed my mother. Even if I'm faking it, just *befriending* him would feel like a betrayal. Anything more would be treason against my own heart. If the plan hinges on me seducing him, you might as well send me home right now. Because I am telling you that it's never, ever going to happen. I'll cut his throat before I'll share his bed."

Larus pulls back to look at me. Then he gets that know-it-all grin on his face that he gets when he's taught me a lesson, but I haven't realized it yet. "See? You do have what it takes."

I'm still practically vibrating with anger when what I've said hits me.

Well, fuck.

I don't know how he did it, but he somehow managed to convince me I *can* kill Ronan. And not just that I can, but that I must.

"You won't fail," he says. "Don't forget who he is. Don't forget what he did to your family. To all of us. And all for a bit of ash." He spits at the ground.

All for a bit of ash. It was true. The phoenix cypress ash was the key to everything.

When Selaran alchemists started buying barrels of the ash, my grandparents hadn't known what to make of it. Our own alchemists used the bark of the phoenix tree to help with a headache, but among our people, the ash had no known alchemical properties.

It was years before they learned the truth: the ash is the critical ingredient for one of the most elusive alchemical processes.

It can turn lead into gold.

It requires more than just the ash, of course, and the entire process is a closely guarded Guild secret. But access to the ash became Selara's highest priority.

And eventually, it became the catalyst for a war that was long overdue. The Selaran crown, then wielded by King Ronan's father Aurelian IV, had long been taking more from Nithyria than it provided. When my grandmother died and my father became the Head of House Verran, Aurelian demanded so much ash that our people could no longer tend their own fields. The fire-born were forced to start massive blazes in the mountains; the water- and wind-born were forced to keep the flames from spreading; and the nature- and earth-born were forced to haul the ash down from the mountains all the way into Selara. Only the shadow-born were left to work the fields, and soon our people were starving.

The Orsa, a savage people who'd raided our lands for generations, took advantage of our weakness and plundered our half-abandoned farms and villages, killing thousands. My father traveled to court a dozen times, begging the king to show mercy. But the king refused. If our people could not deliver what he asked for, he could just get the Orsa to do so instead. In return, he'd give them our lands.

For a fire-born, my father had been exceptionally patient, but there was only one reasonable response to that insult: war. Five years later, when both my parents and King Aurelian were dead, Adria surrendered to the newly crowned King Ronan, and everything King Aurelian promised had come to pass.

We were forced from our ancestral home, Pyka, and the Orsa were gifted it by the crown as thanks for their support in the war. The Machair Plains were lost, and with them, our only ability to feed our people. King Ronan promised to keep us fed as long as we kept the ash flowing into Selara, and for a time, he kept his word.

But shipments started arriving late. And when they finally did arrive, they were often spoiled. The flood was weak, they said. There were problems with pests from Brakkar. But the people of Selara weren't asked to go without. They imported food with the gold they made by razing our forests while they let us go hungry. And every year, they demanded more and more from us.

And that's why Ronan has to die. It isn't just vengeance for our parents. It's for the lives of our people. It's for the lives of all of the people of Selara and Nithyria. Our two kingdoms will remain united, only this time under our rule.

Our spies report division in the capital. Many people are unhappy, not just with the failed harvest but with a number of changes Ronan has made. If Ronan himself were to fall, they say, all the pieces would fall with him.

And apparently, I'm going to be the one to bring him down.

"I won't fail. When it's time, I won't hesitate. I know who he is. I know what he's done.

"And I know he'll pay for it with his life."

Chapter Four

In the morning, we board the ferry down the River Mara to the capital. It's cool outside this long before dawn. Adria and the others have gone below, but I don't want to miss anything, so I stand alone near the bow, taking it all in.

The landscape shifts from marsh to rocky canyon and back again as the Mara meanders on. The river is slow, but our boat makes great time with a wind-born at the sails. We'll be in Faros this very afternoon.

Shortly after the sun rises, I'm joined on the deck by Typhon. As he exits the stairs into the morning air, he breathes in a deep, languorous breath and then sighs an exhale of utter contentment. His Selaran silks billow in the breeze, the thin white of the fabric spreading out behind him like a cape.

It's surprising to see him so at peace. The Typhon I've come to know is an anxious mess, always wringing his hands and pacing back and forth, rubbing his bald head as if the hair might return if he does it hard enough. We've resented his presence ever since he arrived at the end of the war, knowing that he reports our every move to his father, Lord Cyrus, King Ronan's Grand Vizier. I had never stopped to consider that he was as unhappy in his post as we were having him there.

"You'll be able to see the Dalven temple of Kerensa soon," he says as he joins me, pointing to where the ribbon of the Mara disappears into the horizon. "The temple in Faros is larger, but I think Dalven's is the most beautiful."

"Kerensa does admire beauty," I say. It's a dumb response. Of course the Goddess of Beauty admires beauty. *Gods.* But I don't know what else to say, having never been to any temple other than those in Pyka, our old home, and Kalla, our new one.

Typhon is in too good of a mood to care about anything I say anyway. He's happy to have someone to talk to about the sights of his homeland, and for once, I'm happy to listen. I've read about many of the places he points out: the ruins of the Hellenian Palace, lost in an invasion more than two hundred years earlier and never rebuilt; the Gardens of Luminaris, where rare alchemical ingredients are grown by an order of water-born; the Mausoleum of God-Queen Julia, the monarch who reunited Selara and Nithyria after our first civil war. But to see them with my own eyes, to watch the world come alive as it wakes, a world so alike and yet so different from mine, it's fascinating.

It's midday by the time Faros comes into view. From a distance, the city rises in the river's haze like a giant sandcastle sculpted by ancient hands. Warm mudbrick and sandstone structures give the illusion of neat little stairs and whimsical turrets as the city tumbles down from the palace, which rises high on a cliff overlooking the sea. The others have gathered on deck now, but no one else is listening to Typhon as he describes the neighborhoods and quarters of the city.

I take in every word.

"That's the Ivory Spire, home of the Great Library of Faros. It's home to every book in every language in the entire world. I'm telling you, every single book. Oh, and over there, the Palace District. On market days, you can find a trader from every country in the world. There are a dozen markets all over the city, but the best is right there, just steps from the palace. If you go—and you *must*—try to find a man with a red canopy. He sells the most delicious pastry you've ever had in your life. It's layered with walnuts and pistachios and soaked in honey. Heavenly."

"Is that the Alchemists' Guild?" I ask, pointing to a pair of white towers that frame a building with a golden dome.

"Yes," says Typhon, looking uneasy. "A lot goes on there. Very secret, as you know."

Oh, believe me, I know. We all know.

"May I borrow Sylvie for a moment?" asks Larus. He's been watching us from across the deck, but I suspect he joins us now so I don't speak my mind about the Guild, getting us all in trouble before we've even arrived.

Larus, who yesterday wore his usual mixture of loose Enezian clothing and brown leather Nithyrian armor, has opted for a full Nithyrian look for today's introduction to the palace. He's also tamed his locks into a thick ponytail at the base of his neck, a style sometimes worn by nobility.

He looks me up and down: I'm wearing the same armor as yesterday, with the same style tunic underneath, only in blue rather than green. He shakes his head.

"Maybe something a bit softer," he says. "What you wear sends a message. They expect to see a fighter in Adria. Perhaps you'd rather send a *different* message."

I would love to get rid of this ill-fitting leather, if only because of the heat it traps to my skin. I'm dying under the southern sun. But I don't have many better options. With our people going hungry, we haven't had the luxury of having fine clothes made for us. All I've packed are the utilitarian garments sewn by my chambermaids and a few of my mother's dresses they altered to fit me. They're at least twenty years out of fashion.

"I think the only message I can send with what I brought is, 'I need new clothes.'"

Larus laughs and turns to a servant. He takes from him a package wrapped with a white ribbon and hands it to me.

"For me? When did you have time to buy something?"

"I ordered it weeks ago. I was worried I wouldn't be able to get it when we arrived so late last night, but as Arnan's luck would have it, the merchant was having a drink at the bar."

I untie the ribbon, and the fabric releases, nearly slipping from my hands.

Silk. Fine Selaran silk dyed a soft, forest green. A gold cord falls to the ground. The belt, I'm guessing. It's a beautiful garment. And it can't have been cheap.

"Larus, this is too much," I say, but he holds up a hand to stop me.

"What you wear sends a message," he repeats, a lesson in his words as usual.

I think for a moment and then realize his meaning. Selaran silk in a Nithyrian color. The dress is the bridge between Selara and Nithyria, and that's the part I'm meant to play. I should save it for when we meet the king—he's due to arrive tomorrow—but I can't bear to wear my miserable leather trousers for a moment longer when this dress exists and it's mine. I have to at least try it on.

I hurry below deck and find a dark corner that I darken even further to give myself privacy while I change. I'm not sure how to tie the cord, so I settle for the most obvious answer: directly around the waist. Then I wander through the stowed belongings until I find a looking glass.

Good gods. The dress drapes beautifully over my curves, hugging my hips and just grazing the ground beneath my feet. My heavy boots look a little silly peeking out from under it, but I'm certain I can find something better before I meet the king. The soft green looks lovely with my dark hair, which I release from its bun and allow to fall in gentle waves onto my shoulders. I find a gold necklace in one of my chests, a gift from my mother just before the war. It sits between my breasts, drawing attention to them.

I will not be seducing the king. But there's no harm in letting him admire me.

It'll make it all the easier when it's time to stab him in the kidney.

I step back onto the deck, and heads slowly turn as I walk by. Typhon, of all people, is the first to compliment me. "Kerensa's grace smiles on you," he says. His gaze is admiring, appraising without leering, and I feel guilty for having misjudged him all this time. "But let me help you with this."

He gestures to the belt, and I nod, giving him permission to tie it a bit lower so it hugs my hips. "That's the style, or at least it was last year."

I thank him for his help as Larus leaves his conversation with the captain to join us once more.

He stands back and takes me in, then gives his nod of approval. "Different shoes, but it'll do nicely, I think."

"Exquisite taste as always, Larus," says Typhon. They continue to chatter their approval, but I notice Adria smirking at me from across the deck.

"Excuse me," I say and head to her.

On a different day, I might have shrunk from Adria's mockery, but today, I'm in the mood to fight. It's funny, but somehow taking off my armor has given me more courage than wearing it ever did.

"Something funny?" I ask.

"They'll laugh you out of the court in those shoes." To my surprise, she pushes off the railing and starts heading to the stairs. I guess I won't be getting that fight today after all. She doesn't gesture or look back; she just assumes I'll follow her.

And she's right. I find her below the deck, flinging garments from her own chest with reckless abandon. From somewhere near the bottom, she retrieves a pair of sandals. They're made of some kind of reed or jute with long strips of leather that must wind around the ankle somehow.

"Why do you have those?" I ask as she hands them to me. I sit on the ground and remove my boots, but I'm not sure what to do with the leather straps, so I leave them off.

Adria bends to help me. She crosses the leather straps in a pattern I know I won't be able to replicate and ties them behind my calves. "From my last trip to the capital. They stripped me of my weapons and my armor and made me dress up just like this. To show my loyalty to Selara." Her voice shakes with the same barely contained rage I felt just last night.

Adria has never talked to me before about her surrender to Ronan. Seth had taken command of Father's closest forces after Father had lost his duel with the new king, and he quickly surrendered according to their arrangement. But Adria had been hundreds of miles away fighting in the southern desert near Minar. When news had arrived of Father's defeat, she refused to lay down her arms.

I've often wondered why she changed her mind. I'd imagined she'd die before admitting defeat. She was like Father in that way. But she had signed the treaty and given up our lands without so much as an insult, according to Typhon.

I know better than to ask her. I pull myself up and walk to the looking glass. The sandals are a bit too big for me, but I manage to walk in them okay, and I must admit they are a much better fit for the gown.

Adria joins me. I haven't stood with her like this in a long time. I was wrong about our lack of resemblance. While our figures remain as different as ever, you can see the likeness in our faces more with each passing year: not just the eyes, but the same freckles on our noses and cheeks, the same pout of our lower lips. She nods at my reflection, approving, and then she turns me to her.

"This is a costume you're wearing. It's a role that you'll play, that you have to play so we can do what we need to do." I wonder if she said something like this to herself when she entered the throne room. "They can't take who you are from you. No matter what you have to say, no matter what you have to pretend to think or feel, they can't change your heart. Only you can do that."

She stands back from me. I find myself wishing I had Ronan's power to know what she was feeling. She's my sister, but I've seldom felt love or warmth from her. Anger, resentment, disappointment— I've felt those plenty. But what does she know of my heart? How could she know my heart when I don't know hers at all?

Still, the part of me that longs for her approval is ever-present at the back of my mind. I fear her, I envy her, but most of all, I want to make her proud.

"I won't forget," I promise her.

"Put your armor back on," she says, turning back to the stairs. "Leave the silly things for when they'll matter."

I sigh, but I know she's right. My armor hasn't dried much in the dark, humid body of the ferry, but I wiggle back into it anyway. We'll be at the palace soon, and who knows what dangers lurk there in the darkness?

We arrive in the early afternoon, a portcullis rising to allow the ferry into the royal moat. The river meanders into a cavern of ancient stone, reflections of light dancing off the water and up the rough-hewn walls.

The dock is bustling by the time we arrive. All of Selara's nobility will be arriving this week. I'm including us in that list; we're considered part of Selara again, and I need to make sure I remember that now that we're in the capital. We'll all be staying in the palace for three months at least, though a Great Festival can go far longer if the king decrees it.

It's been at least ten years since the last Great Festival, since before the war began. It's said that if you go too long without a festival, the gods will smite you and the people will revolt. Ronan has been pushing his luck waiting this long, so everyone is expecting this to be the longest and grandest festival ever.

I don't know any of the arriving nobility, but Adria recognizes members of House Juni, one of the closest allies of the royal house. They politely nod to us from across the dock and exchange pleasantries about our journey and the beautiful summer weather, but their cold looks betray that they'd rather be talking to anyone else.

A man wearing a long, white garment just like Typhon's approaches us. He's tall and imperious, with silver hair and a silver mustache that curls at the ends, and from the way that he surveys our group as if we're nothing more than a bug under his shoe, I know who he must be: Lord Cyrus, Ronan's Grand Vizier and Typhon's father.

Typhon breaks away from us and approaches him, but rather than a hug or other familiar greeting, he simply bends at the waist and kisses a ring on his father's hand.

"I'll expect a full report after dinner," Cyrus says quietly to his son. It's fairly dark in the cavern, so I'm almost certain I'm the only one who can see Typhon's cheeks turn scarlet.

"Welcome to the Vaylanian Palace. His Majesty God-King Ronan has requested that I personally greet you and show you to your chambers." Lord Cyrus's voice is unpleasantly nasal and full of condescension; it's clear he didn't personally agree with Ronan's request, but what choice did he have when it came from the God-King himself?

"Please follow me and be careful of your step. We wouldn't want you slipping and dashing your heads upon the cavern floor."

I shoot a look at Larus. What an oddly specific warning. Larus shrugs his shoulders in response.

There's nothing for us to do but follow Grand Vizier Cyrus, resident psychopath. He leads us through a torch-lit hallway and up a flight of stairs. "The baths are there," he says, waving a thin finger in the direction of a passage.

"It's almost as if his heart isn't in it," mutters Larus.

I smirk. "There's the kitchen. And here's where we'll hang you if you misbehave," I whisper back.

"Is there a question?" asks Cyrus.

The heat rises in my face in response. I hope he didn't hear any of that.

I make a note to be more careful, especially once the king arrives tomorrow. "Are the baths separated by gender?" I ask, giving Cyrus the question he asked for.

Larus gives me a look that could kill, but gods, if I'm going to be stuck in this miserable place with these miserable people for months, I've got to find a way to have a little fun.

"No," says Cyrus. "All bathe together, except for the God-King, of course."

Well, well, well. There's a little fun, at least. It's been a minute since I've shared anyone's bed. If I get desperate enough, maybe I can find a fire-born to fuck me and then fuck me over like they always do.

We leave the carved stairway for a much larger hallway that appears to be made of the same reddish stone, but in blocks rather than natural formations. It's similar in style and structure to our castles back home; only the materials are different.

That and the nearly endless amount of gold.

It's as if we left the cave and entered a pirate's treasure hoard. Anything that could be gold *is* gold. Torch holders and hinges, the handles on the furniture, frames that hold the portraits, pots holding plants. It's…a lot.

I mean, I get it. I guess if I'd discovered the secrets of one of alchemy's greatest mysteries, I'd put that shit everywhere too.

And I guess there's a chance that it's just brass, and they just want us to *think* that it's gold—

"Everything you see is real gold or at least plated with it. All made just down the road at the Alchemists' Guild," says Cyrus.

Made with the ash they've starved our people for. The price of this gold was Nithyria, and we paid it in blood.

I want to knock this stupid gold pot right off the table onto the floor. Someone in our villages was maimed so that this dumb little plant could sit here where no one ever even looks at it.

But making a scene isn't going to do us much good if we're trying to stay in the king's good graces, so I put my hand in the pocket of my trousers to resist the temptation.

"Ah. Speaking of the alchemists, it's the Guild Mistress herself."

A petite figure treads down the hallway towards us, flanked on both sides by much larger men. All three wear the brown hooded robes and golden medallions of the Alchemists' Guild.

It's the same robe our own alchemist Hermes is wearing, though it barely covers his tall, bulky frame. I hate the man on principle more than due to any actual slight. In truth, he serves our house well in his duties, primarily brewing elixirs and overseeing the healers. But the Guild is loyal to the crown, and the way Hermes in particular fawns over Ronan makes me sick.

It turns out he has a talent for fawning. He bows low to the Guild Mistress, kissing a golden ring on her right hand as she lowers her hood.

"She's so *young,*" I say to Larus. The Guild Mistress looks like she ought to be an apprentice at best, not the head of the entire order. Her features are still soft and rounded, with large brown eyes and golden tan skin pocked with pimples.

"May I present the Guild Mistress of the Alchemists' Guild, Zara of Eki," says Hermes.

Eki. I can't remember where that is exactly, but it's a long way from here. It's somewhere on Velmora, another continent entirely. I wonder how she came to be here and how she came to be the head of the guild while being only…twenty maybe? She can't be older than me.

"Mistress Zara is one of the only light-born living in Selara," says Cyrus, which explains it. "She was gifted by Vayla herself."

"How wonderful," says Larus. "We're honored to meet you."

I'm glad he's here to remind us of our manners, because Adria and I were just staring dumbfounded.

Another light-born at the head of the Alchemists' Guild. Can she feel our feelings as well?

We've never had a particular reverence for the light-born in our family. Our parents didn't give much credence to the ranking of the schools in the Codex, given what the royal House Alta, all light-born, had done to us. Mother believed that the rankings were just the opinions of the person who'd written them down into the Codex, and that they didn't determine our destiny. It was one of her most radical views, pure heresy. Definitely not the kind of thing you mentioned in a temple, or with someone around from the Alchemists' Guild, given their close connection to the church.

Zara smiles warmly at me, if a bit shyly, and suddenly the air between us feels softer, gentler, almost as if sunlight has spilled quietly into the space without brightening a single shadow.

It's…pleasant. Alarmingly so.

"I'm sure you must be very busy," says Cyrus. He doesn't seem to be affected by her presence; if anything, he seems annoyed by her, but maybe this is how he is with everyone.

"As always," she says. "It was nice to meet you all."

"She liked you," whispers Larus after she disappears down another passage. "Did you see her smile? She's probably lonely, surrounded by a bunch of old folks. She could be worth getting to know."

I nod and almost run into Typhon, who has stopped in front of me. I turn to where he's looking and see someone running down yet *another* staircase: a servant, judging by his uniform robes of red linen. He makes a beeline for Cyrus and begins whispering frantically in his ear.

"You're certain? Right now?"

The servant nods and takes off through a door.

Cyrus is flustered, but he quickly regains his composure before he speaks. "It appears that there's been a change of plans. The God-King has returned a day early. Follow me to the throne room; he'd like to greet you himself."

I look at Larus and then Adria, and I see my own panic reflected in their eyes as well.

Oh, fuck.

Here we go.

Chapter Five

The walk to the throne room feels like walking to the gallows. We can't speak to each other, but I know Larus and Adria must be thinking the same thing.

We thought we'd have another day to prepare. Before we left, we discussed a few strategies to keep Ronan from knowing our plans. He's going to expect our anger and even some level of murderous desire. But how much anger would be too much? How many thoughts of the ways I'd like to see him die would be too many?

And how far away can he sense our feelings? Can he sense them even now? He's somewhere in the palace, somewhere in this labyrinth of corridors and stairwells. Had he sensed us when we arrived? What had I thought about since we got here? What had I felt?

Gods, what am I doing? I'm going to drive myself insane with worry, and I haven't even seen the man yet. My head feels strangely light, the way it feels when I haven't eaten in hours. I've got to find a way to calm down before I spend my first time meeting the king passed out on the floor.

"Breathe," says Larus softly so that only I can hear him. "Remember your training."

My training? I've trained in swinging swords, darkening shadows, parrying with a dagger, shooting a bow. I've also trained in formal dancing, the correct silverware to use at dinner, how to play the flute passably well, and how to pray to the gods…How is any of that going to help me when the man I'm going to kill can sense my every feeling? "Oh no, I wasn't thinking of murdering you, your majesty. I was thinking about which fork to use with the salad."

Fucked. I'm *fucked.*

We turn a corner and are faced with a pair of wooden doors taller and wider than the ferry's portcullis, their surfaces etched with gilded swirls. I pause, imagining the impossible weight of them and wondering how in the world they manage to get them open, when two guards stretch out their hands, and the doors shudder, swinging forth into the room. Nature magic, maybe, because of the wood, or earth, if they're somehow using the hinges for leverage. Or air, even, though I felt no gust of wind.

The sight inside is even more spectacular. Ronan's throne room is larger than even our greatest temple. It's a cavernous space with golden candlelit chandeliers hanging high in the rafters, giant columns of pinkish stone, and rows of wooden benches lining the aisles, all pointing to an enormous chair at the very back.

The throne itself is wooden as well, and it appears unremarkable other than its size. From what I remember, it's the original throne built for the original Selaran ruler Queen Elissa from when the lands were first settled, long before the divide that had torn Nithyria into its own kingdom.

I'm surprised to see that Ronan hasn't made himself a new one out of gold yet.

As we're led down the aisle to the throne, it becomes clear that Ronan isn't in it. I glance at Adria, but she simply shakes her head and looks forward.

"God-King Ronan prefers to receive guests in his antechamber," Cyrus explains, his voice dripping with displeasure. "He likes to see his people eye to eye."

His people. We are not his people. We will never be—

No. I stop myself. This is exactly the kind of thing I can't think of.

Gods, it's hard to *not* think of something. As soon as you know you're not supposed to be thinking of it, it's the only thing you can think of at all.

Cyrus leads us to the left of the throne and into a room at the back. It's as different from the throne room as it could possibly be. It's small and quite nicely furnished, with fine rugs in a rich red and tables and chairs carved from a dark red wood.

The wood of the phoenix tree, I realize. Our wood. The wood they burn for their gold.

Is this some kind of power play? To parade us in here and re-mind us of what they took from us? To remind us that they'll always have the power to take it?

I bite the inside of my mouth to stop that line of thinking too.

A door opens at the back, and in he walks.

No trumpets. No fanfare. Only a pair of guards in chainmail and a retinue behind him.

This is the God-King of Selara. The man who killed my father. The man who took our lands from us. Who humiliated my sister. Who starved our people. The man we've traveled hundreds of miles to kil—meet. To meet, and to attend his festival, and nothing else. That's all we're here for.

I hope he felt that.

He's just…a man.

I don't know what I expected. I guess in my mind, I'd built him up to be a monster. I've been hearing about him since I was a child. For the last few years of the war, I'd heard about his every move in the coded letters my family sent Larus. I imagined someone larger than life, someone enormous and hideous and revolting, someone with the soul of a beast and the face of one of Vahlo's demons.

But he's just an ordinary man. Well, not ordinary exactly. He's certainly taller than everyone in the room. That's all I really have time to determine before I see everyone around me bowing, and I bend to do the same.

When I look back up, he's looking directly into my eyes.

The intensity of his gaze sends a jolt of panic through me. What does he sense? What does he know?

Keep it together, Sylvie. Find something else to focus on.

A bead of sweat slides down my neck. It will look suspicious if I look away from him when he's staring at me so intently, so I look back and study his face.

It's…well, it's perfect. There's really no other way to put it. It's almost too perfect. Uncannily perfect, artificial almost. Every proportion is perfect—the spacing of his brown eyes, the length and angle of his nose, the fullness of his lips. The set of his smooth jaw, the size of his ears.

Even the hair on his crownless head is perfect. It's a dark, rich brown with a few sun-kissed streaks of gold, and it has a gentle wave that falls in just the right way onto his forehead to accentuate his perfectly groomed brows.

I can't see much of his figure under his black robes, but I'm willing to bet it's perfect as well.

I can see why someone might find him handsome. Someone, not me. I like faces with a bit more character, with a bit of history in them. A nose broken defending someone's honor. A scar from the time oil jumped out of the pan.

This man looks like he hasn't suffered a day in his life.

A smile flashes across his lips; there and gone in an instant.

Can he feel my disdain?

"Presenting, by the Grace of the Gods, Ronan III; Most High, Most Mighty, and Most Exalted God-King of Selara; Lord of Nithyria and Protector of the Realm. Please stand in line and wait to greet your king."

Of course Cyrus threw that bit in there about Nithyria. It takes every ounce of control that I have not to roll my eyes.

Our small party is made up of the only members of our house worthy of introduction to royalty: our alchemist Hermes, our Guardian Larus, me, and finally Adria. Typhon ignores his father's command and goes to a corner of the small room to greet a short-haired woman in a silk shirt and trousers who entered with Ronan. I guess he's met the king many times before.

I want to ask Larus who Typhon is talking to, but everyone is silent as they wait for the king to approach.

He starts with Hermes. Hermes bows low to the king and is careful not to meet his eye.

Was I not supposed to look at him? I'm pretty sure Larus mentioned that.

Shit.

"Welcome back, Warden Magnus." I wonder if Ronan truly remembers Hermes, who hasn't spent much time in the capital since the war began, or if he's just pretending to do so to seem charming.

Unfortunately, it seems to work on Hermes, who chuckles as he thanks the king for his generosity. This is part of the reason we kept him out of the plan: he's something of a sycophant, and the alchemists on the whole have always been loyal to the crown over their assigned houses.

Next up is Larus. Larus gives a respectful bow, if not as fawning of a bow as Hermes, and meets the king's eye with a face of perfect passivity.

Okay, eye contact must be allowed.

"Guardian Larus Adama," says Ronan. Ronan has a couple of inches on Larus, but he tilts his head forward a bit to diminish the difference. "I heard tales of the elegance of your swordsmanship from my father. I hope you'll do us the honor of entering into the tournament."

Larus laughs at the suggestion, but unlike Hermes, his smile doesn't reach his eyes. "I leave the fighting to the young these days, but I'm sure our girls will do us proud."

"I'm counting on it," says Ronan.

Then he turns to me.

His eyes lock with mine before he even steps closer to face me. His stare is unnerving in its intensity. My instinct is to look away. To sink back into the shadows, to let his light shine on someone else.

But I remember what Larus told me. I can't think of his words, not when I'm close enough to the king to reach out and touch him. Not when I'm certain he can feel everything I'm feeling. But I remember how they made me feel. Defiant. Angry.

Powerful.

I straighten my back, pulling myself up as tall as I can. I'm wearing my armor, not the dress we'd hoped would make a good impression, but maybe it's for the best. Let him see our strength before I try to beguile him.

Then I bow, but I don't break eye contact.

He hesitates for a long moment before speaking to me, his face unreadable. "Sylvara of House Verran," he says, his voice soft. Intimate. As if I'm the only person in the room.

"Sylvie," I say, maybe a little too loudly.

I can see his game. He's sensed my desire to avoid the spotlight, and he's trying to win me over by making me comfortable.

Maybe I should let him believe he has. Maybe I should smile and act like I'm swooning.

I do admit that I feel the same sort of warmth and comfort in his presence as I felt in Zara's. It must be a gift of the light-born, then. And it's an unfair one at that. How easy life must be when everyone likes you simply because they feel good when they're near you.

And I will also admit that his beauty, far too perfect though it may be, is an unfair advantage as well. It's distracting up close. I wonder how long he's spent making his hair fall that way; how many elixirs does he use to make his skin so smooth and soft-looking? Does he have an entire team of servants dedicated to trimming his eyebrows?

I wouldn't be surprised.

Maybe it's a trick of the light in the room, but it looks like his skin is actually *glowing* a little. It's subtle, but with it, I can see the outlines of his arms through his royal robes, the sheer black fabric catching on ample muscle—of course. Of course his body is perfect. How else could it be?

He's standing quite close, closer than I'd expected him to come. I hadn't expected him to come off his throne, to be honest, let alone to meet with him eye to eye on our first day in the palace. He's right here in front of me, only a few feet away, close enough to kil—

Fuck.

Think of something, anything, else.

My mind jumps frantically from the word I want to think, the word I'm desperately trying not to think, and lands somewhere else entirely.

Close enough to…close enough to…close enough to…kiss.

His eyes flash with recognition, and heat rises up the back of my neck. *This is mortifying.* I'm about to pray to any god that will listen to keep my cheeks from turning red.

He smiles with his eyes wide open, no doubt picking up on whatever the fuck is going on with my feelings. "Sylvie. Welcome to the capital. I've heard it's your first visit. I hope you find it to be every-thing you imagined and more."

Then he winks at me before turning to Adria.

He fucking winks. *Gods, save me.*

I'm reeling, my thoughts flying in a panic. I feel sick. I have to get out of here. I can't believe I let my mind think even for a *second* about kissing him, even to save my own life. I don't want to be an-ywhere near him. This is a huge mistake. There's no way I can do this. There's no way I can conceal my feelings. I'm going to doom us all. This is an absolute disaster.

And then, just as I'm watching Adria bow out of the corner of my eye, something occurs to me: I've got him exactly where I want him.

He was charmed by my presence. Wasn't he? What else could the wink have been for? In any case, he certainly didn't seem angry or concerned about us or what we're doing here.

Larus has trained me to observe. To use my senses, to keep out of sight, to speak little and carefully consider my words, to believe in the power of secrets to strengthen my shadows.

Secrets and lies. The key to my power.

My heart is the secret.

My mind is the lie.

They can't change your heart, Adria said.

I don't have to change my heart to do what we came here to do. All I need to do is keep my mind on track. I can lie to him. It can work.

And maybe I can make him feel something too.

Chapter Six

I turn slightly to look at Adria where she waits for Ronan to approach, and I'm shocked at what I see.

Her eyes dart with fear. Her chest rises, her breathing shallow. She's cowering in his presence. I have never, in all my life, seen her like this.

What in the name of the gods is happening?

"Lady Adria," he says as plainly as if he's addressing a servant. "I trust you remember how to bow."

I seethe with anger. Adria looks as though she might cry, but she does as he says. I want to reach for her, to comfort her for the first time in our lives.

And I want to slap that smirk right off his face.

"I can feel the heat coming off of this one," says Ronan, gesturing to me. "Fire-born too?"

The question is for me, and I answer without thinking. "Shadow-born, like our mother."

Like our mother *was*. Like she would still be, if it weren't for his father slaughtering her in her sleep.

My mother's death had been the first real blow in the arms race of vengeance that had torn our families apart. An arms race *we* will emerge from victorious, with the gods as my witness.

My heart pounds in my ears. My words were laced with malice, and there's no way Ronan didn't feel it radiating off of me. The murderous rage boils beneath my skin, and I can't contain it. No amount of rationalizing will stop me from feeling it. No amount of artificial lust will distract me from it.

He could kill me for it. He could take my life right here and now. He could do it himself, slicing through my heart with his light, burning it right out of my chest. He's done it before; he did it to our father on some lonely cliff in the desert wasteland.

But Ronan does not raise his hands. He doesn't reach for his sword. Instead, he looks straight through me, his eyes piercing through whatever foolish defenses I thought I could construct.

And in his eyes?

Only pain.

The moment passes quickly, Ronan excusing himself and pulling away to speak to his Grand Vizier, but I swear I saw it. Not vengeance. Not righteous fury. Not even fear for his own life, the life that he must have known was being threatened.

Just *pain*. I know it because I feel it too. The raw, aching loss that I live with every day. I know that feeling better than anything.

Adria lets out a breath at my side as he exits the chamber. Cyrus comes over to let us know that Ronan has been called into the city for dinner, so we'll be dining alone tonight, but that he'll see us to rooms so we can settle in before it's served.

I barely hear him.

I want to look at Larus, want to talk to Adria and ask her if she's alright, but I can't with Cyrus within earshot, with the eyes of Ronan's guards and servants on us still.

It's only once we're within our chambers that I turn to my sister.

She loosens the armor from her shoulders, and when she turns back to me, she *smiles*.

And then she does the unthinkable.

She pulls me into a hug.

"Excellent performance, Sylvie," she whispers. "He's captivated by you."

I pull away, and suddenly, I can see it: it was all an act for her. The fear, the contrition. She was showing him what he wanted to see.

I thought I'd seen a side to Adria I'd never seen before, a vulnerable side that shared many of my own feelings, but none of it was real.

"I thought I'd ruined it all," I say, stumbling on the words. She shakes her head and holds her finger to her lips. Then she leads me to one of the grand four-poster beds that dominate the small room and takes a seat on the end of it, smoothing a spot for me on the blue velvet bedspread.

"The walls have ears," she says softly.

They also have gold. Paintings in gold frames, gold sconces for the candles. Gold doorknobs, gold latches on the window, which overlooks the city.

I hate it here.

"I was so angry," I whisper, taking a seat beside her. "He must have felt it."

"Of course he did. Exactly as we wanted him to. You're a challenge to him now. He wants you. You hate him. He won't be able to stay away from you."

I do my best not to look shocked. Why didn't she tell me that this was the plan?

But I know the truth: she didn't trust me to pull it off. She didn't believe I could play the part, not as well as she played it.

And maybe she was right.

"Now it's time to go and do as we discussed. He's out today; it's the perfect opportunity."

She squeezes my hand, and I wonder how much of her affection is genuine and how much is for my benefit alone.

But I can't help but be affected by the pride radiating off of her. It feels good to see her happy. It reminds me a bit of our mother. Her praise was rare, too, but nothing felt as good as hearing her say you'd done a good job.

"Go," she says, and without another word, I leave the chamber.

Chapter Seven

There's only so long after you arrive at a new place that you can pretend to be lost in order to get away with being in places you're not supposed to be.

We figure we have about a week before turning up in private quarters begins to look suspicious, and with the king outside of the palace, it's even less likely that anyone will wonder what I'm doing so far from our assigned chambers.

On the way from the throne room, I tried to memorize the route back to it. I retrace those same steps now, glancing out the windows as I go to get my bearings.

It's impossible to map out the palace in my mind. I'm not sure I could do so even with ink and paper, although that would be an entirely foolish task to undertake anyway. All I really need to do is find my way to the king's quarters and then into the servants' passages that lead there.

I make it back to the throne room before I encounter anyone. There are two guards positioned at the door we'd come from; I don't remember them being there after we'd left, so maybe Ronan has returned.

I don't want to see him again. I'm still trying to process what happened earlier. I can't help but feel a bit betrayed by Adria's omissions. I'm wishing Cyrus hadn't shown us to our chambers first so that I could have called on Larus to ask him if he knew about Adria's plan.

And I have no idea what to make of my other feelings, or of the glimpse of pain I saw on Ronan's face. I would give anything to know what he was thinking. Was it simply regret for asking the question, or did it run deeper than that? Was it the memory of his father? Or could he possibly have been regretting his actions against us?

Not fucking likely.

I try not to think about Ronan on the other side of the door, possibly feeling my every feeling once more. I try not to think about how, for all we knew, he could feel everything anyone felt in the palace at any time. Or maybe even beyond its walls.

If that were true, it must be overwhelming. I wonder how he can tell the feelings of others from his own. If he's ever been confused by them. If he's ever felt as confused as I do right now.

The guards watch me approach. I decide to take a page out of Adria's book: I act.

"I'm sorry, but I couldn't find one of the palace servants. I'm trying to find my way to the bathing chambers."

I can't decide whether to try to look simple-minded or alluring. I bat my eyelashes at them a little, hoping it comes across as one or the other.

I probably look insane.

It works, though. One of the guards gives me a very complicated list of directions that I ignore after the first couple of turns send me onward past the throne room entrance the way I was hoping to go.

I imagine Ronan's private chambers must be on this side of the palace. It's near the throne room and away from the guests, and it seems that the bathing chambers aren't far away. Those are down the stairs, so I go up instead.

I pass a lovely balcony overlooking a courtyard filled with exotic plants, a grand ballroom, and a dozen closed doors that must be private chambers. I consider opening one, but the other guests have been arriving, and I'm worried I'll meet someone on the other side. There are other stairways up, but I continue to the end of the hallway until I reach a spiraling staircase that leads into a tower.

It seems a likely place, although I have little excuse for ascending a tower when we did no such thing to reach our own chambers. I hardly want to go in the front door anyway; instead, I search the hallway for a servants' entrance.

I'm standing on my tiptoes, peering behind a tapestry, when something catches my eye out the window.

This part of the palace has windows that face the sea, but when I turned the last corner, I must have turned back towards the city, because it's city as far as the eye can see beyond.

And there, at the end of a street, is a wide-open plaza, filled to the brim with canopies.

The market.

It has to be the same market Typhon described. I try to make out any of the wares, but I can only see flashes of light on metal and crowds of people as small as ants from this distance.

I look back down the hallway. I'm supposed to find a way into Ronan's chambers, but I'm not certain he isn't in them. Maybe he hasn't left for dinner yet.

I'm not even certain I'm in the right place. This could be where Larus is staying, for all I know. If I get caught in the servants' hallways, I won't have any excuse for being there. Wouldn't it make more sense to walk around and observe, trying to catch the servants entering and exiting so that I can know how to avoid them before risking it? I have my shadows, sure, but there's not much I can do if they bump right into me in the dark.

I've found a possible lead. I performed the way Adria wanted me to in the throne room. Ronan isn't even going to be in the palace tonight. Why shouldn't I go to the market for just a little while?

I have a little coin in my pocket. I don't want to buy much, though. To be honest, I just want to see it. There's a whole world out there I've never been allowed to see, and part of it is waiting just down the street.

I head for the stairs and go down them, not up.

I find ground level easily enough, but I don't want the guards to see me going out one of the main doors, so I keep looking for other options. I'm on the way to the bathing chambers again, so I follow the path the guard gave me for a bit until I see a nondescript door that seems to be on an exterior wall.

It's a perfectly reasonable door for me to try, so I try it. Locked.

Not a problem. The hallway is empty, but I deepen the shadow around me just in case. Then I retrieve a small metal rake from my pocket and a pin from my hair, and in just a few seconds, the lock is open.

Thanks, Mom, for teaching me that one.

The door opens into a darkened corridor, which is something of a surprise, but I can smell a hint of salt on the damp air, so I walk inside, locking the door behind me.

Some brooms and cobwebby crates line the narrow walls, leaving only enough room for one person to walk at a time. Thankfully, I don't meet anyone as I travel the passage, and soon I reach another door, this one locked from the inside.

I turn the lock and open the door out into the light of day.

I'm in an alleyway, and judging by the buildings that line it, I'm outside of the palace walls.

I've found an unguarded way out of the palace. Adria will be so pleased with that, I doubt she'll even mind that I visited the market.

Not that I intend to tell her.

The raised voices and the sound of carts rolling on stone give away the market's location even though I can't see it from here, so I make my way through the alleys in its direction. These aren't the streets of Faros that King Ronan wants us to see. They aren't paved with gold or polished to perfection like the palace. They're real, lived-in streets, a little dirty and worn but well-trodden in a way I can't help but find charming. Thousands of people have lived out their lives in these streets over the centuries. Millions, maybe.

They're Selaran, but I don't think of the common Selarans as our enemy. They'll be our people too, once Adria takes the palace.

At the thought, I glance back in its direction. Part of me hopes Ronan can't feel what I'm feeling.

Part of me hopes that he can.

I turn a blind corner, and something moves behind me.

I can feel the heat from their body on my back—they're small like me, possibly a woman—and I can smell something sweet on their breath as they pull me to them, placing a knife at my throat.

Again?

Our encounter on the road yesterday flashes back into my mind. Of how I'd failed. Of how I got away with my life by lucky chance, not anything of my own doing.

This time is different. I will not be a victim. I will learn from my mistakes.

I plunge the alley into darkness and pull my dagger from my belt, driving it right into my attacker's gut before they can even flinch.

Chapter Eight

"**O**w! Ow! She stabbed me! She stabbed me!"

My attacker is screaming behind me like a child. No, not just *like* a child.

They *are* a child.

"I'm dying. I'm dying! Help! HELP!"

The child bends over, clutching his stomach. He's a boy or maybe a short-haired girl, skinny and no older than twelve or thirteen. His ratty tunic is rapidly turning from tan to blood red.

I look around the alley, but no one is there. The market is close. I'm not sure anyone could have heard him over the noise.

I should run. The guards will be here soon, and how am I going to explain stabbing a child in an alleyway when I'm supposed to be getting dressed for dinner in the palace?

But if I leave him, he could die. Judging by the position of the quickly growing patch of blood, I've missed his kidney, but I know a wound like this can still kill a man if not treated quickly, let alone a little boy.

Oh gods, what have I done?

"Hold still," I say. I've got to try to stop the bleeding. I can't cauterize the wound like Adria, but I can slow it down enough to get him to a nature-born healer or an alchemist. I pull a handkerchief from my pocket and try to press it on him.

"Keep away from me!" he yells. Then he shouts again over my shoulder: "She stabbed me!"

"Quit your yelling, foolish boy, and hold still as she says."

I jump at the voice. It's the low, gravelly voice of a grown man, but I hadn't heard anyone coming.

I really need to learn to watch my back.

I turn to the voice and try to explain. "I didn't know it was a boy; he had a knife at my—"

"I saw," he says to me and pushes me out of the way. "What have I told you, boy?"

The boy just whimpers as the man leans down to look at the wound.

It's clear from the man's attire he isn't a guard. He wears a worn tunic as well, though his is much nicer than the boy's. It's made of a rich brown fabric and belted, with a sword sheathed at his waist. Its pommel is plain and unpolished, possibly the standard-issue sword of Selaran soldiers.

The man and the boy must know each other. They're probably in whatever I just stumbled into together.

When the man looks up at me, I nearly gasp.

His entire face has been badly injured. It's healed now, but a violent slash runs from his left brow all the way across his cheek and his mouth to his chin. He wears a patch covering his left eye, undoubtedly lost to the same wound. His nose has been fractured in at least two places, and the skin on the right side has the melted look of a severe burn.

War wounds, I'm certain of it. There are those among our own people who look like this, who had to make do with battlefield medicine and dwindling elixirs near the end of the fighting. With injuries this severe, he's lucky to be alive.

"I suppose you'd like this back," he says, and he gently pulls my dagger from the boy's stomach.

The boy cries out and squirms in pain.

I take my dagger from the man, wiping the boy's blood off with my handkerchief, but my eyes are fixed on the boy. He's bleeding heavily now—removing the dagger was a mistake. I nearly open my mouth to tell the man he's killing him, but he holds his hands over the bloody wound.

I don't smell burning, so he must be nature-born, but I'm not sure nature magic, as powerful as it is, could heal a wound like that quickly enough to save his life.

I also wonder why the man, if he has nature magic, didn't use it to heal himself from his own wounds, although maybe he wasn't conscious to do so until too late.

"It hurts, it hurts," moans the boy, but by the time the man removes his hands, the bleeding has stopped.

"Go on, boy. And don't let me catch you with that knife again."

To my astonishment, the boy gets right back on his feet. I've had wounds healed by a nature-born before, and it's typically slow and painful. It can take days for an injury to heal without an alchemical elixir to speed the process.

The boy stumbles away from us. He's favoring his wounded side a bit, but no more than if I'd punched him rather than stabbed him.

"How can he walk?" I ask the man. "The wound went deep."

"You didn't hesitate, did you?" says the man, not answering my question. "I'm surprised you're still here."

I suppose I'm surprised as well. I should have run ages ago. I should run now.

The man sizes me up, and I do the same. He's a good bit taller than me, but not enough to tower over me, although that appears to be due to his hunched left shoulder more than anything else. I can't tell how old he is, but I don't see any gray in the brown hair that's visible beneath his flat cap. I'd guess thirty, maybe less.

He doesn't seem threatening, but I can't imagine anything good he could have been doing with a child in a darkened alleyway.

I start backing away from the stranger. Just because he helped the child doesn't mean he won't hurt me. "I'm just going to the market. I swear I didn't know he was a child when I stabbed him—"

"I know. Nico thinks he's a shadow rogue. I've told him it's going to get him killed one of these days."

The man grins. It's a little hard to recognize beneath all the scars, but I'm fairly certain it's meant to be friendly.

"I didn't mean to be in your way. I'll just let you get back to, you know, whatever—wait, did you say shadow? He's a shadow-born?" He's so young. My own magic didn't settle until I was sixteen. Nico is thirteen at best. It's not impossible, but it's rare.

"One of a few in this neighborhood," says the man. "And the best at keeping up with the gossip." He flips a coin in his hand. "For a price, of course."

He pockets the coin and then holds out a hand to shake. It's covered in healed cuts, some of them quite deep. "Soren. Thank you for staying and trying to help him."

"It was nothing," I say. It truly wasn't, considering I'm the one who stabbed him in the first place.

I don't offer him my name, and he doesn't ask for it. He does have one question for me though.

"Your accent. Nithyria?"

I nod slowly. It's not going to be possible to conceal my background here entirely, especially not when I'm dressed in our leathers. There aren't many Nithyrians in the capital, although that will be changing soon. Many of our people will be arriving for the festival.

Some of them might be bringing a few sharp objects along with them.

"I'd be careful in the market. There are some merchants who aren't fond of your people."

"I will," I say. "I'm sorry again for the trouble." I turn and walk towards the market, slightly worried that once my back is turned to him, he'll pull a knife on me like Selarans are wont to do.

He doesn't though. I'm halfway down the alley before he calls after me. "I could show you around."

I stop and slowly turn to face him. Is this some kind of a trick?

He approaches then slows when I don't reply. He holds up his hands to proclaim his innocence. "I don't bite, I promise. I can show you which vendors to steer clear of."

I pause. I don't know why he would help me after what I've done to his…spy? His friend? I'm not sure, but I don't read anything nefarious in his intentions.

What I do notice is his eyes lingering on my body.

I did say I was looking for someone to get into trouble with. I'd imagined a fire-born, but a nature-born would do. And I'll admit that I find something appealing about his scars and the way that he helped the boy. And even if it doesn't end up going that way, it would be nice to have a guide.

"Alright," I say. "Lead the way."

I give Soren a fake name—Hazel, a name I'd called one of my dolls when I was younger—and a somewhat ridiculous background story.

"I'm a traveling acrobat. I'm with a troupe performing in the Great Festival."

I say this because it's what I wanted to do the most as a child. A troupe of traveling performers came to the castle once a couple of years before the war began, and I begged my mother to let me leave with them the entire time they were in town.

Their lives seemed perfect. They went from town to town, all over the kingdom, and sometimes all over the world, and all they did was make people happy. I had always been fearless of heights, and my balance was pretty good. I thought I'd make a great acrobat. Though she refused to let me leave with them, Mother did let them teach me some of their routines.

It's enough to make a great lie.

"Will you perform in the palace?"

"I hope so," I say. "That's if we can manage to do well enough in the competition."

I don't actually know how the arts festival or competitions are going to work, but I doubt Soren does either.

It turns out he's a merchant who imports rare items from overseas. It's a competitive business, and so he keeps tabs on his competition with the help of the boy and other shadow-born. He knows these alleys well. I tell him he'd make a fine shadow-born himself, and he laughs far harder than my joke warrants.

And then he gets that look in his eye that tells me I was right when I noticed him looking at my body.

I like it.

When we turn the last corner into the market, I'm afraid the crowd might swallow me whole.

I've never seen so many people in my life. The markets in Kalla are tiny compared to this. There must be at least a thousand people in the square, maybe several thousand.

It's noisy and crowded and there are a million different smells in the air. Fish, meat, strange herbs and spices I can't place, some of them genuinely disgusting. When we pass one stall, the smoke that comes from it is so strong I cough violently. I can barely see anything over the crowd, and I can barely hear Soren even as he stands right next to me.

I love it immediately.

"This way," says Soren. He takes my hand and cuts through the crowd with a finesse that could only come from years of experience, leading me to an area that's a bit more open.

It's strange, but I don't feel the scars I saw earlier on his hand. I realize I didn't feel them when we shook hands either. Perhaps they're worse on the other one.

Soren brings me first to a vendor selling curios from overseas. "She's the real deal," Soren whispers. "And one of my few friends in the market. A bona fide treasure hunter. These are all authentic. No forgeries."

"How do you know?"

"It's my business to know. Come see this," he says. He holds up a dagger. Its blade is black and roughly carved from some kind of shining metal I've never seen before.

"Obsidian. Volcanic glass, likely from the Enez Islands. Practically useless as a dagger. But it's quite nice for a fire-born."

To hone their magic, maybe. I've heard of items that can do that, although Adria thinks it's all superstition. I'm not sure why he's telling me this though.

He offers the dagger to me. "I'm not fire-born," I say.

"More for me, then. She's underpriced this by a lot," he says. He slips a few coins to the merchant without negotiating.

It's not uncommon to share your magic school with strangers, at least not in Nithyria. But Nithyrians are somewhat more tolerant of the shadow-born than the Selarans are from what I've heard, largely on account of our vital role in keeping Nithyria fed before the war. Soren seems friendlier to the shadow-born than most, though I'm not certain if that's because he respects them or simply finds them useful.

I find myself wanting to tell him. There's something about the way he talks to me, the way he looks at me, that makes me want to tell him things, that makes me want to abandon my caution and just let myself be comfortable around someone for once.

But I don't. Not yet.

Instead, I ask Soren about the vendor selling the pastry with walnuts and pistachios, and he knows exactly the place. It's as delicious as Typhon said, if a bit sweeter than I'm used to. I offer a bite to Soren, and he takes it. He's close enough that I can hear him crunching as he eats. There are people all around us, giving us little room to stand. Someone pushes into me, pressing me against Soren.

"Sorry," I say, my words muffled by his chest. The muscle there is surprisingly firm, and there's a lot of it. He must get quite a workout hauling his imports up from the docks.

And he smells really nice, like incense and some of those unnamable spices.

I want to ask him what they are. I want to know him, every little detail.

"Watch your step," Soren says to the man who pushed, a warning in his tone. Then he gently moves me back from him. "Are you alright?"

"I'm fine," I say, but to be honest, I'm a little breathless. I haven't been in close proximity to a man in…well, a bit too long. A year at least.

And the last man who shared my bed was thin and bony, one of our stable boys, someone around my age. Nothing like the body of rock-solid muscle I just felt pressed against me.

"You have a little—" Soren reaches for my face but stops his hand short, gesturing to the side of my mouth.

Crumbs, I'm sure. "Here?" I ask, trying to reach it with my tongue.

He laughs. "No, not quite."

I reach into my pocket for my handkerchief, but when I retrieve it, I see that it's still stained with the boy's blood.

"Let me," he says, and he pulls a handkerchief from his pocket.

It's clean and white, a nice linen fabric, and he dabs it at the corner of my mouth.

My lips part involuntarily from the contact. I look up into his good eye, and it's warm and soft as he cleans my cheek, a shy smile tugging on his lips.

I wonder what it would be like to kiss him.

It took my mind a moment to get used to the disfigurement of his face, but now that it has, I'm growing fond of it. Here is a man with character. A man who has seen battle, if on the wrong side. A man who survived.

No, he's not perfect like Ronan, but he's nice. Approachable.

And I'm unable to stop thinking about how his body felt pressed against mine.

I think about asking him if there's somewhere we can go. I'm not certain of it, but from the way he touches me—gentle, but with an edge of hunger, like he's having to stop himself from going further—I think he would agree to it. I don't have long before I need to get back to the palace, but these things never seem to take as long as I'd like anyway.

But we've only just met, and there's still so much more of the market to see.

I let him guide me through it. He takes me to a fruit-seller and a butcher and a purveyor of fine fabrics, to a booth with rare books and parchments and to a stall with perfumes and oils, which I may or may not have sampled in an effort to find the one he's wearing. At a small cart owned by a water-born, he buys me a flower, a desert rose. It has little fragrance, but it's lovely to look at, a soft pink edged with brighter color. I tuck it gratefully into my hair.

We narrowly avoid a merchant selling Nithyrian wines that I recognize from occasional visits to our market and that would almost certainly recognize me. I explain that I've been home too recently to miss the flavor.

I notice that there are stands that we avoid, including most of the ones selling anything made of gold, of which there are fewer than I had imagined there would be, and a stand selling ornamental masks like you might wear to a ball that I certainly would have stopped at had Soren not warned me against it.

"His are the best masks on the market, but he's not worth the trouble, believe me."

By the time we've covered maybe a quarter of the square, the sun is slipping behind the city walls. It's certainly dinner time, maybe past it even, but I feel no hurry to return to the palace.

I don't want this day to end. I'm trying to remember a better day than this, and I can't.

I know I should go back; I just don't want to. Ronan isn't even there, and I'm sure Adria can make up some excuse once she realizes I'm still occupied in my reconnaissance mission.

I haven't forgotten my duty. I could never forget my duty. But has there been a day in all my life when I was able to do what I wanted?

"Is there anywhere good to eat around here?" I ask Soren.

He grins and takes me by the arm. I like the familiar way he handles me. It never feels pushy or uncomfortable. It's natural, like we've known each other for years rather than hours.

I wonder if I've ever felt this at ease with someone I've just met.

Soren makes one last stop before bringing me to the tavern. It's at a small shop off of the main square that looks to sell ribbons and jewelry, though again, little that's made of gold. I wonder if the Guild keeps it out of the hands of the common folks on purpose.

I twist my mother's ring on my finger, hiding the crest of her house in case it's recognizable to the owner. The air is warm and stale inside, as if we're the only ones who've passed through the door in recent memory.

There's no one behind the counter.

Soren calls into a darkened doorway. No one answers, but there are footsteps on the stairs.

"We're closed," says a woman's voice. "Oh, it's you," she says when she spots Soren. She's an older woman with leathery skin and graying hair, maybe around Larus's age. "You haven't heard? Vesper's not been here in a week. You know how she is."

"A week?" asks Soren. There's concern in his voice.

She? Is this a friend of Soren's?

Or a lover?

My heart flutters at the thought, which is ridiculous. Why should I be jealous? I've only just met the man. I have no claim on him.

"I'm sure you'll find her soon enough, at the bottom of a bottle somewhere by the docks. Or rotting in one of Ronan's cells." The woman spits at the ground.

My interest is piqued. An enemy of Ronan's, or at least someone Selaran who isn't among his admirers.

And someone willing to say it out loud, bold as anything.

"But a week…" says Soren softly.

"I know," says the woman. She sounds as if she's on the verge of tears. "You think I don't know that? She's my daughter."

"I'll find her."

"You better," she says. She looks at the door. "And don't come back here until you do."

We leave in a hurry. Back in the street, I look to Soren for an explanation.

"One of my shadow-born. A young woman, maybe around your age."

I try to ignore the way my heart skips a beat when he calls her *his*. "She's missing?"

He nods grimly.

I'm not understanding. She's just reporting on some of his competitors' dealings from what Soren said. "Do you think one of your competitors did something to her?"

"I don't know," says Soren. "But I intend to find out."

"Could the city watch help? Or maybe Ronan's guards?"

I honestly don't know if there's a difference. The guards I've seen so far in the streets of Faros are dressed about the same as the Royal Guard: chainmail, leather bracers, black cloaks. They just lack the gold crest on their mail.

Soren laughs bitterly. "Not for some lowly shadow-born girl. If her mother were rich, maybe."

Lowly shadow-born. That's what I am to these people. By birth, I'm noble, but I'm from the house that started the war. And I'm just a shadow-born.

Does Soren think the shadow-born are lowly? Maybe he does secretly look down on them like everyone else.

It shouldn't matter. I'm never going to see him again after tonight, and he doesn't even know my real name.

But I have to know.

"I'm shadow-born," I say.

"I know."

How could he possibly know? I haven't told him what I am, haven't used my magic in front of him. Had he guessed it from my personality?

"What gave me away?"

"The way you looked at me when I talked about the shadow-born earlier. I knew you either were one or hated them, and if you hated them, you wouldn't have shown any concern for Vesper. Or for Nico, for that matter."

"Do you hate them? Us?"

Soren lifts an eyebrow in surprise. "No, not at all. I'm not saying the city guard *shouldn't* care about a missing shadow-born girl. I'm just saying that they don't. But there are channels other than through the guards."

That's interesting. It could be good to find out about some of these unofficial channels. And, jealous or not, I can't imagine not doing anything I could for a fellow shadow-born in trouble. "Can I help you?"

Soren smiles. "That's nice of you to ask. Maybe keep an eye out at your shows. She's thin with long red hair and several piercings in each ear." He gestures to the places on his own ears to show me. He's speaking calmly now, but I heard the concern in his voice in her mother's shop. He probably doesn't want me to worry, but I'm an expert worrier. I spent years doing little else while my family fought a war they wouldn't all come back from.

He must see something along those lines written on my face because he says, "Come on. Her mother's probably right about her being at the bottom of a bottle, and there's not much we can do with the shops closing for the night. Let's get something to eat."

I do feel better once I'm in the tavern. It's a lively place, and it reminds me of home, only a little less dour. I haven't spent much time in the taverns back in Kalla; Larus wouldn't let me until I turned eighteen, although I did sneak in once or twice when he was away dealing with house business. But the keep had a small bar of its own, and he'd let me sit there with him while he drank. Sometimes he drank because of bad news, sometimes because of good.

But the news was mostly bad, and the mood was mostly bad.

Here, it's different. It's as if they were never touched by the war. There are people laughing against the bar, people shouting and cheering at tables playing cards, a band playing a lively tune, and a couple in the corner kissing so passionately it makes me blush. The Great Festival is about to begin, and these people have gotten an early start to it.

The food is unusual, or at least it is to me. It's some kind of spongy flatbread with different dishes served directly on it, but it has a pleasant, tangy taste to it, and the company is good as well.

There's a freedom to having only one night with someone. I find myself telling Soren about my sister—without using her name, of course. I tell him about how she commands the attention in a room, about how she's always been the best at everything. I tell him how much I envy her and how I can never seem to measure up to the mark she sets, throwing in some made-up details about her prowess in aerial tumbling.

He asks about my parents and other siblings. I tell him a bit about Seth, but there's not much to tell there, really. He's somehow even more Adria than Adria. I imagine when they talk about the family, they focus primarily on their rivalry, and I'm not even part of the conversation.

And I tell him simply that my parents are dead. He doesn't ask how, and I don't tell him.

His parents are dead too, but that's not unusual. He tells me about his father, a man he both greatly admired and feared. He inherited the business from him, but his father ran things with an iron fist. He's trying to do things differently, and mostly it's working, but some of the people his father paid to cooperate aren't happy with his refusal to do the same.

We don't talk about the war at all. I don't ask him about the scars on his face, and he doesn't ask me whether I fought on the other side.

After dinner and a couple of beers, he suggests we try our luck at cards. I've never played the game before, so I keep my bets low.

It's a game of strategy more than chance, and Soren is excellent at it. He sweeps a large pile of coin from the table: some of it Selaran, much of it not. When he goes to put the coin in his pocket, something falls from his sleeve.

A card.

I see it, but I'm not the only one. I hear the drawing of steel before I see the blade. A man with round glasses stands and shouts, accusing Soren of cheating. The man is right, of course, and he's lost a fair bit of coin to Soren.

There are many differences between Selara and Nithyria, but it turns out how card cheats are handled isn't one of them.

The man challenges Soren to a duel.

The color drains from my face. I know what's coming next. Duels are a matter of honor and can't be declined. There's nothing for Soren to do except agree to the terms and…

He grabs my hand under the table. "Run!" he yells.

He pulls me up and out of the chair before I realize what's happening.

Shit shit shit…

I darken the shadows in the room as I leap over an overturned barstool. All the lying today has given my magic a bit of an edge. It's not enough to stop a shadow-born from seeing, if there are any in the room, but the darkness is near total.

Of course, the problem with that is that Soren is nature-born. He can't see a damn thing either.

He collides with a buxom woman before slowing down enough to allow me to lead. I guide him the best I can as I dodge through the tables of confused and frightened patrons, turning back to see a fire-born cut through some of the shadow with flame.

It's a weak effort, though, compared to mine, and no one seems to be pursuing us with more than just a guess at where we are.

I keep the shadow on us when we're out the door. Night has fallen, so I don't need to do as much as we run through the city streets.

When we make it a few blocks over, I turn into an alley and let the shadow go. The moonlight is dim, but I can see the look on Soren's face: he's highly amused.

I'm not.

"Cheating at cards?" I say, panting from exertion and poking him in the chest. "I thought your business was doing well."

"It is," he says. He can barely talk for laughing and trying to catch his breath. "Believe me, those guys deserve it. And it's just really fun to win."

"It's dishonest."

"Says the shadow-born. Isn't that kind of your whole thing?"

"I'm not a liar," I say. Although I've lied a lot today, I don't typically make a habit of it. "I just…don't tell the whole truth."

"It's the same thing."

"No, it isn't."

"Yes, it is."

"It isn't." There's a huge difference between keeping some things to yourself and lying for the fun of it.

"A lie by omission is still a lie."

This man is infuriating. It was an incredibly stupid risk to take, and now he's arguing with me like a child. We could have been killed. "You're a *moron*," I say.

"Oh, absolutely," he says.

And fuck it, the way he says it is so genuine, I laugh.

I'm still laughing when I hear the voices approaching.

Soren covers my mouth with his hand and presses me against the wall. I darken the shadows again as we wait for the cheated gamblers to pass us by.

I'm listening for them to turn down the alley, preparing for a fight, but I'm also feeling Soren's body against me. He's warm from our run, and his hand is soft on my mouth. I can smell the beer on him, but also that smoky, spicy scent I smelled earlier. It's so alluring it floods my senses.

I want to kiss him. I'm reminded of the slip of my mind when I met Ronan—I'm so starved for affection, maybe I'd want to kiss anyone—but it's different with Soren. I want to kiss him not just out of desperation or to save my life from my damning thoughts, but because I've had a really great time, the best time I've had in years, and I don't want it to end.

The footsteps retreat, and Soren drops his hand. But he doesn't step away from me.

"Is Hazel your real name?" he asks, tucking a strand of hair behind my ear.

"Is Soren yours?" I reply. I didn't see it until now, but there are parts of his story that don't make sense. The way his magic worked earlier, so unlike any nature-born I've ever known. The scars on his hands that don't feel like anything.

Relying on spies when he's able to move freely through the market, checking on competitors on his own.

And where's his store, anyway? Why hadn't we gone there?

But he's standing so close to me, it's hard to focus on the inconsistencies. It's hard to focus on anything when I feel his heat, when his hand combs my hair and then touches my lips, when his own lips part as he leans in. I reach for his face and—

A bell chimes the hour loudly nearby. It's *late*.

"Fuck," he says, pulling away quickly. "I have to go."

So do I. I've been gone *way* too long now. If Adria didn't tell a really good lie, they've probably sent out a search party.

"Until next time," says Soren, kissing my hand. As he turns away, he winks at me.

He winks at me.

And suddenly, I see it.

I don't dare to think it, not until I'm running far away in the opposite direction. I focus on the sound of the bells, echoing their *ding ding ding ding* in my thoughts, desperately trying not to let the name form in my mind.

Because I recognize that wink.

When I turn the corner and the palace comes into view, I can't suppress the thought any longer.

Ronan. Soren is God-King Ronan.

Chapter Nine

F uck. Fuckity fuck fuck fuck.

The moment I realize that Soren is Ronan, I'm completely, one hundred percent certain that I'm right.

Oh gods, what did I say to him?

My mind races back through our conversations, back through every thought and feeling I had near Soren.

Had he followed me from the palace? He must have, right? But then he already knew the boy, so he must have been there before. Maybe meeting the boy was the business he had in the city. The alleyway where he'd found me was near the palace, after all.

What was the boy doing for him then, really? Or any of the shadow-born? Why would he meet with them in disguise? Didn't he have spies for that?

And the *disguise*. It had been so convincing. The injuries had been so real. They couldn't possibly have been a mask or makeup. I've never seen anything that convincing in any traveling show or theatre, although admittedly, I haven't seen many.

His hand was soft. It was soft when it was on my lips just moments ago. It was soft when he took my hand to lead me through the crowded market, when I took his hand to lead him from the mob that wanted to hang him for cheating at cards and declining a duel.

It looked scratched and scarred, but it was soft.

His light magic? Was his appearance a trick of the light?

And, oh gods, no *wonder* the boy was barely hurting when he healed him. He used light, not nature.

The warmth I'd felt near him. The safety despite every sign pointing to danger, the comfort.

That damned light magic got me again.

I've made it back to the door to the palace, but I hesitate. It may not always be unguarded. And what if this is the door he used? Where is he? He must be nearby.

He didn't head in the direction of the palace. Maybe he did truly have someone he was meant to meet in the city.

I feel his eyes on me.

I turn to look, but no one is there.

This is terrible. What is he playing at? Did he spend the entire day with me because of my feelings when we met? Is he trying to get information out of me?

Had I offered him any?

I don't think so. I'd talked a bit about Seth and Adria, but I didn't tell him anything about our plans.

Was anything he said to me true?

I walk along the wall until I find a public entrance, the enormous iron gates hanging wide open and revealing a torchlit path up the hill to the palace.

There are guards at the gate, but one of them recognizes me from earlier.

"I got lost trying to find the baths," I explain. "And then I went to the market to find a mask for the festival ball."

"Did you find one?" the guard asks. I'm suspiciously lacking a box, I realize.

"No," I say. "The vendor wouldn't sell to me."

"I know the man," says the other guard. She's a woman around my age with a pleasant smile. "Try Ibis Street. It's on the way down to the docks."

"Thank you, I will."

I'm surprised by their kindness. I'm sure most of Ronan's guards fought in the war, and I'd expected them to still hold a grudge against us. They must have been instructed to be accommodating.

As I walk through the labyrinthine palace corridors towards our rooms—or in the direction I think our rooms are in, I haven't been this way and have to stop for directions twice—I realize that Ronan may not know that *I* know about his disguise.

That could be something. And the fact that he can disguise his appearance is something too. It's a far more valuable piece of information than the location of his rooms or the hidden exit to the palace.

I also realize that Ronan was about to kiss me. What was his plan then? If he'd done so, surely I would have noticed that his face wasn't scarred.

I doubt my conclusion for the first time. The wink had been so much like Ronan's though. Same brown eye, same expression on his face, even under all the scarring. His hair was concealed under his hat, but what I could see of it was brown, like Ronan's. Soren had a hunched back, and he walked with something of a limp, but the limp had all but vanished when we ran away from the gamblers. If he'd straightened his back, he could've been as tall as Ronan.

And the muscles of his body, the muscles I'd felt when he was pressed against me.

I don't even want to think about it.

I can't be certain, although I feel somewhat certain, but even the possibility alone is worth warning the others about.

I'm almost back to our rooms when I hear Adria's voice through the door.

"I told you. I told you she shouldn't have come."

I stop in my tracks. She's talking about me.

"Adria—" begins Larus. His voice is a bit more muffled, further away.

"Don't 'Adria' me. You know it as well as I do."

"We'll find her. She takes what you say seriously. She's just doing what you asked her."

Adria laughs. "As if she could. You know she's just lost somewhere. She's probably gotten on a boat and made it halfway back to Kalla by now. Or she's lying in a ditch after running from a fight with a child."

Rude. It was a teenager, and I didn't run. I stabbed him.

"Enough. I think it's been long enough. Cyrus must be back to his rooms by now—"

The door bursts open.

"Sylvie!" says Larus.

"Oh, for fuck's sake, where have you been?" says Adria.

"I went to the market," I say, gesturing to them to let me inside.

"The market? You've been gone for six hours at the *market*?" Adria is fuming. I can practically smell the smoke coming off of her.

I tap my ear. The walls have ears here, remember?

"I found a tower," I whisper once I'm close to one of the beds. "It's promising. And I found a way outside. Unguarded."

I thought they'd be impressed with me, and Larus is, at least. He pats me on the shoulder. "Well done."

But Adria is still furious. "Six hours, and that's all you have to say? I lied for you. I told Cyrus you weren't well. Were you seen?"

"I came back in the north gate—"

"You came back in the gate? Past the guards? What did you tell them?"

"I told them I went to the market—"

"I told them you were sick in our room! Unbelievable. Fucking useless."

Ouch.

I hate how much of me cares about what she says. She's being unreasonable. She hasn't even let me explain what happened. But I still *hate* to hear her disappointment.

"Adria, enough. Let her explain."

"Did you find anything at all that could help us? *Anything.*" She's not even whispering now.

I think about Soren and my suspicion that it's Ronan in disguise, but what if I'm wrong? I know what she'll say. I know how much she'll mock me and how foolish I'll feel.

I can't tell her. Maybe I'll tell Larus later, when we're alone again. He would understand if I got it wrong. He would understand why I left at all.

Adria won't. I'm certain of that.

"The door—" I begin.

"That's it. You found a door outside, and it took you *six hours*, and now we're going to have to find a way to account for the fact that you turned up at the gate, having spent the day at the market, after me telling everyone you were sick in our room."

"You could say I felt better, but that I couldn't find my way to the dining hall," I offer. I flinch, waiting for her response.

"You know what? Sure. I'm sure they'll believe you're that *stupid.*"

Larus tries to talk to her, but she storms from the room, slamming the door behind her.

I look blankly at him. I feel something like tears at the corner of my eyes.

"You did good, kid," he says softly. "She'll see it one day."

I won't hold my breath.

In the morning, I put on the green dress Larus bought me. I've missed my chance to use it to make a good first impression, but maybe it will help smooth over any suspicions after my reaction yesterday or my absence last night.

The palace is buzzing with the arrivals of the rest of the court, the hallways filled with servants carrying enormous chests as the courtiers make their way to the throne room for Ronan's opening address.

Our own lower houses, the ones that survived, were largely stripped of their lands and titles after the war, but the other Great Houses have arrived with all of their myriad lower houses in tow. Between the heads of house, the spouses, the Guardians, the siblings, children, cousins, alchemists, and servants, there must be at least three hundred people in the throne room by the time we arrive. The benches have been cleared away to make enough room for everyone.

As we take our place in the back, more than a few heads turn. We don't have many friends in this room. The only reason we're allowed to stand here at all is because of Adria's surrender, the signing of the treaty, and our subsequent contrition.

I don't blame the court for hating us. Our war cost all of them something, although it cost us the most. We have our work cut out for us. We won't reveal our plans to anyone here, but the more of them we can make sympathetic to our cause, the better.

Ronan's throne sits empty once more. I want to get a good look at him to see if I can find similarities between him and Soren while the memory is still fresh in my mind, but it's hard to see from back here. I'll slip forward once he enters, while everyone is paying attention to him alone.

A pair of trumpets plays a fanfare from behind the throne. Grand Vizier Cyrus stands in front of it. He speaks loudly and clearly, his voice echoing through the enormous chamber. "Presenting, by the Grace of the Gods, Ronan III; Most High, Most Mighty, and Most Exalted God-King of Selara; Lord of Nithyria and Protector of the Realm; Sovereign of the Serath Desert and Master of the Palador Mountains; Keeper of the Sacred Light of Vayla; Guardian of the Eternal Oath; Commander of the Royal Orders of the Sun and the Moon; Defender of the Faith; Patron of the Alchemists' Guild and High Arbiter of the Courts of Faros and Minar; Grand Master of the Radiant Legion; Warden of the Eastern Shores; and Champion of the Sacred Covenant that Binds the Kingdom and its Peoples."

Absolutely ridiculous. *This* is more like it. This is the pomp and circumstance I was expecting yesterday. The pageantry. The arrogance.

I guess we weren't worthy of it.

The door to the antechamber opens, and in steps Ronan.

He's dressed in full royal regalia now, black robes concealed by an overcoat in a deep, velvety black with a golden crown atop his perfectly coiffed hair. I slip through the crowd, sticking to the shadows at the edges of the room to get a better look.

My stomach flutters. I'm hoping, praying to Kerensa, that I'm wrong. That the man I spent yesterday with, the man I'd wanted to kiss and maybe a bit more than that, isn't one and the same as the God-King himself.

He looks fucking radiant up there. Literally. The glow of his skin was subtle yesterday, but today, it's as bright as one of the candlelit chandeliers over his head. As he takes the throne, I see the glint of steel at his side.

I wonder if he's used it at all since the war.

He's smiling magnanimously at his loyal subjects, waving to them as they applaud. He points to someone in the front row of the crowd and waves, and she blushes.

The woman must be nearly sixty, and she *blushes*. She wants him. They all do, I realize, as I look around the room. Most of the women and some of the men. They're practically salivating.

I hate how handsome he is. It makes me want to punch him in his pretty face and break his pretty nose.

At the thought, I try to line up his flawless features with Soren's devastating injuries. It's a risk to do so, but Ronan can read feelings, not thoughts, and how much is he going to get from whatever satisfaction or disappointment I'll feel when I reach my conclusion?

It's difficult to say. The eyes and hair are a match, but brown eyes and brown hair aren't exactly unusual; hell, I have them too. Ronan is taller than Soren, but Soren was hunched. It's plausible, at least.

A different guard accompanies him today. Thin and blonde, he wears the typical chainmail and black cape of the Royal Guard. I think little of him until I notice the tattoo on his neck.

He's Orsan. One of Ronan's Royal Guards is Orsan, one of the ancient enemies of the Nithyrians. They've relentlessly raided our villages and slaughtered our people. It was enough of an insult that our lands were given to them after the war. But to make one of them a Royal Guard? Does Adria know? I hope she can't see the characteristic tattoo from her vantage point.

If she does, we might not be leaving this throne room alive.

Ronan holds up a hand, but the applause is still going. I don't get it. This is the damn court. All of these people have been here before, all except me. What are they all clapping about?

How hot their king is?

Ronan tries once again, and this time, the crowd slowly quiets. I listen carefully to his voice. "Welcome, all, to the Great Festival."

The voice is quite a bit like Soren's. Ronan's voice is higher and clearer, but he has also raised it a bit to call out to the crowd.

"The first Great Festival in over ten years!"

There's a lot more applause and more than a few cheers. Ten years without a multi-month party. How ever did they survive?

"The Festival will be in five parts to honor the five gods. The first will be the Festival of Sport to honor Sai, God of War, the Hunt, and the Forge. There will be a grand tournament followed by a hunt. May Sai's best champions reign victorious."

I wonder what we could be hunting. There isn't much game in the city, nor is there in the desert, from what I know. They'll probably bring in some poor creature from our woods, which will struggle enough in unfamiliar territory to give these soft bodies a chance.

"The next will be the Festival of Arts to honor Kerensa, Goddess of Beauty, Love, and Voyages. Artists and performers from all around Selara will delight us with galleries, shows, and countless balls. And, as you all know they're my favorite, one of the balls will be masked, so get your masks now before they're gone."

Interesting. Soren turned me away from the mask vendor—could he have had another reason for doing so? Although the guard at the door seemed to corroborate his story, so maybe it was just a coincidence.

"The third will be the Great Feast to honor Arnan, God of the Sea, the Harvest, and…the Feast."

There's a bit of laughter at that. I'm surrounded by sycophants and idiots. How can they justify holding a feast while my people are starving?

"And the final Festivals will be held together to honor the twin gods Vayla, Goddess of the Sun, Light, and Life, and Vahlo, God of the Moon, Shadow, and Death. The Festival of Night will lead directly into the Festival of Day, a full twenty-four-hour party to round out the season in style."

Round out the season. So it seems the festival will be at least three months then, as we expected. Three months to do what we've planned.

I stop the thought there.

"I hope you will all participate in each festival to its fullest. The past decade has been…"

Ronan pauses, looking around the room for something. A few people whisper. I glance back at Adria and Larus, who look at each other and then at Ronan.

Whatever he's searching for, he doesn't seem to find it. "The past decade has been challenging for all of us."

Challenging? That's what he has to say?

"But we are together now, one people. One kingdom. One glory."

Unbelievable. I know *exactly* what he's saying. We're one kingdom now, and you can fuck off it you don't like it.

Well, I don't like it. I don't feel like joining hands and singing songs about the glory of Selara. I want justice for my people. For what they've taken from us. I want to see our families fed and happy. I'm tired of sitting back and watching our people suffer.

I shouldn't have come here. I don't know how I'm supposed to smile and bow and pretend this man hasn't ruined my life. Our lives. I want to look back to see Adria's response, but Ronan fixes his eyes on me.

The air doesn't seem to be filling my lungs.

Of course he would say that, I try telling myself. *It isn't personal. It isn't just about us. He's trying to keep the peace.*

But it feels personal. It felt personal yesterday when he insulted Adria. It feels personal now, even though he hasn't so much as looked at me today until this moment.

"We will honor the gods and celebrate our—Taran, on my right."

Ronan points directly at me.

Fuck fuck fuck…

My heart is pounding so loudly in my ears I can barely think. He's felt it. He's felt my rage. He knows I want him dead. *Fuck*! It's over.

Gods, I'm going to die. I'm going to die right here in this room, and then what will happen? Will Larus try to avenge me? Will he fight his way through as many of them as he can before they bring him down too?

And Adria. Would she fight for me? Or would she stay her hand?

Does the war mean more to her than I do?

Taran, the Orsan guard, leaps from the dais. I freeze as he closes the distance to me.

I should do something. I should sink the room into shadow. I should pull my dagger or my sword and fight for my life.

But I can't. I'm frozen in place. Not by magic, but by fear. It's a terrible, all-encompassing fear. I can feel death. I can feel how close it is.

But I'm not fighting. It's happening again, and this time, it will be my last.

Just pull your sword. Go down swinging at least.

I can't. I just can't.

I shut my eyes and wait for death to come.

Chapter Ten

But it doesn't.

Death doesn't come. Not for me.

I hear the terrible slicing sound of steel through guts—familiar to me now, this being the third time in three days.

At least this time I'm not the one doing the stabbing.

I peek one of my eyes open to see the man who was standing next to me topple over, the contents of his abdomen spilling onto the stone floor.

A throwing knife falls from his hand to the ground. Was he planning to kill the king too, or did *my* thoughts damn him?

Did I just get this man killed?

Around me, chaos erupts abruptly when his body hits the floor.

There are scattered screams and the drawing of weapons, a stampede of nobility running for the exits, the guards shouting directions that go unheeded.

Taran grabs my arm.

"Let go of me!" I yell, but his grip is tight, and he pulls me with little effort away from the carnage.

I turn to look over my shoulder for Adria and Larus, but I can't see them over the frantic movements of the crowd.

By the time I look back around, Taran has led me into the antechamber.

Ronan is there, his back turned. He's giving directions to the guards, who are escorting an older woman from the chamber.

"Anything?" he asks Taran.

"Just the knife on the ground. Gaius will search the body and his rooms."

"House?"

"Corvinus," says Cyrus. "They've been hit particularly hard by your changes to indenturing."

Why did Taran bring me here? Does he suspect I had something to do with it?

Will they kill me next?

"Did you see anything?" asks Taran.

It takes me a moment to realize he's talking to me. Ronan and Cyrus turn to hear my reply.

"No…I—I don't know."

"Don't be frightened," says Cyrus lazily, as if it bores him to have to comfort me. "You're not in trouble. We just need to know what you saw."

Had I seen something? I try to remember what had been happening around me. I moved up through the crowd. I chose that spot because…"There was a space there, next to him. I was at the back. I moved forward so I could see. And there was a space next to him like someone had been there before, but they left."

"Go," Ronan says to Taran.

"But sir—"

"Send in Stella. He may have an accomplice."

Taran does as he's asked.

Taking a deep breath, Ronan stretches and leans back against the wall, looking at me. He has the nerve to smirk.

Is this some kind of game to him? A man is dead on his order, a man that I'm genuinely hoping was planning to kill him so that I don't have his death on my conscience, and he's just smirking at me like he was dealt the best hand at the table, and everyone else has bet their fortune.

He's slouching now against the wall, and I am once again one hundred percent certain he's Soren. Either that, or the king has a secret, slum-dwelling twin.

Come to think of it, after everything I've heard about how royalty tends to carry on with the common folk, that's not unlikely.

"Cyrus, you too. Go back to your quarters and check on Quinn."

Cyrus doesn't look like he minds being dismissed, nor does he perceive me as a threat. He leaves without so much as a glance in my direction.

Ronan turns to the guard Taran sent in. "Leave me alone with her."

A shiver runs down my spine. What is he doing?

"But your majesty, Taran would—"

"I know what Taran would say. That's why I sent him away."

The guard swallows hard. She's very young, and she clearly doesn't know how far she should push against the king. Even when he's doing something incredibly reckless, like asking to be left alone with someone who wants to kill him.

Maybe he wants to kill me, and he wants there to be no witnesses.

But I don't see why that should be the case. Surely the king's Grand Vizier and his guards would lie for him. Or they would even do the deed themselves.

"Sir, I—" the guard tries again.

"I'll tell him I made you leave. Go."

"Yes, sir."

The guard leaves, shooting a nervous look in my direction.

We're alone in the room.

Ronan looks at me for a long moment. It's unfair that he can feel what I'm feeling, and I have no idea what's going through his mind.

He crosses the room and stands just a couple of feet in front of me, almost exactly in the same position as when we met the day before. He looks different today. Tired. There are dark circles beneath his eyes.

Almost like he was out late.

He crosses his arms. I'm just beginning to wonder if he's doing the Larus thing and waiting for me to say something when he asks, "You know I can feel everything you're feeling, right?"

So he *did* feel me in the throne room. I'm terrified about what he might do, but I won't give him the satisfaction of sounding afraid. "I'm painfully aware of it," I say, feigning annoyance.

Two can play at this smirking game.

He comes in closer and drops his voice low. "So then why don't you even try to disguise your rage? I felt what he felt," he says, gesturing angrily back to the throne room. "And I felt it from you too. Why wouldn't you even try to hide it?"

My heart feels like it's going to beat its way out of my chest. But at least it seems the man next to me also wanted him dead. Thank Sai for that. "If you felt the same thing from me, why am I standing here? Why am I not splattered on the floor in there?"

"Because you're not a killer."

I almost laugh. He doesn't know how wrong he is. Maybe I can't kill just anyone, that much I've proven over the past few days, but I *could* kill him. At this very moment, I could cut his neck and watch that smirk wipe off his face as the blood drained from his body.

My hand itches for my dagger.

But I still it. It's too soon. We aren't ready. "How would you know that?"

Ronan sighs, and I swear I see some of Soren's exasperation in the movement. "I've had this gift for more than a decade. I haven't been able to walk into a room and *not* feel every emotion that every single person has for years. I'd like to think I know people pretty well by now. I know people better than they know themselves. I knew you the moment I met you. Before it, even. I knew you before I'd even walked into the room.

"Rage at me. Tell me how much you hate me. Burn down my palace and curse my name. Gods know I deserve it. But I know—I *know*—you won't kill me. I know it as well as I know how to breathe. I don't fear you, Sylvie."

He stops and looks me right in the eye. "Not for that reason, at least."

I am floored.

I don't know how long I stare at him, how long the silence hangs in the air between us, but it's an uncomfortably long time. "*Gods know I deserve it.*" What did that mean?

What does he think he deserves?

What did he do?

It can't be about what he did to us. Why would he regret that—regret killing my father, taking my home, leaving my people to starve—when it has given him *everything* in return? He is the God-King. He is the living God of Selara, the ruler, the man who has all the power and all the world at his disposal.

Does he regret it? Or is there something else that he did that makes him think he deserves my hatred and rage?

And what does he think he knows about me, anyway? All he has felt from me is my anger. He has never felt my grief. He has never felt my joy.

My anger is all I have right now, but it's not the total of who I am.

"You don't know me," I say to him. "You know how I feel about you, but you don't know me at all. I am more than what I am to you."

Aren't I?

I expect him to say something else arrogant about how he's the only person in this world whose opinion matters, but he doesn't.

Instead, he smiles lightly. A smile, not a smirk.

"Maybe you're right."

And fuck, it disarms me. It's just like Soren admitting he's a moron. I doubt he even believes his own words, and he's probably just trying to manipulate me into liking him, but it works. A little, not a lot.

It makes me ask the question that has been bothering me. I know I wouldn't have asked him, but I think I may be able to get an honest answer out of him right now. "The man next to me. Was he truly thinking of killing you too? Or could it have been my feelings alone?"

"Oh, he was definitely trying to kill me. I'm absolutely certain of that."

"How do you know?"

"Now, now. Let me have *some* secrets." He winks at me again. "Can I escort you back to your chambers?"

"I can find my own way," I say, although I'm not completely confident that's true. I am pleased he asked, though. Adria's little plan seems to be working in spite of my utter failure to act like I don't want to kill him.

"His accomplice could still be out there," says Ronan. There's a slight edge to his tone, almost like genuine concern.

"And if they are, wouldn't I be in more danger walking with the king they're trying to kill than on my own?"

He rolls his eyes, sighing like I'm the most exasperating person he's ever met. "I'm sending one of my guards, at least. I like the dress, by the way," he says, looking me up and down appreciatively in a very familiar way just before he shouts, "Stella!"

Around dinner, we hear from a servant that the accomplice was found, and the threat has been neutralized. Larus was thrilled to hear of my personal encounter with the king, though I leave out the part about him knowing of my murderous intent. Even Adria couldn't help but seem a little interested, although she still clearly hasn't forgiven me for humiliating her yesterday.

I still don't mention Soren. I decide to go and try to find him again tomorrow after signing up for the Festival of Sport events that I want to participate in, and then I'll decide if it's worth telling the others about.

The Festival of Sport promises to be a great bit of fun if nothing else. There will be events for every magic school and class of fighting, but the event I'm most interested in is archery. Larus didn't want me to waste too much time on mastering the bow, considering I'm too small and weak to draw one over and over again on the battlefield, but shooting targets requires a lot less stamina, and it's one of the few martial sports you can practice on your own.

I had a lot of time alone at the castle. I'm really, really good at it.

The next day, I make my way along with pretty much everyone else in the palace to a courtyard where the guards are collecting names on slates. It's a lovely summer day, and the courtyard itself is undeniably gorgeous, surrounded as it is by elaborately carved columns and archways of red and tan stone. Creeping vines cover nearly every vertical surface in brightly colored flowers, while low bushes line the walkways in neat hedges. I feel out of place in my

Nithyrian leathers while everyone ambles about in their Selaran silks and linen tunics, drifting like petals on the breeze.

I pass by a table for the shadow-born trial. It doesn't specify exactly what the test will be, and I'm tempted to find out, but I don't want to draw more attention than necessary to the fact that I'm shadow-born.

Maybe I shouldn't have blurted it out at the king, then.

Okay, my first couple of days in the palace weren't my best. But to be fair, I've never been in a situation like this before. I've never been around nobles outside of Nithyria. I've never even been outside of Nithyria, and I've been dropped into the viper's nest that is Ronan's court.

I'm trying, and that's what matters. That's what Larus tells me, at least.

When I finally make it to the front of the line at the archery table, I recognize some of the other names on the list from Larus's training about the members of the various houses. Most of them fought in the war, so I imagine they're all pretty good at standing in line and shooting people running at them with swords and fireballs.

But shooting at a bale of hay with a target painted on it from thirty paces in a courtyard? I doubt there's *anyone* on this list who has done that as much as I have.

What else can I do? I glance at the other tables, trying to think strategically. Which events would Ronan compete in? What is most likely to get Ronan's attention? What will give me the greatest chance to learn more about him?

I idly question the guards collecting names for the javelin throw and equestrian events, taking a look at the sign-up sheets as I do. Ronan's name doesn't seem to be on any of the lists. Maybe he won't compete at all.

On the one hand, that makes sense. Who would be willing to truly give it their best effort against the king?

But on the other hand, maybe Ronan is afraid of what would happen if he failed. I would pay to see that. To watch someone best the God-King himself.

And I notice there isn't a light-born trial at all, but from what I know, there would have only been two competitors anyway.

After the court has had their chance to sign up, the courtyard will be opened to the common people of Faros as well. Maybe I should wait around to see if Soren shows up. Or the missing shadow-born girl. Vesper? I think that was her name. I did promise I would keep an eye out for her.

I'm about to take a seat to wait for the commoners when I spot someone over at the registration for the trial of the blade. It's the young woman from the day we met the king, the one with short red hair that Typhon was talking to. Possibly a friend of his, or maybe something more?

It's worth finding out. I head over to the table and hear her speaking to the guards.

"I don't know why she's even allowed to compete. She thinks she isn't Selaran. If you're not Selaran, why compete in a Selaran festival?"

Is she talking about me? She hasn't even seen me.

No, I realize, looking at the slate. She's talking about Adria.

"The tournament is open to all," says the guard. It's the friendly guard who gave me directions to the mask seller. I like this one.

"I'm just saying that it shouldn't be. There are *some types* of people that shouldn't be here at all."

Adria and I may not be on the best of terms at the moment, but I'm not willing to stand around and listen to this nonsense. "Perhaps there are *some types* of people that are afraid of getting their asses handed to them."

"Oh, look," says the woman as she turns to face me, her narrow green eyes filled with scorn. "It's Adria's little bitch sister. I heard they kept you locked up with the other rabid Nithyrian animals."

Rude and fucking dumb. You don't lock up a rabid animal. You put it down.

If I say that to her, she'll just say something about putting me down, and the last thing I need right now is to fight a duel against this woman. She's lean and well-muscled, and of course she's taller than me. And, despite a ton of training, I'm not the best with my sword.

"Maybe they did. Do you want to find out?" I ask, but instead of reaching for my sword, I reach for the chalk and add my name to the list.

The tournament swords will be blunted, and chances are I won't have to face her anyway. I'll probably be out in the first round.

But at least this should get me out of fighting her in this moment.

"Save it for the arena, ladies," warns the guard. "God-King Ronan has made it clear that there are to be no duels in Faros during the festival."

I actually hadn't heard that, but I'm relieved to be hearing it now.

And I can't help but wonder if it has anything to do with what happened to Soren last night.

"Of course," says the woman, plastering on a fake smile for the guard. "Go back to your cage, little bitch," she mutters to me, flicking her hand as if she's dismissing a dog.

I look to the sheet to find the name of the woman I'm definitely going to kill when we take out Ronan: Quinn of House Horatio.

Typhon's sister. The Grand Vizier's youngest daughter.

I wait around the courtyard until the light begins to dim, but Soren doesn't show.

I hadn't really expected him to, although if I were the king, I'm not sure I would've been able to resist joining the tournament in disguise for a real chance to compete.

That's if Soren really is the king. Which is a pretty big if.

I see no girl matching Vesper's description either, but I don't really know what I'm looking for. What if she changed her hair or took out her piercings? I wouldn't know her even if I saw her.

I debate going back to the market. If I could find Soren, maybe he could give me more to go on. Or maybe he's already found Vesper, and I'm worrying for nothing.

I can't help but worry though. I know the worst that can happen to a shadow-born spy.

It happened to my mother.

I sigh. The market will be closing for the day soon anyway. I'll have to try to find Soren and Vesper another time. After a day out in the sun of the courtyard, I'm sweaty in my leathers, so I head to the baths to rinse off.

My first visit to the baths was late at night when they were nearly empty. I was grateful for the privacy; I'm not accustomed to bathing in the nude around strangers. Back at the castle, we had a fire-born heat the water in copper tubs in bathing rooms attached to our bed chambers. It was so luxurious sinking into the piping hot water after a long day training with Larus.

The baths here are natural pools within the caves beneath the palace. The water is beautifully clear though, and there are pools of different temperatures you can use depending on your mood.

I undress in a chamber made from a smaller cave, leaving my leathers on hooks on the wall and wrapping in a towel made of finely-woven linen. It's wonderfully soft on the skin. The changing room is busy with courtiers I don't know and who I know don't want to know me.

That's fine. We have plenty of time to change their minds.

I head to one of the cooler pools. The temperature is lower down here, but the heat of the sun seems to linger on you in Faros. There are only a few women in this pool, and they're sitting at the opposite end talking quietly among themselves. I sink into the water, letting my hair down from its bun and diving beneath the surface to wash the day off of me.

Before I can relax, I hear muffled shouting from under the water. I surface, and I recognize one of the voices immediately: Adria.

I climb out of the pool and dry off as quickly as I can. I've barely gotten the towel around me when I catch a whiff of smoke. There's another voice yelling, also a woman. It sounds familiar, but I don't recognize it until I get close enough to hear her words.

"I told that bitch sister of yours the same thing," says Quinn. It's *her* again. This woman is everywhere.

"Leave her out of this. This is between you and me," says Adria.

I round the corner and see them. They're standing across the water in the hot room, both of them wearing only towels. They're unarmed, at least, but Adria is fire-born, and that means she's still dangerous.

And, judging by the flame she's twisting in her fingertips, Quinn is fire-born too.

Great.

"What's going on?" I ask, my voice echoing in the cave.

"Stay out of it," says Adria.

"Too afraid to fight me alone?" asks Quinn.

"Hardly," says Adria.

"If you had dicks, I'd tell you to get them out."

All three of us look around for the speaker. A woman rises slowly from the steaming hot pool. She's old, with curly grey hair that has gone straight at the wet ends and sagging, wrinkled breasts.

She doesn't reach for a towel. Instead, she hobbles naked over to Quinn, who is closer to her. She draws herself up as tall as she can. She barely reaches the top of Quinn's towel, but it doesn't seem to bother her any. "Stop this ridiculous display. You are of noble blood."

Quinn opens her mouth to protest, but the woman gives her a withering glare. "Yes, your majesty." Quinn bows in contrition.

Your majesty? There's only one other person alive who merits that honorific. This must be the Dowager Queen Claudia of House Juni.

Ronan's grandmother.

Queen Claudia glares at Adria from across the water. Adria bows as well and hastily walks back to the changing room, shooting a warning glare of her own at Quinn that says, "Don't even think about following me."

"It's the fire in them," says a voice from behind me. It's Zara, the Guild Mistress of the Alchemists' Guild, back at the palace again.

"Fire or not, there's such a thing as manners," says Queen Claudia. "You seem to have a better sense of that, from what I've heard."

She gestures in my direction. Me? Someone must have been talking to her about me.

Ronan?

"Yes, your majesty," I say. I can't remember if I'm meant to bow to her, but the others did, so I do as well. I keep a tight grip on my towel; I feel exposed enough in front of these people without being literally naked.

"Are you enjoying your time in the palace?"

"Yes, ma'am. Very much so."

"You see? This one has the grace to lie to keep the peace." She smiles at me and looks me over, judging something. But she says nothing else. She's still dripping as she walks back to the changing room with no towel.

With the dowager gone, Zara disrobes and enters the pool.

I hesitate. I have no love for the alchemists, but Larus did mention that it would be good to get to know her. Maybe I should join her.

"Do you know her?" I ask as I take a seat on an outcropping of rock that has been polished smooth by the water. "Quinn?"

She nods, moving closer to talk to me. Maybe she really is lonely. "For a few years now, since I was first invited to the palace after I joined the Guild."

I know the question I want to ask her, but I'm not sure how it will be taken. "Are she and the king…well, are they together?"

Zara laughs. "Definitely not." She leans in conspiratorially. It looks like she wants to gossip, and I'm so glad. "Quinn has been with just about everyone under fifty in the court, and I don't think she plans to stop anytime soon. Maybe they've slept together too, I don't know. But I doubt it. He's not the type."

"What do you mean by that?" I have to ask. I try to appear disinterested, but I'm certain she sees through me.

I decide that's not necessarily a bad thing. Rumors could fuel his interest in me, and if it gets back to him, that will also let me know something about whether Zara can be trusted.

"He's not fire-born," she says. "Whatever his habits are, he keeps them quiet. He doesn't let many people get close enough to know."

Everyone says that about him, but he let me be in a room alone with him after thinking about killing him.

Why?

Zara's waiting for me to say something. "Kerensa save me from the fire-born," I say. It's a common saying in Nithyria.

Zara nods sagely. "A prayer truly worth praying."

We chat for a time, mostly about how she came from Eki specifically to join the Guild and how it's renowned around the world after the alchemy breakthrough.

"Of course, there are some issues here we didn't have back home."

"Like?"

She scratches her fingernails on the ledge of stone behind us, tension growing in her arms. "There are types of magic we aren't allowed to research."

"Aren't allowed?" Who could possibly tell the head of the Guild what they can research? The Guild is on an equal footing with the temples within the church. I thought they governed themselves.

"What's the Selaran saying? 'Speak of Vahlo, and he appears'?" she says, glancing at a group of men entering the room as we're getting out of the water. They aren't the first men we've seen. It was difficult not to stare at first; I haven't seen a man naked in some time, and some of the men at court are in excellent shape.

But the men who enter now are like gods, I can tell even from a distance. Perfectly chiseled bodies of pure muscle in shades of tan and brown. It's a pity they're wrapped in their towels, but maybe they'll get in the water so I can have a better look.

I sigh in appreciation.

"He is very beautiful, isn't he? Too bad he doesn't deign to bathe with the rest of us. And too bad he's…him," says Zara, and I suddenly realize who they are.

It's Ronan, walking with Taran and another guard I've seen before but don't know by name. I hadn't recognized them at this distance with their hair wet and slicked back.

Stupid sexy God-King. His body is literally as perfect as I imagined it. No, not imagined it. I didn't *imagine* it; I just could fill in the blanks from the glimpses I got.

And the parts of it I felt when Soren touched me.

I feel the heat rising in my face *again*, and *oh gods, I'm naked.*

Zara drops a golden bangle on the ground as she puts it back on, and the clinking noise makes them turn.

Ronan spots me, and I want the ground to swallow me up and eat me. I try not to think about him looking at my body. I know I'm meant to seduce him, but not like this. I don't want to be the vulnerable one. I wrap my towel around me as quickly as I can.

He's all the way across the cave so I can't see him clearly, but I could swear he fucking winks.

I'm going to rip that eyeball right out of its socket.

"Slippery when wet," says Zara, holding up her bangle to show it has returned safely to her wrist.

I smile. She seems genuine enough. Maybe she picked up on my "attraction" to the king and was trying to help me out as a friend.

Or maybe she has some other purpose in encouraging our relationship.

I'm feeling crazy again. This place is making me crazy. I don't need to second-guess everything every single person does.

Or do I?

Chapter Eleven

The beginning of the Festival of Sport comes with all of the over-the-top pomp and ceremony that I could have asked for.

The Sacred Flame of Sai is borne down from his temple near the northern wall of Faros to the great arena across the river by fire-born runners, with chariots of the courtiers trailing behind.

Our chariot is at the back of the procession, but I don't mind. It gives me a chance to see the entire parade as it moves down the hill in front of us.

The trail of flame is striking against the city at night. Ronan's chariot is just behind it, but it turns off course just outside the arena. Then it circles around the streets and behind us so that he's the last to enter.

The arena is a great oval of the same reddish-tan stone that the palace is built from, only the entire structure is about the height of the palace's highest towers. We enter through a dark tunnel underneath it, the stomping of thousands of feet over us sending vibrations into the stone walls. I fear for a moment that the whole thing will come crashing down on top of us, but soon we're inside, and I let out a gasp at the sight.

The entire city of Faros must be here. I thought the market was overwhelming, but *this*. This is insane.

"One hundred thousand people," says Larus. I can barely hear him over the noise. "It's the largest arena in the world."

The rows of people stretch all the way into the sky, so high I have to bend my head back to see them all. I had no idea there were this many people here. I had no idea there were this many people *anywhere*.

I don't know where Seth is going to round up enough people to take this city. There are dozens of villages in the mountains, more people than we can feed, but I can't imagine that we have this many prepared to fight.

I stop the thought—although Ronan has already figured out that I'd like to murder him, he certainly doesn't know about the rest of our plan yet, and I'd rather he didn't find out. Though I'm not certain how "planning to start a war" would even feel to him.

Our chariot circles around to join the others as we wait for his grand entrance. I hear the thunder of the horse's hooves before I see him. A hush comes over the crowd. This is what they came to see.

Ronan's chariot rises from the tunnel with the final fire-born flame bearer at his side.

It's fucking Quinn.

Adria's hand goes for her sword reflexively even though she's no threat to us at the moment. The chariot passes us and continues to circle the arena to allow all to see Sai's Sacred Flame, now held suspended above Quinn's bare hand, go by.

The chariot halts before an enormous golden cauldron at the center of the arena. Quinn, wearing red ceremonial robes, ascends the steps to the edge of the cauldron and waits as Ronan follows behind her. It's much too loud in the arena for his voice to be heard even if he yells, but that problem is resolved when the last member of their chariot slowly ascends the steps at Ronan's side.

It's Queen Claudia, almost unrecognizable in her own deep red robes and coronet. She takes her place beside Ronan, laying her hand on his shoulder.

"Welcome, Selarans, friends, and honored guests, to the Great Festival of the Gods!"

Ronan's voice is magically amplified, filling the arena and rising over all the screaming voices.

Queen Claudia must be wind-born. She did seem like a bit of a talker in the baths, as the wind-born tend to be.

"Today we begin the Festival of Sport to honor Sai, the great and terrible God of War, the Hunt, and the Forge." A priestess exits a different chariot and joins him on the stage. Claudia moves her hand to the priestess's shoulder as she leads a prayer to Sai.

"Most holy Sai, King of the Warriors, we ask you to bless us as we honor you with the gifts you have given us. We ask that you select your Champions wisely, lending them your strength so that they may protect us this day and in all battles to come. For Sai, victorious!"

The priestess climbs the stairs near the cauldron and cuts her hand, spilling her blood into it.

Sai's devoted are the most dramatic, I swear. Even Ronan cringes a little at the sight.

"We will see many wonderful competitions in the coming days. But though we honor the God of War, we do so in a time of peace. We come together in unity, and in the spirit that all who participate in the tournament to come are worthy of Sai's blessings, no matter the outcome."

"Sure, Ronan. We're all winners here," I mutter to Larus.

He chuckles. "Are you not inspired to go easy on your opponents? Do you not feel the grace and love of the king and his desire for peace and harmony?"

"Not even a little," I reply.

There's no chance anyone can hear us with all the noise, and if Ronan can feel our disdain, it can't be a surprise to him at this point.

"General Quinn, daughter of our most noble Grand Vizier Lord Cyrus of House Horatio, will do the honors of lighting the ceremonial cauldron of Sai. General?"

General Quinn? I guess that explains her and Adria's animosity towards each other.

Quinn, who has been holding onto the flame above her bare hand the entire time, ascends the final steps to the side of the cauldron to its top. Once she's there, she dips her hand to the rim, and the flame ignites it, racing around the edge of the cauldron.

It's fine, I guess. It's like the torches in the temple, only bigger. The crowd loves it, though. They cheer and stomp their feet so loud I bet they can hear them in Nithyria.

"Then, with Sai's blessing, let the games begin!"

On Ronan's final word, he raises his hand, and an enormous ball of light like a tiny sun flies out from it and into the sky above the arena. A hush comes over the crowd as it rises higher and higher, heading for the stars.

Then it bursts into a thousand smaller lights in every color in the rainbow, each of them flickering and falling into the crowd, vanishing before they touch the ground.

It's *amazing*, I hate to admit. I've never seen anything even remotely like it. The crowd gasps at the wonder of it. And then they cheer even louder than before.

Ronan locks eyes with me as I stare at him. I hope my face isn't too filled with awe. It's not like his ego needs the boost.

He looks so good up there, and he knows it. He's everything a king is meant to be. Tall, handsome, proud. An effortless leader. To the eyes of the public, he's perfect.

Only we know the truth. And we won't let him forget it.

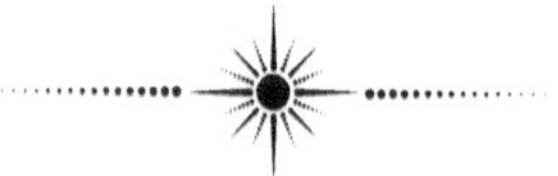

The tournament begins the day following the opening ceremony, but our qualifying events aren't until the end of the week, leaving us a few days to practice.

Adria had been baffled to learn I joined the sword-fighting competition, but it has given her an opportunity to do what she loves to do best: look down on me for being worse than her at something.

She and I find a spot in a secluded cloister near one of the palace's many courtyards with boundaries nearly the same size as those in the arena. The tournament will be scored in what I'm told is a typical fashion: points for each strike landed on the opponent and a loss of points for stepping outside of the boundaries.

I face Adria in our matching leathers. We've been given blunted swords to use for the entirety of the tournament, so we aren't in danger of hurting each other too much, but a blunted blade can still leave a nasty bruise.

And we can't have me looking black and blue if I'm meant to be seducing the king.

I'm coming around to the idea, I realize. It could be fun to get him hot and bothered, desperate to be with me, and then to drop him on his face.

To drop him to the ground. And then *in* the ground.

Adria begins pacing in front of me, meaning we've begun.

The sword in my hand is different than the one I usually carry. That sword is long and thin, with a deadly point made for thrusting, but it's fairly useless against someone wearing chainmail. This sword is a battlefield weapon: broader with a much longer handle meant for wielding it two-handed.

I'm able to parry Adria's opening series of thrusts far better than I can with our own blades: left, right, and then a low cut that leaves us bound. My blunted steel meets hers with surprising accuracy. Adria's moves are almost indetectable with her usual weapon, which is very similar to mine, but with this longsword, I can see her coming from a mile away.

She breaks the bind by charging forward, the strong part of her sword near the handle meeting the weak end of my blade near the point, sending my blade to my right and leaving my chest open for her to strike with a quick attack.

"Not bad," she says as we break. She didn't get me on the first attack, which is a pretty good performance for me. I beam at the weak praise. "Of course, this damned thing has all the liveliness of a child's stick sword."

Of course she would blame the sword.

It's my turn to attack now. She's had me on the defensive for so much of our lives, I'm not sure if I even can remember *how* to attack her. I try taking a high guard, but I move forward too early, and she parries my point and quickly comes around my back to strike while I'm still off-balance.

"Again," she says after she makes contact.

I'm breathing heavier now. I may not be able to beat her, but at least I'm going to get in a good workout.

She comes at me with two quick cuts. I misjudge my parry, and as I dodge backwards from the blow she's about to land on my stomach, I lose my footing and fall on my ass.

"Again," says Adria, not bothering to see if I'm okay.

I hear footsteps approaching as I pick myself up.

"She always feints left, you know," says a familiar voice.

Adria bows as King Ronan rounds the corner, and I do the same. "Does she?" I ask. I wonder how long he's been watching us.

"Do I, *your majesty*?" asks Adria, emphasizing the honorific that I've forgotten. She's acting frightened again, and I wonder if Ronan can see through it, or if he's just accustomed to this response from people because it doesn't seem to faze him.

"Everyone has a tell. Let me demonstrate," he says, holding out his hand for my sword.

To my knowledge, the only person in our family who has faced Ronan directly was my father, and he lost. But Adria is at least as good of a fighter as Father was, and she's a lot angrier than I ever remember him being.

I back out of the way to watch with Ronan's guards. Their exchange is lightning quick, so much so that I can barely follow the different attacks they send at each other. But even at this speed, he can see her attacks coming, and he has no trouble parrying them at first.

And then I see it: just as he said, she feints to the left. He doesn't take the bait like I always do. He anticipates the thrust to the right that always gets me and counters it, nearly getting her neck.

While she's recovering her footing, he attacks with one decisive downward thrust, which he stops just short of her breastbone.

It looks impressive, but I can't help but wonder if she let him do that.

"See?" says Ronan. He holds out the sword to me. "Now you try."

"I think I've had enough for today," says Adria. What is she talking about? She's barely broken a sweat. "But if you'd like to give Sylvie a few pointers, your majesty…"

Adria, what the fuck? Don't leave me alone to make a fool out of myself with him.

Unless he gets off on that. Which…actually seems likely, come to think of it.

"With pleasure," says Ronan. He takes Adria's sword from her as she smirks in my direction, then he holds my sword out to me again. "Shall we?"

Reluctantly, I take the blade from him. I get into position across the floor, measuring him up. He's much taller than me, which means he'll have a major advantage with reach. I'll need to watch out for attacks from above to my head, but that's the case when I fight almost anyone, so I'm quite good at defending against them.

What's more problematic is how good he looks. He's wearing breeches with a grey linen tunic tucked into them, and the laces on the chest are open, revealing the tan muscle of his chest. It's an obscene little shirt, and though my mind is trying desperately to focus on the tactics that could keep me from completely humiliating myself in this fight, my body has other ideas.

Extremely not helpful, I tell my nipples as they harden under my own tunic. Thank the gods my leather armor covers my chest. Although the slight upturn of the corner of his mouth lets me know he felt at least some of what I felt just then.

This isn't a bad thing, I try to remind myself. My body can protect my mind. It can protect my heart. It's not a betrayal. It's exactly what I need to happen.

I'm expecting an attack at any moment, but Ronan lowers his sword instead. "Let's start with fixing your stance."

I look down at my legs. They're bent slightly and angled to my opponent as Larus taught me. "What's wrong with my stance?"

"Nothing if you're fighting with a rapier. But you should face more forward with this sword, and you probably want to open up more to get more leverage for cuts. Try a high cut from here first, and then again wider and more forward."

I try the cut from my current stance. It seems fine, but I am having to fight the blade a bit to keep it straight.

"Now from the front."

I turn towards the front, but he stops me before I swing. "Not quite. Bend a bit more."

I bend my knees further.

"Too far," he says with a laugh. "Can I show you?"

He puts down his sword and begins to walk over. I nod and lower my weapon, trying to ignore the fluttering in my chest as he approaches.

He keeps eye contact with me as he holds out his hands towards my legs. I nod again.

He gently places his hands on my hips to guide them into the correct position. I'm holding my breath, and I'm not sure why. "Move this foot forward a bit," he says, bending to grab my left knee.

His head is dangerously close to the lower half of my body, and it stirs something down there.

Fuck.

He absolutely had to feel whatever the fuck *that* was.

It's good, it's good, I tell myself as I move the foot forward. I can't tell if I'm more aroused or humiliated.

He stands back and assesses. "Better. Take a high guard now."

I do as he says, drawing my sword up and over my right shoulder.

"Chest out," he says, and my heart races for a moment when I think he might touch me *there*, but he just demonstrates himself.

And, well, it's a nice demonstration. His muscles strain against those useless little strings—*seriously, who made this shirt?*—and it's just very nice to look at. Entirely too perfect, but it's impossible to deny how easy he is on the eyes.

As I puff my chest out, my mind starts turning to what would happen if the leather wasn't there, and I shut it down immediately.

Absolutely not, body. Calm down.

"Ass—um, rear out too," he says, for once not meeting my eyes.

"Oh, fuck off," I say, breaking my stance and lowering my sword.

He laughs and holds up his hands, and I see Soren in the gesture. I'm annoyed enough with him right now that I want to come out and ask him, but he takes the stance once more, puffing out his chest and poking out his ass, and it's so fucking ridiculous I lose my train of thought.

Is he a child? I'm not putting on a damn show for him, God-King of Selara or not.

"No way. I'm not doing that."

He's still laughing. "I promise, this is the stance. I'm not being rude. I'll close my eyes if you don't want me to look."

He covers his stupid perfect face with his hand and peeks through it.

"Asshole."

"Stella, come here and show her your longsword stance."

Poor young Stella comes over and draws her sword—her real sword—and she assumes the exact stance Ronan is trying to get me into without so much as a blush on her tan cheeks. Chest out, ass out.

"Ridiculous," I say. "Why can't we just fight with rapiers?" The rapier stance is way less provocative.

"Because they're expensive, and there are one hundred people in the trial of the blade."

And they probably had a lot of these swords lying around after the war ended.

I pout, but I slowly draw myself back into the longsword stance. I puff my chest out, and then…I stick my ass out too.

I may not be able to feel what Ronan feels, but I can see his sharp intake of breath and the way his eyes linger a bit too long on the curves of my body to just be evaluating my posture before they return to mine.

He likes what he sees. The part of me that stirred when he was bending stirs once more.

"Better," he says.

He paces back across the floor and mirrors my stance. He really does stand the way I'm standing, and I envy the guards their position, which offers them a much better view of his ass.

Gods, I need to concentrate. If I keep this up, I'm going to get *my ass* handed to me.

"Ladies first," says Ronan.

I don't hesitate. I'm hoping my sudden movement will catch him off his guard, and it nearly does. I'm going for his hands to disarm him, but he parries my point with the strong part of his blade at the last moment and comes in for a quick riposte to my shoulder.

"That was actually very good," he says.

And godsdammit, that's nice to hear, even coming from him.

"Try the same again, but this time, be ready for my riposte."

I do as he says, and he goes for the same attack after he parries, but I take a step back and knock his sword away.

"Very good."

"As long as my opponent tells me what he's going to do beforehand, I'll stand a chance."

He drops his guard. "You're very good at this. You do know that, don't you?"

"I don't need your pity."

"It's the truth. I watched you. Adria's one of the best sword fighters in the kingdom. She's more practiced, but her training happened on the battlefield. This isn't a battle. It's a sport. Adria knows how to go for the kill. You're smart enough to see other options."

He watched me.

"And you know that how? My feelings? Do I *feel* smart?"

He smirks. "Among other things."

Heat drifts down to my core instead of my neck this time. I know exactly which feelings I've been having around him.

We continue for several more rounds, and though our exchanges are lasting a bit longer, he wins every last one.

I do appreciate that he doesn't just let me win. Although I'm not sure if it's for my sake that he doesn't or his.

"I'm dying," he says, wiping the sweat from his brow. It's a bit past midday, and the sunlight has started to shine into our covered alcove. It gave me a small advantage in our last exchange when my sword glinted in his eye: I finally managed to make contact with him, but unfortunately, he got me in my belly at the same time.

I am melting in my leathers, though. I'm not sure what he's complaining about in his clothes, which are so thin they might as well not be there. "Do you mind if I…?" he asks, pulling at the hem of that absurd shirt of his.

"Go ahead," I say a little too quickly.

There's a hint of a smile on his lips as he pulls the tunic over his head.

Fuuuuuuck.

I thought I'd seen it all through the laces, but I hadn't even scratched the surface.

I can see why they call him the God-King. It isn't because he's the end of a long line of nobility believed to be descended from the goddess Vayla herself.

It's because of his abs.

The whole chest area, really. I don't know the names for all the muscles, but they're all there, and they're exquisitely cut and hard and—wait, is that a scar?

It is. There's a scar there on his left side. It's long and deep, from a brutal cut that must have nearly killed him.

I wonder why he didn't have it healed with the others he got in the war.

I struggle to keep thinking of it as my eyes follow the V-shaped crease of his muscles to his thin, silky breeches and…let me stop my thoughts right there again before I make a fool out of myself.

He chuckles a little, and honestly, fuck him. It isn't fair that he gets to know every embarrassing feeling I have.

And it isn't fair for me to be the only one distracted.

"Do you mind if I…?" I say, reaching my fingertips under the ties that hold down my leather chest piece.

"Go ahead," he says.

I take my time removing the chest piece and pauldrons, keeping myself turned to him so he has a good view. Then I unbuckle the leather leg guards I'm wearing over my pants. I feel much cooler but also much more exposed.

I hope my gamble pays off.

I get back into the stance he taught me, and this time, I feel my breasts move with my chest as I push it out. The undergarments I wear when I'm wearing my leathers don't do much to keep them in place, which isn't going to feel great when I'm fighting, but I'm hoping it will be worth it.

"Like this?" I say, though I know perfectly well how to stand by now.

He tilts his head unblinkingly. "Just right."

There's a soft, sultry quality to his voice that tells me this was *absolutely* the right decision.

I go for an attack from waist height. I cut down towards his legs and duck under his blade, which works.

It actually works. I hit him in the thigh, and he misses me entirely.

"Yes!"

"Good, but it was a risk. I shouldn't have missed that."

"Shouldn't have, but you did," I gloat. I can't help myself.

"Are you a sore winner, Sylvie?"

"I think you're about to find out."

I've noticed something in the way he attacks. It's like the way Adria loves to do a feint to the left. Ronan loves to leave something, usually his left side, unguarded as bait so he can get you with a quick parry and riposte.

I'm usually so busy parrying his furious movements that I fall for it, but he's moving a bit slower this time.

My breasts bounce on my chest as I lunge forward and back for a quick attack and then a parry for his counter, and I can guess what's causing the slowdown.

I'm finding it hard not to stare at his chest as well. And his arms. And his back when he cuts down. The muscles tighten and ripple beautifully.

And then there's the way he looks at me, especially when I get close to him. It's not just hunger or excitement, although that's there too. It's something like fascination. Like he can't believe that I'm real.

It makes me feel bold. Powerful.

It makes me feel like I could bring him to his knees.

"Something the matter?" I tease.

"I don't know, is there?" he replies as he manages a glancing blow on my shoulder.

"Touché."

He smiles then, really smiles, and it makes his skin glow a little. I wonder if he knows how appealing that is. "One last time?" he asks.

I nod. I'm exhausted, but there's a part of me that doesn't want to stop. I have to admit that this was a good idea. I'm getting in good practice with the longsword, and I'm learning a lot about how Ronan fights.

I may or may not share that information with Adria. We'll see how nice she is to me tonight.

I prepare for his attack. He lunges, I parry, he lunges again, I parry again. I bring my sword up for a high cut, and he rushes forward. But he's got my blade to deal with, so he doesn't take the thrust he intended to my side.

Instead, he takes his left hand off the sword and grabs me by the shoulder.

He pulls me to him, trying to control my sword arm. I grab the blunted blade with my left hand to control it and thrash against him.

But he's too strong. He abandons his own sword and overpowers me quickly, forcing the blade from my hand.

He pulls me against him.

My head is pressed against his bare chest. It feels so good, I nearly forget that I've lost the fight.

"You're dead," he whispers in my ear. He has my own blade pointed at my side, but he doesn't take the point.

I don't know what makes me do it. I don't know if it's something about his magic or the proximity or my desperation or the way that looks at me or the way flirting with Soren made me feel.

But I see my opportunity, and I go for it.

I shift my hips to meet his. *He's rock hard.* I rub myself against him, lightly, just once.

He inhales sharply in surprise.

Then I snatch the blade from his hand.

I jump back and land the point directly on his heart.

"No, you are."

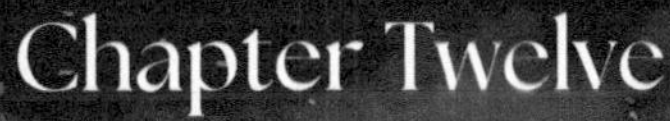

Chapter Twelve

It takes a moment for him to compose himself. He's frozen there in front of me, vulnerable at the end of my blunted blade, his eyes running from my sword to my lips to my hips and back.

Oh, I've won alright.

He looks like he's seriously considering tossing the sword to the side and taking me in his arms.

But he controls himself, his mouth twitching as he backs away, laughing. "Well done."

I lower the sword and give him a little bow. I try not to think too much of the feeling of him hard against me, of how satisfying it was to hear his little gasp of surprise.

Of the way my body stirred in response.

Of the way it pulses with warmth to see him smiling and clapping for me.

All part of the plan, I tell myself. It's the plan and nothing more.

Off to the side, someone clears their throat.

It's Taran. He must have arrived at some point during our last exchange.

My mood shifts instantly, and I know Ronan can sense it because he asks, "Something wrong?"

"You know what's wrong. I don't understand how you can have someone like that as your guard."

After everything his people have done to mine. To parade an Orsan around us.

It's insulting.

"Someone like what, exactly?" says Ronan. He quickly puts his shirt back on, and I do the same with my armor.

"Someone like him. He's Orsan." As I say the words, I hear how dangerously close they sound to what Quinn was saying about us.

But it's different. We're the victims of them both: the Orsa and the Selarans. It makes sense for us to hate them.

Ronan's lips press into a thin line. He draws himself up into his full regal posture and crosses back to me.

He towers over me.

"What do you even know about the Orsa?" he asks, an accusation in his voice.

What do I know? Is he kidding?

"What do I know? What I know is that they've killed my people for generations. I know they've raided our lands and stolen our home."

King or not, I won't be insulted in this way. My father started a war for this.

"Taran, come here."

Taran does as his king commands. I've been too distracted with everything going on to pay much attention to him, but I get a good, long look at him now.

Admittedly, he doesn't look that threatening. He's not a tall man, only an inch or so taller than Adria, I'd guess, his body all lean muscle. His hair is a bright, sun-bleached blonde, almost as light as an infant's. His eyes are a clear baby blue, and his face is even more freckled than mine.

But I don't let his boyish appearance fool me. I can tell everything I need to know about him from the dark tattoo on his neck. The shapes of it are geometric, but they follow the curve of his body in an organic way. I might be impressed by the artistry if I wasn't so repulsed by everything it stands for.

"Tell her about when we found you."

Taran looks to Ronan in confusion. "Your majesty? I came to tell you Queen Claudia is looking for you—"

"She can wait. Tell her about what happened to your people."

Taran and I have at least one thing in common: we don't know where the king is going with this.

But Taran can't refuse him, so he does as he asks, even though it clearly makes him uncomfortable. "They came into my camp in the night while we were sleeping. I was eleven. We'd been there maybe a month, following the game down into the valley."

Poaching illegally, more like it. Poaching was punishable by death.

"We had no real fighters among us. They'd been lost in previous raids on our home, leaving only a couple who knew their way around a sword. Our hunting bows were no use in the ambush."

Those previous raids had likely been in response to their own.

Ronan's eyes are on me, and he scowls in disapproval at my emotional response.

Let him.

Taran swallows, looking down at his boots as if it can prevent him from having to picture what he's saying. "I was in the forest when they came. I'd gotten up in the night to relieve myself, and I hid when I heard the screams. It…it wasn't quick. They kept some of them alive for hours. My parents, my sister—"

He chokes a little on the last word.

And it slaps me awake.

Neither his words nor his response to the memories should come as a surprise to me, but they do. I've never spoken to an Orsan before. I've never thought of what the stories would sound like from the other side.

I've heard about our righteous slaughter of the Orsan raiders who attacked our own people many, many times. Every story felt like vengeance. Every story felt like victory against a savage foe.

But Taran, even now many years later, doesn't look savage.

I know how he feels, I realize. I know how it feels to lose your family to something that you have no say in. To be powerless to do anything to help them because you're too young.

"I found their bodies in the morning. They—they had no clothes. They had wounds in places…I couldn't leave them like that. The Nithyrians had taken everything—our skins, our linens. But I found a shovel, and I dug them a grave."

"And that's where we found him," said Ronan. "My father and I, out on a hunt in Nithyria like we did sometimes before the war. We found him dragging his mother's naked body into a shallow grave." His look pierces me. "Eleven years old."

My stomach twists and lurches upward, a cold, sick wave flooding my chest until I feel like I might retch right here.

I don't have anything to say to that. I can't think of *anything* that could justify what happened to him. What happened to his people. It's one thing to stop poachers. That's necessary, especially when people are starving. But what happened to them—if it's true?

It's inexcusable. Dishonorable. Vile.

Who had done it? Was it my own father?

My mother?

Larus?

"Sylvie?" says Ronan, lifting a hand in my direction but stopping himself.

I lean against a pillar for support. The world feels as if it's tilting beneath me, my breath coming in shallow, uneven gasps. It takes a minute, maybe longer, before I can steady myself enough to find my voice, to push past the tightness in my throat and speak.

"I'm sorry," I say quietly, knowing it isn't enough. It could never be enough to make up for what he lost. What my people took from him. I look up into Taran's blue eyes, so vividly clear and piercing I feel exposed beneath their gaze.

We took everything from him, just as Ronan and his family had taken everything from us. "I didn't know."

I've hated the Orsa since I was a child. I was brought up with warnings about leaving our lands, told countless times by my parents, by Larus, by Adria, by Seth, and even by our servants, about the danger they posed to us. That they would kill me in my sleep without a second thought. That they'd drag me off in the night and force me to bear their children. I accepted it as true without question.

And I still believe them, but I can't help but think about why Taran joined the fight against us. It wasn't because he was inherently bad. He was just a child; how bad could he have possibly been? It was because we had taken everything from *him*, and in a brutal, horrible way.

We took out our enemies that day, and in the process, we made a new one.

"I tried to fight Ronan when he found me. I thought he was one of you."

His words sting, but I can't blame him for seeing me as one of his enemies.

I had seen him that way until only moments ago.

"Thankfully, all he had was that shovel. But my father was so impressed with his courage, he asked him to join his guard in training, and the rest is history," says Ronan.

Taran clears his throat, an awkward smile tugging at his lips at Ronan's praise, searching for something to redirect the conversation and lighten the mood.

"If we're reliving the past, you should at least tell her about the birthday when you challenged me to a duel because you thought I'd drunk the last of your beer."

Ronan laughs, and I can see the years of friendship between them. Taran is more than Ronan's guard. He's a confidant, a companion whose loyalty is rooted not in duty but in their history together.

I'm embarrassed by what I've said about him.

But I'm also angry because it all comes down to the food. Maybe if we'd had enough food, we wouldn't have needed to treat poachers so harshly, and we could have shared more of our land. "I am sorry for what happened to you. No one should have treated you or your people that way. But my people were starving because of what Selara demands of us. My people are *still* starving because of what Selara demands of us. We have done what we have to in order to survive."

Ronan and Taran exchange a look I can't read. "Is that what they've told you?" asks Ronan.

My blood boils at the implication that we'd lie about that. "I've seen the hungry people myself. I've seen the spoiled grain."

Ronan's brow furrows, genuine confusion spreading over his features as he studies me. It's clear this revelation unsettles him, and for a moment, he seems at a loss for words. "But have you yourself ever gone hungry?"

"I—"

No, I hadn't. The castle had many mouths to feed, all of them vital to keeping the country—*province*, whatever—running.

Just because there was enough to feed the castle, that didn't mean there was enough for everyone.

"There was a problem with the grain last harvest," Ronan explains, "but we increased our imports from Brakkar to make up for it. Your stores should have kept you going in the meantime. That's the report I have from Typhon. Was it inaccurate?"

Shit.

I may have just revealed something I shouldn't have. I know we've kept Typhon out of our plans. I'm not sure what we told him to report back to the king. It sounds like we managed to hide the problem with the grain from Typhon.

But…why? I thought we'd asked Ronan for help, and he'd refused. He's acting like he didn't know there was a problem at all.

"Just because things are better now doesn't mean we've forgotten the past," I lie, hoping he doesn't notice my confusion.

"I wouldn't expect you to," says Ronan. "But I hope you'll also think of the future."

He looks at me intently, and Taran backs away a bit to give us some space.

Ronan drops his voice so it's very low and soft, the same sort of intimacy he offered me on the night we met. "We have lived with these feuds all our lives. There are scores being kept that have been kept since long before we were born, and if we don't do something to change it, they'll keep going long after we die. We can tally them all up, measure whose loss hurts the most, find out who is owed the most in repentance. A point here, a point there. Weigh the missing grain, count the parents taken from their children. Gather up all the blood, sweat, and tears and see whose make the deeper ocean. But to what end? Where does it stop? Are we doomed to repeat this pattern for all eternity?"

It's easy for him to say this from the top. He won. If we let the feud end here, he's triumphant. Would he feel the same way if our rebellion had been a success?

A wrinkle forms between his brows. "You don't believe me?"

"It's not that I don't. It's just that I think it's a lot easier to say what you're saying when you're the winner."

"It didn't feel like victory." There's a raw edge to his voice, the same bare, painful look on his face as when we first met. "What I'm saying is that there is no winner. There shouldn't be. This world was built on violence. On slavery, on conquest. On the backs of the other, the outsider, the stranger. The enemy. There's always an enemy. The alchemists tell me it's in our nature. The strong over the weak. The pure over the tainted. The priests tell me it's destined by the gods. The righteous will triumph over the unworthy.

"But the gift I was granted has taught me one truth: there are no others. Whatever it is that we are, we're the same. And this beautiful, terrible world has enough for all of us, or it did until we destroyed it. Until my family destroyed it, and yours too."

My family didn't destroy anything. What little we had was taken from us. His *father* is the one who destroyed it all.

"But I believe it can have enough again, if we nurture it. If we work together to build something better than what was given to us. This festival isn't just for fun. We were born into a fight that doesn't have to be ours. We can choose another path."

What is this? Some kind of trick? A pretty speech to make me feel like he cares so I won't do what I came here to do?

If it is, he's a better actor than even Adria. He's wasted on the throne. He should have been on the stage.

And if he's being genuine, if he really believes what he's saying, what does he intend to do about it? Pretty words won't save my people. Pretty words won't feed them. It's nice that he wants to build a world where we all have enough one day, but what about right now?

And what am *I* meant to do about what he says, anyway? "Why are you telling me this?" I ask him. "I'm not the head of House Verran. I'm not even the heir."

"Because I know you'll listen. Because I know you're smart enough to see I'm right. And I'm hoping it makes a difference."

I shake my head. "You don't know me, Ronan," I say again.

"Maybe not," he says. But this time, he adds, "But I want to."

Chapter Thirteen

I stumble through the courtyard in a daze, not sure which of the things that has just happened to process first.

But I know exactly who I need to talk to in order to work it all out: Larus. He'll know the truth of the grain situation, and better yet, he won't judge me for slipping something potentially damaging to Ronan.

I head to his rooms to find him, but instead, I find Adria, on her way from our wing of the palace in a hurry.

"Have you seen Larus?" I could ask Adria about what Ronan told me, but to do so would mean facing her wrath.

I need Larus there, in case she loses it.

"He's down at the docks greeting Felix," she says. "I'm heading there now."

I join her, both for my own needs and out of curiosity. I've never met Felix March, but I know him by name and reputation. He's one of Larus's contacts from the Enez Islands, and he's well known both here and abroad for his ruthless mercenary tactics. Some call him a pirate; others call him a savior. He'll say he's here to join in the celebrations of the Great Festival, but he's really here to update us on the naval blockade. Having lost our limited naval forces in the last war, his ships will be critical to ensuring our siege of Faros is a success.

I tell Adria about practicing with Ronan as we walk through the bustling streets of Faros. About his tendency to bait an attack, about the things he taught me in case they're useful to her eventually, if she faces him in battle.

But I keep the rest to myself, for now.

I can't bring myself to ask her about the Orsa, not because I'm afraid of finding out the truth, but because I'm afraid she'll try to justify it.

There are no others, Ronan said.

To Adria, there are only others. There's us, and then there's everyone else.

She may not approve of what happened to Taran's people, but I don't think she'll feel bad about it, either.

And I don't know what to do with that knowledge.

Or the fact that some of what Ronan said made sense to me, even though I'm not sure how any of it changes anything, at least not right now.

But I can't ignore his words, not completely. He's having an effect on me, as much as I hate to admit it. Whether it's his magic or something about who he is, I'm not sure.

I thought I had him where I wanted him.

But maybe it's the other way around.

The Faros docks are even more chaotic than the docks under the palace. Hundreds of people rush about, shouting over the din of carts rumbling over wooden boardwalks and anchors splashing into the waves. Ships rise up from waters cloudy with sand and debris, their white sails as tall as the temple towers.

This is where all the gold has gone. It's being loaded into the ships, drifting from our shores in huge, heavy crates that strain the arms of the dockworkers. I wonder how much this festival is costing us. How much of our land and labor will be devoured for the sake of the Feast.

We're passing a row of cliffside shops and a rowdy tavern when everything goes eerily quiet.

Then, there's shouting.

"Duel! Duel on the south dock!"

Adria's eyes fill with uncharacteristic panic. The south dock is where Larus is meeting Felix.

Larus is beyond his dueling days, from what he's told me, although I don't doubt he could hold his own if it came down to it. He'd managed the bandits on the road just fine, but they weren't armed and trained as well as the typical seafarer.

But it's not Larus who's fighting.

"Great," groans Adria. "There goes our navy."

Two men stand on the dock in tense opposition. The first is wearing the salt-bleached linens of a dockworker, his fiery red-hair pulled into a knot. His knuckles are white around the hilt of his blade.

Opposite him stands a strikingly handsome man with a dark complexion and short-cropped black hair. He smiles confidently, as if this was nothing but a minor inconvenience. He wears a far finer version of Larus's typical Enezian attire: an open coat with gleaming gold buttons, black breeches, and an undershirt in a rich green.

Felix, I presume.

"Are we here to fight or fuck? Pick one. I haven't got all day," he jeers.

Larus is standing off to the side with a small crowd behind him, shaking his head. We join him as the red-headed man curses and spits at the ground, drawing his sword.

"What happened?" I ask.

"The usual," says Larus. "There was a higher bidder."

"He sold that man out to someone?"

Larus nods. "I wouldn't pity him. If he was dealing with Felix in the first place, he likely deserves what he gets."

I wonder what that says about us.

The red-headed man drives his blade forward to attack Felix. He's raging and uncoordinated, and Felix parries almost out of boredom.

The man then attempts to grapple, but Felix holds out a hand like he's blowing the man a kiss.

It knocks him flat on his ass.

"Wind-born?" I ask. Larus nods. "Isn't it dishonorable to use magic in a duel?"

It's also against Ronan's rules to be fighting a duel during the festival at all.

"Felix isn't exactly what you would call an honorable man," says Larus with distaste. Then he turns to yell at him. "Quit toying with him and finish this. Some of us have business to attend to."

"I told him I haven't got all day," says Felix, lazily knocking the man down again when he gets back up. He makes eye contact with me and smiles. "But if you insist."

Before the man can pull himself completely upright, Felix drives his sword into his chest. The man chokes and sputters as Felix withdraws it, tossing him to the ground like garbage.

A woman rushes over to see to the dying man. "How could you?" she cries at Felix.

"Hey, he challenged me." He tosses her a bag of coins and wipes the blood from his sword with his handkerchief before he comes to greet us.

"Now Larus, how can you talk to me about business without introducing me to this simply stunning young woman?"

It takes me a moment to realize he means me.

Sure, I've been looking for trouble, but even I'm not that insane. "I'm Sylvie of House Verran, and you can fuck right off if you think I'm getting involved with the source of whatever *that* mess was."

Larus and Felix eye each other, and then they both laugh. "Larus, I like this one."

"I didn't train a fool," says Larus with pride.

"Forgive my impudence, madam," says Felix, taking my hand and kissing it. I snatch it back. "And allow me to introduce myself. I'm Felix March of the Enez Islands, Admiral of the Third Navy and sword for hire."

"The pleasure is all yours."

"It usually is," he replies. "Now, let's talk business. You wanted grain, and darling, I brought the bread. Only there's a small issue with some of the rye."

This conversation is coded to conceal the true purpose of securing ships, but there's also some truth to it. We've been importing some goods from the Enez Islands as a cover for our renewed interest in dealing with them. The loss of our harbor made imports prohibitively expensive for us to manage, limiting us to what was made available in our markets by traveling merchants. But it's well known that Felix is willing to deal with anyone who can pay, no matter the inconvenience. If Ronan or Cyrus asks where the money is coming from to pay him, we'll say we sold some of our hunting rights in exchange. And this, too, is partially true.

But the entire truth is that we've promised Felix and the Third Navy—which, despite its name, isn't truly a military force sanctioned by the Enez Islands government but rather a mercenary company that controls much of their defense—a portion of the Selaran gold production once we take control.

"Don't tell me," says Larus, understanding something from the coded exchange that I don't.

"It won't be long. A month, maybe. She just wants to see you."

"Larus?" Adria asks.

"I have to return home," says Larus, and my heart sinks. He's my only real ally in the city. My closest friend. I don't know if I can do this without him. "My mother wants to see me, and we need her…rye." *Ships.*

"Your mother is alive?" I ask, and Felix laughs. I've never heard him mention her. Which is odd, now that I think about it.

"We didn't part on good terms, let's just say that," says Larus, ignoring my accidental insult regarding his age.

"We don't have to leave right away," says Felix. "The winds are good at this time of year. Better when I'm on deck." He does the same blowing-a-kiss gesture to me that he did to the man, but it simply lifts my dark hair from my shoulders rather than knocking me over. "Exquisite," he says. "A true beauty."

"Fuck you," I say.

"Are you offering?"

"I'd rather just get this over with," interjects Larus. "When can we sail?" He looks from me to Felix with apprehension. I think he's trying to protect me from disaster.

He doesn't need to worry. Even I can see that particular disaster coming.

"Come now, Larus," says Felix. "My crew needs a few days on shore at least."

"It looks like you managed to do enough damage with just a few hours," says Larus, gesturing back to the corpse.

"It only takes a few minutes, my good man."

Gross. I'm actually relieved that he's gross. It makes it easier to avoid his charms.

"The weekend, and no later," says Larus.

"Deal," says Felix, and they shake on it.

That only gives me a few days before Larus leaves to talk to him about everything that has happened. But it won't be tonight by the looks of it. Felix is already talking about all the places they need to drink to catch up. Adria and I are being invited, but for once we seem to be on the same page about something.

"We're heading back to the castle to rest," she says. "The qualifying events are in just a couple of days."

"Ah yes, the Festival of Sport. Absolute waste of time if you ask me. What's the point of fighting without the blood?"

"The girls are both excellent fighters. Sylvie is doing archery as well," says Larus with pride. I love to hear him show me off.

Felix looks me up and down *again*, his eyes lingering on my chest. Absolutely shameless. "You know what? You might have changed my mind about the festival. I'll see you soon, ladies."

I don't think that was Larus's intention, but it's done now. "Hopefully not *too* soon," I mutter, and Felix laughs like it's the best thing he's ever heard as we walk away from him.

I follow Adria back to the palace, but on the way, I hear the familiar sounds of the market. "You go on ahead," I tell her. "I wanted to get a lighter pair of trousers for the tournament. It's too damn hot here." And, if I happen to find someone else there, all the better.

She tosses me a couple of coins. "Get me some, too."

I'm relieved that she doesn't have anything to say about me going to the market again after the debacle the first night. Maybe she's starting to trust that I can handle what I'm here to do.

Or she's just glad not to have to spend the evening with me alone. Probably the latter.

Chapter Fourteen

It occurs to me once I make it into the market that tracking Soren down might not be easy.

There are even more people here today than the first time I came, and I only know the places he showed me. I don't even know his last name.

If he even has one.

I'm not sure why I'm so desperate to see him again. The thought that he might truly be Ronan unsettles me. If it's true, I can't even begin to imagine what I would say to him.

I realize what I'm really hoping is that he *isn't* Ronan at all. That I can find some comfort in him, in someone whose life isn't woven into the web of lies and schemes that surrounds me.

"Have you seen a man with a scarred face recently? Or a woman with red hair and pierced ears?" I try asking each vendor I visited with Soren, but no one has seen them.

Or at least no one will admit to having done so. I'm certain some of these people must know or remember Soren. Maybe they're refusing to help me because I'm Nithyrian.

I stop by a clothing vendor and pick up the trousers I told Adria I was here for and a couple of light dresses as well. They're nowhere near as nice as what the rest of the court wears, but they're in the Selaran style, which should help me blend in better the next time I return here.

I'm thinking of what else I could do to find him again when I realize I'm being followed.

The past few days have left me increasingly paranoid, always wondering if someone is lurking just out of sight behind me. I recall the lessons my mother taught me when I was a child about how to discreetly check for a tail using reflections. I scan the market with careful intent, peering into the many gleaming surfaces around me. I check a silver service, then a glass case holding jeweled necklaces, then a looking glass with an ornate rim, and finally a vase made from polished brass, before I see him.

It's a boy, and though it's difficult to make out his features in the distorted yellow reflection, I think it may be Nico. Did Soren ask him to follow me if I came back here?

I decide to keep browsing to see if he follows. I head from the vase seller to a stall with a metal cart, a water-born selling an ice-cooled cream dessert. The metal is frosted at the bottom, but at the top, I see the boy again in the reflection. Definitely Nico. I'm glad he's recovered from my stabbing. I consider confronting him, but I decide to let him get some practice in. He's darkening the shadows around us a bit too much to look realistic, but it's not a bad effort for someone so young.

He vanishes eventually, and I debate how long to wait here, wondering if he even has a way of communicating with Soren, or if they only check in periodically. Would Soren come even if he had a way to tell him I was here?

The answer is no. I wait until the market closes, but he never arrives.

Then the next day, and then the day after that, I do the exact same thing. Larus has roped Adria into discussions with Felix, but he's kind enough to keep me out of it, and I have nothing better to do.

And I like the market. I like the movement and the noise and the way I melt into the crowd there, unseen and unremarkable.

"I thought it was you," says Soren, seeing me.

It's nearly nightfall by the time he arrives. Soren stands before the bench in the central plaza where I've been sitting, looking almost exactly as he did when we first crossed paths in that shadowy alley. He's wearing the same brown tunic and trousers, the same patch on his eye.

I'm determined to discover whether Soren truly is the person I suspect him to be, the person I don't dare name, but before I confront him, I allow myself to have a moment to just enjoy his company.

"I'm glad to see you. I was hoping you'd come back," he says, winking his good eye at me.

Damn that wink. "I thought I might see you at the Festival of Sport registration," I say. "Are you not competing?"

"No, I've had enough of all of that." He gestures at his scars. "But I was hoping to know if you saw Vesper there. She's good with a throwing knife."

I ignore the tinge of jealousy that hits me when he talks about Vesper. "No sign of her at the registration, although I'm not sure I would have known her if she did show up. She still hasn't turned up, then?"

Soren drops his gaze to the dusty ground, slowly shaking his head. "No. I've asked around in every tavern, inn, and watering hole in town. And even some beyond Faros's walls. And worse, she's not the only shadow-born missing."

Dread cuts through me. "More of yours?"

"One of them. Her name is Marcella, and I have a lead on her."

That's all I need to hear. "Where are we heading?"

Soren smiles grimly, taking my arm in his gentle, familiar way and pulling me off the market square into an alley. "It's not that simple, I'm afraid. It's going to be dangerous. I don't know what they're doing, but there's a chance they've kidnapped these women."

"Who? And where?"

"It's an importer with a warehouse down by the docks. They deal mainly in spices and exotic goods. Someone saw a woman matching Marcella's description being dragged into the warehouse."

"Lead the way," I say.

"Hazel," says Soren, and I forget for a minute that it was the name I gave him. His voice is gruff, but the intimacy is alarmingly familiar. "We can't just run in there, swords screaming. There will be a dozen people working there at least, many of them armed. Spices are expensive, and they're sure to have them well protected. I don't doubt that you're capable—I remember what you did to Nico—but we need some kind of plan. *I* need some kind of plan. You don't need to do this at all. It's not your problem."

"They're like me. And even if they weren't, how can you expect me to do nothing after you've told me this? I can help. You said you wanted to see me again. For what other reason if not this?"

"There were other reasons," he admits, and something stirs within me.

Not now.

"The plan is I find a way inside and sneak in there and tell you what I find. Then we can come up with something—"

"Absolutely not. I'm not letting you go in there alone."

"But I can move in complete darkness. I can stay hidden. You'll be blind."

"You led me out of the tavern."

"Barely!"

Soren crosses his arms, standing firm. And tall. Standing taller than he ought to be able to with his shoulder injury. "You don't know where to go, and I'm not going to tell you if you don't agree to take me in with you."

"Fine," I snap. "But if you get us killed, don't say I didn't warn you."

"If I get us killed, I doubt I'll be saying much of anything."

"I will," I say. "I'll bribe Vahlo and haunt your reborn self from the underworld."

The death god is choosy about who he allows to leave his domain. The best souls are reborn into a new life, but some of the worst are sent to haunt the living to remind them of what they'll miss out on if they don't behave.

"You don't believe you'll be reborn yourself?"

Not a chance. Not after I do what I've been sent here to do. "I'll be lucky if my soul isn't devoured." A fate that awaits the very worst of us, those who fail Vahlo's final judgment.

I only hope Vahlo understands that the ends justify the means.

"Let's go," I say, not wanting to discuss my anticipated sins any further, and I try to lead us off in a direction Soren still hasn't given me.

He takes the lead, and I follow him through the bustling evening streets, weaving between tired shoppers and vendors hurriedly packing away their goods as colorful awnings come down for the night. When we finally leave the main thoroughfare, the noise drops away, replaced by a heavy, unsettling silence. The alleys Soren guides me through feel unnaturally deserted, their shadows stretching long and deep as we near the docks. Every movement startles me. The brush of a cat against my leg. A door opening, a man sweeping dust outside. A woman drawing laundry in from a clothesline.

"Are you alright?" asks Soren, and I jump at his voice.

It's a bit of a slip. There's no way for Soren to know I'm afraid. It's too dark for him to see my face.

But Ronan would be able to tell.

"Fine," I say, although I'm not. I had been too focused on the missing girls before to think of it, but it occurs to me this could be some kind of trap Ronan set to expose me. He could be leading me into danger on purpose in hopes of getting rid of me, or of finding out what we're up to.

Or what if Soren isn't Ronan, and he's leading us into danger he's really not prepared for? I have my sword and my dagger. I have my shadows. I'm wearing my armor. But is it enough? There's no way I could beat a dozen people on my own.

"You don't have to do this."

"I know," I say. "But I sort of do."

The girls are shadow-born like me. My age, give or take a few years. Soren told me about them. Vesper: a red-head with a love of beer and breaking the rules. Marcella: a scrappy girl who wears her hair in braids to keep it out of the way when she fights. They're gone, and no one else is looking for them. They could be in the warehouse. They could be frightened or hurt.

It also occurs to me that Ronan, if Soren really is Ronan, could use the immense power at his disposal to find them. But there must be a reason why he hasn't. Maybe, after we've found them, he'll tell me what it is.

"Just down there," says Soren, pointing to a large building at the bottom of the hill. It's close to where we met Felix earlier in the day, and a couple of new fears make themselves known: that we might encounter Larus or Felix nearby, or that the plot we're uncovering might involve them in some way.

This is a disaster.

"Hazel," murmurs Soren comfortingly. "You can just go home. I'll go in and scope it out."

Time to teach him a lesson for using my feelings when he's not meant to be able to do that. "I don't know why you think I'm scared. I never said I was. I'm just thinking about how we can get in."

"Sorry," he says, reaching up to run his hands through his hair but finding his hat instead. "It was just the tension…your silence…"

Riiiiight. "Quiet. I'm thinking."

I can see far more clearly in the dark than he can. There are several doors into the building. The double doors at the front, which will obviously be guarded. Two doors on the left side into an alleyway—likely better options, although not completely safe. A stairway from a deck on the right side down to a dock with a door on each level. And who knows how many in the back.

The only good thing about the setup is that it's a lot of doors to guard. If they have around a dozen people here, like he suspects, it's unlikely that there are more than one or two per entrance. We could maybe take them in a fight, but there's a problem with that.

"How are we meant to get the guards out of the way without killing them?" I ask. My weapons are not meant for intimidation or knocking sense into people. They're meant to kill, and even if I try not to, I can't guarantee they won't.

If the guards are involved in trafficking the girls, I won't feel bad about taking them out. But if they aren't…

"With this," says Soren, pulling a vial out of his pocket. "An elixir that knocks someone unconscious if inhaled. All I need is for you to get me close enough to them that I can open it beneath their noses."

"So which door are you thinking?" I ask him. It occurs to me that once we're close enough, if it's Ronan, he'll be able to tell if someone is on the other side of the door by their feelings.

Let's see what he has to say about that.

"The alley is the darkest. Let's get closer. Maybe we'll be able to hear something."

Hear something. Sure…

I wait until the lone woman in the street passes us and lead Soren down the hill to the warehouse. I stick to the shadows of the buildings, avoiding the streetlamps and only darkening our surroundings when I absolutely must in case someone is looking.

As we approach, I check for movement in the alley before I darken the shadow there. I grab Soren's hand—smooth as ever—and lead him into the inky black of total darkness.

The secrets I'm concealing, including my knowledge of his identity, are really making a difference to my magic. I can usually feel a bit of a drain on my energy when I darken a shadow, and that pull is greater the larger the area or the longer I hold it. But I feel almost nothing in this alley. It's the difference between running up the stairs and a leisurely stroll on level ground.

Soren gestures to the door furthest away, or roughly where it is given that he can't see it. I take it that means the one closest to us is guarded. We creep along the alleyway, moving extra slowly as we pass the guarded door. My shadows have no impact on noise. One wrong step and our mission is over before it begins.

We approach the unguarded door and stand perfectly still, listening.

Silence within.

I try the handle, expecting it to be locked.

But it isn't.

The door clicks open just a crack. I pause, completely motionless except for the pounding of my heart.

There's no light coming from within the doorway, not even without my shadows. I move to step inside, but Soren squeezes my hand and doesn't follow.

He pulls backward, and I understand his meaning. Slowly, softly we creep a few feet back, the door still hanging open.

"I don't like this," he murmurs so quietly I can barely hear him. "Why would they leave the door open?"

"Maybe someone was just careless," I whisper, but I can't ignore the shiver that goes down my spine. "Did anyone know you were coming?"

"No," says Soren. "A friend of Marcella's told me. I can't imagine she'd send me directly into a trap."

"What do you want to do?" I ask. I know exactly what we should do: turn around and go back to the palace and come back with two dozen armed guards to turn this place over.

But there are so many exits, it's possible that they would escape with the girls before we ever set foot inside. And if they're in there—just feet away from us—and I turn around and leave them?

"I'm willing to take a look if you are."

I nod, then tell him, "Alright," because he can't see in the damn dark.

It's honestly quite brave of him to let me guide him while he's totally blind. Brave, and also incredibly foolish.

I lead us back to the threshold and pull the door open a bit further, keeping us behind it initially in case someone comes running.

But they don't. It's only silence behind that door. Silence, darkness, and hopefully two shadow-born girls who don't fear it.

Soren nudges me and drops my hand for a moment, pulling out the vial of elixir. I take it from him and open it without giving it back.

He reaches for me and gives my hand an angry squeeze when he finds it empty.

I pull his head to me and whisper impossibly softly into his ear. "You can't see."

What good will the elixir do if he can't see where the enemies are?

Of course, he can sense where the enemies are, but he thinks I don't know that. I smile in the darkness, grateful he can't see my satisfaction.

Elixir in one hand, Soren's hand in the other, I lead him around the doorway and into a narrow hall.

It looks as if this area is used for storage or maybe disposal. There are a handful of crates and empty barrels lining the walls, but there's nothing else in the room except a doorway that looks to lead deeper into the building.

It's too narrow in here for us to be side to side, so I stand in front of Soren. I back up to him until I feel him against me. I breathe deeply, willing the part of my mind that wants to focus on the sensation of his body against mine to shut the fuck up.

I need him to stay close to me, or he'll knock something over in the room and give us away. I move forward, and he follows, our bodies moving in sync with each other. My pulse pounds in my ears, and I can't tell if it's from the situation we're in or the way he feels. The heat of his body on my back. The warm breeze of his breath on my neck, brushing the wisps of my hair aside.

We make it to the door, and I reach to try it. He doesn't stop me, which makes me feel that it's unlikely that there's anyone on the other side.

This door is locked.

What a relief.

Carefully, with agonizing slowness to avoid making a sound, I retrieve my rake from the coin purse in my pocket and a pin from my hair, and I pick the lock.

Soren's face registers surprise, but he says nothing.

I crack the door open slowly and peer inside the room before entering.

The main room of the warehouse sprawls before us, dark and expansive. It's filled with shelves and racks, each of which is covered in wooden barrels and crates, some of them stacked to the ceiling.

The darkness is broken only by the distant flicker of a single candle in a window on the opposite side of the room. There's no hint of movement, not a footstep, not a shifting shadow. Wherever the guards are, it's not here.

I move slowly along an aisle between shelves, and Soren reluctantly follows. There's room enough for us to walk together now, and I feel the lack of him the second he moves out from behind me. We pause as we reach an aisle that extends to the front door. I darken the shadow as deep as it will go as I lean out to check for guards.

No one. Even the front doors have been left unguarded.

This feels all wrong. The goods they store here are valuable. The shelf beside me contains several crates labeled as saffron, a spice so rare and expensive that I've never so much as seen it, let alone tasted it. And the city is busier than ever with festival goers coming into town. Why would they take such an unnecessary risk?

Did someone else get here first?

There are no signs of a struggle. Nothing looks the slightest bit out of place.

Soren squeezes my hand and walks a step in front of me, urging me onwards. It's brighter on this side of the warehouse because of the candlelight, bright enough that he drops my hand and begins to lead.

I try to ignore how empty my hand feels without his, how his warmth lingers on my skin.

We're nearly to the candlelit window now, although an aisle separates us from it. I peek through a gap in the crates to see an empty desk with an overturned chair within.

Here's the fight we were looking for. It's difficult to see from this angle, but something caused the occupant of the office to leave in a hurry.

"Let's go," I whisper. The office has a door that leads outside on the dockside of the building. If the girls were here, they could be on a boat by now.

"Wait," says Soren, and he grabs my arm and pulls me back to him forcefully.

Then he pushes us both to the ground, urging me into the bottom shelf between a stack of wooden boxes.

He's sensed someone. It takes a moment before I hear their approaching footsteps. At least two of them, moving quickly and with no regard for the noise they're making.

The door slams open, banging into the wall.

"Gods, it's heavy!" yells a man. His voice is accented. It reminds me a bit of Larus, the accent of the Enez Islands, though I know it's not him. I could recognize Larus's voice anywhere.

Please don't be Felix.

Something crashes to the ground with so much force that it shakes the containers we're hidden between.

"Careful with it," replies a woman, her accent Selaran. "There's a lot of coin in that crate."

"Yes, madam," the man replies. He says it without a hint of sarcasm, and I breathe a sigh of relief that it's unlikely to be Felix. After our encounter today, I can't imagine him taking orders from anyone.

This is our chance. We could knock these two out and then wait for the others to check what happened to them, picking at least a few of them off one by one.

I put my hand underneath me, beginning to push myself up.

Soren grabs me by my shoulders, pulling me to him tightly so I don't lose my balance from the loss of momentum.

I can barely breathe, for a couple of reasons. There's the terror of being caught, of knocking something over and getting their attention before we're ready to take them on. And there's the physical sensation of being crushed against Soren, robbing my lungs of the space they need to fill but also sending a rush of excitement through me.

It's hard to focus when he's holding me this close, when I can smell him, incense and spice.

But his action works: they don't hear us.

"One more," says the woman.

"Don't bloody remind me," grumbles the man.

Their footsteps retreat, but they don't shut the door behind them.

"Quick," says Soren, pulling me to my feet. "Before they return."

We rush over to the crate. It's large and unmarked, roughly the size it would need to be to hold an adult woman. But there are no air holes.

I'm terrified to see what's inside. Soren looks around for something to open it while I peek through a hole in the wood.

"It's not the girls," I say. "It's…bricks of something."

Soren pries the crate open with a crowbar and then removes one of the bricks from its paper packaging, smelling it cautiously. "Joy plant," he says, dropping it back into the crate in disgust. "Dried and purified."

A powerful alchemical ingredient. I've seen Hermes use it to ease the passing of the horses. "For the Guild?" I suggest. Perhaps they're only intending to sell it to the alchemists. There has to be a trade in it, and it's likely a lucrative one.

He shakes his head. "Only the Guild can import it. Come on, before they come back."

We slip through the open door and onto the deck. There are barrels and columns of wood here that offer cover, so we crouch behind them to get a better view of the dock.

"It's Marcella," says Soren.

"In the crate?" In front of a small sailboat at anchor sits a single large crate, identical to the one we saw brought into the warehouse earlier.

And in front of it are all the guards. I scan their faces and bodies as quickly as I can, grateful not to see Felix among them. Whatever is in that crate, it must be so valuable that everything else in the warehouse pales in comparison.

Soren shakes his head. "I thought I recognized her voice earlier, but I didn't want to believe it. It's her. The one in charge."

The woman who was giving the orders. It's one of the missing girls.

Marcella stands tall and commanding at the end of the dock, conversing with the captain of the sailboat. Her dark hair is in braids as Soren described, and she's wearing tight leather pants and a leather chest piece over a dark red tunic. If I hadn't already heard her voice, I might have guessed she was Nithyrian.

She's certainly ready for a fight.

"What do we do?" Could Vesper be here too? Is it possible that they're working together doing whatever this is?

Or maybe Marcella could have kidnapped Vesper and is holding her against her will.

Or maybe Vesper isn't here at all, and we've stumbled upon a dangerous smuggling operation manned by people willing to risk everything for a bit of coin.

"We get out of here," says Soren. "Vesper isn't in that crate. We can figure the rest out later."

Around the corner, there are two more guards positioned at the end of the deck to block access to the dock from the street. "Not that way." The only way back is through the still-open warehouse door behind us.

I lower the shadow to lead us through it.

"Soren," calls Marcella from below just before we reach it. Ice runs through my veins at the sound. "Did you come to make me an offer?"

Of course. She's shadow-born. She can see us through my shadows.

Down at the dock, the captain and crew of the sailboat hurry to launch. The warehouse guards rush over to Marcella, but she stops them before they climb the stairs.

Soren steps forward. "I came to rescue you. Though it appears I'm a little too late."

Marcella's laugh is melodic and dark. "Poor naïve Soren. A man who thinks he's his own master, and yet he's nothing more than the God-King's slave. Or did you think I didn't know who you were working for all these years?"

"What do you want, Marcella?"

"The same as you. I'm just doing business. I'll give credit to Ronan for one thing: the man knows how to create a black market. I would have cut you in only—well, you would've just run right back to your master, wouldn't you?"

She doesn't know who she's talking to. She sees the connection, but it doesn't occur to her that she's talking to Ronan himself.

His fingers twitch for the blade at his side. He shifts his weight, blocking more of me from sight.

"Don't think I don't know you have another shadow-born back there. It's a nice little trick that she has, but it won't work on me."

She's right. Against another shadow-born, the only weapons I have are my blades. And we both know how good I am with those.

Well, those and the uncapped elixir I'm still holding.

"Lift your shadow," Soren mutters to me, and I understand why he asks.

It'll weaken his light.

"I'm sorry it went this way, Marcella," he says, and the quiet scene turns violent all at once.

Soren raises his hand and fires off a tiny burst of magic which only misses Marcella because a guard rushes up in front of her, falling to the ground before he can even pull his sword. Marcella plunges the area around her into darkness, causing another guard to stumble and trip over the first one as he falls. She flings a knife, which narrowly misses Soren and clatters somewhere within the warehouse as he takes my hand and flings us back behind the barrels. The guards from the street race down the deck, and I drop a shadow over them just before they reach us. They stumble forward, and Soren impales one with his dagger while I shove the elixir into the other one's face.

The guard collapses to the deck, and I take the dagger from her hand and throw it into the fray on the staircase, almost striking another advancing guard but just missing to the left.

The guard who had been carrying the crate makes a dash for the dock and leaps from it, swimming after the rapidly escaping sailboat. Marcella ducks behind a pile of crates.

Soren takes out the guard I'd missed, who had nearly made it to the top of the steps in the darkness, with a bolt of magic.

It's as precise as Adria's tiny burst of flame, hitting him in the side of the head and dropping him instantly.

"Come on." Soren grabs my hand and pulls me towards the deck that leads to the street.

"What about Marcella?"

"The guards can deal with her. There are too many of them left. We've got to go."

We round the corner into the street, but there's movement to our right, near the alley where we entered the warehouse. Some of the guards from the dock have come around.

There are so many of them. Six, at least. I drop the shadows around us to give us cover.

"Run, Sylvie," says Soren.

My real name.

My heart stops.

He said my real name.

The guards stumble forward out of Marcella's shadow and begin to charge, flinging flame and lightning at us as Marcella retreats towards the alley. Soren fires off a bolt of light at her and misses, but he doesn't run after her.

He stays at my side, preparing for the incoming assault.

Run, Sylvie, he said. I wonder if he even realizes he said it.

I don't run, though. I draw my sword, keeping the vial of elixir in my other hand, covering it with my thumb to keep it from spilling.

I lift my shadows as the first three guards reach us. Soren lunges forward, his sword flashing through the air to cut down the first guard in a single, fluid motion as a flame dies in his hand. The second doesn't even have time to raise her blade before Soren releases a bolt of crackling light, striking her square in the chest and sending her sprawling backward. As the third guard swings his sword at me, I meet his attack with a swift parry, the clang of metal ringing in my ears. Before I can counter, Soren spins around and dispatches the last guard with a clean strike.

"Good gods," I say, looking at him. He was definitely holding back when he fought me. He turns and takes out another advancing guard with another bolt of light.

There's a delay between the bolts, and it seems he can only send one bolt at a time. So it works similarly to Adria's fire magic, then.

"Don't follow her," he says, as he sees me eying the corner Marcella retreated to.

But who else will be able to track her? It's not like he needs my help here.

In the time it takes me to decide, he takes out another guard, leaving only one remaining.

"I think you've got this," I say, and I head for the alley behind the warehouse in pursuit of Marcella.

As I round the corner, an arm reaches out and grabs me.

"Too easy," says Marcella. "Disappointing, really."

I thrash against her. I drop my sword, which is useless in these close quarters, and go for my dagger.

"Let's not," she says. We struggle with it, but she manages to get it away from me. Then I jam my elbow back into her ribs, and she doubles over, letting me go. "Bitch!"

I hear the front doors open into the street and then the clash of steel as Soren fights what must be even more guards. I have a choice: back into the street to help him, or try to take Marcella on my own.

I know what I should do. If he dies now, if Ronan dies now, the plan fails. I should protect him.

But Marcella is right here. If she gets away, we may never find her again. And we may never find Vesper.

I retrieve my sword from the ground and hold it out at Marcella, keeping her at a distance.

She laughs at my hesitation. "Another one dumb enough to fall for Soren's little game. You know what he's really after, don't you?"

I don't, but I do want to know that. Would he tell me? I'm not sure. He'd said my name, so the rules had changed. But would he tell me the truth? Or would he go on keeping his secrets?

"No? Drop the sword, and I'll tell you," says Marcella.

"No, thanks," I say. I'm not *that* stupid. "Kick me the dagger, and I'll let you live."

She also declines. Fair enough.

She lunges for the dagger just as I sprint toward her, sword raised and ready. She makes it there first. I try to dive out of the way, but she's too close for me to dodge.

The dagger flashes through the air, spinning toward me. My breath catches, expecting the cold bite of steel, but in the split second before it hits, something impossible happens. The dagger stops mid-flight, suspended just inches from my cheek. A tendril of darkness shooting out from my chest holds it there. The air hums with its power.

My shadow.

"What the fuck?" says Marcella, as shocked as I am.

The dagger hangs there in the air, and I realize I'm controlling it. I can feel it, just like it's in my hand.

I could stab her with it. I could end this right here.

Instead, I let it clatter to the ground.

And I grab the vial of elixir with my shadow and shove it in her face.

Marcella's knees buckle, and she collapses onto the cobblestone pavement as Soren rounds the corner.

"What the hell—what's that?" he asks, seeing the tendrils of my shadow given form retract back into me.

"I don't know." It's the truth. I have no idea what just happened.

I retrieve my sword and dagger from the ground. "The rest of them?"

"Dead," says Soren. "Or near enough to it. A damn shame." He shakes his head as he approaches me, hands out, "Sylvie, I—"

"Don't," I say, backing up with my weapons still drawn. "It's time for you to tell me what the fuck is going on, Ronan."

His hand flinches at the sound of his name. "As you wish," he says with a sigh. He fires a burst of light into the air, a smaller version of the spectacle he created at the opening ceremony of the Festival of Sport.

When I look back, Soren is gone.

In his place is the God-King of Selara.

Chapter Fifteen

onan's light flickers, casting erratic shadows over the ware-house before slowly descending to the ground, illuminating the alley with a pale, trembling glow as it fades.

"Calling someone?" I ask.

"Taran and some of the others are nearby."

I seethe, my heart still pounding from the fear and exertion of the fight. "And you didn't think that would have been useful five minutes ago?"

He steps closer to me and waits for me to lower my weapons, which I do. Reluctantly. He comes even closer then, standing close enough that I can hear his still-heavy breathing, his eyes pleading with me to listen. "I will explain. When we're back in the palace, I'll tell you everything. But please, Sylvie. I'm asking you to keep quiet about what happened until I do."

I want to say something smart about not needing to listen to him, but something in his expression stops me. It's not a command. He's *begging* me. He's afraid of what will happen if I don't listen to him.

"Fine," I say, and he breathes a sigh of relief. "*Everything*, Ronan."

Taran arrives then with five other guards in tow. Six trained Royal Guards waiting…where? Down the street?

For fuck's sake, this better be good.

"Take her to my chambers," Ronan says, gesturing to me. "Gaius, go with them. The rest of you are with me."

Taran comes along beside me. "This way, my lady."

"I'm not a lady," I say to him. "That's my sister."

I'm just Sylvie.

"I'm sorry, I didn't mean to—"

"It's fine."

I follow Taran into the street. Bodies are strewn across the cobblestones, some twisted and contorted, others bloodied. But a few of the fallen—the ones taken down by Ronan's light magic—look eerily peaceful.

"Quite a fight," says Taran. "He should have called us sooner."

"That's what I said."

Taran gives me a shy smile and then leads me up the hill, tracing our steps back to the market with the other guard trailing behind at a bit of a distance.

We walk in silence for a time. Taran rolls his neck, running his hand through his blond hair. He looks tired. From the ringing of the temple bells, the hour is late.

"How long were you out here?" I ask him.

"A few hours."

"Were you watching the warehouse?"

"No. He wouldn't tell us where it was meant to happen."

Interesting. I had the impression that Ronan trusted Taran, but it sounds like he keeps some things from even his closest guard.

I can sense there's more that Taran would like to say, but he says nothing.

I can imagine why. The last time I saw him just a few days ago, I had been deeply insulting.

"I'm sorry for what I said," I say to him.

He doesn't turn his head to look at me. "You don't need to apologize."

"I do," I say, and I stop, forcing him to stop and face me. "I'm sorry. Not just for what happened to you, but for what I said about you and your people. I'm realizing now that there are a lot of things I don't know."

"You weren't wrong," he tells me. "Not entirely. The history between our people…it's long, and it's bloody, and there have been terrible losses on both sides."

His eyes are full of a deep sadness that I can't comprehend.

"But that's history," I say. "It's not you, and it's not me. I know how it feels to have people hate me just because I'm Nithyrian, because of what my family has done. I see it in their faces. I hear it in their whispers. And I did the same exact thing to you, and that's not fair."

I knew it when I said it, knew that it sounded like what Quinn had said to me, and I said it anyway.

The people at court and in the streets of Faros aren't wrong to whisper about me. Even Quinn isn't wrong, as much as I hate her for it. They see me for what I am. I want to believe that I'm better than what they say, but deep down, I know I'm not.

"Ronan says—" He stops himself, looking into the distance. Is he worried that he's betraying Ronan's confidence? "His majesty says that you're different. I didn't see it at first, but I think he may be right."

I'm not different. I'm just like the rest of my family, just like the people Ronan spoke about, the people keeping score. I tell myself I do what I do for the good of my people, but is that really true?

Or am I doing it for my own good? For my selfish need to see Ronan suffer for what he did to us. What will his suffering give me? What will it give our people?

Another war. More death, more hunger. What will it cost us all?

I can't say any of that to Taran though. "I don't know if I'm different. But maybe things can be different one day. Like Ronan said."

I don't believe my own words, but unlike Ronan, Taran can't feel that.

He nods, and he leads me back into the palace.

The entrance to Ronan's private chambers is not exactly where I expected. Taran guides me past the tower I stumbled upon my first night here through a series of dimly lit hallways, our steps echoing on stone. Finally, we reach a discreet door nestled in the shadow of a marble archway, its heavy wooden frame inlaid with subtle carvings.

The guards that protect it don't question why I'm with Taran. They simply let us enter.

Inside, I expect to see more of the same décor from the rest of the palace: tan stone and garish amounts of gold, with a clutter of tapestries, paintings, and a thousand other decorative things that I'm sure are worth more than my life.

But the first room we enter is closer to the antechamber to Ronan's throne room. It's about the size of that room, big enough for only a pair of cushioned benches in a rich red fabric, the legs made from Nithyrian wood.

I had thought Ronan had brought us to the antechamber full of Nithyrian things the first day to intimidate us, to remind us that he controlled Nithyria and our lives within it as well.

But perhaps he just prefers our aesthetic.

"You can sit," says Taran. "Ronan should be here soon."

I'm not sure which bench to sit on. They appear roughly equal, although maybe the one on the right has bit more wear in the cushion furthest from the door. Ronan's preferred seat?

I take it. Because I'm annoyed with him, and because I'm petty at heart.

Taran raises his eyebrows but says nothing.

He stands in front of the door at the back of the chamber, the one that must lead into Ronan's bedchambers and other rooms beyond.

It's a pity that Taran is there to guard me because I'd really like to sneak a peek into those private chambers.

To find a way in. A servant's passage we can use when the time is right.

And for no other reason.

I am *not* thinking about Ronan's bed or how near I must be to it. I know it's good for the plan, but there are limits to how far I'm willing to go. I try to find something else to think about before Ronan gets here, but there's little else in the room. A seascape on the wall. A potted plant in the corner. Taran. I didn't notice it before when I was still blinded by prejudice, but he's not a bad-looking guy. His features are soft, almost boyish, but the tattoo gives him a bit of an edge. Not exactly my type, but like the goddess Kerensa, I enjoy beauty for beauty's sake.

The door opens, and Ronan enters, looking unamused. I imagine he felt my wandering eye from the other side of it.

Good.

"Leave us," says Ronan. Taran exits back into the hallway, and I take a shameless glance at his ass as he leaves.

Then I flash my eyes back at Ronan, who is doing his best to conceal the fact that he's seething.

Even better.

"When did you realize?" he asks tersely. He stands across the room, arms crossed over his tunic. He's still wearing Soren's clothes, and in them, it's so obvious that they're the same man, I can't believe I ever doubted it.

"Realize what? That the king of Selara was prancing about darkened alleyways posing as a war-wounded?"

"I wasn't posing. I was a war-wounded." He turns, and Soren's face flashes onto his so quickly it makes my stomach queasy. "These are my own scars. Or they would have been, if the healers hadn't gotten to them."

I suppose he wants me to feel sorry for him.

I don't.

"They did incredible work. I suppose that's what happens when all of the best healers in the land are at your disposal."

"Unlike your own sister and brother, who have to wear their wounds on display for all to see," he says sarcastically. Adria and Seth have no scars either despite the fact that we lost the war.

"When you left me because the bells were ringing," I say, returning to his question. "You winked."

He raises his eyebrows in surprise, a hint of a smile playing on his lips. "Did I?"

I roll my eyes. "You know you did."

"I hadn't realized…well, that probably explains why I lose so often at cards. It seems I have a tell."

"Or you're bad at cards when you're not cheating. Why do you even need to cheat if you can feel what everyone feels?"

"I'm not a mind reader. As amazing as I am, it is actually possible to deceive me. If you play your cards right."

Another wink and a gods-awful joke.

"I can't *imagine* why anyone would try to deceive you." I need to rein in the sass, but he's really pissing me off right now.

"Are you angry with me?" he asks. He takes a seat on the bench across from me, leaning forward a bit in my direction.

"You truly are an idiot. Of course I'm angry, Ronan. You lied to me—"

"*You* lied to *me*—"

"And you dragged me into something that could have gotten us killed—"

"I told you it was dangerous. I told you not to come. You *forced* me to take you—"

"And you acted like you were my friend, and you tried to kiss me! How did you think that was going to go, exactly? When I touched your face and realized the scars weren't real? What was going to happen then?"

Ronan leans back, and a soft blush blooms across his golden cheeks.

It's really, really attractive.

Fuck.

"I don't know. Honestly, I don't," he says as I start to protest. "No one has ever come onto Soren before."

"Come onto Soren? Soren came onto me!" I cross my arms and turn towards the door, a bit too embarrassed to meet his eye.

"Eh." He leans forward again as though he might reach for me, but then he shrugs his shoulders to cover the motion. "I think it was mutual. I can feel things, remember."

"How could I forget?"

There's a long pause that feels uncomfortably tense. I'm terribly aware of how he must be sensing every emotion I'm having, how he's been sensing them all night. "When did you realize I knew?" I ask, to break the silence more than anything.

"When I told you I'd be able to hear them behind the door. I felt your doubt. I knew you'd guessed how I could tell if anyone was there."

"Why didn't you say something then? How could you let me go into that warehouse when your guards were ready and waiting just down the street?"

"I wouldn't have let anything happen to you," he says so quietly and seriously that it takes my breath away. "I didn't take any pleasure in doing what I had to do tonight. I didn't think it would get out of control so quickly. I thought we could knock them out one by one…But I couldn't let something happen to you, and my guards couldn't know where I was. Not until I could be sure—"

He stops himself. He looks at me appraisingly, and I can tell he's trying to read something in my feelings. Trying to judge what he can or should say to me.

The answer, of course, is nothing. He shouldn't trust me, and I'm sure he knows it. But he doesn't seem to be able to stop himself. It's as Adria said it would be: he can't resist me.

There's something about that I like, in spite of everything. In spite of what I know about him and what we're planning. In spite of his actions tonight and his deception when it came to posing as Soren.

What can I say? It's nice to be liked.

He stands, making his decision. Then he crosses to the entrance and opens the door.

"Down the hall," he says to the guards stationed outside, and I hear the rustle of their movement as he shuts the door again.

He's sent them away. Not far, but far enough that they can't overhear.

"Sure of what?" I ask.

"I'll get to that in a second," he says, tilting his head towards the guards moving in the hallway. "One of the reasons was that I knew the secret would strengthen your power, and it looks like that worked. Unless you've been keeping the true power of your shadows a secret as well."

"That was new," I admit.

"A rare gift," says Ronan, "even among the shadow-born. Light has energy. It can be as harmless as an illusion—" He turns his hand, and a fig appears in his palm.

My mouth falls open in shock. I've never seen anything like it. It's like he plucked it straight out of the air.

He takes a bite of it, but his mouth goes straight through it, and it vanishes.

"Or as deadly as the bolts I used against some of their guards. But shadows have no energy on their own. They're a lack of it, a lack of light. I've encountered a number of shadow-born, both on and off the battlefield, but I don't remember ever seeing one capable of shaping the shadows into something with form. I've heard of it, but I thought it was a myth."

"I don't know how I did it. Or if I'll ever be able to do it again." It would be a very valuable skill to have, but I don't see why I, of all people, would have it.

"I'm certain that you will. I did want to try one thing, if you wouldn't mind darkening the room."

I do as he asks. Then he sends a small ball of light into the air.

It's bright, surprisingly so. It doesn't illuminate my shadow, not all of it, but the shadow doesn't nullify it either. If anything, it looks a bit *brighter* in the shadow when I lift and lower it to test it. "That's what I thought. I saw it happen out there. Strange."

"I didn't think it would work like that," I say. "Adria's flames are weaker in my shadows." And my shadows can snuff some flames entirely, depending on who's stronger.

"It doesn't usually work like that. In fact, I've *never* seen light and shadow work like that. It's worth asking someone about. Maybe the Guild Mistress. She knows more about the nature of magic than anyone."

I lift the shadows as he extinguishes the light, standing and crossing the room, then taking the seat next to me on the bench.

I can feel the air change with his closeness. I almost kissed him. I let him touch me, let him hold me; gods, I *pressed* myself against him, *again…*

"You told me to tell you what the fuck is going on."

I did say that, although I didn't entirely expect him to do so. I wonder what he decided. How much of what he'll say now is the truth, and how much of it is an invention to get me off his back.

"As I'm sure you can guess, I don't pose as Soren to keep an eye on what the merchants are doing."

I'd guessed that, yes. "Go on."

"And you've probably also noticed that you aren't the only one around here that hates me. Hated me?" He raises one eyebrow, the brow that was his good one when he was Soren.

"Hates you," I say, but I must not say it very convincingly because he smiles.

"Of course. You aren't the only person around here who hates me. In fact, I have many enemies." He shifts, and the humor drains from his face. "Information is leaving the palace, but I don't know how. I don't know who it is, but someone within is acting against me. Revealing my movements, my weaknesses. My plans and edicts before they're announced. And they're good at it."

My pulse races. This is incredibly revealing information. "Why would you tell me this?" Ronan is a self-admitted idiot, but surely he's not this stupid. He knows how I feel about him.

"Because I know it's not you. It began long before you arrived. Nithyria may hate me, but you've always been open in your disdain. I find it oddly comforting."

"You find it *comforting* that we hate you."

"I mean, I'd prefer it if you didn't. But you can't make everyone happy at the same time, and I know you must realize what another rebellion would cost us. What it would cost your own people."

I had just been thinking of that very thing. Vahlo damn him, he's getting into my head.

"But there's someone among my own people who is using their position to undermine me. That's what my shadow-born are doing. They don't know why they're doing it—although apparently some of them suspect more than I'd realized. They keep tabs on my advisors. My friends. Even my own family."

Ronan had little family left. Did that mean they were tailing his own grandmother?

"You think I'm insane," he says with an empty laugh. "I think I am too. I'm going insane, at least. I have no idea who I can trust. Someone is lying to me, and it's someone that knows me well enough to be able to hide it from me." He sighs, and the weariness in it is bone deep. "I'm tired, Sylvie. I've been at war for a decade, and much of the worst of it has been *off* of the battlefield. I was delusional enough to think this would be easy. I thought I knew better than my father. What I told you about him as Soren was true. He was a good father, but he wasn't a good king. There were things he did while he was in charge that made things worse than they had to be. I don't blame Nithyria for rebelling."

I'm certain he can sense my shock. And my distrust. He's telling me everything I want to hear, and that fact isn't lost on me.

"I know you don't believe me. I don't blame you for that, either. But I thought it would be simple to set things right. To undo the damage he did, to right his wrongs. But every change I've made has backfired. Even things I've done that I know I'm right about—the changes to indenturing law, for example. You remember the man in the throne room?"

How could I forget the man who died in front of me just days earlier?

"Indentured servants had no rights to petition the magistrate, even if they were abused by their masters. That happens often, unfortunately. I gave them those rights. It seemed so obvious. And yet it cost the masters—many of whom are in my own court—greatly."

"Good," I say. Someone who abuses their staff doesn't deserve to keep them.

"I agree, but they're nobility. I need their support to keep the people fed. To keep commerce flowing. I can't strip everyone who does something immoral or illegal of their lands and title."

"Of course you can. You're the God-King." He'd managed to do it to most of Nithyria. Why should these Selarans get special treatment? Especially after they've abused their position of power.

"I'm trying not to plunge the country into another war. We're barely recovered from the last one."

"You said yourself you can't make everyone happy."

"You sound a bit like Quinn."

I bristle at the suggestion. "I'm nothing like her." In fact, when he'd mentioned someone was betraying him, hers was the first name I thought of.

"No, you're not, but on this at least you're agreed."

"Do you trust her?" I can't help but ask. Not just because I suspect her, but also because I'm curious about the nature of their relationship despite Zara's assurances that there's nothing between them.

My curiosity is purely intellectual, of course. It's good to know what—or who—I'm up against if I'm trying to ensnare the man.

There's a burning twinge in my throat almost like jealousy. I resist it at first, but then I think better of it. I lean into it. Maybe it would be good to let him think I'm jealous.

"As I said, I don't know if I can trust anyone. I've had to keep all of this from even Taran, my oldest friend, in case one of the guards is involved. That's why I went myself in disguise."

"Do you think you can trust me?"

"No," he says with a wry smile. "But at least I'm certain of how you feel about me. And I think there's a part of you that agrees with what I'm saying even if you dislike me personally. I want you by my side."

This is exactly what I wanted. What we wanted, Adria, Larus, and I.

I'm not sure how to play it. If I seem too eager, he'll see right through me. But I don't want to refuse him outright either.

I think of what Larus would tell me if I had the chance to ask him. He'd suggest I play up my insecurities. Fish for a compliment.

"Why? It's not like I'm great in a fight," I say. And this is true. I've had my ass handed to me by every single person I've faced in the last several days. I hate it, but Adria was right about that much.

"You would've killed Nico if I hadn't been there, and you beat Marcella. Don't let her arrogance unnerve you. She talked down to you because she knew you were the only one who could've stopped her. You shouldn't sell yourself short."

Perfection. And deeply satisfying to hear, although I hardly think besting a literal child counts for much.

Gods, I hate how much I love to hear his praise. I wish I could forget that Soren had existed. There was something about him that was so validating, so empowering. To know how much he trusted me. To feel the way I impacted him, the way he wanted me...

It hurts a little to imagine that it was all part of whatever scheme Ronan isn't sharing with me.

Because there has to be a scheme here. I refuse to believe he's being open and honest with me for fun, no matter what he says. He seems like a fool, but I don't doubt that he would play one if it gave him an advantage.

It's what I would do.

Maybe what we want is the same thing. I want to get close to him to have the chance to strike. He wants to keep me close so he can stop me from doing so.

Although if he wanted to, he could eliminate me as a threat at any time. And maybe Adria would start a war over it, or maybe like the house of the man who died in the throne room, she'd take it as a lesson.

I almost laugh. Who am I kidding? She'd definitely start a war over it, even if she had no way of winning.

It's the way she shows her love.

Staying close to each other benefits us both. I can think of one thing that could keep me there, at least temporarily. "What about Vesper?" I ask. "What do you think happened to her?"

"I'm hoping Marcella will be able to tell us something. I'm very grateful to you for keeping Marcella alive, by the way."

"She seemed willing to talk," I say, not mentioning the fact that delivering the killing blow seems to be something I struggle with.

"I thought that someone had found out about my shadow-born, and that they were tracking them down one by one. But either that isn't the case at all, and the fact that Vesper went missing around the same time that Marcella stopped showing up is a coincidence, or Marcella was involved in her disappearance. Either way, I'll find out."

There's a knock at the door then.

"It's Taran," says Ronan, and it disturbs me a bit that he can do that. "Come in."

"She's awake," Taran says without opening the door all the way.

"Be there shortly."

Ronan looks from me to Taran and then down into his own lap as Taran closes the door. "I hate to disappoint you, but I'm afraid he's a lost cause." He clenches his jaw and looks into my eyes. I see a hint of jealousy there. "He loves men. And I do mean 'loves.' A hopeless romantic, that one."

My heart sinks a bit more than I expected, but not because of Taran. "Do you mean that you and he—?"

"Oh no," says Ronan. "No, that's not my preference. And he's like a brother to me. Although I do suspect he loved me a little once, but then, who doesn't?"

"Oh, fuck off," I say, rising to my feet.

"I'm glad you still feel you can say things like that to me. It would be a pity to get anything less from you than your whole self."

He's right—I shouldn't say things like that to the king. Even Adria treats him with respect.

But he likes it, and I enjoy it *greatly*, so I don't intend to stop.

Then I think about the rest of what he said. About getting my whole self.

I know I won't be giving that to him, but I can't help but think of what it would mean for him to "get" me, even the part of me I'm willing to give. As a friend? Something more?

I swore I wouldn't take him into my bed. But I was ready to take Soren there. And Ronan *is* Soren.

How much of it was real? How much of any of it is real?

"Did you tell me about Taran because you're jealous?" My heart pounds as the words leave my lips. I can barely believe I've dared to ask him, but there's a part of me that's desperate to know.

For the sake of the plan, I tell myself.

His hand twitches at his side as he rises to face me. He speaks softly again, that same damned voice that feels like bathing in sunlight on a cold winter's day. "Maybe there are some parts of Soren's life that I'll miss."

And gods, maybe it's just manipulation, but it absolutely melts me.

The air between us is still and heavy. I scarcely dare to breathe it in. He hasn't moved, but I can almost imagine him reaching for me. I can picture his hand grazing my cheek. Feel his phantom fingertips on my skin, warm and smooth.

I can feel the pull of him. The way his light draws me in. A soft, inviting glow.

I am a moth, and he is the moon.

"Good night, Ronan," I say, and I bow to him, my eyes lingering on his lips as I do. I feel an ache in my chest, a hunger. And, just like the twinge of jealousy, I lean into it.

It can only help, after all.

"Thank you, Sylvie," he says, his voice breathless.

Chapter Sixteen

Adria's bed is empty by the time I wake in the morning. Warming up already, I'm sure. It's the qualifying day for the events we're competing in, and I'm deeply, deeply regretting staying out so late last night.

Not just because I'm exhausted, physically and mentally, but because in getting the answer I wanted about Soren, I've only raised further questions.

The one that weighs the most heavily on my mind is how much of what Ronan said can I believe.

I need to speak to Larus. He'll be able to help me sort out what's going on here. That's if he can get away from Felix long enough to have a real conversation.

But first, the tournament. I dress quickly, donning one of my rougher old tunics, my leather armor, and the new tan pants I bought in the market. I keep my breakfast light in hopes of avoiding revisiting it later if I'm hit in the stomach. Adria is waiting for me at the palace gates, where chariots have arrived to carry the competitors to the arena. The palace's competitors, at least. The common folk mostly walk.

"You were late last night," she says, more curiosity in her voice than accusation this time. She's wearing the pants I bought for her, so at least I have that going for me. "And you-know-who wasn't at dinner. Did you manage to find each other?"

My thoughts race. I'd planned on telling Larus everything, but how much should I tell Adria? "I saw him when I returned from the market," I say in a panic.

Alright, good start. That much is true. But do I tell her about Soren?

It's important information about him. It would be good for her to know that he can disguise himself. There's a chance he could do it and try to deceive us into revealing something about our plans.

So why don't I want to tell her?

"Well? What happened?"

What happened? What happened? "He was returning from the market too. Some girls have gone missing. I'm not sure how he knew them, but they're shadow-born like me."

"I can guess how he knows them." She makes a rude gesture with her hand and lowers her voice so it can't be heard over the pounding of the horses' hooves. "Can't keep track of his whores?"

That's really unfair of her to say. She doesn't know anything about him—

Oh, *fuck*. What am I doing?

His little manipulation routine *worked*. The game he's been playing, a game that he's been aware of all along while I was left guessing. He's gotten to me. I'm actually debating how much to tell my own sister.

"I did find out something very interesting," I say. I gesture then to the chariot driver. It's unlikely he'll hear us, but it's not worth the risk.

But I am going to tell her.

Later.

Adria raises her eyebrows and nods. Then she smiles broadly and pats my back, and I'm reminded of how good it feels to please her.

The chariot drops us outside of the arena, the track we took the first night now occupied by a variety of races. This time, we walk the darkened tunnel on foot.

By daylight, the arena is almost unrecognizable. It's half empty now; the qualifying events must not have the same draw as the opening ceremony, though perhaps that's due to the royal box sitting empty more than anything else. I breathe a sigh of relief at Ronan's absence—that's one less thing to worry about today.

With the crowd huddled largely in the shadows, avoiding the sections of sunlit stone, the scale of the arena is even more apparent. It's impossible not to be awed by it, and yet I can't help but think of the men and women who built it. Slaves mostly, I'd guess, since the arena was built long before Selara ended slavery. I wonder how many people toiled to dig the enormous stones out of the ground, how many of them broke their bodies dragging them here hundreds of years ago.

What did they think of what they made?

Adria snaps me from my reverie by pointing to the great torch, which had been dragged off to the side to accommodate the dozen events happening simultaneously on the arena floor. "So much for that honor," she snarks, taking a dig at Quinn, though I doubt the location of the torch has anything to do with her at all.

We're shepherded by an official through the swirl of noise and action to a towering slate board propped against a pillar. The order of every trial and every individual competing is written on it in white chalk.

My archery trial will be first, along with Adria's qualifying sword fight. The sword-fighting tournament is seven rounds of single elimination. Based on our placement in the bracket, we'll only face each other in the semifinals, and the chances of me making it that far are slim to none.

I read through the other names until I finally find the one I'm looking for: Quinn of House Horatio. She's on the other side of the bracket entirely. Neither of us will face her until the final, assuming any of us makes it that far; thank Sai for his mercy.

I wish Adria luck as I join a line of archers preparing to fire their qualifying shots. The target is painted on a bale of hay at a distance of thirty paces, exactly as I practiced all those years in the castle courtyard. The standard issue Selaran bow has a bit less give than I'm used to, but I quickly adjust to it during my practice shots.

"SYLVIE!" someone screams from the crowd.

My heart races as I look into the stands just to my left to see Larus, but it isn't him yelling.

It's Felix. "Sylvie! Over here!"

Oh, for fuck's sake. The swashbuckling idiot is swaying on his feet and jumping haphazardly around, drunk before noon. He's wearing another ridiculous maritime coat, this one in a bright yellow that makes him look like a dying canary as he flits around, waving like a lunatic.

I cover my face with my hand.

"Your husband?" asks the woman in black leather qualifying to my right. I don't recognize the style of her armor or the way she wears her dark curly hair, piled onto her head with a strap holding it in place. Brakkari, maybe, or from somewhere beyond?

Wherever she's from, they must spend a lot of time practicing archery. Her practice shots are nearly all bullseyes.

"Gods, no," I say, watching Felix tumble into a man seated in front of him in the stands.

The woman laughs. "He's a mess, but he's handsome. Tell him to cheer for Calliope instead if you don't want him."

"Gladly."

Despite Felix's distraction, I manage to sail through my qualifying shots. I notice that Calliope does just as well as I do. Better, in fact. She splits one of her own arrows right in the bullseye.

"It will be a grand competition," she says, pointing to my target where three arrows are grouped closely dead in the center. She holds out her hand to shake, her grip firm and unyielding.

"To victory," I say. It's a message of goodwill and good luck that I hope isn't lost on her, assuming she isn't from here.

"And to the victor," she replies, the customary Selaran response.

By the time I meet Adria again at the sword-fighting ring, she's already won her qualifying bout 5-0.

"Don't get in your head," she tells me as I take a blunted sword from the rack. "Most of these people have never had a day of training in their lives."

"Most of them had five *years* of training during the war."

"Just hope you get someone young, then," she says, and she's in such a good mood from her triumph, she gives me another rare smile.

I don't get someone young.

What I do get is a man at least a foot taller than me and twice my weight, with a scarred bald head and arms the size of tree trunks.

"Fuck me," I whisper as I step into the circle.

He's a behemoth. One of the Seven Champions of Sai, legendary chosen warriors of the war god made flesh.

How the fuck am I supposed to fight *this* guy?

The monster of a man lunges at me the moment the bell is rung, his sword waving wildly in his massive hand.

It's fucking terrifying, but it's also a piss-poor tactic. He's got so much momentum that he can't change course easily, and it would be obvious to anyone who isn't blind where he's heading.

I lunge out of the way at the last moment, thrusting my own sword behind me into his back as he nearly falls to the ground.

"1-0!" yells the closest judge.

Was that…for me? It had to be, right?

Did I just score a point?

The man grunts as he rights himself. I offer him a hand, and he slaps it away.

"Nithyrian cunt," he spits at me.

"He can't do that!" yells Adria from the sidelines. "No contact outside of a fight." Adria has little patience for the rules except for when they benefit her.

Or me, in this case. She's on my side. Probably just making sure I don't humiliate her, but I'll take what I can get.

The slap would have been a point deduction if he had any points to begin with, but he doesn't, so we go again.

I'm debating what tactic to use to keep him at a distance and parry anything incoming when he charges again.

And…it's exactly the same as before. Like, exactly. Same angle, same momentum.

And I dodge in exactly the same way.

And it *works*.

"2-0!"

"Fuck!" he yells from the ground. He did get in an extra step this time, which nearly led him outside the circle. Which also would have lost him a point, if he'd had a point to lose.

Which he didn't.

"Sylvie!" yells Felix again. They've followed me across the arena to spectate in the stands nearby. "Sylvie!"

Fuck it. I pump my fist in the air in his direction.

He lets out a primordial scream in response, stumbling over a step, and even Larus claps a little after he gets Felix back upright.

I'm winning. I'm *winning*, and Adria was right—it really is easy.

The bell rings, and I swear to Vayla if this man lunges again…but he doesn't.

He stands there waiting unguarded. His sword arm is lax at his side.

A trap? Perhaps he's trying to see what I can do.

I charge forward, preparing to adjust to whatever guard he takes, but I don't reach him.

The ground beneath me moves.

It's just like when we were attacked on the road. The dirt floor of the arena cracks open and slides forward, putting me on my back in mere moments.

Magic. He's an earth-born, and he's using magic against me.

It's not allowed. Someone should be here to stop him in a minute—

I can't finish the thought before he's on top of me. He sinks a knee into my stomach, knocking the wind from my lungs. My sword is still in my hand, and I use it to thrash at him, but he grabs it by the blade and tosses it aside.

"Tell Vahlo who sent you," he says as he reaches for my throat.

He's going to kill me. He's actually going to try to kill me in this arena in broad daylight, surrounded by judges and guards and my family and friends.

His hands are squeezing my throat. I sink my nails into his skin, clawing at his hands, trying to get them to release me, but it does no good. He's going to crush my windpipe before anyone can get to me. Through my fading vision, I see Adria's flame ignite the sleeve of his tunic, but it's too soaked with his sweat to catch.

His hands squeeze again, and panic shoots through me as I thrash helplessly beneath him. I can't beat him, not with sheer strength and no weapon, and while I'm certain Adria will eventually light him up like a bonfire, I could be dead before it happens.

Thankfully, my survival instinct has gotten quite a lot of practice in recent days. It takes over then, and I release my magic, tournament rules be damned.

I drop a shadow over us. The darkness isn't total, not out here in the broad daylight, but it's still disorienting enough for the earthborn that I'm able to punch him hard in his vast stomach before kneeing him where the sun doesn't shine as he stumbles forward.

My lungs fill with a painful, shaking gasp.

I'm alive. I'm still alive.

"Sylvie!" yells Adria. She's close now. I release my shadow so she can find me.

The blinding sunlight disorients me, and I nearly collapse into her arms. My throat aches and burns where he choked me, the narrow passage of my airway swelling as the blood rushes to my wounded neck. I try to say something to her, but the words don't come out.

"She's hurt. Healer!"

A judge gestures to someone in a distant white tent almost boredly, as if my serious injury is just an inconvenience to him. The other judge doesn't look at all. She turns to face the crowd. "Disqualified for use of magic during a non-magical event—"

Well, at least there's that, I think as I pray to Vayla the healer gets here soon. He tried to kill me, but at least I'm alive, and I'm still in the tournament.

"—Sylvie of House Verran. Victor: Leon the Smith."

What?

"But I—" Fuck. My voice croaks and hisses, the sound barely coming out. It's really getting hard to breathe…"He. Used—"

Adria puts her arm underneath me, trying to move me towards the healer tent, but I can barely walk. I see Larus making his way through the crowd, trying to get down to the floor to help.

Adria is furious. "Where is the fucking healer? She's hurt. Disqualified? He used magic first!"

"Please clear the area and wait for the healer."

"ABSOLUTELY NOT." Adria is about to start the war right here in the arena if they don't start helping me soon.

"Excuse me," says a quiet voice from behind the judges.

The judges bow to the woman, who is wearing the brown robes of the Alchemists' Guild.

I see her face in the shadow of her robes, and a weight on my chest lifts even as my lungs scream for air.

"Guild Mistress," says a judge. "The healers are on their way."

"That's not why I'm here," she begins, but seeing the state I'm in, she rushes over to us, helping Adria hold me up. "Gods, she's dying."

The healer arrives at nearly the same time, and he tries to hand Zara an elixir, but she refuses it.

She places her hand on my neck, and the relief is nearly instantaneous. A comforting warmth spreads through my skin, reaching deep into the damaged tissue. Something stretches and snaps painlessly back into place. When she finally lets go, I can breathe freely. My throat no longer aches at all.

"Thank you," I say to her, my voice now clear.

This must be what Ronan did for Nico when I stabbed him. It's nothing like the slow nature magic of the typical healer. It's nothing like the agonizing burn of the fire-born. It's even better than most of the alchemical elixirs. It was *painless*, and unbelievably fast.

Light magic is truly incredible.

Zara rounds on the judges then. She stands as tall as she can, and though her voice is soft, there's an edge of power to it that I've never heard from her before. "The God-King will be hearing about the healer situation. He's made it very clear that no one will be dying for the sake of our entertainment. And as for the misunderstanding regarding the match, I must conclude it's simply due to the angle you were watching from." What Zara says makes no sense: the judges were positioned on opposite sides of the circle with a full view of everything. There's no way they didn't see what happened, but her words do give them an excuse for their behavior. "I saw everything from the stands. The man—Leon? He's earth-born. He caused the damage to the circle. Sylvie was only reacting to his threat. If anyone should be disqualified, it's him."

The judges look at each other tensely. "Of course, Mistress," says the man. "We're grateful you were here to illuminate us."

A light pun. Zara flashes a smile at me so quickly I nearly miss it.

The female judge turns to the crowd to redo the proclamation. "Disqualified: Leon the Smith. Victor: Sylvie of House Verran."

Larus finally makes it to us then. I'm glad he's left Felix back in the stands, but I realize as I look for him, it's because Felix is flat on his back.

"He'll be fine," says Larus as he sees where I'm looking. "Are you alright?"

"I'm fine, thanks to the Guild Mistress."

She smiles. "Any time. Anti-Nithyrian prejudice runs deep in Selara still. A pity, and when you were doing so well. I'd wish you luck, but I don't think you'll need it."

I open my mouth to reiterate my gratitude, but she bows her head and slips away with all the subtlety of a shadow-born.

"Look who lives to fight another day. Well, barely," says the jeering voice of Quinn of House Horatio. I know her before I even see her. I'd recognize her mockery anywhere.

"Fuck off," says Adria. "You'll see who barely lives when we fight."

"Then you admit I'll make it to the end?"

I glance at Larus. As much as I'd like to see what Quinn is up to, I'd really rather not get pulled into this argument. In fact, what I'd really like is to sit down.

"Come on," he says, and he leads me into the stands, but further up beyond where Felix is resting. "Let the fire-born do…whatever it is that they do."

As I take a seat next to Larus in a part of the stands empty enough to afford us privacy, I breathe a sigh of relief. Not just because I've survived yet *another* attempt on my life, but because it's Larus. All of the confusing things I've been feeling will make sense once I've had a chance to speak with him. I just know it.

"I've heard you've been busy," he says, waiting for me to speak as usual.

He's not talking about today. He's talking about my encounters with Ronan, which I'm sure he's heard about from Adria, although she barely knows more than he does. "I fought with him. Not a real fight, but he came up to us while we were practicing. I told Adria about some of his favored moves."

"That's good. Although if he had any sense, he wouldn't show you everything he's capable of."

That was true enough from what I'd seen of him when our lives were truly threatened.

Gods, there's so much to tell Larus. As much as I want to hear what he thinks about the rest, I'm afraid to admit everything to him. Will he think I'm a fool for befriending Soren?

And how do I let him know what's happened without confessing to every embarrassing detail?

I decide to avoid the topic for a bit longer while I work out what to say. Instead, I mention the way Quinn seems to be everywhere that we are as I watch her walk away from Adria, unfortunately not on fire, and Larus thinks it's no coincidence.

"Keeping an eye on you, I'm sure. For her father or the king, maybe both. She and Typhon are nearly twenty years apart in age. The rest of their siblings died in the war, along with their mother.

Whatever begrudging affection Typhon has for our family after his years with us, I wouldn't expect her to share it."

I hadn't realized until our encounter on the ferry that Typhon *did* have a begrudging affection for us. But it's good to know. We need every ally we can find around here.

Including, I realize, maybe even Quinn herself.

"There's a chance she's more amenable that she seems. Someone is. Someone on the inside, working against him. *He's* trying to find them."

Larus shakes his head. "Not one of ours. But good to keep in mind. We know from the throne room that there are others with similar goals."

How many others are plotting to do the same? If they succeed, our own plans could fail.

That's at least one good reason to help Ronan.

I ask Larus why he invited Felix here—he didn't intend to, but he thought it would put him in his place once he saw how good we are in a fight, although it's unclear how much of the day he'll even remember. And then I talk at length about the palace, the food, and the sights of the market, still avoiding the true topic of conversation.

But Larus knows me too well. As I dive into my third mention of the bathing caves, he holds up his hand to stop me. "This isn't what you wanted to speak with me about."

He's right, of course, but it's unnerving how easily he sees right through me.

"I met someone the first night we arrived in the market," I say, my pulse thrumming in my ears as I look around us. Even though we're at a distance from the nearest spectators, there's always a risk that a wind-born is near enough to hear. I drop my voice low. "It was him. In disguise."

"Disguised how? Wearing a wig? Did you recognize him immediately?"

I shake my head. "His magic."

"There were rumors," he muses. "Not about him, but some of the old kings and queens. Never verified."

"Or perhaps stricken from the record."

Larus nods slowly, stroking his beard. "When did you know?"

"That night, although I wasn't certain until last night."

"When you saw him again."

I nod.

"Did he follow you there? To the market?"

"I think so."

Larus claps for someone emerging from the water-born trial. The sudden movement and sound startle me. I hadn't even noticed they were swimming. "It seems he shares our idea," he says as I join his applause.

"What do you mean?"

"I mean that he wants to keep you close just as we want to keep you close to him. Convenient, but also dangerous. Has he done anything to endear himself to you?"

I blush, remembering the near-kiss. "Maybe once or twice."

"And did it work?" Larus has been keeping his eyes forward, but he shifts them to me then, and I know he can see the answer before I say it.

"I liked Soren," I admit. "That was who he pretended to be. But I don't know the real him. I've only spoken to him a couple of times."

That was the truth of it. No matter how much I'd liked Soren, Ronan wasn't Soren, and I had no real idea how much they had in common. It could be everything or almost nothing. The entire existence of Soren could have been made to appeal to me specifically, for all I knew. Ronan couldn't read thoughts, but it seemed like more than a coincidence that my impression of him as too perfect when we met led to meeting a version of him with flaws fully on display.

"Be careful," whispers Larus, his hand twitching over his sword reflexively. "It benefits him to win you over. Don't forget it."

I nod, but I know Larus can see something else is on my mind. He pauses, waiting for me to speak, but I don't. I cheer for a man who hit a bullseye with a spear instead.

He sighs at me. "Say it," he says.

I swallow, trying to force the panic that's rising from my chest back down my throat. Of everything I've said to Larus, this is the thing I'm most afraid to talk about. "It's about the Orsa. And Taran, in particular."

Larus uncrosses and crosses his legs, switching which one is on top. For most, it would be a casual gesture. The kind of thing you do one hundred times a day without attracting any kind of attention. For him, a man completely aware of his appearance at all times, it's the peak of agitation.

"What did he say to you?" he asks, his voice clipped.

"He told me about how his village was slaughtered—"

"Poachers. I remember."

"You were there?" I can't hide my shock and disgust, and I know Larus sees it too.

"No," says Larus. "Your uncle's men." My uncle Theron, father's younger brother. Lost in the war with the rest of them. He had been a favorite of my brother Seth's, although Mother wasn't fond of him from what I remembered. "Theron kept his men on a longer leash than your father liked."

"So it's true what they did? Slaughtered all of them, even the children?" I'm unwilling to ask what else had happened to them, what reason they had for stripping them naked. I can't bear to even think of it.

"Yes, and it was disgracefully done. And with the king nearby on a hunt. Aurelian took no issue with it; no laws were broken after all. They were on Verran land. Their lives were forfeit. But your father was angry, both at Theron and at the king taking Taran as a ward. It never should have happened, but to keep the boy was a terrible insult."

Their lives were forfeit. Even the children, who had no choice in the matter. I didn't—couldn't—understand. "Taran was only eleven. There were other children there too. What could they have possibly done?"

"Their parents knew what the consequences were, and they trespassed anyway. The blood is on their hands."

"But they were starving—"

"Sylvara." Larus *never* uses my full name. Not ever. Not even the time I climbed the highest castle tower as a child, a castle the Orsa now control, nearly falling to my death. I've always preferred Sylvie, and he has always respected that.

Until now.

"You don't understand what you're talking about, and that's my fault, not yours. I protected you from it. I shielded you from what the Orsa do, what they *are*. But make no mistake, Sylvie, they are *monsters*. They are not like us, no matter what Ronan would like you to believe. They have ravaged your family's lands for generations. They have plundered your villages. They have slaughtered your children in their beds. Everything we did to them in that village, they've done to us one hundred times over. They are savages, and they will stop at nothing until Nithyria is ground to dust.

"I have served your family faithfully since I was no older than Taran. I have fought and bled for you because I believe in you. If you had seen the things I've seen—if you had watched your dearest friends die at their hands—you would never dream of defending them."

I have never heard Larus say so much at once. He's a man of few words, seldom prone to lecture. He likes to let me come to conclusions for myself. And yet here he is, telling me I'm wrong.

I trust Larus beyond anything. Beyond even my brother and sister. He's more than twice my age, but in many ways, he's my closest friend in the world.

But what he's saying just doesn't make sense to me, and I won't lie to him and pretend that it does. I respect him too much for that.

"You say they're not like us. But you also admit my uncle's men did the same—"

"Because of what *they* did first." His voice is sharp and impatient, and hearing it makes heat rise in the back of my neck.

It hurts me to hear his disappointment. I'm ashamed to argue with him, ashamed enough to consider letting it go, but I just can't. "Does that make it right? It isn't what you taught me."

Larus sighs. "I hoped you would live in a time of peace. Of reconciliation. I prepared you to fight a war, but I didn't prepare you to live in one. They took your home, Sylvie. We are at war with them, no matter what they say here. They are your enemy."

The enemy. The other. I think of Adria's words, and then of Ronan's. I think of Taran on the road back last night. Shy, almost painfully so. Never drawing attention to himself, serving his king without complaint or question. Beyond that, he's grateful to him. He serves Ronan out of love, not fear. If the heart of a killer beats in his chest, Taran hides it better than anyone I've known.

"The man who nearly killed me down there thought the same thing about me. Was he right?"

Larus opens his mouth to speak and then closes it. He furrows his brows and crosses his arms in front of him, opens his mouth *again* and closes it *again*, and then shakes his head. "Sylvie," he says, and he softens, his eyes wrinkling at the corners as he almost smiles. "Who taught you to be so wise?" He sighs again, a deep, heavy sigh that moves his entire chest. Then he slowly stands up. "There's a part of me that knows that you're right. Maybe not about everything, but you could be right about Taran, at least. I know it, I *know* it, but still I can't agree. I'm an old man, Sylvie, and the wounds they made have been there longer than you've been alive. It's not my mind you need to change. It's my heart."

"Can you change my heart instead?" I ask him. I stand to face him, and I see a mixture of pride and confusion. At the end of the day, he loves me, even if he doesn't understand me.

"I don't think I can," he says. "And I wouldn't even if I could." He places his hand on my shoulder. "Trust yourself, Sylvie. I have served your house most of my life, and I will continue to serve you as long as you let me. I have always believed in House Verran.

"But I have never believed in anything more than I believe in you."

Tears spring to my eyes. I slowly nod at him. I don't know if I believe in myself right now, but his faith in me gives me courage. *Thank you,* I think, but I don't say it.

I don't need to.

Larus returns to help Felix, whose dark skin has taken on a pale, greenish hue as he's woken, and I check the arena floor for Adria so we can return to the palace together.

I've had enough of the tournament for one day.

There's no sign of her near the sword-fighting ring, and no scorch marks leading away from it, so I take it her battle with Quinn was purely verbal. She probably guessed that I would return with Larus, so I head into the tunnel we entered to take a chariot back on my own.

I spot her there, standing against a wall just past the tunnel entrance. If I hadn't been able to see in the dark, I'm not sure I would have noticed her. "Waiting to pounce?"

"Something like that," she says. Her voice sounds rough, but that's not unusual. Where there's fire, there's smoke. She must have gotten into something with Quinn after all for there to have been enough fire involved to make her voice hoarse.

"You alright?" I ask. I see no obvious burns, though her clothes are a bit disheveled.

"You should see her." She grins.

"Come on." I want to tell her what I've learned about Ronan and what I'm thinking about Quinn, but I can't if she turns her to toast before I get the chance.

"I'm not heading back just yet."

I roll my eyes and keep walking. There's no point in arguing with her when she takes that tone. She just can't help herself. "Keep an eye on her," I say. "She could be up to something."

"Like what?"

There are a few people making their way through the tunnel, so I don't tell her about my suspicions that she could be leaking information about Ronan, and that if she is, she may even be an ally. "She's keeping an eye on us," I say, echoing Larus's words. "Try not to kill her before we can find out why."

"Look at who's giving the orders now," she says. She mockingly bows to me, and I give her a rude hand gesture. "Before you go, those shadow-born girls," she says. "What does he think happened to them? Are you going to help him find them?"

That's odd. She showed no interest in them before. "Did Quinn ask about them?"

"No," she says, sighing impatiently. "Just tell me what he said."

"We found one of them. No sign of the other."

She doesn't seem surprised when I tell her *we* found them, even though I hadn't told her that part of the story yet. "Got it."

I really don't understand why she's asking, unless she's thinking that his shadow-born spies have been compromised in some way. Maybe she even had a part in it without telling me.

"Do you know where she is?" I ask. I remember the sound of Vesper's mother's voice, her worry and fear for her daughter. If Adria did something to her…

"For fuck's sake, no. Now fuck off, before Quinn comes back."

I shake my head and leave her there to play whatever stupid game she's playing.

Fucking Adria. When they go low, she goes straight to hell.

Chapter Seventeen

Back in the palace, I'm hanging my armor to dry in our chambers when there's a soft knock at the door.

I must look like hell because Taran's mouth falls open in shock when I open it. "He wishes to see you."

He does, does he? "Tell him after I bathe."

Taran shifts his weight, his armor clinking from the movement. "He said to bring you to him right away."

"And you will, right away, *after I bathe.*"

I am not going to talk to him about whatever it is he wants to talk about in this state. My hair is half-fallen from its bun, half-caked in dirt from my time on the ground, and my clothes are stiff with dried sweat.

Even if it's just a game that we're playing in getting to know each other, I am not playing it like this.

The servants have already taken my change of clothes down to the changing rooms, so I finish hanging my pauldrons on their rack and head out the door.

Taran is still waiting there.

"Are you going to oversee my bath?"

Taran blushes a deep red that covers his entire face, neck, and even his ears. I both feel sorry for him and feel validated in my assertion that this poor, shy man can't possibly be bad just by virtue of his birth. "No, ma'am. I'll tell him you'll meet him straight after."

"Good man." It takes him a minute to leave even after saying that he will, and I imagine he's trying to determine if he's failing to follow an order of Ronan's, or if my defiance is something that can't be helped no matter what Ronan told him to do.

I take my time bathing, not only because the heat of the hot cave feels particularly nice on my sore muscles and bruised back, but because I'm thinking of what Larus said to me about Ronan benefitting from me taking his side.

It's interesting because it's well beyond what I had been thinking. It made some sense to me that Ronan might want to keep me close to see what Nithyria was planning and if we had anything to do with the information leak, or to be able to stop me himself if I tried to make a move. I'm the weakest link in our chain, the person with the least experience on and off the battlefield.

But it hadn't occurred to me that Ronan might think there's a chance of winning me to his side entirely. We would never try to do the same; we know there's no chance of making Ronan give up his crown willingly. The very notion is absurd. So wouldn't he consider trying to win me over equally ridiculous?

Or is he so arrogant that he thinks there's actually a chance?

I'm still drying my hair with a towel—*where's a wind-born when you need them?*—when I hear the same faint tap on the changing room door.

"I'm nearly finished," I say through the crack as I hold the door ajar. "But I'm hungry. I thought I'd stop by the dining hall—"

"He told me to throw you over my shoulder if I have to, but I *must* bring you to him immediately."

I open the door a bit more to get a better look at him. "Would you throw me over your shoulder?"

He winces. "Please don't make me."

So that's a yes.

I let him squirm for just a minute thinking he might have to, then I toss the towel back inside and follow him up the stairs to Ronan's quarters.

The door opens before we approach it. Of course it would. He could feel me from down the hall.

"What took you so long?" he says to Taran, and the poor man stammers an apology.

"It's my fault," I say, interrupting him. "I dared to insist on bathing before I was granted my royal audience."

"Come inside," says Ronan brusquely. I shoot a regretful look at Taran—*sorry I got you in trouble*—before following Ronan.

We're back in the sitting room again, but this time, he opens the door at the back and leads me through into his chambers.

The room we enter isn't what I imagined at all. There's no bed in it, I notice entirely too quickly, so he must sleep elsewhere. This is a lounge of some kind, a space meant for gathering and relaxing.

There are clusters of chairs and low divans in luxurious velvet fabrics, some of them angled to face each other in conversation like the benches in the receiving room. Shelves reach to the high, vaulted ceiling, filled with books, scrolls, and beautiful objects carved from stone or crafted from silver, all of them worth more than everything I own, I'm certain. On the far wall, curtains of a delicate, gauzy material billow in the cool evening air to either side of a wide archway.

But what catches my eye the most is a desk in the corner with a great map of Selara hung on the wall behind it. The map is filled with pins and markers that must relate to the stacks of paper below somehow, important trade routes or military installations or maybe just places Ronan likes to visit. The answers must be there, right on that desk.

I could learn so much in this room. And he let me in here willingly. He invited me.

Ronan stops just inside the door and turns to me. He's wearing a sheer black tunic similar to the robes he wore the first time we met. It's tight through his shoulders, revealing the tension in the muscles there. His beautiful, flawless face shifts from annoyance to concern and then returns to a careful neutrality. There's a war happening in his mind as he tries to decide how much to give away. It's a feeling I know well.

His composure falters as he looks at my neck. Someone must have told him about what happened in the arena. Did he send someone to keep an eye on me, or had Zara come straight here after the fight? It's only been a few hours since then.

Instinctively, I try to hide my throat from his gaze. There's no wound there anymore, but it feels too vulnerable to let him see where someone hurt me.

Did he ask me here to check if I'm alright?

He steps closer, close enough for me to feel his heat, to feel the warmth of his light. Then he reaches out quickly, and then suddenly slows before he makes contact, as if he can barely restrain himself. As if he needs to feel me to be sure that I'm okay, but he's afraid of how I'll respond.

I look into his eyes, and there's something so vulnerable there, so worried, that I lift my chin, granting him access.

Gently, with an almost unbearable delicateness, he brushes his fingers on my skin.

His touch is different than Soren's. Soren's touch was familiar and comforting, like the embrace of an old friend. This touch lingers on me, warm and intoxicating, the feeling of it new and rare and sacred. It tugs at me, pulling me into him.

My lips part involuntarily. A droplet of water from my damp hair runs down my neck and onto my chest. I can feel his eyes follow it, and I want him to keep looking. I want him to watch as the water traces the curve of my breast before disappearing beneath my evening gown. I want him to wonder where it is when it doesn't soak into the thin linen fabric.

I want him to envy it.

He exhales softly, and I know his eyes have done as I hoped without even looking up. "Her work was good," he says, his voice low and sultry, "but there's still some bruising. Here." He wraps his arm around me and rests his hand on the small of my back, his fingers slipping into the gap between the buttons.

I gasp as his fingertips graze a bruise just below my waist. My skin tingles painlessly as their heat repairs the damaged blood vessels. In moments, the bruise is gone so completely that my only indication it was there at all is the lingering touch of his hand.

I want more.

Am I even pretending now? Do I even need to remind myself that it's good to give in to this feeling? Or have I somehow managed it without any convincing?

I still don't know how much of anything that's happening is real, but I would let him touch me, I realize. He could slide his hand down my back and pull me to him. He could angle my chin up until my eyes meet his, and he could kiss me. Soft, at first. Tentative.

And then harder, wilder, until I'm breathless and gasping for him.

Can he feel that?

I wait for a moment, but he doesn't move. He's as frozen as I am, transfixed by the contact of his skin on mine. When I look into his eyes, I see another war being waged there. He wants this—he *needs* it—but…what? I can't tell what holds him back. Maybe he's afraid? Maybe he's uncertain if this is a step too far.

Maybe the line between real and pretend is getting a little too hard for him to find.

I know the feeling.

I take a step back, and he pulls his hand from my dress. "Thank you," I say, my voice barely a whisper. "I'm alright now."

I turn to leave. I can't be in here anymore; my feelings are overwhelming my thoughts. I'm not sure if they even are my feelings, or if they're just the desires of my body.

I feel lightheaded. I feel a heaviness in my core that desperately wants to drag me down with it.

I feel like I should wrap my arms around his neck and kiss him.

I feel like I should run out the door and never so much as look at him again.

I take a step forward, a step away from him, a step towards the door and my sanity.

And he grabs my arm.

It takes every single ounce of my strength to turn around slowly. To not throw myself into his embrace. To wait and hear what he has to say before losing myself in him entirely.

"Wait. Don't go."

I stare at him, unblinking.

I can't move. I can't even breathe.

His hand is still on my arm. He rubs a gentle circle there with his fingertips, then they still as he thinks better of it. The war in his mind has spread to his hands, to his body.

I know that feeling as well.

Finally, he speaks, the battle won. "Have dinner with me." He's trying desperately to regain his composure, to return his voice to its normal tone and cadence, but it only half works. It's half "have dinner with me," half "come to bed with me."

He found a middle ground. Something between what he truly wants and what he knows is best. I admire that. It's a sensible thing to try, a de-escalation of whatever it is that's happening here without running for the door entirely.

But I can't stay. I shouldn't. I need to leave; I need to get out of here and clear my head, to think about what's happening before I do something—"Alright," I hear myself saying.

What am I doing?

Is this his magic? Is it the reason for the pull he has on me?

"No," I say more firmly than I truly feel. "I don't know. I need some air."

"Come," he says, and *godsdammit*, did he have to say that word?

"Did you have to say that word?" My eyes widen as I realize I've said that thought out loud.

But wonderfully, miraculously, it fixes everything. It's so silly, so *stupid*, that he can't help but laugh, and finally, blessedly, the tension breaks.

Kerensa, thank you for helping me in my hour of need.

I'm back in the room. I'm back on solid ground. I feel the cool stone through my thin sandals, feel the cool breeze from the open archway.

That's where Ronan leads me, straight past the shelves full of insights into Ronan's character that I might have been able to explore if I could've kept myself together for five fucking minutes, past whatever hidden doors the servants use that I could have been finding if I'd remembered *anything* useful at all, and through the archway onto a balcony overlooking the sea.

It's an incredible vista, of course. Deep blue water stretches to the horizon, a streak of gold shimmering in the last light of the setting sun. Rocky cliffs jut out from the sides, lending the balcony their natural protection, although we're up far too high for anyone to climb anyway.

It would be difficult to access his chambers from here. Difficult, but not impossible, I realize, as I see other balconies to the sides.

"What are you thinking?" he asks me, and my thoughts scramble, trying to land on something connected to my feelings but not quite so incriminating.

"I'm wondering whose rooms those are, and what they did to earn the view."

Gods, what a dumb question. Possibly anything but, I don't know, waging a war against his throne?

He looks at me quizzically. "You know, I never wanted to read thoughts until I met you."

A strange thing to say. "What do you mean?'

He leans over the railing, and I join him, doing the same. At a safe distance. "Usually I can guess what someone's thinking by the feelings that they have. People aren't terribly complicated. The feelings they have are largely the same. Anger, fear, joy, anxiety, desire." His eyes flash to mine on the last word, and I'm desperately willing the blood in my neck to stay there and not rush into my face. He swallows, tilting his head to cover the movement. "It's not hard to connect their feelings, to guess at the cause of them. Sometimes it's the sequence of them that gives them away, sometimes it's the things they say, even if they don't match the way they feel."

He turns to look at me and then shakes his head. "But you're a mystery to me sometimes. It's infuriating. I can feel so much from you. Gods, it's like you're shouting at me with everything you're feeling, but I have no idea what any of it means."

"I'm shouting at you with my *feelings*?" That doesn't seem good.

He laughs. "I'm not saying you're doing it on purpose. But when you're in the room, it's like I can feel no one else. It's nice, actually. My power—it can be overwhelming when a lot of people are around. You quiet the noise."

I smile a little, and he leans a little closer. He looks so lovely in the dying sunlight. It catches the gold strands of his hair and illuminates them from behind, casting a faint glow around him.

Or maybe it's his own internal glow. It's hard to tell.

"If you want to know what I'm thinking, just ask," I say.

"Will you tell me the truth?"

Not likely, but maybe sometimes. "I'm shadow-born, like you said. It's in my nature not to."

"I don't believe that for a second."

"Sacrilege? And from the God-King himself?"

He smiles mischievously. "All day, every day."

The aspects of the schools of magic are written in the Codex. They're sacred. The crime of sacrilege has rarely been punished in the last one hundred years, but at a minimum, it will get you a good talking to from a priest, which is reason enough to avoid it.

I want to ask him more about that—how does someone manage to lead the national religion, a religion that holds him to be the reincarnation of a literal god on earth, and also speak against it? But a pair of servants arrives then, one holding a tray and the other a tablecloth and utensils, and I realize I missed how he summoned them and where they came from.

Maybe Ronan is right. I may be a shadow-born, but I'm also the world's worst spy.

"Just against the railing there," he directs them as they set a small table and move it onto the balcony. "Perfect."

"I'm sorry to make you wait," says Ronan as he takes the seat across from me. "But you can never be too careful." He gestures, and one of the servants lifts a cover and takes a bite from something that smells like perfectly fried fish as another lights a candle.

My mouth waters, and my stomach growls angrily. I'm starving.

"I'll take my chances," I say, reaching for one of the covers, but he smacks it back down.

"I have to insist that you don't. It won't be long."

I don't see why I should have to wait for the royal taster. It's not like someone is going to poison me.

"Finally, a feeling I can read loud and clear. No, I don't think someone is going to poison you, but they could certainly poison us both."

"Have you ever eaten anything warm in your life?" I don't know how he can stand eating cold food. I always made Seth heat my dishes if they took too long coming from the kitchens.

He lifts the cover off the fish and holds his hands over it. In just a few seconds, it begins to sizzle. "I manage."

"Cover it back up. It smells too good."

After an agonizing wait, the servant appears to be very much not dead, and Ronan finally lets me gorge myself, which I do with great enthusiasm after he reheats my food for me.

"Tell her servants to make sure she has food to take with her to the arena on tournament days. She's starving."

I open my mouth to protest, but I really am starving, and it's a nice gesture.

There's a slight pause after we're both done, and it reminds me a bit of Larus waiting for me to talk. I take a sip of wine—damn, it's delicious; Nithyrian for sure—and fire away. "So what do you want to know, Ronan? You asked me to dinner. You want to know what I'm thinking. Ask me."

"Are you liking it here?"

Here? "In the palace? Or Faros?"

"I take it you don't like one of those. Which is it?"

"The palace," I admit. "I don't mind your chambers—"

"Good. You'll be back here," he says, wiping his mouth and then freezing, napkin still in hand, as he realizes what he said. "For dinner. I meant you'll be back here again for dinner—"

"I like the décor here," I explain, ignoring the way my pulse races at that little slip-up. "The rest…"

He leans over the table, moving the candle to the side and dropping his voice low. "I'll tell you a secret: I hate the palace too. I had these rooms redone to my own taste."

After the war. These rooms had once belonged to his parents. For once, I'm grateful that we lost our home. I never had to see the rooms my parents slept in pass to my sister. I couldn't imagine using them myself, feeling their presence every time I was in them. I don't blame him for changing things.

His parents. My parents. Gods, we'd all lost so much. I wonder what they would say if they could see us sitting at this table together.

His brows furrow. "You're doing it again. Feeling things at me that I don't understand."

"I was thinking of our parents."

"Ah," he says, and he takes a deep sip of wine. "That explains it."

"Can I ask you a question?" I ask after another pause.

"Go on."

"How did you know about the bruise on my back?"

He looks off across the sea, searching for a way to explain it. "When I touch you, I can feel the blood flowing through your body. It's like a map in some ways, the way it appears in my mind. I can feel when something isn't flowing as it should, when it collects somewhere or exits through a wound."

When it collects somewhere. Like a bruise, or...

Like arousal.

"Exactly," he says, tilting his glass to me. "I got that one. And yes, it's every bit as embarrassing as you're imagining."

Gods. I tell myself to never, ever let him touch me again.

Or maybe to let him touch me right now.

Godsdammit, keep it together.

"I'm sorry I wasn't there today to heal you. I was following a lead on Vesper that led nowhere, unfortunately. We didn't get anything useful from Marcella; it seems like the two going missing weren't related. I won't miss another of your events."

"Please don't," I say. "You don't need to come." I don't really want him to come. I'm not sure how well I'll perform, knowing he's watching.

"I won't let something like that happen to you again." He leans back and crosses his arms, defiant.

I scoff. "You sent me into danger yourself."

"That was different. I was there."

His mouth sets into a firm line. Fine, I'll let him have this one. But I still want to know how he knew what happened. "Did you send someone to keep an eye on me?"

"No," he says, picking up his fork and flicking it across his empty plate. It's an obvious lie. "Alright, yes. I did."

My face flushes, and for once, I can't tell if it's from embarrassment, anger, or some kind of primal appreciation for being protected.

"And don't tell me you didn't need it because you did. It's a good thing she was there, from what she told me."

"Wait, are you telling me you sent Zara to protect me?" The head of the Alchemists' Guild? He sent the head of the Alchemists' Guild to protect me during the tournament?

"She offered to go, to be fair. She pointed out that House Verran has a lot of enemies, and I agreed it would be best to have someone with light magic there to help you. Honestly, I think she just wanted to see the sport for herself. I don't think either of us thought she'd truly be needed."

Zara had volunteered. I make a mental note to send her something as a thank you. She had been absolutely right.

"That's two questions you've asked me. It's my turn," he says. I reach for the wine bottle at the same time he does. Our hands touch, sending a shock through me like lightning. I pull away suddenly, remembering what he said about feeling arousal.

I'll let him pour.

His breathing falters for just a moment before he regains control. "What do you like to do?" he asks me once our glasses are full again.

I laugh. "All the buildup for that?"

"I'm serious. I told you I'd like to know you. Tell me what you like."

"Well, you know I'm not great at sword-fighting, but I'm not bad at archery. I can embroider, dance, the usual things. I can actually do a bit of acrobatic tumbling, that part of what I told Soren was true. Oh, and I can play the flute."

"That's not what I meant, although I am fond of music. There's a lute in there." He gestures back to the living area.

"Don't tell me you're one of those guys that plays the lute at the party."

He smirks. "I would have been, in a different life. I might have been a bard. Can you picture it?"

"I can, actually." He's just the right amount of charming and smarmy.

"I can picture you playing the flute as well," he says.

I can't let that opportunity pass. "Is that a euphemism, or…?"

He nearly chokes on his wine.

"I'm sorry," I say, being anything but. My shadows hum their approval at the silly little lie. "I don't know where that came from. What were you trying to ask me?"

He opens his mouth, blinks, looks back into the palace, bites his lower lip in a way that sends a tingle between my legs, and then recomposes his face, remembering. "Those are things you *can* do. But what do you *like* to do? If you had one day left to live, how would you spend it?"

What do I like to do? The truth is, I don't have a great answer to that question. I've spent so much of my life doing what I was told to. So many years being told that what I wanted didn't matter, that I needed to focus on the good of the house or the people. My duty. My responsibility.

What am I, other than that?

The only thing I can think of is how good it felt to go to the market. How it felt when Soren showed me around. When he told me about all the vendors and the wonderful places they'd come from. "Well, I'd—no, it's stupid."

"Tell me." He reaches across the table and nearly takes my hand in an automatic gesture that sends my heart racing. But he stops short.

Control.

"It would take more than a day," I say.

"A week, a month. Whatever. It's a hypothetical, Sylvie. I won't hold you to the timing."

I gaze out over the ocean. It's beautiful out there, waves crashing in the darkness. I wish he could see it too. "I would get in a boat and sail anywhere. Everywhere. I want to see it all, all the things I've read about in books. All the beautiful places that are painted in our pictures and embroidered in our tapestries. I want to climb mountains and go to markets and learn how to say hello in a dozen languages. I want to journey to the Five Wonders of the World and measure them with my own eyes, to decide which one is the most wondrous. I've spent my entire life in Nithyria, and I loved it there, but my father used to promise me that once it was over—once the revolution was over—he'd take me to all the places I wanted to go. And then he never came back, and we never went. If I could do anything, it would be that."

Ronan stays silent for a long time. His fingertips brush the stubble on his jaw in deep contemplation. When he finally speaks, his voice is low, but it doesn't carry the warmth I'm accustomed to. It's raw, almost to the point of breaking. "I'm sorry he never got to take you. I took that from you."

He did, of course, but the rage I felt towards him for doing so is hard to find right now. It's strange to be without it. My rage has been my constant companion these past few years. Somehow, it's been slipping away from me, and I failed to notice its absence until this moment.

Yes, Ronan killed my father. He killed him in a duel my father requested, a duel they both agreed to in order to end the war and save the lives of their people. And I've hated him for it for so long, but…

This isn't the man I hated.

He isn't the same as the monster in my head. If there's a version of Ronan that relished killing my father, either he's hiding it very well, or he's long gone too.

Because all I can see in his eyes is regret.

"I can't give you him back, but someday, maybe, I could take you. To honor his memory. I would take you, if you'd let me."

I don't know what to say. I should be insulted. To take the trip I'd planned with my father with his killer instead? I should be raging.

Where did my rage go?

Who am I without it?

I can't trust him. I need to remember what Larus said about how it benefits him to have me on his side. He could be using what I want to win me over. It costs him nothing to make empty promises.

But…his face. The soul-deep sadness in his eyes. The way his voice cracks when he speaks. The tension in his arms, the control he's holding onto so tightly it looks like it might rip him apart.

There's a part of me that believes him.

There's also a part of me that knows that what Ronan said about the endless war between our families—the crimes on both sides—is true. He took my father, but my father took his. To honor my father would be to honor the man who took his father from him, for my sake.

Either he means what he says about ending the cycle of violence between us, or he's the best liar I've ever met.

Either way, the trip he's imagining won't happen. But I don't think about why. I refuse to disgrace this moment, this moment of compassion that I do not deserve, with thoughts about our plans.

"Maybe someday," I say, but I know he can feel the truth.

Chapter Eighteen

During the weeks that follow, I keep a careful distance from Ronan.

The first time I see him in the courtyard of the palace after our dinner a couple of days later, he asks me to join him again that evening.

"I can't," I tell him. "I need to focus on the tournament."

It's a pathetic lie, the kind that doesn't require the magical power of empathy to detect. But I can't tell him the real reason I choose to stay away.

I tell him no because I want to say yes. And I don't know what to do with that feeling.

I do ask him when I see him in the dining hall a few days later if there's been any news about our friends. He tells me Marcella has been released to a city jail to await trial, and that he gave the city watch the order to find Vesper. Although, as he suspected would be the case, they haven't been able to turn up anything new yet.

Ronan is there at the tournament every time I compete, as he promised, though he does keep his distance as well. He watches from the royal box as I defeat a baker with a surprisingly accurate thrust, then a member of the city guard who fights as if he'd just woken up, and then a young cousin of House Juni, who flourishes her sword so wildly in sweeping spins and daring flips that I'm terrified of her until I realize that she actually can't fight worth a damn. And he's there watching as I finally fall in the fifth round to the heir of House Faber.

I give him—and the crowd—a good fight, at least. Titus, like me, was too young to fight in the war, but also like me, he clearly spent his entire life training for it. His house is renowned for their smiths, and his handling of the issued weapon is the best of anyone I've fought with or witnessed. It flows from his arm like it's a part of him; he never fumbles with the balance or his grip. He dominates me in the beginning of the fight, taking a quick 4-0 lead and nearly ending it there before I make a miraculous parry that causes us to double hit each other, negating the points.

I can almost hear Ronan from across the arena repeating what he taught me weeks earlier. Everyone has a tell. If I had days to practice with Titus, maybe I could find his, but I only have one point before it's over.

I'm not sure why I even care about winning. If I win this, I'll have to fight Adria next, and that will be the end of it either way. And I'll have to deal with listening to her gloat endlessly, or at least until she beats Quinn, who she's nearly guaranteed to face in the final, just as they predicted.

Titus flicks his red hair back over his shoulder—it's long, and for some reason, he hasn't bothered to pull it back. And then I think back to the last point, the one I parried. He flicked his hair, and he took a high attack. It's like he cleared the weight of it to enable his guard. It's the kind of automatic movement I doubt he even notices himself making.

And sure enough, he attacks from a high guard so fluidly that I wouldn't have seen it coming. Except that I do. I parry and throw off his sword, coming in for a thrust to his neck before he can regain control.

"4-1!"

The crowd, which is much fuller at this later stage of the tournament, begins to shift to this side of the arena.

On his next attack, he doesn't flick the hair. He's favored a low guard that baits me to attack when he doesn't go for the high guard, and that's exactly what he does. I don't fall for the bait. I keep my distance, using my point to protect me as he moves to the side, looking for an opening. He finds one, but I guess that he's feinting, trying again to bait me again into a futile attack, and I withdraw further, nearly touching the line out of bounds.

He laughs. "Come on."

Then he flicks the hair again.

I lunge for a low attack while he's taking his guard, and it connects with his thigh.

"4-2!"

There are some scattered cheers from the crowd. Not many, both because I'm Nithyrian and I'm still losing, but I don't think even the most patriotic Selaran can resist a good comeback story.

I win over more of them as I score once again, this time by landing a lucky cut that I definitely shouldn't have gone for.

"I thought you were a better fighter than that. And you were, I guess," he says with an appreciative nod. "Well played."

At least he's nice. "Thanks," I say while gasping for air. He, on the other hand, has barely broken a sweat.

The point I land to tie the match is the one I'm most proud of. My middle guard forces an attack from him, which I bind, and I manage to win the bind despite the weaker position by sidestepping and going for a cut above his blade to his arm. It's a risky move that leaves me open on the left, but I think about what Ronan said: this isn't life or death; it's a sport. The worst that could happen is he lands a double hit, and we're back to square one.

The best that could happen is I land a clean point, and that's exactly what I do.

"4-4!"

Titus smiles as I back away from him. "You are fearless."

He's right. Knowing he won't hurt me, knowing he can't hurt me, not with Ronan watching, frees me to enjoy what I'm doing.

I'm having fun now, but I wish it had happened earlier because I'm also exhausted. My arms feel like jelly as I try to get back into position. This fight has gone on for far longer than usual, and I'm apparently the only one feeling it. Titus looks as fresh as when we started.

Titus takes a middle, point-first guard this time—a first for him—another stance that will force an attack from me. It's a strong position, one where attacks from above or below can be easily parried to the side or to the ground. I can bind him easily enough, but he'll have the reach and strength advantage, and I can't count on my last move working again.

I haven't paid much attention to my stance until now, the desperate fight to remain in the match drawing most of my attention, but I decide to take a moment and recenter myself before attacking. I do exactly as Ronan showed me: I stick out my chest and my ass, tightening my core and flexing my sword arm, testing different guards.

Titus loosens his guard a bit, distracted by…well, me, by the looks of it.

It's my opening. I lunge to his left, but he sees me coming and blocks me by grabbing his sword with his free hand. It's a very strong parry, and I reel back and off balance upon impact. He reaches out for the grapple, and I almost manage to bring my point back down in time, but there's too much backwards momentum.

He takes hold of my sword arm, and I have no choice but to do the same. But this is a disastrous position for me. He's at least a foot taller, and though he's trying to be gentle, he overpowers me easily, forcing me to drop my sword.

He doesn't pull me to him as Ronan did when he grappled me. Instead, he backs away and taps his blade lightly on my shoulder. It's very gentlemanly. "Well fought," he says.

"Not quite as well as you," I say with a bow.

"Victory! Victor: Titus of House Faber!"

The roar is deafening; the entire arena has moved over here to watch us. Adria comes over to help me after I shake Titus's hand and exit the ring. Larus has gone with Felix to the Enez Islands, and part of me is glad he wasn't here to watch me fail.

"You know, that wasn't as bad as I thought it was going to be," says Adria. High praise from her. "And you exposed a lot of his weaknesses." Which will help her when she fights him in two days' time.

"Happy to be of service." A servant hands me a canteen of water, and I gulp it down gratefully. Then they refill it from the air with their magic. Arnan bless the water-born.

We head into the section of the stands reserved for the Great Houses to watch the shadow-born trial, which I'm grateful I didn't participate in, given the timing. At the center of the arena, an elaborate set of metallic hoops has been constructed. Each hoop holds a lens or a mirror; their purpose is to concentrate the sunlight to levels of increasing brightness. The shadow-born succeeds if they can darken the area enough that the judges can't read a word displayed on a slate.

I don't recognize any of the participants, nor did I expect to. The only other shadow-born I know are Ronan's spies, and of those, only Nico could have participated. I'm clapping for a young woman who's doing remarkably well with only a couple of lenses to go when someone clears their throat beside me.

It's Taran. "He wishes—"

"To see me," I finish with him. I don't argue with him. There's no point with much of the rest of the court around. "Lead the way."

Taran takes me through a tunnel and up a stairway to the entrance to the royal box. It's guarded by four of Ronan's guards, and there are an additional two stationed at the door into the arena.

Inside, Ronan sits with Grand Vizier Cyrus, Typhon, and Quinn. Quinn, who won her own fight earlier, smirks as she sees me, but she keeps her mouth shut in front of the king.

"A valiant effort," says Typhon. "And Larus told me it's not even your best event. I'm looking forward to the archery final in a few days."

"As am I," I say, bowing to him. Archery has gone much more smoothly than sword-fighting, that's for sure. It's been clear since the first couple of rounds who the finalists would be: the woman I met during qualifying, a man from House Santori, and myself. The others are a bit better than me in most of the trials, but only just. Any of us could win.

Typhon shifts in his seat, rubbing his bald head and trying to act casual. "When will Larus return, do you know?"

I'll have to tell Larus he was missed. I wonder what he'll think of Typhon's interest. Will he think it's merely polite conversation, or is the Grand Vizier's son harboring certain suspicions about the absence of our Guardian? "In a few weeks, we're hoping. Assuming his mother is well." We've explained Larus's time away from court as being due to his mother's illness, which is close enough to the truth that no one has questioned it.

Until now.

"Of course. If you hear from him, send her my best wishes."

Ronan has been watching this entire exchange with immense curiosity. He rises from his seat—cushioned, the only one to be so in the entire arena—and gestures for me to head back into the hallway.

It's dark here in this private area near the royal box; only a single candle burns in a sconce on the wall. It gives me a moment to look at Ronan before he can see me clearly.

He looks as rough as I've ever seen him. His eyes are hollow and rimmed with fatigue, his shoulders slumped but filled with tension. Even his hair is a mess.

He's exhausted.

"Are you okay?" he asks, reaching for my arm where Titus gripped it on the final point.

I don't offer it to him. "I'm fine," I say. Although the flesh there is a little sore, I doubt it will bruise. Titus was a lot gentler with me than he could have been.

Ronan doesn't press the issue. "You did well today."

I can hear in his voice that there's more he wants to say. He wants to talk to me again. He wants to touch me again.

He misses me. It's been more than three weeks since our dinner on his balcony, and he misses me.

The realization pulls at me. It draws me in; it makes me take a step closer to him.

No. "Are you doing that?" I ask, alarmed to feel myself moving forward. "Is that your magic?"

Ronan is perplexed. "What do you mean?"

"That pull. Is it you?"

"There's a pull?"

"You can't feel it?"

Ronan's laugh is hollow. "I didn't say that. But I'm not doing anything, magic or otherwise, if that's what you're asking."

"You can't influence emotions? Only feel them?"

"No, I can't influence emotions. Gods, imagine if I could. It would make a lot of things easier. Unfortunately, all I get to do is know what everyone's feeling all the time with no ability to understand why or how to change it."

"But the way that light magic feels. That's something, right?"

His eyes snap to mine. "How does it feel?"

I scowl at him. "You know perfectly well. Like a warm glow. Comforting, inviting."

"Ah. Not everyone experiences that. But some do. Do you think it's my magic pulling on you somehow?"

"I don't know," I say, withdrawing a step.

"Tell me when you figure it out." His response is unusually curt, so much so that I think I've been dismissed.

I begin to bow.

"Wait," he says, sighing. He holds his forehead in his hand in frustration with himself. "I'm sorry. I'm not trying to influence you with my magic, I promise. But if you think it's making you act in ways you don't like, I'll continue to keep my distance. If that's what you want."

It's not what I want. I know it as soon as he says it. I don't want to walk away from him now, but I know that I need to.

Not because of the plan, but because I need to figure out what the fuck is going on with me.

"I don't—I just—ugh," I try to say. "Just for a bit longer."

"For as long as you need," he says, and he lets me go.

Two days later, I watch from the stands as Quinn advances to the sword-fighting final with ease.

Adria faces more of a challenge with Titus, but even his height advantage doesn't help him as she defeats him 5-3. At least it's her closest match yet, so I'm not completely humiliated.

The week that follows is the tensest since we arrived. Adria and Quinn take every opportunity to antagonize each other, to the point that I'm not sure we'll make it there with them both intact. It's only their joint arrogance at wanting to humiliate the other in front of a huge crowd that stays their hands.

I gift Zara a bottle of Nithyrian red for saving my life and spend some time watching tournament events with her on days she isn't busy with Guild business. She's about the only person willing to talk to me with Larus gone, Adria preoccupied with Quinn, and Ronan off limits for my own sake. I don't talk to her about him. Instead, we discuss more of her life in her homeland of Eki.

"There's no such thing as sport in Eki," she explains. "No such thing as a fight for practice. They put real blades in the hands of children. If you make it to adulthood, your training is complete."

"The Festival of Sport was like that too once. My mother told me that hundreds of people and thousands of animals would die at a single festival back in her great-grandmother's day." It was the abolition of slavery that ended the barbaric practice. It turns out people who aren't in chains aren't as happy about putting their lives on the line for the entertainment of others.

By the time the archery final comes around at the end of the week, the crowds in the arena are near capacity. It's the next-to-last day of the tournament. Only tomorrow's finals in chariot racing, the 100-foot dash, the fire-born trial, and trial of the blade will draw a larger crowd.

The sound is deafening. From the arena floor, which has been cleared of all except the torch and the three targets, I can barely hear Ronan's amplified voice, his grandmother lending him her power once again.

"Welcome to the archery final! Our three competitors have bested a field of over one hundred, but only one can reign as Sai's Champion of the Bow."

He pauses for a cheer, which is so loud I nearly drop my bow. I've skipped my armor tonight, wearing instead the light Selaran clothes that keep me much cooler in the late afternoon heat.

"Will it be Linus of House Santori?"

The man on the far-left waves to the crowd. He's about ten paces away, but I know his face well now after five rounds of the tournament. He's a small, slim man of around thirty with a sharp goatee and tightly proportioned features. His House, Santori, is a minor house loyal to House Alta, the Royal House, and he receives an enthusiastic reception from the home crowd.

"Or will it be Calliope of Parthis?"

The response for Calliope is a bit more tepid, which isn't surprising considering that Parthis is quite a distance from here. At least I think it is. I don't recall the geography of Velmora in much detail.

Calliope is unfazed. She waves enthusiastically, her dark curls shaking. She's dressed in the same black leathers as the first day of the tournament, and she seems unaffected by the heat. I bet it's hotter in Parthis, wherever it is.

"Or will it be Sylvie of House Verran?"

A shiver travels through me at the sound of my name on Ronan's lips.

There's a much bigger cheer than I was expecting considering my House. There are some heckles, but they're largely drowned out by the cheers. Maybe I won some fans at the sword fight after all.

"Archers, take your mark."

This is it. I step up to the white line that has been painted on the dusty arena floor. There will be three rounds with three arrows each round. If the scores are tied, and they're likely to be considering everyone's performance so far, we'll go into sudden elimination where we shoot one after another until someone fails to get a bull-seye. The last one standing wins.

"Nock—"

The crowd noise fades as I nock the first arrow. Nine arrows between me and victory. There isn't much of a reward for being Sai's Champion other than pride, but I find myself wanting it anyway.

I want to hear Ronan say my name again. I want him to place the laurel wreath on my head.

I want him to tell me how proud he is of me.

"Draw—"

I take a deep, stilling breath as I draw my bow. The target is just like the targets in the courtyard of the castle where I was raised. I'm there again, eleven years old. Everyone is still alive. I'm passing time waiting for them to come home. Larus is on the sidelines, telling me to keep my arm steady.

The bullseye is in sight. I stare at it, unblinking. I line the arrow up with it, aiming just above to account for the drop. The afternoon wind is still.

Even the crowd is silent.

"Loose!"

I shoot the bow, and I know immediately that something is wrong. Not with my shot—it's a bullseye. But the other arrows don't hit their targets.

A blood-curdling scream comes from the crowd, and then all hell breaks loose.

The stands echo with shouts and trampling footsteps as I look to my left. Linus is on the ground, bleeding.

There's an arrow in his ear.

Calliope, shrouded in shadow, is running for the track.

She killed him. Holy fuck, she killed him.

Why?

"There!" I shout in her direction, and a dozen guards run towards her.

I should chase after her. I don't know how many of the guards are shadow-born, but I doubt it's many. I could even loose one of my arrows at her retreating figure.

I nock my arrow, but something stops me from shooting.

Why would Calliope shoot Linus in the middle of the tournament final with one hundred thousand witnesses? Why, when it won't win her the tournament? She'll be hanged as soon as they catch her.

Why would she risk her life for this?

And then it occurs to me.

There's only one reason to do something that would cause this much chaos.

It's a distraction.

I look into the royal box. Ronan is standing at the front, giving orders to Taran. Claudia is being herded out the back by Quinn and Typhon, and the Grand Vizier is shouting to someone in the stands.

None of them see the man on the right, creeping up to Ronan. How could they?

He's hidden in the shadows.

I look around me, but no one else is looking in that direction. No one can see him but me.

Calliope killed Linus as a distraction. This man is going to kill Ronan.

I don't hesitate. I don't think of the consequences.

I nock one of the competition arrows.

I draw the bow.

And I loose the arrow into the royal box.

Chapter Nineteen

My arrow hits its target.

The man collapses to the ground next to Ronan, his shadow dropping as he falls. I survey the box for other threats, but the shadows look clear, and Ronan, seeing the dead man on the ground beside him, lights it up anyway.

The man is dead, and I killed him.

My first real kill.

I thought I'd be sick with regret. I thought I'd agonize over what I'd done, and maybe I still will later.

But for now, I'm just relieved.

Ronan is alive.

Several of the guards rush into the box and start overturning chairs. One kneels to examine the dead man, and then another points out onto the arena floor.

Points at me.

Ronan, who keeps shrugging off the guards to stop them from moving him, looks out at me and starts gesturing and yelling.

"Go!" I yell, motioning for him to get to safety. I'll be fine.

I watch as Taran finally convinces him to head to the exit, then I make my way to the nearest tunnel out of the arena. The crowd is half gone now, just as the amplified voice of Grand Vizier Cyrus urges them to calm down and not to push, assuring them there's no danger.

I'm not sure I believe him. I didn't see if the guards managed to get Calliope, but she certainly wasn't working alone.

I'm nearly at the tunnel when I see movement to my right, and I just glimpse the guard's charging figure before he knocks me to the ground.

"Wait! I'm trying to—"

I feel the heel of his blade impact my skull, and everything goes black.

I wake in a carriage. It's enclosed, like the carriages we use in Nithyria, but there are bars on the windows.

"Go back to hell, Nithyrian cunt," the same guard as before spits at me, and then I'm under again.

I wake again in a jail cell.

The stone floor is cold and hard beneath me, and my head and body are in agony. Based on the way the pain radiates along the side of me that's on the ground, they threw me in here.

The cell reeks of blood and shit and vomit. I nearly vomit myself as I pull myself upright, my arm screaming in pain when I put weight on it.

What the fuck is happening?

"There you are, Nithyria," says a woman's voice from beyond the bars. It's dark in the cell, but that's not what's making it hard for me to see. The guard must have hit my head pretty hard. "I'd keep my mouth shut if I were you. They think we're in it together."

That accent. I recognize it.

"Calliope?"

I pull myself up using the bars and peek through a gap.

It's her, alright. She's in a cell across from mine, slouched against the wall.

"No talking," says a guard. He raps my fingers with his sword where they're clutching the bars.

The impact stings. I pull back, but I lose my balance and fall to the shit-stained floor.

"You heard the man, Nithyria," says Calliope.

The guard rattles his keys. "Speak again, and I'm coming in there."

It takes a minute for my thoughts to collect themselves over the pain in my head.

They think I did this.

They think Calliope and I planned this together, both of us shadow-born, that we were all working together with the assassin who went for Ronan. That has to be the reason I'm in here.

Fuck. What am I going to do?

I was there with her on the floor. I shot an arrow in the royal box, right next to Ronan.

I'm from fucking *Nithyria.* Of course they think I was trying to kill him. *He* probably thinks I was trying to kill him.

How can I possibly prove that I wasn't?

There's only one tiny speck of relief in the shitstorm of my panic. Ronan is alive.

Is he alive? He was alive before they knocked me out.

I know I shouldn't antagonize the guard, but I have to know.

"Is he alive?" I call out, my voice smaller than I expected. "Ronan. Is he alive?"

The guard laughs, a cruel, bitter laugh. "Oh, you better believe he is. How does it feel, bitch? Your little plan failed. It failed, and you'll die in here. That's if he doesn't kill you first. Both of you."

"Please, I didn't—"

"SHUT THE FUCK UP BEFORE I KILL YOU MYSELF."

I shut up.

Ronan is alive. He's alive.

I saved him. I came here to kill him, and I saved his life instead.

Oh, fucking hell. Why did I do that? Even if I ever manage to get out of here, Adria is going to kill me.

I should have just let him die.

No, I shouldn't have. I couldn't have, and I know it.

What I don't know is why. Why did I save him? What made me shoot my arrow at his assassin instead?

Has he gotten to me so thoroughly? Has his plan worked that much better than mine?

Godsdammit.

"—right now, so help me Vahlo if you don't let me in there, I swear I'll—"

There's a voice coming from down the hall. It's female, and it's familiar, but it's not Adria.

It's Quinn.

Great. Just great. Just what I need, another person who hates me. Did she come here to gloat? To spit in my face? To kick me while I'm down as low as I can go, so low I can barely sit up?

Quinn's short, red hair is plastered to her forehead with sweat. She's wearing a full set of Royal Guard armor, and there's dried blood on her cheek, maybe hers. "I always knew I'd find you here one day."

"Go to hell, Quinn," I say, but I cough up something that looks suspiciously like a blood clot as I do.

"Shit, Sylvie," she says, rushing to the bars. "Let me in there now. RIGHT FUCKING NOW!" she screams at the guard.

He fumbles with the keys, and she snatches them from him, flinging the door open.

Oh gods, she's going to kill me.

She rushes over to me, and I cower away from her, trying to drop a shadow but failing. "I was going to mess around with you for a bit, but I had no idea what state you were in. Can you walk?"

"What?" Is she…is she trying to help me?

"Oh, fuck it," says Quinn, and she picks me up. She *picks me up* like I'm nothing. "Vayla help me, you smell like death."

"What are you doing?"

"I'm getting you out of here. I saw the whole thing. I know you saved him. Just hang on."

The guard tries to protest, but she raises a hand beneath me, and I feel the heat of the flame in it. "Don't even fucking think about it."

"Bye, Nithyria," yells Calliope as the guard lets us out the door.

Quinn runs me up the stairs and out of the dungeon. I can't believe how strong she is. We pass a servant in the hallway, and she shouts at them, "Alchemist. King's quarters. Right now!"

I moan as the room seems to darken.

"What the hell! Sylvie, did you do that? I can't see."

I think I might have. I try to let it go.

"Don't you fucking die on me. I promised him I'd get you. He's going to *kill* me if you die."

We enter into a passage—it has to be one of the secret passages I've been looking for, but I'm too incoherent to see it—and we emerge in Ronan's living room.

"Help!" yells Quinn. I raise my head weakly in time to see Ronan leap from across the room.

Quinn lowers me onto a couch, and Ronan places his hands on my body.

The relief is immediate. He touches my leg, my hip, my arm, and the pain just fades away. His hands are so warm, and the light is so bright and comforting.

"Ronan—"

"Don't try to talk yet." He gently lifts my head and reaches the big, angry bruise at the back where the guard hit me. Twice.

I flinch at the touch. The pain is deep there.

"I know," he whispers soothingly. "It won't take long."

I let him touch me, and it hurts for a moment, but then the warmth spreads bone deep until it tingles and then vanishes, taking the pain with it.

"Ronan," I say again. He's looking at me, and his beautiful, perfect face is terrified. He's so terrified of losing me.

I didn't want him to die, I realize.

That's why I shot the arrow.

I *don't* want him to die.

I reach up and throw my arms around his neck, pulling him to me.

I hear a soft grunt as I knock the air from his lungs. Then he relaxes into my embrace. His body is so warm against mine with the weight of his chest pressing into me, holding me tightly against him. "Thank you," he murmurs, again and again, his voice low and soft. He gently strokes my back, and I just stay there in his arms for a long, comforting moment.

"Told you," I hear Quinn whisper as I part from Ronan. Taran slips her a coin.

Ronan doesn't ask them what they were betting on. I suspect he already knows.

Zara presses an elixir into my hands. "The light doesn't always reach everything internal," she explains. "This should help with the rest. You'll need to take it every six to eight hours for two days, maybe three, just to be sure."

"Thank you," I say, and I take a sip from the cup she hands me. It's warm, and it tastes of honey and a strange, woody herb that reminds me of the temple.

"Frankincense," she says. "For the bleeding."

"Sir, we need to discuss the tournament—" Cyrus begins. There are a lot of people in the room, I realize with some embarrassment.

"Quinn, can you take her to my bath? And see about those guards when you're down there before I do something I'll regret."

"I'll go too," says Zara.

"I can manage," I say, standing up. Really, there's nothing wrong with me now, and I hate to miss whatever is about to be discussed. But I do absolutely reek of the dungeon floor. "I'm feeling fine."

Ronan ignores me and nods to Quinn and Zara, who lead me through a passage—this time I see them press the stone on the wall to open it—down a spiral staircase and directly into Ronan's private bath.

It's a small chamber, but it's not claustrophobic. The rock formations arch over the pool, which steams with heat. The servants there undress us all, and Quinn and Zara help me into the luxuriously warm waters.

Quinn narrates the entire sequence of events of the tournament to Zara, who was down at the Guild Hall when it happened.

"She loosed one arrow. One fucking arrow! Perfect shot. I couldn't believe it. I thought she was trying to kill him but missed—so did the guards, apparently—until I saw the body hit the floor. Right there in the fucking shadows."

"Ronan couldn't feel him?" asks Zara.

It's a great question, I realize. Ronan had no trouble feeling the man in his throne room. This man was even closer to him.

What had changed?

"Probably too much going on. Too many feelings all at once," says Quinn, but the way she says it makes me think she's hiding something.

Zara doesn't seem to pick up on it. "I hate to run, but I need to get back to the Guild. Sylvie, don't forget the elixir. It's important that you keep taking it even if you feel better. There's a lot going on inside our bodies that we can't see. That even the God-King himself can't see."

"Understood," I reply. "And thank you, Zara."

"Thank *you*, Sylvie. Without you, I fear we'd all be in a very different situation tonight."

Quinn splashes some water in my direction after Zara has left for the changing room. "Come on, we should get back too before he thinks I've kidnapped you."

The servants dress me in a loose Selaran evening gown I don't recognize. It's a soft linen fabric in a dark navy, and it feels wonderful on my skin.

Quinn whistles. "I can see it. I mean, I hated you, but I get it now. Sorry I was an ass. I thought you wanted to kill him."

I'm grateful Quinn can't feel my feelings. I *did* want to kill him.

Oh shit, that reminds me of Adria. "Can someone tell Adria what's going on?" I say to the servants. I don't want to see her right now, not until I can figure out what I'm going to say to her, but she's probably setting fire to the dungeons as we speak. "Can you tell her I'm okay, that they know I saved the king, and that I'll be back to the room soon?"

"Yes, miss," says a servant. She hurries off into another passage, again pressing on a specific stone.

At least I'll have that bit of information to share with Adria when I see her. Maybe it'll help soften the blow of saving the life of the person we're meant to kill.

By the time we return to Ronan's chambers, everyone but Taran has gone.

Ronan takes my hand, leading me to a different couch. It feels so good to have him touch me again. I didn't realize how starved of it I had been these past few weeks.

"Your majesty, I'm sorry to interrupt—" says a guard as they enter.

"Godsdammit," says Ronan. He turns to me apologetically. "Give me a moment."

I nod. It's fine.

He's the king.

Ronan slips out the door, and Quinn takes his place. "I didn't want to ask with the servants around, but you and Ronan—"

"Quinn," warns Taran.

"What? I'm not blaming her. Look, Sylvie, we've all been in love with him at least once. I thought I only liked men because of him, for fuck's sake, Sylvie. *Men.*"

I blush furiously. I also have to restrain myself from rolling my eyes—he told me everyone had been in love with him, and I thought he was just being arrogant, but I guess he was telling the truth. "I don't know what you're talking about—"

"I promise you're with friends here. Taran, tell her."

"Leave her alone, Quinn. She's been through enough without you barging into her personal life."

"Oh, get off your high horse. She's one of the girls now. Look, Sylvie, he's amazing. Idealistic and naïve, sure, and way too trusting, but he's the God-King for a reason. I don't think there's ever been a God-King that deserved it more than him. Which is ironic—"

"*Quinn.*" Taran can't stop looking at the door. This must be something Ronan doesn't want me to know.

"She needs to know, Taran. She's going to be protecting him now at times when we can't be there. You know it as well as I do. Have you ever seen him like this? Ever in your life, Taran?"

"No," Taran admits, sending a frisson down my spine.

"What do you mean?"

"Oh, just that he's *obsessed* with you. And look, I won't lie. I've been a skeptic. Openly hostile to the idea, you might even say. But after tonight, I'm onboard. Sail us the fuck away, Sylvie. Sail us into the fucking sunset. It's about time he gets to be happy."

Obsessed? My heart is pounding. Quinn is practically bouncing on the couch next to me; she's so enthusiastic, and I'm feeling sick.

He's *obsessed* with me. He has talked to them about me.

Fuck fuck fuck…

"There's just one problem—godsdammit, Tare, tell me I'm wrong. Tell me you think she doesn't need to know."

Taran is clutching his head like dealing with Quinn is physically hurting him. "I just think he'd want to tell her—"

"What are you two doing?" asks Ronan as he reenters the room.

Quinn and Taran—Ronan's best friends—try to look innocent but fail, unsurprisingly.

"I'm trying to explain to Taran that Sylvie needs to know what happened tonight. What really happened."

"Leave us," he says, and Quinn and Taran exit without a word, although Taran does, at least, look apologetic.

"I hope you realize what kind of friend you've made there," he says to me once we're alone, gesturing to where Quinn went. "She's never going to give you a day of peace."

I don't care about that right now. Not when I finally get to be alone with him again.

"Sylvie," he sighs as he sits down next to me, wrapping his arms around me.

He leans back on the couch and pulls me to his chest, and I rest my head there against his heart. It's beating fast, but it relaxes some as I stroke his arm. He strokes my back in response and idly runs his fingers through my hair.

In his arms, nothing else seems to matter. Not our plans, not the war, not what happened tonight, none of it.

It feels so amazing just being held by him.

But I'm greedy. I want more. I want him to kiss me. I want him to push me down on the couch and kiss me until the sun comes up. Until I'm begging him to show me where his bed is—

"I have to tell you something. Quinn is right; you need to know."

He groans regretfully as he lifts me off of him and turns me to face him. When he looks at me, I can tell I wasn't the only one thinking of needing more.

There's a moment before he speaks where I think he might change his mind and just kiss me. I can see it in the purse of his lips, the tension in his jaw. He's so lovely in the candlelight. The way it catches on the gold in his hair, the honey in his eyes. The way it glimmers on his skin. I want to touch him so badly, and I know he wants to touch me…

But he stops himself, letting out a breath. He scowls, and shame washes over him. It hunches his shoulders.

It makes him look small.

"I couldn't feel the assassin tonight," he finally admits. "The man in the royal box. I didn't sense him there."

Is that it? "Quinn said it was because there was too much going on—"

"Quinn lied because others could hear. Only she and Taran know the truth. I'm losing my magic, Sylvie. I couldn't feel him because I'm losing my magic. If you hadn't acted, I would have died tonight."

What, and I can't emphasize this enough, the fuck.

"You're the God-King. You're a living god. How can you lose your magic?"

"I don't know. But I think it has something to do with the actions I've been taking, the changes I've been making—"

"I don't understand. Those changes are good, and light is good. 'And she, the lady of light, gave her gift to the best among them.'"

I recite the Codex to him out of habit.

"I don't think that's true." He pauses, and his eyes dart with the memory of something that haunts him. "I *know* it's not true."

More sacrilege.

"Light isn't good. Light is power. The most ambitious, ruthless actions I've taken? Those are what strengthen my power. Everything I do out of compassion seems to weaken it. My father knew it. He tried to teach it to me, but I didn't listen."

"But your gift is empathy. You can feel what others feel. That isn't power. It's kindness. It's good."

"It can be, or it can be used to manipulate. When we met—" He looks away. He doesn't want to say this. "When we met, I thought about using the attraction you felt at our first meeting to get you to like me."

So he felt it then, the slip of my mind that made me think about kissing him.

And he thought about using it against me. To get close to me, like Larus suspected. Like I suspected.

"But I couldn't do it. I didn't want to *trick* you into liking me. I meant what I said. I could feel who you were before I ever walked into the room. Quinn wanted me to keep you close, to keep an eye on you because she didn't trust you or Adria. And I wanted to keep you close because…because I wanted to know you. So I followed you as Soren. I thought if I could get to know you without the attraction getting in the way, that would be kinder. Easier on us both if it turned out I was wrong about you."

Does admitting this now make him more trustworthy?

Or less?

Do I want to trust him because he's being honest with me, something I haven't been willing to do with him, or because the very manipulation he claims he hasn't done has worked on me?

Could this be a part of the same manipulation?

He leans forward a little, and I can see he's fighting not to touch me. "But then you were attracted to Soren too, for fuck's sake. And my magic. Gods, it wanted me to deceive you. It strengthened when I lied to you. It weakened when I told you the truth. It's weakening even now, but I need you to know this. Lying isn't a shadow-born thing. Not exclusively. I don't think the distance between shadow and light is as wide as we think it is."

Is this something he really believes, or is it just something I've always wanted to hear?

Did he know that? Could he feel it when we met?

"I can feel your doubt," he says.

"How can you feel me if you're losing your magic?"

"It's not constant. It comes and goes, though I can't predict when or why. I can still feel most people most of the time, if they aren't actively trying to hide things from me. I felt the assassin in the throne room. And with you…it's different. You're like an alarm bell ringing in my ear. There was a point when I wondered if your presence was the reason for the change. If your voice was drowning out the others. As nice as it is to focus only on you, it's dangerous. But even when you pulled away from me, it didn't stop wavering. And the decline started before you ever came."

So he'd definitely noticed when I pulled away.

He must be feeling for my reaction, but I don't know what to think. The way he talks about me, the way Quinn and Taran were talking. Quinn said he's obsessed with me. She also called him naïve and idealistic.

There's a chance that he's genuine. I would be a fool not to see that. There's a chance this isn't a game to him, and that he has meant exactly what he's said since we met.

He turns to face me, and a feeling washes over me. It's strange but familiar. Loneliness. A desperate need to be understood, to be accepted.

To be believed.

It's there for a moment, and then it's gone.

"I wish I knew what to say to let you know you can trust me. Maybe there's nothing. Maybe all I can do is prove it to you, over and over, as many times as it takes. I'll do it if you'll let me." He touches my cheek, just a brief brush of the fingertips, but it makes me tremble with longing. "But I'm choosing to trust you. Not just out of gratitude for saving my life, though I don't know how I can ever repay that. But because I believe you can be trusted. I'm trusting you with my deepest secret, something that can and will destroy me in the wrong hands."

"Those hands could be mine," I say, but the words ring false. I look into his eyes. There are little flecks of gold there right in the center. So warm. So lovely. Could I really take the light from them?

Or would I sooner let him destroy me first?

"Yes, they could be yours," he says, picking up my hands from my lap and studying them. He strokes a finger along my palm, and I shiver.

I can't think straight with him touching me, and I know he can feel it. If I don't do something to break this moment, I'm going to end up pulling him to me, and I don't know if I'm going to be able to stop.

"Well, then," I say, forcing the words from my mouth before I do something else with it. "There's really only one conclusion: you're a moron."

"Like I said, absolutely yes."

Can he stop being charming for five minutes?

"I know it's a lot to take in," he says. "But I told you I want you at my side. And after today, it seems like I need you there. But I don't care what my magic is trying to demand from me. I won't take your choice from you. I'm going to ask you to do something, and I only want you to do it if you want to. Deal?"

I nod my head slowly.

"I want you to join me in the royal box tomorrow. And for the rest of the festival as well."

"The tournament is continuing?" I had thought they would cancel it after tonight's events.

"That's what all the commotion was about earlier. They wanted me to cancel it, but I refused. I made a promise to my people, and I intend to deliver on it. There will be extra security, but the show will go on."

Adria will be happy, at least.

"Oh, gods. We have to watch Quinn fight Adria."

He laughs. "Absolute nightmare scenario. Either Quinn wins and she's insufferable forever—"

"And Adria burns the arena to the ground. Or Adria does—"

"And Quinn roasts her on the spit at the after party."

I laugh with him, and I know what my answer will be.

"I'll join you, Ronan."

There are so many things for me to sort through after tonight, so many thoughts and feelings that I don't know how to even name, let alone what I should decide to do about them.

But I know one thing quite clearly: I want to be at his side.

The rest I can think about later.

Chapter Twenty

dria is waiting for me when I finally make it back to the room. She stands near the window, arms folded tightly across her chest, her expression unreadable.

I brace for her response. She hasn't hit me since we were children, but if anything is going to provoke violence, it's this.

"Un-be-fucking-lievable," she begins, meeting me at the door. Her blonde hair is dark and wet, fresh from the baths, and she's already in her nightgown. I guess she got the message that I was alright. "I can't believe you did it."

I try to move past her into the room, but she stops me. "You did it. You saved the plan."

Come again?

"You're not mad?"

Adria laughs, and then she pulls me into a hug.

A hug.

"Are you kidding me? I can't believe you made a shot like that! Sai's fucking champion indeed."

I'm not following, but I'm afraid if I admit that, I'll make her angry somehow, so I just go along with it. "Well, Larus made sure I got a lot of practice—"

"Larus is going to be *so proud* when he gets back! It all could have fallen apart tonight. All our planning, everything we sacrificed. It all hinges on—"

She remembers her surroundings and pulls me to the foot of the bed in case someone is listening.

"—it hinges on Ronan dying at the *exact* right time. If they have time to gather their power behind a new king or queen, we're fucked. It was so close."

It *was* close. And there's a part of me that hates Adria for the gleeful way she talks about it. The way she talks about his death like it's just a step in a process to her. Something fun, too, like baking a cake. Add eggs, flour, sugar, murder the king, and stir.

I can't tell her how it made me feel to save him. I can't tell her that although I did know that the timing had to be precise, I didn't think of it tonight.

I can't tell her about the war that's raging inside of me.

She won't understand.

When she asks what we talked about, I only tell her that he wanted to express his gratitude and see what I knew about Calliope. I don't tell her about the fact that his powers are waning, or that even so, he can still feel what I feel. I don't tell her that if we want to kill him, we need to change the plan to make sure she can do it because he's unlikely to see her coming.

I don't tell her because I don't want her to do it.

And it makes me a traitor to my people. It makes me a traitor to my family. It makes me a traitor to the memory of my parents and everything they fought for.

I don't tell her because if she knew, she'd kill me.

Adria waits for me before going to breakfast for the first time since we arrived. She's in the best mood I've seen her in in a long time. As far as she knows, the plan is going exactly as she'd hoped, and today is the day she gets to humiliate Quinn.

I don't know who I'd rather see win. I don't think Quinn has suddenly changed her mind about Nithyrians, but I can't help but appreciate what she did for me in getting me out of the dungeons. And I admire her loyalty to Ronan.

But Adria is finally being nice to me, and it's hard to silence the part of me that relishes her approval in spite of everything.

Still, I don't want to see her victorious. Or Quinn, for that matter.

Is there a way they can both lose?

Adria invites me to join her at the arena, but I tell her I've already promised Ronan that I'll be joining him today. I didn't find out when, though, and he's not at breakfast for me to ask him.

Adria is *thrilled* to hear Ronan asked me to join him. "I'm sorry I ever doubted you," she says. This…this might be the first apology I've ever gotten from her. "I hope you have the *best* time together."

I feel a wave of nausea churning in the pit of my stomach. The first time I've ever had her respect, and it's because she thinks I'm finally not fucking something up, when in reality…

I'm definitely fucking something up.

I head towards Ronan's chambers to see when he'll be heading to the arena, but I'm stopped by a servant.

"For you, miss," they say, placing a slip of paper in my hand.

Meet me at the market.
- Soren

My heart starts pounding when I read his name. Soren.

Why would Ronan want to meet with me as Soren now that I know who he is?

Unless he's found something out about Vesper.

I race down the steps and out of the palace. I don't bother to hide who I am or where I'm going; there are far too many people around for anyone to notice what I'm up to.

The market is so incredibly full of people that I can barely enter it. It seems that everyone from the entire region is in Faros today for the end of the tournament. There are new merchants selling pennants and banners for spectators to wave, and I realize some of them are in our house colors. Nithyrian green and blue.

People are actually buying flags in Nithyrian colors. Are they going to cheer on Adria?

"You'd better get over here before they see you," a familiar voice whispers.

Soren. It's so wonderful to hear his voice.

It's Ronan's voice really, I know, and it's Ronan's face under the illusion, but there's something just so comforting about seeing him like this again.

I let him lead me into an alley near where I first encountered him. "That was lucky. If they spotted you, we'd be in trouble."

"What? Why?"

He tilts his head as if I've said something stupid. "Sylvie of House Verran, the hero of Selara? The savior of the king?"

"Is that what people think?"

"Some of them do, at least. We leaked that you saved me this morning to some of the town's biggest gossips. It was that or face people who thought you were trying to kill me coming for your head. Though I can't guarantee that won't happen, not until the ceremony later."

"Ceremony?" He's talking about it like I should know what's going on, but I don't.

"The crowning of Sai's Champion of the Bow?"

I think he means me, but that's absurd. "We didn't even compete. I don't need a pity trophy."

"You killed a would-be assassin with a single arrow during the archery competition. With one of the other competitors disqualified and the other unfortunately deceased, I'd say that makes you the winner. And judging by the colors on sale, the people seem to agree."

The Champion of the Bow. The hero of Selara. The people will recognize me after tonight, if I go along with it, assuming they don't know me already. I don't know how to feel about it. I was known in Nithyria, but as the third child in a noble family. Almost everyone who knew me had met my family personally. They worked our lands or kept our house.

But the people here don't know me at all, except for what I did for Ronan.

How can I be a hero to them?

"Can you disguise me?" I ask him. If we're getting closer to the mole or at least what happened to Vesper, we should try to avoid being noticed.

"Not unless you're sitting still. The illusion works because it's on my own body. I don't think I can keep it close enough to you. Here," he says. He takes his hat off, the hat that hides his perfectly coiffed hair, and hands it to me. "Put your hair up in that. It will help."

"Mess your hair up, then. You look like you spent an hour on it."

"Two hours, thank you very much."

"Come here," I say, reaching my hand into a planter filled with sandy soil and a very dead succulent, the only thing in this alley that seems reasonably sanitary. "A bit of this will do."

"Absolutely the fuck not," says Ronan, dodging me.

"You have to. You literally look like a god fell down to earth, even with the scars."

"You think I look like a god?" He drops Soren's voice in surprise.

I roll my eyes at him. "You know you do."

"But *you* think so?"

He leans a little closer to me, and I can't resist the opportunity. I shove my dirty hand into his hair, messing it up as best as I can.

"Fuck!" he yells. He tries to get away from me, but I have years of experience wrestling with much older siblings. I manage to make him look very reasonably human in just a few moments of mussing.

"Better," I say, appraising my handiwork.

He brushes some of the dirt away, but it's still pretty effective.

"Did you get a lead on Vesper?" I ask him now that we're sufficiently disguised.

He nods. "A man came in saying he saw someone of her description struggling with someone in an alley. We're going to see what he knows."

"When?"

"Just two days ago."

Then there's a chance she's still alive. I'd nearly given up hope.

"But there's something else. One of the shadow-born from the trial was reported missing yesterday. And a second one this morning."

Two more shadow-born missing. Maybe I was right to avoid the trial.

"It could be another coincidence like Marcella," he says. "There are a lot of people coming and going right now. It's easy to get separated."

"But possibly not," I say.

He nods.

He leads me through a series of alleys that seem to follow the city wall. Twice we cross busy streets, but the disguises seem to hold, or maybe it's just that people are too preoccupied with the festival celebrations to give us much notice.

We finally come to a nondescript door near a guard tower. We're close to one of the city's northern gates, and there's a lot of foot and chariot traffic coming and going nearby. But no one seems to notice as Ronan knocks on the door in a strange rhythm.

"*Selara, Vayla's Favored Land,*" he explains. It's not the official anthem of Selara, but it's a fairly common hymn. I recognize it the moment he says it.

A woman with a gruff voice opens a slat at eye level. "Business?"

"Soren Solinus to see Mery."

"Token?"

Ronan removes something from his pocket and passes it through a lower slat on the door. I don't get a good look at it, but it glints in the sunlight like a coin.

"Ten minutes."

The woman closes both slats. Then there are a series of *clinks* and *clangs* as she unlatches a dozen locks. Finally, the door swings open.

We step inside to find what at first glance could be any ordinary home. There's a bench for greeting guests, a dining table with six chairs, and a kitchen built around a stone hearth. In the back corner, a staircase leads to an upper level.

In Nithyria, the residents of a home like this would be considered solidly middle class. Merchants or healers, maybe.

I wonder who Mery is and why we're here.

"Safe house," says Ronan, feeling my curiosity. "A place where assets can be kept protected without bringing them to the palace."

"Assets?"

"Witnesses, errand-runners. Spies."

People like my mother. I'm sure she knew all about safe houses. She probably operated some of her own back home in Pyka before the war.

I wish I'd known to ask her about it then. There were so many things I could've talked to her about if only I'd known to ask before she died.

"Are you alright?" Ronan mutters. The woman from the front door is opening another under the staircase at the back. She doesn't seem particularly interested in our conversation, but I've learned to be careful who I say things around.

I nod in response. I can tell him what's on my mind later.

The door at the back opens onto another stairway that leads to a cellar. "No weapons," the woman says, holding out her calloused hands.

I look at Ronan for confirmation before removing my sword and dagger. He removes a dagger from his waist and another, smaller knife from his boot.

The woman is satisfied. There's no reason not to give up everything; it's not like we can remove our magic.

I follow Ronan down the narrow stairwell to a corridor at the bottom. There are at least a dozen doors here. Though they're windowless, there's a gap at the bottom that lets light through. Only a couple of them appear to be occupied.

"Third room on the left," calls the woman from upstairs.

Ronan knocks on the door, and a boy greets him.

He's a teenager, twenty at best, with deep tan skin and black hair shorn razor short. His loose clothes swallow his lean build and have a faint smell of fish about them. A dockworker, I'd guess.

"Mery?"

"Are you the man? I really hope it's you. I'm late. Maxima will have my head if I'm late. You get that, don't you?"

Mery gestures us into a small bedroom. It's sparsely furnished, with only a simple single bed, a small dresser, and a single chair. Mery takes the chair and gestures for us to sit on the bed.

Which we do.

Together.

"We won't be long," says Ronan, carefully avoiding looking at me. "And you'll be free to go once we leave."

"Oh, thank Arnan. I want to help Vesper, I do, but it's my job, sir. I can't lose it."

So the boy knows Vesper, then. This isn't just some random stranger seeing someone who matches her description.

"When did you see her?" asks Ronan.

"Day before yesterday. It was just after the noon bells. I was making a delivery near the temple—the Vahlo temple, that is. They order from us more than the others. I was running with my cart through one of the back alleys, trying to get back before I got a boxing 'round the ears, when I saw her. Her hair was cut short, and she was even thinner than usual, but it was her, sir. I know it."

"How do you know her? Describe her to me."

"I saw her at the docks. There's a tavern there she comes to some nights. A couple of them, really. Before they took her, her hair was long and red. Now it's real short. Almost as short as mine. Her earrings are gone too, but I was real close. I could still see the holes. Two up here—" He gestures to the top of his left ear. "—one over here." The middle of the right ear. "And two each on the bottom. I know 'em because I asked her about 'em. She told me a story for each one. She worked hard to get the coin for 'em all."

He knows Vesper well, and from the way he talks about her, he admires her a great deal. Maybe even loves her.

"Who took her?" I ask.

"I don't know who they were, begging your pardon, miss. But they come running after her. She ran into a door, and I pushed the cart to try to block 'em, but they threw me back with magic. By the time I got back up, they were all gone. Not a trace of 'em. I looked as long as I could, but I had to get back—"

"—to work. We understand. The alley and the door, they're the ones you showed the guards? You're certain of it?"

"Aye, sir. I know it real well."

"Did you see the people who took her at all? Could you describe them?"

"Not well, sir. One of 'em was wearing a robe. I thought they might be from the temple, but it were brown instead of black like they wear there. He was a big guy. She didn't stand a chance, Vayla help her."

A brown robe. An alchemist? Or maybe a priest of Kerensa, although Kerensa's temple isn't close to the temple of Vahlo.

But with the festival going on, it could be anyone from anywhere. Brown robes aren't exactly uncommon in other kingdoms.

Ronan asks a few more questions, but it's clear that the boy has told us everything he knows. He says something to the woman upstairs that causes her to release him despite originally limiting us to only ten minutes, and the boy gratefully rushes past us as we're leaving.

"I really hope you find her. She's a good one," he says.

"We'll do our best," says Ronan.

I wonder what the boy would think if he realized he'd just spoken to his king.

"To the alley?" I ask Ronan once we're outside.

He nods. "The guards have already checked it out, but I figure another pair of eyes can't hurt." He checks his weapons, which the woman returned to us, and I do the same.

But we had no need to be concerned. The alley is as empty as the boy described. Ronan carefully shines a light in the dark corners, but I grab his hand and stop him. It's too risky to be seen doing light magic around here. "I can see in the shadows just fine. What are you looking for?"

"Blood, hair, a scrap of fabric. I don't know."

"It's a city alleyway. Even if we find something, it could be from anyone. What about the alchemist angle?"

"I'd be surprised if it's someone there. Zara runs a tight ship. I don't want to ask them directly or to even let them know we're looking, but it would be good to find out which alchemists match the description. Tall and heavyset, male."

"I can think of one alchemist that matches that description." Our own alchemist, Hermes Magnus. And, come to think of it, I haven't seen much of him since we arrived. He's been spending a lot of time down at the Guild.

"Yours?"

I nod. "I could try to see if he's up to anything. Tell him I need more silphium elixir or something."

Not that I was looking for an opportunity to mention an elixir known for its contraceptive properties or anything.

Ronan-as-Soren looks reasonably shocked to hear me mention it. "Do you? Need more of it?"

"No, we brought plenty," I say matter-of-factly. Not that he should remember that fact later. It's just information that happens to be true. "But it makes him uncomfortable to hear me speak of it, so I could take advantage of that to poke around a bit."

"Devious," says Ronan with admiration. "I'll see if Quinn can think of any other alchemists that fit the description. She has a better memory for names and faces than I do."

"What about the priests of Kerensa—"

He holds up a finger to silence me—there's a noise down the alley.

My hand reaches for my sword, and I lower the shadow we're in just a bit. It's not perfect cover, but it should do well enough without being too obvious.

We wait together for a long moment, dangerously close to touching. I shouldn't have mentioned the silphium. Now it's all I can think about.

There's another rustling sound a few doors down from where we stand. Ronan tenses at my side, his hands up and ready to strike.

Then, there's a commotion: a flurry of wings and a cacophony of terrified screeches and squawks. From the eaves, a black bird with subtly iridescent feathers swoops and dives at a smaller grey bird with long wings. They appear to be fighting over a small, shadowed hole beneath a window ledge.

It's a vicious fight. The smaller bird can't untangle itself from the black bird's talons, can't escape the relentless pecking of its yellow beak. Feathers fly in unnatural whorls, drifting to the ground as the smaller bird twists and turns, its efforts only tightening the black bird's grip.

Ronan races towards the battling birds, caution be damned. He shouts, arms raised, and the black bird shrieks in protest but finally flutters off. The grey bird lies awkwardly on the window ledge, its breathing shallow and labored, too hurt to even attempt to escape.

I approach Ronan slowly, on the lookout for any more surprises hiding in the shadows. When I reach him, his hands are cradling the injured bird, his fingertips bathing it in soft, golden light.

He's healing it.

I watch in amazement as the beak wounds on its back, its neck; its eyes close in only moments. The bird, now whole again, pauses for a moment in confusion, unsure what to make of being helped rather than hurt.

I understand its feeling. It has no context for its situation. There's nothing in nature that can do what Ronan did for it, nothing in nature but violence and survival. It doesn't know to be grateful. It flits away, frightened, but it doesn't go far. It perches near the roofline as Ronan approaches the gap in the wall they fought over.

A little woolen nest woven with bits of straw, leaves, and lint is hanging from the cavity, half broken. There are two cracked white eggs inside, each about the size of a gold coin.

"Damn," says Ronan as he sees them, shaking his head. They're beyond saving. Then he leans forward and picks up something from the ground beneath the nest.

It's another white egg. He holds it gingerly in his hand, turning it over. There's not a crack on it.

Light flashes from his fingertips, brief and bright. Ronan carefully tucks the nest back into the cavity, placing the warmed egg back inside.

Then he backs away. "I don't know if that will make any difference. The starling will be back. But it was worth a try."

I stare at him for a long moment, speechless.

I've never been more captivated by anyone in my life.

"What?" he asks, his good eye amused.

"It's just...you're not what I expected."

"What did you expect?"

A monster. A villain. "I don't know. Just not...that."

Ronan, wearing Soren's face, smiles shyly. Then, his expression shifts to something more playful. "I'm sorry to disappoint you."

I laugh at that.

With neither of us sure what we're looking for, we abandon the search. Ronan leads us through the alleys back to the palace.

"Am I like you expected?" I ask as we walk, unable to resist. There's something about seeing his face as Soren that frees me to speak with him in a way that I can't with Ronan himself.

"Better," he says, and it sends a shiver through me.

"Soren, I have to tell you something," I say with mock serious-ness. "I met someone."

"Oh?" He looks fake-puzzled. "Was it a red-headed man, about this tall, quite a good duelist?"

He's describing Titus, the man who beat me in the sword-fighting tournament.

A man who flirted with me. "You noticed that?"

"Oh, I wasn't there. Far too busy with the imports. But I heard the two of you had quite a bit of tension. I've heard they're placing bets on whether you end up married."

"They aren't." They better not be. That would be absolutely mor-tifying.

"They are. But there are rumors that your heart belongs to an-other."

That very same heart begins to pound. "Oh?"

"Are they true?" Ronan faces forward, unwilling to look me in the eye.

"Well, I don't know about my heart. But there is a man. He's difficult to describe."

"Ruggedly handsome? Roguish with a heart of gold?"

"Definitely not. More like disturbingly perfect. Uncannily gor-geous. In a way that makes your eyes hurt when you look at him."

He feigns being stabbed in the chest. "Thank the gods you aren't talking about me. I'd be absolutely insulted." He pauses. "Not even the heart of gold?"

"Well, there is a lot of gold involved, I guess," I say lamely. It's true, but it sours the mood almost immediately.

Ronan grimaces. "You want to know something stupid? I fuck-ing *hate* gold."

I stop in the middle of an alley underneath a clothesline. "What?"

"I hate it, the whole damn thing—"

"Are you fucking kidding me?" Gold is the key to everything. It's the reason our forests have been stripped, the reason my people are starving, the reason we fought a war. It's all so Selara can have their fucking gold, and he *hates* it?

I've never been so insulted.

"Wait, Sylvie. Fuck, I mean Hazel. Let me explain."

"My kingdom has lost everything for something you *hate?*"

He has the sense both not to correct me for calling Nithyria a kingdom and not to touch me.

He speaks quickly, moving back in front of me, which is good because I actually have no idea where we are or how to get back to the palace from here. "I know how important gold is and what it costs Nithyria. Believe me, I know it. What I hate is *why* we're all in this mess. I hate that my father, in his infinite wisdom, destroyed so much of our lands—your lands and his own—that we have no *choice* but to keep making it. One poor harvest, and we'll starve without it. All of us, not just Nithyria. It's the only thing we produce in any real quantity. All the alchemists tell me is how we need more ash, we need more gold, we're going to run out any day now. I've begged them to come up with another solution, but they've failed. The entire Guild has ground to a halt. They do nothing now but make it; there's no time for anything else. Our greatest minds, and this is all they do. So yes, Sylvie, I hate it. More than anything in this fucking world."

I don't believe him. I can't believe him. Ronan, the God-King of Selara, the ruler who succeeded his father and finished his war, all to control our ash, our lands, and our people, all for the sake of the fucking gold.

And he doesn't even want it.

"I know you're angry," he says, and I *am* angry, and I'm even more angry that he can tell what I'm feeling. "But I'm still trying to find a solution for us. I'm trying to find another way forward—"

"Go to hell, Ronan." My people are dying, they're starving, and for what? For fucking what? "If you wanted to find a solution, you would have. You would have let us go! You had every opportunity. After your father fell, you could have ended it. You could have given us our freedom, and you didn't."

"I couldn't. Sylvie, I couldn't. I just told you why. Everyone would have starved—"

"My people did starve! They're still starving!"

"They aren't," says Ronan quietly, bracing for my reaction. "Or at least they shouldn't be. I looked into that when you told me about the grain a few weeks ago. The grain has been arriving. There were spoiled shipments, but that was almost a year ago. Bandits get them sometimes, but we always send more. There shouldn't be anyone going without. I don't know what they told you, but I'm certain of that. It's the one thing I've been focused on the entire time I've been on the throne. It's the thing that keeps me up at night. I know you think you don't know me, but from everything you've seen me do so far, do you really think I'd let people starve? Do you think I'd starve them on purpose? Really, Sylvie?"

We're nearly back at the palace now, and it's a good thing, too, because we've completely forgotten to use our codenames. Ronan stops me in an alley, and I realize it's the alley where I met Soren.

I think about Soren saving Nico. Soren leading me into a warehouse, trying to find Vesper. Ronan saving Taran when he was a child. Ronan giving rights to the indentured. Ronan inviting everyone to participate in the festival, even us. Even after what we did. He welcomed us with open arms.

Would Ronan let people starve?

No, I don't think so.

But would Adria?

My first thought is no, of course not. Adria wants a war, not a famine. She wants to take control back from Selara, and she knows that the only way to do it is by taking control of Selara itself. If what Ronan said is true, Selara and Nithyria are dependent on each other, our fates intertwined. We can't have the independence my parents fought for, but we can ensure our freedom by ruling everything for ourselves.

But what would she do to make that happen? Or, more importantly, what *wouldn't* she do?

Would she starve our people to win their support? Would she let them go hungry if it meant they'd rise up against the Selaran oppressors? Would she carefully control the grain shipments to make sure the people were fed enough to fight, but hungry enough to want to?

And if she did, would she tell me about it? Or would she leave me in the dark, knowing that she might lose my support if I knew the truth?

It's plausible. I hate to admit it, but it's plausible.

And I could see Seth going along with it. Hell, I could see Seth proposing the idea himself.

Larus, though, that's where I'm having trouble. Because Adria and Seth would do anything for revenge. I can see that clearly now. Could Larus have been so blinded by his loyalty to them that he went along with it? Or has he been kept in the dark like me?

Are people actually still starving, or was that just last year, as Ronan said? Is this all just a lie they told me?

Or is *this* the lie? Is Ronan lying to separate me from my siblings? From my people?

Fuck.

I don't know what to believe. I need to talk to Larus desperately, but he won't be back for another week.

"Do you think I'd let people starve?" asks Ronan again. "It's really important to me to know what you think."

I can see the raw hurt on his face. He's not accustomed to being doubted, not openly at least. But it goes well beyond that, and we both know it. He wants to know if *I* doubt him. It matters to him. He can feel what I feel, but he doesn't know what I think.

And it's tearing him apart, not knowing what I think about him.

I look at him, and I see exactly who he is, maybe for the first time.

"No, Ronan," I tell him truthfully. "I know you wouldn't."

Chapter Twenty-One

A dria has already left by the time I arrive back in the palace, which is probably for the best. I don't know if I'd be able to stop myself from confronting her, and doing so as she's preparing for her highly anticipated fight with Quinn could be disastrous.

I don't even know *how* to confront her. If I ask her, would she tell me the truth? I doubt it. Maybe I should think of some other way to get her to admit what's really going on.

The more I think about it, the more it makes sense. What would Ronan have to gain from starving our people? Sure, it would save some coin, but at the cost of unrest and lost labor. And judging by the way no expense has been spared for the festival, Selara isn't that short on coin, despite what the alchemists have told Ronan.

Perhaps he wants to weaken us to allow the Orsa to control our lands completely. That's what Adria might say, and it's what Larus likely believes.

And I could see it being true. I should believe it's true. They took our home from us and gave it to the Orsa. Maybe they asked us to come here so they could expose us and justify taking the rest of our lands from us.

But there's a part of me—it's small, but it's growing—that believes Ronan. More than that, that *wants* to believe Ronan. That wants to live in the world he envisions. A world made of the best of us doing the best we can for each other. It's naïve, as Quinn said. It's foolish, and it's beautiful, and I'm having trouble believing that it's all a lie he made up for my benefit.

I'm having a hard time believing he's lying to me at all.

I take my time bathing and dressing. My favorite of the palace servants assigned to us, a sweet young girl named Hilaria with bouncy brown curls and big green eyes, helps me apply makeup in the Selaran style: light eyeliner, a peachy balm for the lips, and a shimmering powder for the cheeks flecked with silvery sparkles. She tames my wavy hair but leaves it down. "To accent the laurel wreath," she says. "You're so beautiful. They're going to see you as their queen after tonight."

As I prepare to dress in the gown Larus bought me before we arrived, there's a knock at the door. One of Ronan's servants arrives with a box. It's finely packaged, wrapped in a white silk bow.

For the hero of Selara.
- R

I'm certain it's a gown, and when I lift the top, I find that I'm right.

But I couldn't have guessed how lovely it would be.

Hilaria squeals. "It's so pretty!"

The gown is made of delicate white silk threaded with glittering silver. It's long and flowing, with silver clasps inlaid with opal, or maybe mother-of-pearl.

Not a bit of gold in sight.

I have no idea how to put it on, but Hilaria is happy to help me. She drapes the material over me, crossing it over my shoulders to preserve my modesty. Then she cinches my waist with a silver cord.

It's a beautiful dress. And, as Larus would say if he were here, it certainly sends a message. It says, "I am Selaran. I am proud to be Selaran." It's something I wouldn't have even considered wearing a few weeks ago, plan or not.

But now?

I hope Adria sees me wearing it and chokes.

Hilaria leads me to a palace entrance I've never used to meet Ronan, who's waiting for me.

He takes a long, lingering look at me as I walk down the stairs. I feel a jolt everywhere his gaze touches as if it's his fingertips on my skin instead of his eyes.

I can't tell if it's his magic or simply my overwhelming attraction to him that makes me tingle when he looks at me.

He looks glorious. He's wearing a crown tonight, a thin band of gold that sits in hair that has clearly been labored over intensively to undo the mess I made of it in the alley. His face is back to its ordinary, uncanny look of absolute perfection as well, but I'm starting to get used to it. As time goes on, I'm starting to notice little flaws that I find endearing: a tiny white scar on one of his cheekbones, a little asymmetry in his eyebrows. It isn't a face with history; the healers have done too good of a job for that. But it's human in a way I couldn't see at first.

And the way he looks at me, as if he wants to grab onto me and never let me go, makes him all the more beautifully flawed. He's an absolute idiot for trusting me. For believing in me. For seeing something in me that I'm still not certain is there.

But I want it to be.

"You are radiant," he murmurs to me as I join him. "So beautiful it's hard to look at you."

"You don't seem to be struggling."

"I'm struggling to *just* look at you," he clarifies, and it sends a wave of nervous pleasure to my core to hear it.

We travel to the arena by enclosed carriage, the ordinary chariots abandoned due to the possibility of further danger. It gives us some degree of privacy, but it also creates an incredibly tense atmosphere as we look at each other without touching for the sake of Queen Claudia and Grand Vizier Cyrus, who accompany us.

They congratulate me, thank me, and chatter at me about I don't know what. I'm not really listening. I'm watching Ronan, watching the way his lips pout when he waits to speak. The way he brushes his hair back from his eyes. The way his hands seem to twitch in my direction. The way his entire body seems to point to me.

The carriage enters the arena to thunderous applause. In the center of the arena, an elaborate stage of painted white wood has been constructed to hold the ring for Adria and Quinn's final match. A viewing box awaits us off to one side, draped in red velvet and gold. And in front of the stage, a raised platform stands ready for the crowning ceremony.

The carriage runs the track of the arena and then returns to the royal box. Ronan helps his grandmother out of the carriage first and then returns to take my hand. "Are you ready?" he whispers to me.

"I'm not sure if I am, but I'm here."

"That's enough for me," he says.

When I step out of the carriage, I swear the arena is going to collapse from the noise and energy.

The rumor mill must have been working overtime: there are blue and green banners everywhere. The entire arena is filled with them.

And people are chanting my name.

I wonder if any of them are Nithyrian themselves. If any of my people are here to witness my betrayal, or perhaps to cheer on my companionship with Ronan.

Am I a traitor to them? Or a savior?

Either way, everyone knows where I stand now. Ronan guides me to the seat directly to the left of his, his hand lingering on mine for a moment before he releases it. He faces the arena with a regal composure as Claudia joins him to elevate his voice.

"Friends, Selarans, and honored guests. Today is the final day of the Festival of Sport. Our incredible competitors have graced us with amazing feats of strength, astounding tests of endurance, and some of the finest combat Sai has ever seen.

"But, as it seems some of you already know, our celebrations were nearly brought to an untimely end yesterday. To those of you who witnessed yesterday's events, I am sorry that our festivities were marred by an act of senseless violence. To House Santori and the friends of Linus, we grieve with you. And to those who would stand against us, let me say one thing quite clearly: we will not be broken."

The crowd erupts into cheers. It takes a moment before Ronan can quiet them enough to speak.

"We have come here together to celebrate our gods and the world they have made for us. Though we honor Sai tonight, we do so in the spirit of togetherness. We do so in the knowledge that war should be the last resort. It's a path we will not walk lightly. We know its cost."

He glances towards where Adria is waiting off to the side. I wonder if she notices.

"But to our enemies, let me also say this: if it's war you want, you will have it. The champions of Selara, the champions of Sai, will rain his wrath down upon you. The people of Selara will take up the cause with righteous fury. And let me be perfectly clear about this: we will be victorious."

The cheer is so thunderous it hurts my ears. If Adria thinks the people are going to join her side once the fighting begins, it looks like she's severely underestimated their patriotism.

"I stand here before you not because I was born to do so but because I choose to do so. Because I have accepted the mandate you have given me. Because I respect the covenant with which my family has ruled this kingdom for more than six hundred years. I do not rule you for my personal gain. I rule to make sure each and every person in this nation can live the life they were born to live with liberty, prosperity, and as much happiness as the gods will grant them."

Where's Larus when you need him? I remember how just a few short weeks ago, we mocked a speech just like this one. But, as much as it pains me to admit it, I sort of like what he's saying now.

Kerensa, save me. I think I like this fool.

"Tonight, we honor the gods. But we also celebrate their creation. The people who are the foundation of this nation. My family. My court. And each and every person in this arena and beyond. And tonight, we honor the champions. As we crown the final champions this evening and close the Festival of Sport with tomorrow's hunt, our next celebration begins. Are you ready to be entertained?"

The crowd screams in affirmation.

"Then let us witness the final fight. Who will be the champion? Is it Lady Adria, Head of House Verran? Or Quinn of House Horatio?"

The response to them is surprisingly even, considering Adria's past. I'm fairly certain it's my coattails she's riding.

The judges pull both of them into the center to chat. Adria is wearing her typical leathers, her blonde hair pulled into a tight bun on the top of her head. She looks like a lion ready to pounce as she takes her place in the circle.

Quinn, who's dressed mostly in black, has borrowed the pauldrons of the Royal Guard to protect her shoulders. She lacks some of Adria's confidence, but in its place, she wields some of that righteous fury Ronan was talking about.

I can't believe it, but now I'm hoping she can pull this off. I still don't know if I trust her, but it would be such a treat to watch Adria lose.

"Talk about fighting fire with fire," Ronan says with a wink as they begin, taking his seat beside me.

Because they're both fire-born.

I shake my head at him. "Who told you that you're funny?"

"What do you mean? I'm hilarious."

"We need to find the person who told you that. *That's* your enemy."

Taran, who's standing to my left, chuckles.

The fight moves so quickly that it's difficult to follow. They're fighting fairly, at least, not a hint of fire magic in sight. Adria takes an early lead, but Quinn manages to score a couple of points in there, making it 3-2.

Ronan sighs next to me. "She's feinting to the left still, but Quinn has either forgotten what I told her, or she's too distracted to notice. It'll be over in a minute."

Taran nods.

"Have you so little faith in your friend?" I ask. I am sorely tempted to shout out to her, to tell her about Adria's weakness.

But I need Adria to believe that I'm still on her side. I *am* still on her side. Aren't I? Isn't there a chance that it's all a misunderstanding and there's a perfectly good explanation for the food shortages?

Why do I find it so hard to believe the best in her and so easy to believe the best in Ronan?

"4-2!" says the judge. I didn't even see the blow.

"Like I said," says Ronan.

Quinn looks well and truly defeated out there. I want to see a glorious comeback from her, but I know Ronan's right. Sometimes, no matter what you do, the wrong person wins.

Adria takes a low guard to bait an attack. Quinn falls for it, Adria feints to the left, then—

Quinn somehow dodges the cut that follows and dives for Adria's hips.

"Oh, shit," I say as they end up on the ground.

Grappling is allowed in sword-fighting, but the goal isn't to knock your opponent out. It's to score a hit on them with your weapon.

Someone forgot to tell Quinn and Adria that.

They're wrestling violently on the ground. Quinn has Adria by the bun, dragging her as Adria knees Quinn in the stomach.

"Enough!" yells Ronan, but either they don't hear him or don't care if they do.

Adria kicks Quinn's sword away as she reaches for it, going for her own.

But Quinn tackles her again. She pins Adria down, and for a moment, I think her superior strength will win the day.

"Stop!" yells Ronan. "No exchange!"

Quinn lifts her head in his direction, and Adria takes the opportunity to sock her in the jaw.

"You fucking bitch!" screams Quinn, spitting blood and punching down at Adria, who rolls to the side to avoid her.

Ronan gestures to the judges to step in. From their hesitation, they're reluctant to do so, likely fearing for their own safety. But they finally do manage to split them apart, much to the disappointment of the crowd.

"You're dead," says Quinn.

But between her bloody face and her inability to observe what Adria is planning, she can't make anything out of their next exchange, and Adria scores a quick tap to Quinn's leg to end it.

"Victory!"

Ronan looks at me, and I don't need to feel his feelings to know he's thinking *I told you so.* "At least she won't be as insufferable as Quinn," he says as Adria takes a victory lap around the stage.

"Not for you, maybe," I say with a groan. "I have to share a room with her."

"There are other rooms in the palace," he says with *another fucking wink.*

"I think there's something wrong with your eyelid," I say, trying to ignore the little surge of excitement that pulses through me at his words.

"Maybe so." He winks again, just to annoy me, as he stands to announce the victor.

"I give you the Champion of the Blade, Adria of House Verran! All champions, please take the stage."

One by one, the champions of each event ascend the platform at the front of the stage. Ronan announces each of them in turn, placing a laurel wreath in their hair with steady hands.

I'm not sure what I should do. Ronan said he would crown me Champion of the Bow, but I'm still not certain I deserve it. I keep my seat until he crowns Adria.

"Behold, your Champions of Sai! Truly, Sai has honored us by giving us these incredible athletes, mages, and fighters."

Maybe he changed his mind?

"But of all the people we honor tonight, there is one who we honor above all others. She is the reason I'm standing here before you."

Oh, shit. We're doing this.

"I give you the Champion of the Bow, the Hero of Selara, Sylvie of House Verran!"

Ronan gestures to my chair. Instantly, I feel every eye in the room fall on me.

I slowly rise from my seat, my body stiff and heavy, crushed under the weight of their collective gaze.

The roar is deafening, of course. But what surprises me is the sudden flurry of color and movement descending from the stands above.

Flowers, I realize. They're throwing flowers for me. Hundreds of them. Thousands, maybe. A wind-born gusts up an incredible breeze of heavily scented petals—lotus, jasmine, water lily. The blossoms float around me in a fragrant whirlwind, bathing me in their perfume. It's so beautiful and so kind it brings a tear to my eye.

"Come here, Sylvie," says Ronan, gesturing to me.

Slowly, as if in a trance, I move towards him, overwhelmed with emotion. The other champions move aside to let me have the stage to myself.

I bow to Ronan, lowering my head to receive the laurel wreath.

He solemnly places it in my hair, and then he leans in, bringing his mouth to my ear. "You look good in a crown."

My heart stops. Everything stops.

There is nothing here but us. Nothing here but him.

He says something after about Sai's Champions, the parties that will follow, and the beginning of the Festival of Arts, but I don't hear it. I don't hear anything, not even the deafening noise that continues through his announcements.

It's like the arena emptied when he spoke to me.

This is real.

He wants me. And maybe it's just a game. Maybe it's all part of a plan or a scheme, but he put a crown on my head in front of the entire city. And he knew exactly what that would mean to them.

I feel two-hundred thousand eyes on me. I feel their pride and admiration.

I feel the weight of their expectations.

And I'm certain there's no way for our plan to work, even if Adria tries to go ahead without me.

How could we possibly get these people on our side now? I saved Ronan. Me, a member of House Verran. Me, the daughter of the rebels, the traitors that plunged Selara into a five-year war we'd barely begun to recover from. Me, the sister of the woman who surrendered.

And I'd chosen to save his life when I could have let him die.

All Adria can see is what revenge against Ronan will feel like. But what happens after? Even if we can conquer Faros and take the rest of Selara before they can mount a response, what then? How do we rule over these people after that kind of betrayal?

These people who love me.

What was it that Hilaria said? "They'll see you as their queen?"

I never wanted to be queen. But when Ronan holds my hand up in the air and they raise their voices in exultation, I can see it.

At Ronan's side, I can see it.

Chapter Twenty-Two

Quinn joins us for the carriage ride back, her anger so palpable it practically smolders.

"Fucking *bitch*," she says. "Sorry, Sylvie."

"No, do go on," I say.

She laughs and then clutches her jaw where Adria punched her.

"You know I could heal that," says Ronan. When I look across the carriage at him, he isn't looking at Quinn anymore. He's looking at me. Our eyes meet, and he looks away quickly out the carriage window, half a smile on his lips.

Gods, it feels good to see him smile like that.

"Not a chance," says Quinn, and it takes me a minute to remember what we were talking about. "I want them all to see what a lunatic she is. I can't believe you two grew up in the same house."

"My parents didn't really raise me," I say without thinking.

"I guess they wouldn't have had the time," says Queen Claudia.

Shit. I brought up my parents, also known as the traitors that they all nearly died fighting against. "I was raised by our Guardian, Larus Adama, primarily," I say, hoping to smooth over the conversation.

"That makes sense. We love Larus. Or Typhon does, at least. I mean, he *really* loves Larus," says Quinn.

This comes as a shock to me. Typhon asked about him, but I thought it was due to his suspicions about what we're doing, not romantic interest. And maybe it was, and Quinn is just reading what she wants to in it.

"He's been pining ever since you lot arrived. Probably long before it, even. There's been a *lot* of pining going on around here." Quinn looks pointedly at Ronan, who glares at her.

He's been pining for me.

"Quinn," he says in warning.

I can't help but smile. I copy Ronan's move and look out the window to avoid making eye contact with him, but I'm certain he can feel my reaction.

"Everyone could stand to be a bit more forward is all I'm saying. Believe it or not, it's possible to see something you want and just go for it."

"She has a point," says Queen Claudia.

Ronan buries his head in his hands to avoid looking at them. "Remind me to never let the three of you in the same carriage again."

"That's not fair. Sylvie didn't do anything," says Quinn.

He shakes his head at her, exasperated. "I'm not blaming Sylvie."

"He's no fun," says Quinn, shifting so she isn't facing him. "Queen Claudia. Let me tell you what I heard about Thad of House Nauta and his scullery maid."

Quinn and Queen Claudia spend the rest of the carriage ride gossiping about the court, filling me in on the context wherever I'm lacking it.

I catch Ronan staring twice more. It sends a thrill through me each time, so much so that by the time we arrive at the palace, I'm considering following Quinn's advice and taking matters into my own hands.

But we don't get a chance to be alone before we're ferried into the ballroom with the rest of the court. I've passed this room a few times during the day, but it was nowhere near as spectacular as it is at night. Thousands of candles flicker in a dozen golden chandeliers suspended over a floor tiled in an elaborate geometric pattern, the light catching on the embedded stones and glittering. It gives the room the effervescent appearance of a glass of sparkling wine, and the flashes from the courtiers' jewelry only enhance the effect.

It's so beautiful I somehow forget to hate it, if only for a moment.

"It is lovely," whispers Ronan, sensing my awe. His hand hovers over the small of my back, the heat and light of it sending tingles up my spine. "But nothing is as lovely as you."

I turn to him. I want to ask him to leave this room, to take me back to his chambers and finally show me where his bed is, but the next moment, the court realizes I'm there, and I'm pulled away from him to meet everyone Quinn and Queen Claudia were just gossiping about. We've been here for weeks, but everyone treats me as if I just arrived yesterday.

I tell the story of how I saw the assassin in the shadows and shot the arrow a dozen times before someone finally rescues me.

It's not Ronan.

It's Titus, the man who defeated me in the trial of the blade. Like most of the court, he's out of his armor tonight, wearing a silver tailcoat and black breeches, the house colors of House Faber. His long red hair has been slicked into a low knot at the back of his neck. It suits him. "Can I get you a drink? You've been talking for so long by now, you must be thirsty."

"Wine," I say. "And some of those little cheese puffs, if you wouldn't mind. I'm starving."

"Good choice. They're delicious."

He returns with a glass of red and an entire tray of pastries, including several of the cheese ones.

"My savior." I give him a little bow of my head as I stuff my face with cheese. He was right—they *are* delicious.

"I'll admit I had an ulterior motive in saving you. Well, two, actually."

"Did you?" I ask, sipping my wine.

"I did. First, I'll admit that I've been getting quite a bit of grief for being the one who defeated the hero of Selara, and I was hoping to show everyone there are no hard feelings. There are no hard feelings, are there?"

"Of course not," I say. "You were more than fair."

"It was a good fight. My second motive—"

I catch movement out of the corner of my eye. It's Ronan, lurking off to the side near an arched doorway. A Guardian from one of the lower houses is talking to him at length about something he appears to care nothing about. His eyes flutter to mine again, his expression troubled.

"—is also a selfish one. I hoped that by freeing you from the clutches of the court, I might be able to convince the most incredible woman in the room to dance with me."

"Oh," I say. "Where is she?" I smile coyly. I know exactly what he meant.

"She's standing in front of me, covered in crumbs."

I laugh as I wipe my mouth. It reminds me of Ronan dressed as Soren wiping them in the market after we met.

"Sure. I'd love to dance," I say, more to get my mind off the memory than anything else.

I don't think much of it. I haven't been to a ball like this before, but I was instructed in the etiquette. It's customary to dance with many partners in one night if you're unmarried.

Judging by Ronan's white-knuckled grip on his glass, he didn't receive the same instruction.

"Ah," says Titus, catching my glance. "You know, there's a rumor going around that you're more to him than the woman who saved his life."

He says it matter-of-factly, but it's really a question he's asking me. One that I'm definitely not at liberty to answer. "I have no idea what you mean."

"Of course you don't," he says. "I can't say that I blame you. He's him, and I'm, well—"

"A very talented fighter, the heir to a Great House, and quite a gentleman besides. There's a rumor going around about us as well, I believe."

He beams at that and takes my hand, leading me to the dance floor.

I can't help but try flirting with him a little. He would be an excellent match for me under different circumstances. A better match than Ronan in many ways, not least of which is that he isn't doomed to be assassinated, if not by us, then by one of the many others Ronan has managed to piss off.

Across the room, Ronan scowls.

"If nothing else, I'm grateful I had the chance to dance with someone as beautiful and gracious as you," Titus says.

It's nice to hear, but it doesn't send my pulse racing, which is unfortunate. A part of me had hoped that it would. It would have allowed me to believe that what I'm feeling for Ronan is simply physical frustration, something that could be satiated by someone else.

But if I've reached the point where I can't even flirt with someone else without thinking about Ronan, I'm in trouble.

The dance floor is full of courtiers—mostly the young, but some of the older crowd as well. I know most of the dances, having been trained by an instructor for my court debut at a time when things were going so well for us in the war that we'd believed we'd be holding our own court. Titus dances as well as he sword fights, with similar grace and fluidity. And better yet, he's fun. He laughs and jokes with me much like Larus does, taking advantage of the moments when we're near each other to point out where a cousin of House Nauta has spilled sauce down his shirt or to speculate as to why the Lady of House Modesto is smoothing her dress so much after returning from the latrines.

I do like him even though he doesn't excite me. With him, I can almost picture a different future, one where there is no plan. Where I marry Titus, have a few kids, and eventually become the Lady of House Faber. It would be so much simpler.

It's the life I was born to as the third child of a noble family, or the one I would have been born to if my parents hadn't started a rebellion. When I was born, I wasn't the heir or the spare. I was just there. I'm not needed to keep the family line going, and I'm not able to take up a common profession. As much as I would have loved being a traveling acrobat, to do so would have been a scandal. And it would have been a difficult life, estranged from my family and the resources they provide.

Because of that, like most younger sons and daughters, my only real option is to marry another noble, preferably someone with a higher status than mine. Much of my training, the parts that weren't meant to be used on the battlefield, concerned the keeping of a fine house. How to entertain other nobility, how to be interesting enough to attract a suitable spouse.

Titus is exactly what my parents would have wanted for me, if he had been Nithyrian. He's what Larus would want for me now, assuming that he survives the war that follows. If we execute Ronan and win, he's the future I could have.

But I don't want it.

I didn't know it until I came here, having never spent much time thinking of anything but my duty, but I don't want an ordinary life, war or not. Not now that I know that something better is possible.

All the danger, all the intrigue of the palace. It should terrify me, but it's the first time I've felt alive. How can I be content with the ordinary when the extraordinary exists?

I can't be with Titus. And not just now because it jeopardizes the plan. Not ever.

Because of me.

Because I can't stop feeling Ronan's eyes on me as I move. When I dance, it's for him. When I laugh at Titus's words, it's Ronan that I look to, wishing he could share in the joke.

I don't know what I'm going to do about the plan or Adria or Larus. I don't know how I feel about what I came here to do or what it will mean for my people if I fail to do it.

But I know one thing: I'm done pretending. I don't need to pretend anymore. Maybe I was never pretending at all.

I want Ronan.

He arrives at my side the moment after I think it.

"Excuse me," I say, curtsying to Titus, who bows to Ronan, understanding without explanation.

"I was wondering if you had forgotten me," I say, moving off the dance floor.

His jaw twitches as he leans in closer so we're not overheard. "Me? When you've spent the entire evening with someone else?" There's heat in Ronan's words, more than I had expected.

I haven't been with Titus for long, really. Four dances, maybe five, all of them fast with minimal contact. I'm reminded of his reaction to me thinking of Taran in his sitting room. "Are you always this jealous?" I ask. I hate to admit that it thrills me a little if he is.

He rubs his thumb over his mouth as he thinks of a response, and I find that I'm jealous of it. I want to be the one touching his lips. "Not always. Just when—"

"Ronan, you know what I'm feeling."

"But not what you're thinking."

"The only thing that matters is what I'm feeling." The music slows, and I take his hand. He takes a moment before he follows, but eventually, he lets me lead him back to the dance floor.

Gods, he's beautiful, even when he's angry. Even when he's being ridiculous. The tightness of his jaw. The darkening of his eyes. He's so gorgeous it's difficult to look at him. Difficult to breathe around him.

I wonder how I could ever have felt differently.

He takes my hand, his fingers straining against the urge to hold it tightly, and places the other one on the small of my back, his touch agonizingly light.

I think of the bruise he healed a few weeks ago, the way his fingers slipped into the fabric of my dress.

He's keeping me at a distance now as we begin to step to the music, and I hate it. I want to be in his arms, pressed to his chest. Safe.

"I flirted with Titus because I wanted to see if I could feel anything for him," I say to him. He looks at me but doesn't meet my eye.

"And did you?"

"No." It's the truth. As much as I enjoyed spending time with Titus, it wasn't the same. I stroke Ronan's shoulder. "I'm sorry," I whisper. "I didn't think it would upset you. I thought it would be obvious what I was truly feeling. And who was making me feel that way."

"Don't," he whispers. His hand clutches at the back of my gown.

"Don't what?"

"Don't do that." He presses his other hand over mine to still it.

Is he this angry with me? Over a little flirting?

He sighs. "Come on." He leads me from the dance floor, through a door, and onto a balcony. He drops my hand and leans against the stone railing, facing out to Faros.

"Is this about Titus?" I ask. "Really, it meant nothing—"

"No, it's not about Titus." His shoulders tense. He won't even look at me. "I can't do it, Sylvie. I can't take it anymore."

"I can't do it, Sylvie. I can't take it anymore."

I freeze, my mind reeling. What is he talking about? Fear clutches at my throat, making it hard to get the question out. "What do you mean?"

He shakes his head slowly, his hand clenching in front of him. Then he turns suddenly, taking my face in his hand, his grip trembling. "This. I can't take this. I know you've been pretending. I felt it when we met. I let you…I thought maybe your mind would change eventually. But I can't go on like this if you're still lying to me."

My breath catches, guilt coiling in my chest. I am lying, at least about some things. I still haven't told him the truth about the reason we came here. The plan we had.

But does it truly matter now? Now, when I know in my heart I can't do it anyway?

He brushes my cheek and then my lower lip with his thumb. My lips part at his touch.

"I'm desperate for you," he whispers.

His words burn through me, lighting me up like a candle. The heat and light travel down my neck, down my back, and settle in my core. I sigh as he wraps his arms around my waist, pulling me to him.

He leans back, closing his eyes. "I can feel it when I touch you. I can feel your body respond to me, ache for me. I can feel your desire.

And I want to give you what you want. I want to give myself to you. I want to take you, body and soul. But I can't, not if you're pretending. Not if it isn't as real to you as it is to me."

He removes his hand from my waist and pushes me away.

I take him by his neck, and I pull him back.

I press my body to his. He groans, and his body betrays him, the length of him moving, reaching for me. I take his hand and move it back to my face.

He leans in, closing the remaining distance between us. The heat of his body envelops me. The smell of him, spicy and woody, like incense. It's heady and intoxicating. It feels like the entire world hangs in the distance between our lips, in the anticipation of a kiss that I want desperately, dangerously badly.

I know he can feel it. How can he imagine that I'm faking it? How could he believe that any of this is anything but real to me too? That I would even consider giving my body to someone I didn't desire?

But I can't bring myself to say it. I can't, not while I'm still lying about other things. Even if the truth is that I want him as badly as he wants me.

Maybe worse.

"I know what you want from me," I say as he backs away again, feeling my hesitation. "But I can't give it to you. Not yet. Something *has* changed. But to be with you the way you want me to…"

I pause, looking into the distance. About this, at least, I can't lie to him. "The way *I* want you to," I say, looking him right in the eye. He swallows. "It's a betrayal, Ronan. Of my people. My family. Even if I'm right about you, I can't let go of them. Not yet. Not while I still believe there's a chance to fix things. To make everything right."

I realize this truth as I speak it. If everything Ronan has told me is true, it means I've been lied to. But it doesn't mean there isn't a chance for us to find a way forward together. I have to give them that chance. Adria, but especially Larus. I have to know what Larus has to say before I can turn my back on them completely.

"I'm not asking you to let go of your people—"

"You are, Ronan." I think for a moment of how to put it without revealing too much. "You said yourself you know how much we hate you. How much *they* hate you." His eyes flash at my correction. "My people would never accept us together. They would treat me as their enemy, my own family included."

"I won't let them," he says, but I can tell he knows that even the God-King himself doesn't have that power.

"That's not the only reason," I admit.

"No?"

My heart pounds as I look up at him. "I can't be with you because if I do, I won't be able to let you go. It will consume me."

"Sylvie." He pulls me to him again, but this time, he doesn't lean forward. He pulls my head to his chest and holds me there, his head bending behind my back. I stand on my toes, reaching up, and he obliges me, bending down so that our heads are on each other's shoulders, holding each other in a tight embrace.

"I should walk away from this," he mutters, his breath in my hair, his fingertips stroking my back. "But fuck, I don't want to."

I feel his words deep within me as he breathes, the heat of his body pressing into my chest. I breathe with him, our bodies rising and falling together. "I'm not pretending," I tell him. Here, in his arms, I can tell him that much. I can't look him in the eye and say it, but I can say it with my body against his. I breathe him in—spice and cedar and smoke—and I sink my hands into his back, pulling him harder against me.

He takes a deep, shuddering breath, and I unfold. "I want you," I say, my voice quiet. "I've wanted you for a long time."

He sighs against my shoulder, his lips brushing it as he speaks. "I want you so fucking badly it hurts."

So take me, I think, but I don't say it. I can't say it.

But I know he can feel it, and I can feel his growing desire for me between us. He lifts his head a bit until his lips hover over the bare skin where my neck meets my shoulder. Then he presses the softest, faintest kiss there. It's tentative and full of restrained longing, full of the need that pulses within him, the need he's trying desperately to hold back.

"Go," he whispers. "Go, before I stop you."

I don't want to go. But he's pushing me away from him, putting distance between us again, and I know he's right. I need to go. If I don't go, I'm going to surrender myself to him. I'm going to give him exactly what he wants. Exactly what I want. I'm going to give in to my desire. I'm going to let it consume me, let it take me over until the only thing that's left is my primal need for him.

I take a slow, reluctant step away from him. It hurts physically to do it. The distance between us is cold and cruel, a biting chill that reaches the bone even though the night air is warm around us. I feel as though I'm being torn apart, like a part of me is being left behind.

I hear him shift behind me, hear him struggle as I hesitate.

I hear the moment he loses the war within him.

"Fuck it," he says.

Then he grabs my arm and yanks me back to him, pushing his mouth on mine with so much force I gasp.

Chapter Twenty-Three

He kisses the gasp from my lips as he knots his hand in my hair, pulling my head to him so he can claim my mouth.

I wrap my arms around his neck as he reaches his other hand in my dress, kneading his fingers into the small of my back. The kiss is deep, relentless. Searing. He tastes of wine and honey, of longing and lost control, of sunlight and the warmth of a candle's glow.

I kiss him back with equal desperation, with darkness and forbidden desire and damnation, with an aching need for the one thing I can't have.

His lips take each of mine one by one, sucking and pulling at them, memorizing each of them, the feel, the taste, as he reaches lower and pulls me closer to him by my hips.

I fling the laurel crown from my head and then clutch at his collar, tugging on it, needing him closer. Testing me, he darts his tongue between my lips. I open for him. I let him in, meeting his tongue with mine, letting him explore my mouth. The thrust of his tongue between my lips sends a wave of heat down my spine. It pinches my nipples, leaving them hard and needy against the smooth silk fabric of the dress he gave me.

I reach my hands into his perfect, golden-brown hair, relishing its softness, my fingertips grazing his crown. And then I press them at the nape of his neck. I urge him deeper into my mouth, and he gives me what I want, opening himself into me, devouring my tongue.

I lower the shadows around us. Not so much that he can't see me, but enough that we shouldn't be visible from inside.

My breasts are heavy and hot against him. I want him to touch them, to taste them. "Is this what you want?" he asks, kissing my neck and reaching a hand up between us, grazing my breast, touching the peak of my nipple with agonizing softness through the white fabric.

"More," I beg.

He takes my mouth again, his lips warm and wet against mine. "Greedy," he whispers. My nipples ache with need. He touches one lightly again and then gives it one soft squeeze.

I groan in frustration.

Fuck. He's teasing me, and I love it.

And from the feel of him hard against my stomach, he loves it too.

He kisses me again, harder now, more insistent, as he reaches lower still and lifts my thigh to his hip. I wrap my leg around his back, angling myself so that I'm pressing my most sensitive area against his length. The layers of fabric between us are thin, and I'm wet already with desire.

"Fuck," he says, moaning into my ear. He licks the shell of it and sucks on the lobe, teasing my nipple with one hand as he presses the other onto my ass, pushing me to him until I'm rubbing the soaking flesh between my thighs against him.

White hot desire floods me. I want to shove the layers of fabric aside. I want to free his cock, to feel the head of it against me—

—to lift her by her hips and lower her onto me, sinking myself all the way inside of her until I'm drowning in her—

What the fuck?

"What was that?" I say, lowering my leg and pulling away from him.

My heart thunders in my chest. I feel the cold absence of him again as he releases me, confused.

"What's wrong? Fuck, Sylvie, I'm sorry—"

He covers his face with his hand, shocked. Ashamed.

"No," I say, taking his hand and pulling it from his face. "It's not that." I kiss his hand, and he melts into me with relief. It wasn't the kiss that was the problem. "Did you make me feel something?"

I felt something just a moment ago. It was a feeling, clear and present as my own, but it wasn't mine.

It was his.

I felt it coming from him, felt his desperate desire for me. Felt what he wanted to do to me, how he wanted to take me. I couldn't hear his thoughts or see an image, but I knew exactly what he wanted.

I knew it like the feeling had come from my own body instead.

"I don't understand," he says. "What did you feel?"

"You. I felt what you wanted. Did you do that?"

He looks at me as if I'm speaking another language. "Did I do what? Did I want you? Yes, very much—"

"No," I say, sighing in exasperation. "I felt your feelings. Your power. Can you give it to someone else? Can you make them feel things? I thought you said you couldn't."

"I can't," he says. He's looking at me with wide-eyed earnestness, and I can tell he's telling the truth. At least, what he believes to be the truth. "Are you sure you felt my feelings? I know you're feeling conflicted. Fuck, I shouldn't have done that. If you felt something and then regretted it—"

"No," I say firmly. I reach my hand behind his neck, and he shudders at my touch. "It wasn't regret. I don't regret it." I plant a small kiss on his lips, and he freezes, fighting the urge to reach for me again. "It wasn't my own feeling at all. I'm certain, Ronan."

He knits his eyebrows, trying to find another explanation for what I'm saying. "What did you feel?" he says in a small voice. He's nervous. Exposed. Afraid of what he showed me.

"I felt…"

I don't know if I can say it. If I say it, I'm going to need it. I'm going to need him inside me more than I already do.

And what I need to do is walk away.

Fuck, I don't want to walk away.

I wonder if I could feel it again. I desperately want to. I lower his hand to my ass and hitch my leg up around him once more. He groans and kisses me, lifting me up by the hips until I've wrapped my legs around him.

I kiss his cheek and whisper in his ear. "You want to push me against the column behind me. You want to take my nipple into your mouth and suck it the way I wanted you to. You want to feel me arch my back and press myself against you. You want to put your hand between us and shove my dress aside so you can feel how wet I am on your fingers."

His eyes close, picturing it, and then jerks his head back in surprise. "You can feel that?"

I nod. It's more specific than I had imagined it being. I can see now why he thinks he knows someone based on their feelings alone. "I can't feel anything now that you've pulled away. Maybe it's only in the heat of the moment? Has it happened before…?" With someone else? I want to ask, but I don't want to think of him with anyone else right now.

"No," he says firmly. "Never." He stares at me in wonder. Is it his power, or is it mine? Is there something special about us? Something beyond even whatever this is, the intensity of this connection?

He brushes his fingertips on my cheek, looking at me as if he doesn't believe I'm real. "I always wanted to. I always wanted to share it with someone, to let them feel me like I feel them."

"I want you to do it," I say to him, leaning forward and pressing my lips against his jaw. I whisper in his ear, "What you want."

"Fuck, Sylvie." He moans a kiss against my lips and carries me to the column. He puts his hand behind my head to take the impact as he shoves me against it, kissing me wildly on my lips, my jaw, my neck.

He presses himself against me, bucking against my core, which burns with heat. Then he lowers his mouth to my breast, freeing it from my dress. He sucks it, hard, his lips insistent as his tongue licks circles around my swollen nipple. I gasp, feeling it deep within me, feeling it send a pulse of need through me, the need to be filled.

"Can you feel that?" he asks as he moves his hand between us, his fingers feeling for an opening in the damp fabric.

"You want to..." My breath catches in my throat. I'm overwhelmed by his desire. "You want to be inside me—"

"Yes," he hisses. "Fuck, I—"

The door opens behind us, and we spring apart. Ronan puts me down and turns to face out to the city while I turn to the column to smooth my dress, hoping whoever is there can't see the flush on my skin as I lift the shadows to reveal us.

"Oh, fuck," says Quinn. "Did I just—"

"What do you want, Quinn?" says Ronan, his voice husky and edged with frustration.

"Sorry, I thought I saw you come out here. It's the Brakkari ambassador. He's looking for you, says it's important."

Ronan gives me a quick look, and though I can't feel it, I can read it: apology, penitence, longing. "Lead the way," he says to Quinn, and he follows her from the balcony, taming the muss from his hair with another regretful backward glance to me as he goes.

I'm left there, cold and reeling, alone in the night.

What the fuck just happened?

I try to collect myself so I can return to the party before I'm missed. I rub the damp spot of my dress against a dry part of the fabric near my hip until it isn't as obvious. I run my fingers through my hair, smoothing it back into shape.

His fingers in my hair. He had knotted them there, pulled me by it—

Fuck, the desire for him is still close. The shock of Quinn's arrival splashed cold water on it for a moment, but it's lurking beneath my skin, hot and ready for him.

I've got to get out of here before I run after him and beg him to carry me to his bed, Brakkari ambassador be damned.

Everything inside looks too glaringly bright when I reenter. The party is still underway, people dancing and chatting as if nothing happened on the balcony just now.

As if the entire world didn't shift on its axis, as if everything didn't come sliding down off its surface, spilling out into the cosmos, forever changed.

They clink their glasses of beer and wine and chat and flirt and smile while I desperately try to moor myself. There must be something, anything, here that can put me back on solid ground.

My eyes catch someone moving in the shadows. He's wearing a brown robe, an alchemist's robe, and he's tall and heavyset.

Hermes.

Just the alchemist I've been looking for.

I hadn't seen him earlier, although would I have even noticed him with Ronan around? But here he is now, and by the looks of it, he's heading somewhere.

Somewhere I will follow.

Chapter Twenty-Four

Hermes walks the halls of the palace alone. At first, I think he's heading to the alchemy wing, maybe sent by Adria to fetch her an elixir of some kind, but he keeps going past it and down some stairs to a familiar door.

It's the locked door I went through when I arrived.

I don't follow him through it—the hallway is too narrow, and he'll be able to hear me within the passage even if he can't see me in the shadows. But I know exactly where the passage leads, so I head through the palace gates to the same alley, stopping only to ask one of the guards—it's Stella, thankfully, one of the few that I recognize—to borrow her cloak.

Stella gives it to me without question, but then she offers to accompany me wherever I'm going.

"No need," I say. "I'm just heading to the market."

"It won't be open, ma'am." Stella gives me a sideways glance. I hadn't realized it before, but she doesn't look much like your typical guard aside from the armor and closely cropped hair. While she's clearly strong enough to wear her chainmail day in and out without complaint, her facial features are petite, almost delicate. Her brown eyes lack the sort of glazed look many of the guards take on after standing in the same place all day. They're shrewd, cunning. Something about her reminds me of my mother.

"Fine," I say, seeing no point in trying to lie. "I'm not heading to the market."

"I have to go with you," she says with zero hesitation.

"Did he order you to? If I ever left the palace alone?"

"Yes."

"And if I tell you no, you'll follow me anyway?"

"Yes."

Ronan won't like this. There's a chance, albeit slim, that Stella could be involved in whatever Hermes and the alchemists are doing. But I don't have time to argue with her, and I don't have the time or the inclination to get his permission.

"Keep a distance from me. I'm trying to remain unseen."

If she can manage to track me in the darkness, I'll be impressed.

I slip her black cloak on and vanish into the shadows just in time to see Hermes emerging through the passage. I follow him through a series of alleys, concerned at first that he's leading me into a trap, but eventually I realize it hasn't even occurred to him that he could be followed. He heads directly to the alley where Ronan and I were just this morning.

There's someone else waiting there for him in a brown robe. The other person is turned so I can't see them, but they're smaller than Hermes. A tall woman, perhaps, or a smaller man.

They don't stop for conversation. They enter a door—the door Mery must have shown the guards—and close it behind them.

It *is* the alchemists, then. Or at least some of them. If Hermes is responsible in some way for kidnapping Vesper—

Did Adria put him up to it? She asked me about the missing shadow-born that time, although she's never mentioned it since. I can't see why she would take an interest in them, unless she somehow knew about their connection to Ronan.

But what other explanation is there for Hermes being here?

I decide to leave somehow getting information out of Adria for another time. I have an opportunity right now to find Vesper, and I don't intend to miss it.

I wait until Stella arrives in the alley, and then I creep along the shadows to her.

"Shit!" she says when I drop them. She has her sword halfway drawn before she realizes it's me. "Sorry, ma'am. I lost you somewhere back there."

"They went in that doorway," I whisper. "I'm going to follow."

"Who did?" she asks. "What are we doing out here?"

"It doesn't matter. Just wait a few minutes, and if I don't come back out, come in after me. Or let Ronan know where I went."

"No," she says. She sheathes the sword and stands in front of me, defiant. "The king would never allow it. Either you take me in there with you, or I'll take you back to the palace myself."

She's bold for someone so young, much bolder than she was with Ronan. She'll learn her lesson about defying nobility at some point, but right now, I'm actually glad she wants to go in there with me. I'm a little scared of what's inside.

"Come on then," I say, leading her to the doorway.

I listen through the door before we enter. Silence on the other side. I wish Ronan were here, and not just because he could tell how many people were waiting in the room.

I try the handle. Locked.

"Let's go," says Stella, looking around the alley anxiously.

I don't have my rake with me, but I do have some pins in my hair from where the laurel crown was placed. I take them out and begin fumbling with the lock.

After a moment, Stella takes the pins from my hands. But rather than lead me away from the door, she begins to pick it. She makes quick work of it, even quicker than I typically manage with better tools.

"Where'd you learn that?" I ask her as the door pops open.

"I grew up in the palace," she says, as if that explains it.

I swing the door in slowly. It creaks a bit, which makes me wince, but if Hermes and whoever he was meeting are still there, they don't come to investigate.

"I'll just go in first in shadow—"

"No," says Stella, brushing past me. She draws her sword and looks around, the dim moonlight coming through the door the only light to guide her.

The room is small and sparsely furnished, with no doorways in sight. Shelves cling to the walls at odd angles, their contents long since removed. Between two battered desks with drawers hanging open and empty, a cluster of crates sits beneath moth-eaten fabric. A few frames linger on the walls, their pictures gone. Everything is coated in a layer of dust.

There's no sign anyone has been here at all.

"There must be some kind of trap door. Some kind of passage. See if you can find anything."

"Can I light a candle?" Stella asks, pulling one from her pocket.

"No." It's too much of a risk. If a candle is seen from within, they may realize we're onto them. "Take this side." I let her search the side of the room nearest to the door while I look in the dark corners.

It's tense for the first few minutes, but we eventually relax somewhat once we realize no one is coming.

"How did you become a guard?" I ask her as we're each combing over the walls for gaps or secret buttons. "You don't seem much like one."

"I grew up in the palace, as I said. My mother was one of Queen Calia's chambermaids."

Queen Calia, Ronan's mother. "Was?"

"Until Queen Calia died. King Aurelian dismissed all of her staff a few months after her passing. I was eight years old. It was just before the war began. The harvest had been poor that year, and there wasn't much work around. We struggled for about a month before Ronan found us."

"Found you where?"

"At a boarding house near the docks, sleeping in a bunk room with a dozen others. He tracked down all of his mother's dismissed servants and invented reasons to bring them back. He hired my mother to teach him the lute. She was playing in the tavern for a bit of coin at the time."

So that's how he learned to play. "Why did he do that? Just to be kind?"

"Maybe. But maybe also to keep his mother's memory around for a bit longer. When the war began, my mother served with him, in his army."

I can guess how the next part of the story goes. "She died in the war?"

Stella nods, looking at me out of the corner of her eye as she examines the desk in the corner. "With her gone, they let me stay in the palace as long as I did some chores and stayed out of the way. After the war, I asked Ronan to train to be one of his guards. I didn't want to be a maid, but I wanted to be around him. I didn't realize it at the time, but I think it was for the same reason that he saved us: to keep the memory of my own mother alive a while longer. He still plays her lute sometimes." She smiles as she says it for a quick moment before straightening her expression and returning to the task at hand.

She loves him, like they all love him.

And I'm beginning to understand why. The thought of him play-ing Stella's mother's lute just to make Stella happy is almost unbearable.

Everything I thought about him was wrong.

I think back to the time he told me that everyone loves him. I'd dismissed it as the sort of cocky nonsense that someone like him would say, someone who had been brought up to believe that he was better than everyone else by nature of his birth.

But he was right: everyone does love him. And they love him not because they have to or in spite of who he is or what he does, the way that I love Adria and Seth. They love him because he cares for them. Because they all have a story just like this one, a moment where he saw something he could do to help, and he did it. Because he's kind and good. They choose to protect him because they believe he's worth protecting.

I'm beginning to believe it as well, and that thought scares me more than anything that's happened tonight.

We search the room until the bells chime the next hour, finding nothing. It's like Hermes and his companion never even came in here.

"Come on, Sylvie," says Stella. "There's nothing here. Let me take you back to the palace."

I let her, thanking her for helping me even though we failed and asking her to keep quiet about it to anyone other than Ronan. I'm heading towards Ronan's chambers to wait for him to give him the news about Hermes when Adria finds me in the hallway.

She's wearing one of our mother's dresses, a navy-blue gown that fits awkwardly on her muscular shoulders, and it looks like she's coming from the party. "I heard you put on quite a show to-night before I arrived. Titus and then Ronan. They say Ronan was furious when you left the dance floor together."

"Somewhat," I admit.

"I really have to hand it to you, sis. You are *far* better at this than I expected."

She's been drinking heavily, by the smell of wine on her breath and the sway of her step.

I change my plans. I can tell Ronan in the morning about Hermes if Stella doesn't tell him first. But I have a chance here with Adria while she's drunk.

A chance to get some answers out of her.

"I have so many things to tell you," I say. I stop a servant and ask for another bottle of wine to be sent to our chambers.

We change into our nightgowns, and I pour us each a glass once the bottle arrives. She drinks hers indulgently, but I merely sip mine.

I start by congratulating her on her victory over Quinn.

"It was too easy, really," she tells me. "Titus was a better fight. I bet he'd be a better fuck too."

She never talks to me like this. Either she's really happy with me or truly drunk, but either way, I take it as a good sign.

"I think Quinn has a bit more experience than Titus on both counts."

"He's a baby, isn't he? Same age as you, I think. You're twenty-two?"

Almost. My birthday is in a month, right at the end of the Festival of Arts. I hadn't even thought about it. "Twenty-one until next month."

"That's right. Quinn's twenty-seven, same as Seth. I'm surprised her father didn't force her to marry with only Typhon left to inherit."

"I don't think there's much forcing that you can do with her."

"I managed well enough today. Forced her to make a fool out of herself." She laughs harder than her own joke merits.

I pour her another glass. "Why haven't you married?"

"You want to know something fucked up? The only good thing about Mother and Father being gone is I don't have to get married. They would have made me if they were alive, but they aren't, so they can't. You and Seth can carry on the family name. I don't give a fuck about any of that. Although I guess you won't be getting married anytime soon with Ronan there blocking anyone decent from having a chance."

I shush her; she's being loud, and the servants could still be nearby.

I don't know how long I have until she's incoherent or passed out, so I decide to try my luck with some of the things I want to know.

"I have some good news," I tell her. "Ronan is increasing the grain shipments. I told him about our shortages, and he's promised to send as much as we need to make up for the losses."

"Oh," she says. She sways on the edge of the bed. "That's good. Good news."

Her delivery is entirely unconvincing. I decide to press on.

"I thought you would want to know. So you can do something about it."

"What do you mean?" She sits upright, suddenly alert. Is she faking being drunk, or is she just having a moment of lucidity?

It's such a risk to say what I'm about to say, but I have to know the truth. "I mean that whatever you've been doing, you're going to need to do more of it. To the grain. Whatever scheme you have going, it's about to get harder."

I clench my jaw and take a tiny sip of wine through thin-pressed lips, grateful she can't feel what I'm feeling.

She starts to laugh. Then she stops, and she starts again, pointing her finger at me from around her wineglass. "Well, well, well. Look who's finally living up to the family name. Even Larus hasn't worked that one out yet."

I do my best to appear nonchalant, unbothered by this sudden confirmation. "I figured he didn't know. Or Typhon. That mustn't have been easy."

"You have no idea," she says. "I've had to ride Seth's ass about it for more than a year. We hire bandits, they send more guards. We let water into the storage, they send more grain. It's a fucking arms race. But they handed us the opportunity with those rotten shipments, and we couldn't let it go to waste."

"It's a delicate balance," I say, trying not to let her see my disgust. My horror. "Keeping the people fed enough to fight but hungry enough to want to." It's exactly the thought I had when Ronan told me, but deep down, I didn't believe it.

But it's true. They did this, my own siblings. They let our people sit on the brink of starvation—let some of them starve—on purpose.

For what?

Revenge?

"Those bandits on the road," I ask her, piecing something together. The people who attacked us when we were on our way here—she had ordered me to kill one of them when she started talking. "Were they some of yours?"

"Probably. I don't even know. Seth has one of his men hire them. Fuck, Sylvie, we underestimated you. *I* underestimated you. I thought Larus had made you soft. I hated that you grew up with him. You needed Mother's grit and Father's firm hand to guide you. I thought you were a lost cause. But you figured it out, and all on your own. You're clever. Cleverer than Seth by far. Maybe cleverer than me."

"Maybe I will be someday," I say. She takes it as a compliment, but it's not.

It's a promise.

Chapter Twenty-Five

I find Ronan in the dining hall in the morning.

He's dressed for the hunt: a long tan tunic, sturdy trousers for riding, and heavy boots that almost look Nithyrian. I'm wearing nearly exactly the same thing down to the colors. We make quite a pair, and I'm sure he notices as well because his eyes light up when he sees me approaching his table at the head of the room.

"Your majesty," I say, remembering to bow this time.

Quinn, who's seated a few chairs down to his right, coughs a little. My ears heat at the memory of what she walked in on.

"Did you need something?" he asks.

"A word in private before we head to the temple." We'll be stopping at the Temple of Sai for a blessing before the hunt begins, but I'm not sure if I'll be accompanying Ronan, and even if I am, I doubt I'll be alone with him to give him the news about Hermes.

Several heads look up at my request. I don't know how I feel about being at the center of all this gossip, but I suppose it's just the cost of being with someone like Ronan.

Or, not being *with* him, per se. Being near him. Being around him. Wanting to spend every waking moment of every single day in his company—

Gods, I'm fucked.

Ronan wipes his mouth with his napkin—his beautiful, perfect mouth that felt *so good* on mine, not that I'm thinking about it— and gestures to a door at the back of the room.

I walk around the long table and follow him to it, letting him hold it open for me. I smell the scent of his cologne as I pass him, and it takes me back into his arms. Resisting the urge to reach for him, I follow him through a courtyard and into the small antechamber to the throne room where we met.

He looks around the room and then at me, unsure whether to sit or stand. Unsure of how much distance he should put between us. Without feeling it, I can sense his confusion. Have I brought him here to admonish him for his behavior last night? Or to continue it?

Neither, unfortunately.

"I saw Hermes leaving the party last night, and I followed him. I followed him back to the alley Mery told us about."

"On your own?"

"No, Stella followed. You ordered her to do so."

He nods. "She knows where you went? And why?"

"Not why, but she knows I was looking for someone there. I'm sorry. I didn't want to argue with her and miss the chance."

"It's fine; I'll handle it." I don't ask him what he means. I know him well enough to know that it won't be bad for Stella. "What did Hermes do in the alley?"

"He met someone. Another alchemist. I couldn't see their face. They went through the door, and then nothing. I followed after them—"

He puts his hand on his face. "On your own? Sylvie—"

"Yes, yes, I know. I shouldn't have done that. But there was nothing there. Stella came in and had a look as well. Nothing but undisturbed dust. I don't understand it."

"Some kind of magic or elixir, most likely, to cover their tracks."

Again, I find myself wishing my mother were still around to ask.

"I haven't seen Hermes back yet this morning," I tell Ronan. "He was supposed to be joining the hunt."

"He may know you're onto him. Damn, I hate that we're leaving the palace today. I need someone to keep an eye out for him."

I don't want to say it, but I have to offer. For the sake of the shadow-born. "I can stay. I can follow Hermes if he comes back." I don't really enjoy hunting anyway.

"Do you want to stay?" he asks. But the real question he's asking is, "Do you want to stay away from me?"

And there's only one real answer to that. "No," I say, taking a step forward. "I want to go with you."

"Good," he says, his shoulders relaxing. "I'll ask Taran to stay, maybe. He won't ask questions. Or Stella, since she already knows some of what's going on."

Now that I've taken care of business, I'm deeply aware of us being alone in the room together again. "Ronan, I—"

"If I let myself talk to you about what happened last night, I'm going to try to pick up where we left off. And if I do that, I don't think we're going to leave this room. And as much as I want to tell Sai to go fuck himself and his damned hunt, I can't. The court has been looking forward to it more than anything else. We have to go."

"Yes," I say, inching a little closer. "We have to go."

"Don't do that. Stop feeling things at me."

"What am I feeling?" I ask him, my voice pure innocence.

He groans. He knows he shouldn't say it. He knows what's going to happen if he says it.

But he just can't stop himself.

"Something along the lines of 'I want you to kiss me, you fucking moron, and then bend me over that table.'"

"And I thought you weren't a mind-reader."

"I'm not going to do it." He shakes his head and avoids looking at me. "I'm not letting them down."

"Too bad," I say. I start walking towards the door. "I guess we'll just have to—"

He crosses to me and slams me against the door with a kiss. It's even hungrier than last night. It's the kiss of someone who has been doing nothing but thinking of kissing me again since we were interrupted. It's the kiss of someone who cannot get enough of me, whose hands can't stand being off of me for even one minute longer.

It's possessive and territorial and demanding. It's his tongue claiming my mouth, his hands in my hair, pulling and begging and opening me to him.

It's my arms wrapping around him, pressing him against my body, my hands on his back scratching at his skin beneath his shirt, trying to bring him closer—

And then it's a touch of light on the back of my head where it hit the door. "Sorry," he mutters to the side of my mouth as he heals me. He takes a gasping step back and then reaches for the handle.

"Let's go," he says, and I can see it takes every ounce of his strength to do so.

"You're a selfless ruler," I tell him.

"Don't fucking remind me," he says, pinching his brows in disbelief that he has to walk away from this again.

I follow him into the courtyard. He turns to look at me, then he stops to smooth my hair.

"Fuck it, just one more," he says, and he kisses me again.

This one absolutely thrills me. We're here in a public courtyard in the light of day. Anyone could see us. He wants me so badly, he doesn't even care.

I let myself get lost inside of it for a minute, maybe two. Okay, maybe three. And then I finally break away from it because I can tell he's close to not being able to.

"Come on," I say. "There's always the carriage ride at least."

We share the carriage with Queen Claudia, who does not get the heavy hints Quinn drops to allow us some privacy. I should have some shame and try to avoid thinking lurid thoughts about Ronan in front of his grandmother, but it seems I'm somewhat shameless when it comes to him. I spend the entire ride thinking of what I want him to do to me, watching his face as he tries to hide what he's sensing. Gods, it's so fucking hot watching him squirm, watching him shift his legs and twitch his jaw. Sorry, Queen Claudia. What you don't know won't hurt you.

"I hope you're having fun," he whispers as we arrive once Queen Claudia has left the carriage. "I'm going to ruin these pants if you don't stop."

Fuck. My core is already heated from my own fantasies, but that image sends it molten.

It's hard to focus on the rites of Sai. They've always been my least favorite anyway, although even Kerensa's beautiful ceremonies would have seemed like a nuisance under these circumstances.

The Temple of Sai is near the northern wall, and this ceremony is my first visit since we've arrived. The practice of religion is quite personal in both Selara and Nithyria. Some families tend to adhere to one god or goddess over the others, participating in services honoring the others only on significant holidays or occasions like these festivals. Others devote themselves to all equally, alternating days of worship or even attending services for each on the same day.

We adhered more to Vahlo and Sai than the others, due in part to my parents' preferences but also their locations. The temples of Vahlo and Sai are joined in Pyka, the city where I grew up. I suspect the reason is more logistical than anything else. Sai's rites involve fire and blood, and Vahlo's ash and bone, and those things tend to go together.

Ronan, as the embodiment of Vayla on earth, holds dominion over all the gods and goddesses, and so he performs the rites of Sai along with the head priestess of the temple at an altar draped in rich red fabrics. It's a lot of burning wood and pouring blood and ritual incantations, ancient forms of magic that supposedly once opened the doors to the magical abilities that now manifest in each person without such efforts.

I think of the heretical things Ronan has said. About how the schools of magic aren't as concrete as the Codex says, about how the qualities of people may not align as well as it seems. I think of what my parents said about how the hierarchy was nonsense.

Zara is in the front row just a few seats down from me. She gives me a tiny wave to avoid attracting attention when I meet her eye.

I think of something she said to me once about forbidden forms of magic. About the way she acted like Ronan was a hindrance to her work.

Could she know something about what Hermes was doing with the shadow-born? Could it have been at her request?

"The blood of the fallen," says a priest as he approaches with a cup. It's just red wine, thankfully. This was the only part of Sai's rites that I enjoyed as a child. I remember playing with a little servant boy after the service, pretending we were drunk from a single sip.

I take the cup offered to me and drink from it.

Poison, I realize. Not the cup I just drank from. (At least, I hope not.) But what's happening to Ronan. It could be poison, couldn't it? The thing that's making him lose his magic. It's not a constant decline. Maybe whatever they're poisoning him with doesn't last long. Maybe it's difficult to get access to him, so they can't always keep his powers suppressed. But as long as he's weak at the right moments, moments like the other night in the arena, that should be enough eventually.

But what about the taster? He has a taster eat and drink everything he touches, including this very wine. They would know if the taster was being poisoned, unless…unless the poison didn't make them ill in any way. Would the taster even notice their powers were diminished? Or could an alchemist, an alchemist like Hermes, make a poison that would only affect the drinker's magic? Or even one that could only affect the light-born, so that the taster remained unaffected?

Could it be in the very cup I just drank from, the cup Zara is drinking from now?

I try to ignore the nausea that begins suddenly after I have the thought. *It's not poison*, I tell myself; *it's just anxiety.*

Unfortunately, telling yourself not to be anxious doesn't tend to do much for anxiety except amplify it.

After the rites have concluded, Cyrus stands at the altar to announce the hunt to the court. As always, he sounds vaguely annoyed to be delivering the message. "In consultation with the priests, we have selected a most excellent quarry for today's hunt. The griffin of the Red Cliffs, a creature revered by Sai for its brutality and power. By taking it down, we honor Sai and the champions he has chosen. Hunting group assignments are available on the board in the back. Chariots are waiting outside to take each group to the hunting grounds. May Sai bless this hunt and the hunters."

We're hunting a griffin? I thought we'd be after an alligator or a heron or something. I've never even seen a griffin outside of the pages of a book. I'm trying to remember which two animals it is—eagle and horse? Eagle and goat?—when Ronan approaches.

"I took some liberties with the hunting groups," he says, his hand grazing the small of my back in a way that makes me shiver. "I hope you don't mind."

"You've assigned me to Lord Cyrus's group then?"

He smirks. "Cyrus isn't that bad. He thinks I'm a complete imbecile compared to my father, but he does what I tell him."

Does he, though? Or could he be the poisoner?

I'm really understanding now what Ronan was saying about being unable to trust anyone. There are so many people here at court who have reason to act against him.

"You'll have to tell me what that feeling meant when we're alone later," he mutters before greeting Queen Claudia, who wants to wish him luck.

I wait for him by our assigned chariot with Taran, who has conveniently been placed in our group as well. There are three others in the party, who are in their own chariot just behind ours: Nona of House Alta, Ronan's aunt and current heir to the throne, Lucas, the second son of House Modesto, and a member of Ronan's Royal Guard named Rhodes that I haven't met yet.

"Keep an eye on him," says Ronan as he joins us at last. He glances at Lucas. "He was caught near my chambers this morning without cause."

"So you thought you'd bring him with us when we're all bearing deadly weapons?" I ask.

"Just another day in Selara," he replies with a shrug.

I get to see some of Selara today as the chariot passes through Faros, leaving the city walls and heading to the cliffs to the north where the griffin dwells. Beyond the reaches of Faros, there are only a few scattered structures amid the sprawling farmlands, where the little grain that Selara still grows is nearly ready to harvest. Herds of lazy cattle, goats, and sheep lounge in grassy fields under expansive blue skies. I envy them their naps—it seems a much more pleasant way to spend a late-summer day than hiding behind rocks, trying to kill something.

Civilization ends abruptly as we venture away from the life-giving River Mara. The fields give way to low, scrubby bushes and then empty patches of dusty land in shades of brown and grey. Then the chariot climbs hills that are low and gradual at first, like the barren desert we crossed when we arrived, but that become increasingly steep and jagged the further north we go. Before long, I hear the ocean again, crashing into the base of the Red Cliffs, which are appropriately named, somewhere to the east beyond sight.

We approach a small circle of tents on the hilltop. "The scouting party," explains Ronan as we exit the chariot. "They've been tracking the griffin."

"That seems like cheating." I've never been on a hunt like this before. My father took Adria and Seth before the war, but I was too young to join them. The only times I've been hunting were with Larus, who was teaching me to use my bow to bring down deer and small game. We were rarely successful, largely because I couldn't bring myself to hurt the animals. At the time, I thought I had Larus convinced that it was just because I had poor aim. But looking back, I'm certain he knew the truth.

"We'd be out here all month like them if they didn't do it," says Lady Nona. She's a tough-looking woman: leathery tan skin, greying brown hair, and the kind of lean build that says she's no stranger to these circumstances. She's a war survivor, one of the few from her generation. "I, for one, would rather sleep in a bed than a bunk."

The scouting party equips us with bows and arrows. When they hand me mine, they smile. "You're the one to beat, they say," one of them, a young servant girl, whispers to me.

I'm touched that she looks up to me, but unfortunately, she's wrong. I'm about as likely to kill the griffin as I am to kill anyone, which is to say not likely at all.

Not unless it tries to kill Ronan. Then I might be motivated.

Ronan, for his part, looks about as uncomfortable as I am. I wonder if this brings up memories of his father. He said they once hunted together on our lands.

We hear from the scouts that the griffin was last spotted half a mile or so northwest, but that since it can fly, it ranges quite a bit during the day. It tends to dive to the shore for fish in the afternoons, and since it's no longer mating season, it doesn't roost anywhere in particular.

There are twelve hunting parties, most of them around the same size as ours, made up of everyone in the court who wanted to attend, along with their guards and servants.

"Twelve parties and one griffin?" I ask. "Is that typical?"

"Griffins are solitary creatures at this time of year, but it will likely take more than one party to bring it down, unless someone makes a very good shot. They have a thick hide, and they're ferocious predators on their own. I wouldn't be surprised if we end up empty-handed," explains Ronan.

"What happens then?"

"We declare that Sai has protected the beast, which means it will live out its life and never be hunted again. And then we feast on pheasant or something and pretend it never happened."

Ronan takes the entire endeavor with about as much irreverence as I had expected from him, at least when he's speaking with me. He's much more effusive to the rest of the court, giving a stirring speech about Sai's champions and their noble cause in slaying the foul beast. From that, I glean that the creature is part eagle, part *lion*. I see now what he means about turning up empty handed. King of the beasts and king of the birds in one.

Ronan is pulled away to talk to some courtier or another, with his guards trailing behind, and he calls over his aunt to join him, leaving me alone with Lucas.

Lucas is around my age, maybe a few years older, with narrow blue eyes that are a bit too close together. He's lean and of average height, although he holds himself up higher, his jaw jutting upwards as he speaks. "You have them all fooled," he says.

I startle when I realize he's speaking to me. "Come again?"

"The king. His aunt. All of them. But I was there that night in the arena. You missed."

He says it with a high degree of confidence. I know I should walk away from him and tell Ronan what he said immediately, but I would like to know why he was hanging around Ronan's chambers, so I keep talking.

"If you believe that's the case, why tell me?"

"So that you know that I'm watching you. So that you know that if you try again, I'll be there."

Well, I guess that's good news for Ronan. It seems unlikely that Lucas is trying to act against him, unless he's telling me this now to throw me off his trail.

Which isn't a bad strategy, come to think of it.

This is *exhausting*. When I was thinking last night of how I wanted a life with Ronan, I wasn't thinking about this. Never knowing who your friends are. Having enemies lurking around every corner. Treating every interaction with suspicion, always looking for some secondary meaning in the things people say.

It's terrible.

I decide to leave it to Taran to keep an eye on Lucas. I can't deal with him today.

Most of the hunting parties head off in the northwest direction the scouts indicated, but Ronan doesn't want to go that way. I wonder if he picked up on a feeling from one of the scouts, or if he has another reason for avoiding the rest of the court.

We head over a ridge to the north and down a rocky path into a canyon. A narrow blue stream runs along the smooth stones at its bottom, meandering around bends out to meet the ocean. There are signs of griffin activity here: discarded fish bones, desiccated piles of droppings. Abandoned nests as big as our chariot.

Ronan examines these, trying to see if any are fresh. We march up and down the stream for nearly an hour with no sign of anything.

"We should head back to the hills," says Lucas, shifting the quiver on his back. "There's nothing out here."

"You can go," says Ronan. "Rhodes, go with him."

"Yes, sir."

"I'm with him," says Nona. "I think we all ought to go."

Ronan shakes his head at his aunt. "Not yet. But we'll meet you soon. Go ahead."

"Suit yourselves," she says with a curtsy and a meaningful glance at me.

Taran backs away a little as the others leave to give us some space.

"I thought they'd never leave," Ronan says once they're well out of earshot on the path out of the canyon.

"Did you bring us here on purpose so that they'd get bored and leave us alone?"

He winks.

I glance back at Taran. He's looking at a pebble near his foot as if it's very interesting, only glancing up on occasion to make sure Ronan is still safe. Poor man. I don't want to make him uncomfortable, but I'm not certain I can keep my hands off Ronan for long now that we're almost alone together.

I'm getting ready to reach for him when I hear the clatter of a small rock falling into the canyon.

"What was that?"

Ronan holds a finger to his lips. Taran, closer to the noise than we are, turns and draws his sword.

We creep along the canyon floor, the crunching sounds of our boots on stone suddenly amplified by our heightened awareness. When we get to Taran, Ronan places a hand on his shoulder, and we all three crouch down behind a large boulder.

There's a long silence, so long that Ronan laughs and begins to rise.

And then there's the unmistakable flap of great wings from fifty feet above us. I lean back in time to catch its enormous silhouette cross the sky.

Oh, gods. We're fucked.

Chapter Twenty-Six

The griffin stands before us, as beautiful and deadly as the cliffs it came from. Its head is that of an enormous brown eagle, with a curved beak and sharp golden eyes that track our every breath. Its feathered wings rest on the ground before it, talons flexing. Behind it, the golden tail of a lion swishes, the dark tuft of fur at the end moving so rapidly my eyes blur the motion.

It's at least twice as large as I was imagining. It's bigger than a horse, bigger than my father's destrier had been. Now I see why Ronan said we'd be lucky to take it down with a single party.

And all we have is half of one.

I can't help but think what a pity it would be to kill it. It's a majestic creature. What must it be like to see the world through its eyes? To soar above it, taking in a view so few get to see? I have an absurd notion that it would be fun to ride on its back. Maybe I can convince Ronan to spare it. We can scare it away so the others never find it.

Beside me, Ronan places a hand on Taran's shoulder to still him from reaching for his bow. He must have felt what I wanted. "Not yet," he says.

Then he begins to rise.

What the hell is he doing?

"You can't mean to approach it," says Taran. "If we have any shot, it's from back here."

"I can feel her," he says. Taran and I both turn to look at him.

"What?" we ask together.

"The griffin. I hardly ever feel animals. Just their fear, and rarely. But I can feel her. She's curious about us."

Oh, gods, he's gone insane. "Did you feel me wanting to ride it? I wasn't being serious. It was just a silly thought. You don't need to do this."

"Listen to her, sir. Listen to yourself. Do not go out there—"

Ronan ignores us. He rises, and the griffin scratches the ground with her talons.

Its talons. I do not believe he can tell that it's female.

Taran looks at me, and I look back at him, our bewildered faces mirrored. "You're the one who's supposed to protect him," I say to him.

"*Kronor, sotero,*" he says, a curse in the Orsan language, judging by his delivery.

Taran slowly stands to the side of Ronan.

"It's alright, girl," says Ronan, the absolute imbecile. He holds out his hand in front of him in a nonthreatening gesture.

The griffin scratches the ground again, huffing.

Ronan takes a step back to walk around the boulder, and I grab his wrist. "I will not let you die out there, and neither will Taran. If she attacks, we'll kill her."

Ronan tucks a strand of my hair back in place and kisses my cheek. It's so soft and familiar that I forget my worries for a moment. "Trust me," he says.

I do trust him, but I don't trust anyone or any*thing* else.

Which is a shocking realization that I'll need to come to terms with later, assuming I'm still alive to do so.

Ronan creeps slowly along the stream bank. He keeps his hands out in front of him, miles away from his weapons. Taran and I sink back down behind the rock. I don't draw my bow in case it frightens the griffin with Ronan so close to it, but I reach for my power, my shadows. I don't know if I can make them take form again, but eagles are active in daylight. I doubt griffins, with their eagle eyes, see well in the dark.

"I can make the water rush," says Taran, pointing to the stream below us. "If he stands on the shore, it might be enough to take her off her feet or to make her take flight."

Taran is water-born, then. That's unexpected. I'd been guessing fire, although his adaptable, patient nature should have given me a hint, I suppose.

We wait, watching as Ronan slowly approaches. At one point, she stirs and cuts a large scratch into the gravel that goes all the way to the sand. She looks ready to charge. "Wait!" Ronan calls back just as Taran starts to raise the water and I begin to lower the canyon into darkness.

The griffin stands still.

"She's fine, aren't you, girl? Just a little closer."

This may be the most anxious I've felt since I arrived in Selara. I'm losing my mind watching this man, this man I swore to kill and am now struggling to imagine living without, approach a beast that can take him out in one fell swoop.

My stomach is in my throat as he closes the final feet between him and the deadly creature. She backs away suddenly, maybe five feet back, and lets out a loud, low screech.

"Ronan!" I cry. "Just let her go. We'll tell the others we didn't find her. You don't need to do this for me. She's scared."

Godsdammit, I want him to get back here. Maybe I could pull him back with my shadows.

Ronan bends low, showing her his neck. "She's scared, but she wants me to approach her. Trust me, Sylvie."

I shake my head, my heart pounding in my ears, as he reaches for the griffin. I can barely look. Maybe he'll get lucky and she'll only take his hand off. He could live without a hand if he could heal himself with his magic.

When I found out I was meant to kill Ronan, I imagined it would be a difficult undertaking. A dangerous game of cat and mouse, racing to keep one step ahead of him, searching high and low for a weakness, for any opportunity to strike.

If I'd known he would voluntarily put himself in situations in which he could be killed repeatedly, even against my strongest urging, I wouldn't have worried so much.

Except that now I no longer want him to die, and he's making it very difficult to stop him from doing so.

The griffin inches closer. She stalks forward with feline grace, her body lowered near to the ground in position to strike.

If he dies right now, I'm going to kill him.

The griffin waits a couple of feet from Ronan, as still as a statue. He flexes his hand in her direction in invitation.

And then, to my absolute astonishment, she lifts her head forward to meet his hand.

"Hello, sweet girl," he says as he lightly brushes her feathers. "I'm Ronan."

Taran and I look at each other in disbelief. He's talking to a damn monster.

"It's alright," he calls back. "She's calm now." He looks at her again. "Can they approach you? They're my friends."

Who is this man? This is supposed to be the tyrant ruling with an iron fist. The man who starved Nithyria, who stole our lands and ground us down to nothing as punishment for the war.

How did I ever believe that? How does *anyone* believe that?

"Come on," he calls. "I've made a friend."

The griffin paces around Ronan, sniffing at him and nudging at his clothes. I'm not as certain as he is that she isn't trying to find which parts of him to tear apart first, but I'll admit that there is a certain level of curiosity in her intelligent eyes.

"Nope," says Taran. "I'm fine right here."

"Sylvie?"

I hesitate. I know he's done this for me because I thought about riding her. And, I admit, there's a part of me that's curious. I wonder if anyone has ever ridden a griffin before. I can't remember reading about it. I wonder if anyone ever even thought to try.

Ronan's eyes are filled with childlike glee. Kerensa save me, he's adorable. He's just so excited, and he did it for me. I can't resist him.

This is what I want my life to be like, I realize as I approach him. Adventure, a little danger, a lot of excitement, and the feeling I get when I see him smile.

"Come on," he says. "She likes you."

I swear if this man is delusional, I'll—

"Oh," I say as she nudges my shoulder with her head. It's feathery but firm, a powerful push that nearly knocks me off my balance.

"See?" says Ronan. He catches me by the waist with one hand and pets the griffin's eagle head with the other.

"Very good," yells Taran from behind the rocks. "Can we go now?"

The griffin lowers herself so that her hindquarters, the lion bits, are on the ground.

"What is she doing?" I ask.

Ronan smiles in response. "Didn't you say you wanted to see the world?"

"No!" shouts Taran, understanding what Ronan is doing before I do. He cautiously approaches us, his sense of duty overwhelming his fear. "I'm sworn to protect you. I can't let you do this."

I really want to, but I'm terrified. It wouldn't be like riding a horse. Griffins *fly*. People don't fly. Not even the wind-born can fly. We're just too heavy for it.

"She wants us to," says Ronan, already moving to her side and getting ready to put me on her.

The sensible thing to do would be to turn around and head back to the palace, leaving the griffin to her griffin business. The main problem with that is that I *do* want to see the world from the sky. I've thought about it since I was a child climbing the castle walls. Since I pretended I was an acrobat, soaring and tumbling through the air.

And I know Ronan knows it.

"Taran, tell the others where we've gone. Tell them the hunt is off. Tell them something like Kerensa appeared before me and asked me to spare the animal, and that out of love for her, Sai agreed they should hunt some fallow deer on the way back to the palace. Or make up something better, I don't care."

Taran stops, hand furiously rubbing his tattooed neck. It's a direct order from his king, but I can tell by his continued defiance that this wouldn't be the first time Taran had to save Ronan from himself. "If you die—"

"We won't die," says Ronan. "She won't let us. I know I sound insane, as usual, but you've learned to trust me. I'm right, at least half of the time."

Taran remains unconvinced.

"At least a third of the time? Look. If you won't believe me because of me, believe me because of her. I won't let anything happen to her."

Me. He won't let anything happen to me.

Taran nods, shoots me a look that says *that's what you get for encouraging him*, shakes his head, and walks away.

"Ready?" says Ronan.

I nod, trembling. My body shakes as he helps me onto the griffin's back. It feels a bit like riding a horse bareback, something I've only done once or twice when I had to share a horse with my sister. But her body runs hotter than a horse's, and the feel of her long feathers beneath my hands as I grip her large neck is strange and somewhat alarming.

Ronan mounts the griffin behind me, her wings making it a tight fit. He wraps his hands slowly, luxuriously around my waist as he presses his body against mine.

"Hold on tight," I say. My heart nearly explodes out of my chest from terror and excitement as the griffin takes to her feet.

The great eagle wings spread behind us and begin to flap.

Then, with a stomach-turning lurch, she launches into the air.

I scream involuntarily as the canyon floor recedes beneath us. I grip her neck, hoping I'm not hurting her, hoping Ronan doesn't slip from her back as she soars through the valley.

Ronan laughs and cries out in joy as we come out of the canyon.

Selara lies before us. It's a view no one has ever seen before, and it takes my breath away. Even those that have climbed to the top of Faros's tallest towers and the highest cliffs have never been this high. From up here, I can see how unforgiving the land truly is. The Serath Desert stretches on seemingly endlessly, the vast sand dunes reduced to mere ripples at this height, like ridges on a great golden feather. In the far, far distance the Palador Mountains rise like a mirage, their craggy, forested peaks barely a silhouette against the sun-drenched sky.

The griffin flies towards the snaking River Mara, the glittering blue jewel flanked with strips of green. Faros and the cities along its banks reduce to dusty patches of brown amid the green, almost indistinguishable from the desert, only the temples rising in shining white marble above the dust.

It's shocking how small the palace seems from up here. How tiny and fragile all of Selara seems, more than a million people steps away from certain death at all times.

I wonder how small Nithyria would seem from up here if we could see beyond the mountains. I imagine it must look like the land swallowed us up, our miniscule structures nearly invisible beneath the dense canopy of the forest.

A gust of wind sends the griffin tumbling suddenly, her course veering sharply east towards the sea. My legs grip, but I feel Ronan slide behind me.

"Hold on!" I cry into the wind. My hair whips into my face like a lash as I feel Ronan scramble to keep his grip on my waist.

The griffin must feel his struggle because she fights against the wind, trying to right herself, and for a moment, he manages to regain his balance.

But then another gust comes, even more violent than the first. The griffin dives, looking for a place to land amid the cliffs. I cling to her neck, grabbing Ronan's arm and trying to make him do the same, but I feel one of his legs fly up behind me as he loses his seat on her shoulders.

"No!" I shout, and I feel my power pressing into my palms. My shadows. I can feel them begging to be released.

I let them go with an anguished cry. They spill out from somewhere deep within me, somewhere vulnerable and full of terror.

They don't envelop us in darkness. Instead, they reach around us with whirring tendrils, binding us to the griffin.

They wrap around Ronan's hips and push him down onto the griffin's shoulders and forward against my body.

He wraps his grateful arms around me and around the griffin's neck as her wings slow, the edge of a cliff overlooking the sea beneath us. She lowers us the final stretch deliberately, touching down with a softness that must be for our benefit.

My arms are numb when I pull them from her neck. The tendrils of shadow slowly retract, releasing us from their hold.

"Amazing," murmurs Ronan, his mouth against my shoulder. I can feel the sweat on his skin, the thrashing beat of his heart against my back as he relaxes his grip.

He dismounts first then helps me down. We're on a high cliff facing southeast, with the sea in front of us and to our left and Faros to our right.

Once we're on solid ground, he takes me into his arms.

I jump up, laughing as my legs wrap around his waist. He laughs too, a relieved, shaking laugh that I feel all the way in my core as I hold him as tight as I can.

"See? We didn't die," he says, kissing my forehead firmly, like it's the solid ground neither of us appreciated until this very moment.

"That was insane," I say, my voice trembling.

Ronan slowly lowers me down to look at me. "But did you enjoy it?"

I nod, the energy flowing in my veins making it difficult to find the words. "A lot, up until the point you nearly died."

"You saved me again," he says, his hands still on my hips. "Although I don't think she would have let me fall."

The griffin is peering over the side of the cliff at the ocean below. She certainly seemed to be trying to help us. Maybe she really is as intelligent as Ronan believes.

"What's she doing?" I ask, realizing that I trust him to interpret her feelings.

"Getting ready to hunt, I think. Shall we watch?"

I worry for a moment about whether she will return to carry us back—or how we're even going to get her to carry us back, considering our communication with her is one-way—but when she dives to the crashing waves below, she returns with a large fish in her lion's paws before I can even finish the thought.

She looks at us, and I could swear she's offering us some. "No, thanks," I say. I'm getting a bit hungry, but not enough for raw fish.

"See? She's trying to take care of us. I know you can't feel her, but you can tell, can't you?"

He does seem right about her, I have to admit. Maybe it truly was Kerensa's hand that led her to us instead of to any of the others, all of whom would have taken her life instead.

"I'm glad it was us," I say. She begins to tear into the fish, and Ronan leads me to a boulder far enough back from the cliff's edge that I feel comfortable taking a seat on it.

We look out together at the sea for a long moment, listening to the waves crash beneath us, the shoreline invisible beneath the cliffs.

"I missed the ocean," I say.

"From when you lived in Pyka?"

"Yes. But it was different there. There are cliffs like these, but they're covered in grass and moss. And the sand is dark."

He looks wistfully out at the water, not meeting my gaze. "I remember. We visited a few times before the war. You were never there. I remember thinking they made you up." He gives me a slight smile.

"They sent me away a lot." While they were planning the war, although I don't say that part out loud. "To my aunt's in Kalla, mostly. It was like a second home to me. It wasn't that hard for me to leave Pyka. All the memories…most of them of empty rooms. Of closed doors and waiting. Of training. I think what I miss the most isn't what happened there, but what didn't. What could've, if things had been different. Does that make sense?"

He looks at me with deep affection. "Yes. Yes, it does."

"I wish I had met you then," I admit. "It would have saved me a lot of grief."

"How so?"

I weigh what to tell him. I know I want to stop the plan Adria and Seth have put in motion, but if I tell Ronan about it, he'll have no choice but to arrest them. They'll likely be executed for what they've done, and Larus and Felix and everyone else involved as well.

But there's a chance I can stop it from happening. They need the Third Navy's ships to blockade the harbor, and Larus has control of some of those. There will still be time when he returns to stop them from coming. From Seth's latest message, his forces won't be ready until after the end of the Great Festival, which is still weeks away. All I need to do is get Larus on my side.

And he's always been on my side.

"I've spent the past few years blaming you for everything," I say. That's true enough. "If I'd met you before, maybe things would have been different."

"I doubt it," he says with a humorless laugh. "*I* was different then."

"In what way?"

"I was arrogant. Angry. I felt like the world belonged to me, that it owed me something."

"Angry? At what?"

"The world. My father. The last time we came to Pyka, it was shortly after my mother died. I was sixteen. You would've been—what, nine? Ten? It was a year before the war started."

"Ten. Your mother died of cancer?" Ronan has never spoken about Queen Calia to me before. I think of what Stella told me about how he tried to keep her memory alive after her death.

"Yes," he says, his voice strained. "The visit was tense. It was easy to see why, later. But at the time, I thought I'd made it that way. I was so angry. My magic had settled, but it wasn't enough to save her. There are some things beyond even light magic to heal."

I can see the anger in him still, in the tension of his shoulders. I touch one of them, and he twitches reflexively. "Sorry," he says, his hand brushing mine.

My heart aches for him. Ronan, just sixteen, blaming himself for not being able to save his mother. "You know it wasn't your fault, right? You know that now."

"Yes, I know that now. But I didn't then. I had so much rage in me."

"I did, too," I admit. "Even then, when I was a child. And much more later."

"At my father? At me?"

"Among other things. At my parents for abandoning me, for choosing war over their child. At my siblings for going with them."

He nods and looks into the distance again. The sun is lowering in the sky behind us, bringing a golden tinge to the light as it meets the water. We should be heading back soon. But there's something else I've been wanting to ask him.

"What drew you to me in the beginning?" I ask. He'd said he'd felt me before he even came into the room the first time. That he'd known me even then. What did he feel?

"Loneliness. Not mine, yours."

I turn to look at him. He meets my eye this time, and it's like he sees right through me. Right through whatever walls I've tried to build, right down to the core of who I am.

"I could feel the way you felt standing there with your family. With them, but apart from them. The way you were trying so desperately hard to be something that you're just not. The fear of them finding out. And the deep, heartbreaking knowledge that no one will ever truly understand you or love you for who you are. I recognized the feeling because I've felt it every single day since your father died."

Since he killed him. I freeze, my breathing shallow. We've never spoken about that day, about what happened out there on that cliff.

I realize I want to know. I *need* to know. I can't be with him without knowing. "Would you tell me about it? The duel?"

He turns to me but doesn't reach for me. "Are you sure? I've been wanting to tell you the truth, but…it's going to be hard to hear."

My mouth runs dry. My vision narrows to his face. "What truth?"

He rubs his hand through his wind-blown hair, trying to find the right words.

"What truth, Ronan?" I ask, my body so tense I feel lightheaded.

"I'm sure you heard what led up to it. The duel. Our armies had been at a stalemate for a week. We'd lost so many already—we were down to the dregs after more than four years of war. Half of my legion were green. The horses were gone. The city had been under siege for two years, and it looked like my campaign to end it all in the field was going to be a 'success': everyone would be dead by the end of it. Everyone on both sides. Your father sent a message that if I faced him in single combat, he'd honor the result."

I nod, slowly. This I knew.

"It was…" Ronan stands and turns around towards the setting sun. "Just over there somewhere." He points to the west, near where we'd been ambushed on our way to Faros. "We'd kept your soldiers to the sand—the desert. I could have starved him out, eventually. We had supplies coming in from the Mara, although not many of them, and he had nothing but blighted fields and desert behind him. But I was arrogant, and I was tired, and I thought it could all be over if I could just beat someone three decades my senior. I thought it was a joke. I thought he was a fool to ask."

"My father was an excellent swordsman," I say. "And an honorable man."

"Both of those things I knew, but I thought I was better."

"And you were." Clearly, that must have been the case. I want to listen to him, but I'm anxious to know what truth he's been concealing.

"Barely," he says. "But yes, I had him. A fight to the death isn't like the tournament. It's a quick and bloody thing. Every strike may be your last. You don't make a single move unless you're certain it's safe. Your father knew this. We clashed a dozen times before he made contact." He lifts his shirt to show me the long scar at his side I'd noticed when he practiced with me. "I didn't let the healers near it. I wanted the reminder."

"Why?"

"Because the next moment, everything changed for me. It's the line between what I was and what I am."

He sits back down on the boulder, keeping a bit of distance between us. "I spent my entire life believing my father was a god, and that I would be a god once he was gone. But when he died—"

"When my father killed him." On the battlefield, in a bloody, brutal defeat with a spear just a few months earlier.

"When your father killed him, I didn't feel any different. I didn't feel like a god. I felt like a boy, a broken little boy that wanted his dad back. And then, just like with my mother, I got angry. But this time, it wasn't the world I was angry at."

"It was my father."

He nods. "I spent days and nights fantasizing about revenge. I thought of one thousand different ways to kill him. It was sick. I could think of almost nothing else. Every time I ran my sword through someone, it was his face I saw. Every time my light hit its mark, I imagined the life fading from his eyes. It consumed me. And when he hit my side, I saw it all fading away from me. But there was an opening in his attack. A chance to take out his legs, and I took it. It brought him to his knees."

I nearly vomit thinking of it. I want to hit Ronan for telling me, to pound my fist into his chest and tell him to stop.

But there's a part of me that wants to hear this. To know what happened, even if it kills me.

"He knelt there on the ground in front of me, and it was over. I'd won. I was bleeding but not dying. He was unable to stand. All I had to do was raise my sword and end his life, and it would all be over."

He turns and looks me in the eye. "But I couldn't. I couldn't do it."

"What?" I can barely hear him over the pounding of my heart.

"Your father died that day, Sylvie, but not at my hand. I stood there in front of him, thinking of my righteous victory, thinking of the satisfaction I would finally have to see him dead on the ground, the end of the war, the triumph of my revenge, and what I felt was…nothing. It's like a lever flipped. All that fury, that need for justice, it just vanished. There was something about him there on the ground, something about the way his grey hair fell from his helmet, something painfully human about him. I saw the real man and not the version I had created in my mind. And I knew that killing the man wouldn't give me what I wanted. It wouldn't give me my father back. It wouldn't ease my pain. I wish I could say I thought of you in that moment, but I didn't. I didn't even consider what it would have done to you. I didn't consider what my people needed from me either, how much they'd suffered and how much they deserved an end to the fighting. I'd killed hundreds by then, thousands maybe, but this one man I couldn't kill."

There are tears in my eyes. The real man, not the version in his head. The man, not the monster. It was what I thought of Ronan when we first met. I wonder if he could feel it then. If it was part of what drew him to me. "What happened to him?" I ask, my voice trembling.

Ronan shakes his head slowly, sighing. "He told me to finish it. To finish it, or he would. That he'd never stop fighting for Nithyria. That if I wanted an end to this, I had to kill him. I argued with him. I told him to surrender, to lay down his sword, and we'd end the war together. We could negotiate. He laughed at me. He didn't believe me, and I couldn't blame him for it. He kept telling me to fight him. I could smell the smoke on his breath, feel the heat rising off of him. He was too honorable to use magic to end our duel, but he was so angry with me for denying him his warrior's death that I thought it might rise out of him on his own like a child. When I refused again, he picked up his sword."

His voice chokes on the words. "And still I couldn't do it. I was so lost, so broken in that moment without my vengeance to guide me. I was such an empty shell of a person that I wanted him to end me instead. It was Taran, in the end, that saved me."

"Taran?"

"He was my second. It was only the four of us: your father, his General Sullius, myself, and Taran. Just us four on those rocks. When I refused to act, Taran rose and defended me. He stabbed your father in the back as he reached out to strike me. Then he fought the general too, all while I stood there and did nothing. I was nothing. Beyond nothing."

"You forfeited the duel," I say. Seconds aren't allowed to step in after the duel begins. It's dishonorable. "Which means that you didn't win. Which means…"

"That Adria has a claim to the throne."

The words hang there in the air between us like poison. Taran, sweet, kind Taran, a man I'd defended to Larus, had killed my father, not Ronan. And they'd lied about it, killing my father's second to cover the lie.

We had won the war. Or we should have, there and then.

But Ronan *had* defeated my father. It was his mercy that cost him the victory.

I don't know how to feel. On the one hand, Nithyria should have its independence. There are rules of engagement, and Ronan and Taran broke them. They dishonored the arrangement my father made with them, and in doing so, Ronan forfeited the crown.

But on the other hand, he was trying to spare my father's life. And I can't blame him for that. Whatever stayed his hand, I can't blame him for it. I know now what it takes to take a life. I know it isn't easy. And part of me feels immensely relieved that he wasn't the one to do it. He's still the reason my father is dead, but he didn't die at Ronan's hand. I don't know why that matters to me, but it does in some visceral way.

But either way, I know one thing for certain: Adria can't be queen. Not now. Not knowing what I know about who she is and what she would do to get the crown. What I know she'd do once she had it.

"I need some time to think," I say to him.

"I understand. No one knows, apart from Taran. Not even Quinn."

I nod. "I won't tell anyone."

"I know."

Why did he tell me? He could have lied to me. He could have refused to tell me about it at all. Instead, he told me this secret, a secret that could cost him everything. Why?

"Because I trust you," he says without me even asking the question. "Because I trust you more than I even trust myself."

He closes the space between us. "And because I want to be with you." He doesn't take my hand, but I can feel the phantom touch of the gesture that I know he wants to make. "And I can't be with you and keep secrets from you. So this is me. This is everything I've kept hidden from the world. It's up to you to decide what you want to do with it."

What I want to do with it.

I could use his words to end his reign, or I could carry them with me to my grave after spending a lifetime at his side.

The choice is mine. The power is mine.

But I don't feel powerful.

What I feel is…

I don't know. I don't know what to feel.

"Take me back, please," I say, and he nods without another word.

Chapter Twenty-Seven

He takes me back to the palace on the griffin, talking to her and tugging on her feathers like he's guiding a horse.

Which works, shockingly enough. We don't speak for the ride, but I know he can feel my awe in spite of everything as we pass through the darkening sky. As we glide over Faros, sparkling with candlelight. As we take in another view no one has ever seen before.

I want to be with you, he said. The words echo in my mind.

My desire for him has not waned. If anything, I feel it more than ever knowing what happened out there with my father. The way he felt when confronted with the reality of killing him. The knowledge of what he needed to do, what was best for his people, and his inability to do it. It's exactly how I feel when I look at him.

I'm also grateful to him for trying to show Father mercy even if he wouldn't accept it. He gave Father a choice, and Father chose to fight rather than to return to us. To return to me. I don't care about whatever nonsense code of honor was broken. If showing mercy is dishonorable, then what's the good in honor?

But Ronan had nothing left when he stood on that cliff. He had no siblings; both of his parents were gone. I have people I still care about despite everything terrible they've done, people who will die if I give them up. If I can't find a way to stop them.

I want to be with Ronan, too. I know it, as much as it terrifies me to admit it. But I need to take some time to think, to find a way to have both him and my family.

"Will you keep her?" I ask him as we dismount on his balcony.

"If she'll let me," he says, and I wonder if he's talking about the griffin.

In the morning, Adria wakes me early to hear what happened during the hunt. Apparently, our change of plans regarding the griffin caused quite a controversy.

"I thought Cornelius was going to shoot one of us instead," she says. "You know him. Big guy from House Gallus."

I shake my head.

"With the weird little beard?"

"Oh, sure," I say. I know exactly who she's talking about now. "What did he do?"

"He tried to snap his bow in half, but it didn't break. So he threw it down and stomped on it. You should have seen it. A full-blown tantrum."

Another enemy made. Ronan has a talent for it, that's for sure.

Speaking of enemies, there's something I've been meaning to ask her. "Hey, have you seen Hermes around? I've had this headache that keeps coming back. I wanted to ask him about an elixir."

The lie comes to my lips so easily, I wonder if there is something to my shadow-born nature. Maybe the reality is that I'm quite good at lying, even lying not by omission, when I feel justified in doing so.

"No, I haven't seen him in a while, actually. He's barely been around since we got here."

I take it from her casual tone that she doesn't know what Hermes is involved with. Or she's lying to me about it, which is always a possibility around here.

I don't tell her about our theory that he's somehow involved with the missing shadow-born. She's never brought it up again after that time in the arena, and I no longer trust her enough to risk exposing something to her that could help her, if she is involved in some way.

I part with her on the way to breakfast, taking a detour to the bathing caves. By the time I arrive in the dining hall after my bath, she's already on her way out with Titus of all people following behind her.

I should have warned him about her. Gods, she'll eat him alive.

I meet Ronan's eyes the moment I walk in the room, and it sends my pulse racing again. He has such an effect on me even from such a great distance. I look at him for a long moment, and then I take a seat at my usual table.

He goes back to his conversation with Cyrus, and I turn to my plate, trying not to look up again.

"He's gone and fucked it, hasn't he?" Quinn saunters over with a steaming mug in hand. She takes a seat beside me without invitation and puts her hand on my shoulder.

"No, I—I don't know what you—"

"Oh, yeah, I thought so. He's been moping around all morning. What did he do? One near-death experience too many?"

"No," I say. "I actually enjoyed the griffin ride."

She nods in appreciation. "A bit of a thrill-seeker, are you? I like that. I'm really jealous, actually. We saw you from the ground. It pissed a lot of people off, but it looked like it was worth it."

"It was," I say. I'm not sure how much or what to say to Quinn about what happened with Ronan. We aren't friends, and he told me she doesn't know the truth of what happened.

But without Larus around, it would be nice to have *someone* to talk to, even just a little.

"Did he confess his undying love or something? Too much too fast?"

I nearly spit out the grapefruit I'm chewing. "Does he do that often?"

"Hardly," she says with a snort. "He never lets anyone get this close. It's probably the only reason why he's still alive. But it seems like the kind of thing he might do with you."

I take a sip of tea, trying to keep my hand from shaking at hearing that. "It wasn't that." I know I should say more, but I'm struggling to think of a good lie. Instead, I turn the question on her. "Have you ever been in love?"

"A few times," she says with half a smile. "You see that girl over there, the one with the baby?" She points to a woman around her age with dark hair holding a chubby little infant in her arms, trying to get him to drink something from a mug. "She ripped my heart out of my chest. I cursed Kerensa for about two years before I could stand to be in the same room as her."

"What happened?" I ask.

"She married—where is he? Oh, there he is. That guy." She points to a large man with a weird little beard that doesn't cover his chin. Cornelius, the man who'd lost his shit when the hunt was called off.

"Adria said he's an asshole."

"He is. But he'll inherit the lands and the title, and I never will."

"I know the feeling," I say. We're both the youngest children in our families.

"Listen, you don't have to tell me," she says. "But judging by the way you two are looking at each other, it's not over for good. Tell me what I can do to help. Do you want to make him jealous?"

"No!" I say a bit too forcefully. "No. I agree with you. It's not over. I just...I just need a bit of time to think."

"A distraction then," she says, pointing to me with her pastry, her mouth half full. "The good news is the best festival is about to start."

"I thought you'd be more into the Festival of Sport than the Arts, to be honest."

"Are you kidding? This is the *beauty* festival. Have you seen the dancers? The acrobats? The theatre folks in their skimpy little costumes?"

I smile. "I do like music. I was thinking about joining the court band—"

"Oh hell no. No, Sylvie." She looks at me like I'm insane for suggesting it. "That's not for you. It's all old people and quiet kids obsessed with patriotic songs. If you want to play, there's a music competition that should be fun."

"I don't want to play on my own, though."

"Getting sick of the attention?"

"Yes, actually."

"Look, participating is fun and all, but it's far more fun to just watch. Come on. Ronan is about to kick the whole thing off in the throne room. Then we can make a plan. You can at least stand to be in the room with him. That's better than I could manage."

I wasn't planning to go to Ronan's announcement of the Festival of Arts, but I let Quinn drag me along with her. Honestly, it feels good to have someone else decide what to do. And I'm sure I'll appreciate the distraction, right after I watch the man I'm deeply conflicted about talk to his court like nothing is happening between us.

Ronan takes his time getting to the throne room to make the formal announcement. They've brought in benches this time since the room will be used for some of the performances, so at least we get to sit while we wait.

When Quinn and I take seats in the front row—at her insistence, though off to the side at mine—Zara comes over to join us. I realize I didn't have a chance to mention my suspicions about poison to Ronan yet, and doing so now is going to be awkward.

Great.

"I heard you had quite the encounter with a rare animal last evening," she says to me. I'm not surprised this news has reached her since it seems like nothing stays quiet for long in this palace. "I asked Ronan if we could collect some of its feathers. Not many, of course. But griffins are rarely encountered, and there could be much to learn from them."

"Good luck," I tell her. "He's pretty attached to her."

"He didn't seem fond of the idea. I should have asked you first, it seems."

When Zara looks away, Quinn gives me a look I can't fully interpret. It seems like she doesn't want me to tell Zara that something is going on between Ronan and me. Does she suspect something too? Or did Ronan tell her about Hermes, and that's made her suspicious about all the alchemists, like I am?

I don't get time to give it much thought because Ronan arrives then, and we all get on our feet to greet him. I'm reminded of the last time we were in this room when I watched someone die right beside me.

When I watched Taran kill him. Just as he'd killed my father.

Taran enters behind the king. His face is red, from embarrassment or exertion, I can't say. It's such a kind face. The Taran that killed the man beside me took no pleasure in it. His face was emotionless as he sliced through the man's heart.

Was it the same when my father died?

We take our seats again as Ronan sits on the throne. He's wearing his crown again today, along with a somewhat nicer tunic than I've seen him wear before. It's the same black he prefers, but there's a sheen to it. A subtle embroidery in a floral pattern, to honor Kerensa, no doubt.

"Before we begin today, let me first address the outcome of yesterday's hunt. While we sought to give a final honor to Sai, it was Kerensa, our breathtaking goddess of Love, Beauty, and Voyages, that stayed my hand. It seemed that she could not wait even one more day for the beginning of her festival, and so while I'm only just announcing it to you, I feel the Festival of Arts has already begun."

There's some scattered applause. Letting the griffin live was a very unpopular decision, judging by the response. And he did it for me. I imagine the room isn't feeling as kindly to me as they were a couple of nights ago.

Ronan continues to announce the various competitions, performances, and galleries where the festival will be taking place over the next few weeks, but my attention lapses quickly. Quinn is hanging on his every word, despite likely having heard it all before, and I'm content to let her decide what we'll attend.

My mind is in the antechamber. I know it should be on what Ronan told me last night, but I'm finding it difficult to work through. I want to lean into my feelings of relief at finding out my father didn't die at Ronan's hand, but what it means for Adria—what it means for Nithyria—haunts me. We could have had our independence. He could have given it to us there, but he chose not to.

And I know he says it was out of necessity, that our kingdoms need each other, but was it really his choice to make?

Although he did give my father the opportunity to work it out with him, and he declined, at least according to what Ronan told me.

Ronan could have lied about that. But to what end? What he told me wasn't flattering. It didn't justify his actions or put him in a good light.

It's too much to think about. And so I keep drifting back to the other side of the door, back to where Ronan kissed me—

A wave of heat flashes over me. It's sudden and terribly strong. It's—passion. Excitement. And it isn't just mental, it's physical. I feel it in the warmth on my neck. The peaks of my nipples beneath my dress. A slickness between my legs.

"—the fourth week. Then, the final show—" Ronan stops mid-sentence, leaning forward suddenly. His skin flushes red.

"Sir?" asks Taran, approaching the throne.

Ronan looks at me. What the fuck is happening?

Whatever is happening to me, it looks like it's happening to him too. He shifts in his seat, gripping the armrests with his hands.

"Sir, are you alright?"

"I'm fine," says Ronan through his teeth. "I'm fine," he repeats, his voice leveling out.

The flush leaves my body as quickly as it came on. I breathe heavily, suddenly dizzy from whatever caused my blood to change its flow so quickly. Poison?

"What the hell?" whispers Quinn, looking at me. "Are you okay?"

"I don't know," I say. If it were poison, it seems like it wouldn't have gotten better. Magic of some kind then, maybe?

Ronan shakes his head and resumes his speech as if nothing had happened. There are a couple of murmurs in the crowd, but no one dares say anything.

At the end, when we all rise for his exit, I feel it again.

"It's both of you," says Quinn, looking between where I put my hand down on the bench to steady myself and where Ronan has done the same on the throne. "Come on," she says, taking me by the arm and marching me towards him. "Zara?"

"What's going on?" asks Zara.

"Something with these two. We may need your help."

"Quinn, I don't think—" Fuck, I can hardly speak, it's so strong. But I'm not about to say anything in front of everyone. Not with the way it's making me feel. It's mortifying.

I need to talk to Ronan alone.

"Out," says Ronan when we enter the antechamber. "Not you," he says to me.

"Something is wrong with them," says Quinn, ignoring him. "They need a healer. Zara, could you take a look?"

"Of course," she says.

I'm extremely grateful that Zara doesn't share Ronan's power at this moment.

"Don't touch her," says Ronan, but Zara ignores him too, and we're both overcome by another wave of whatever this is before he can push her away from me.

"Her face is flushed. Her heart rate and breathing are fast. What did you eat? It could be an allergy you share."

"It's not a fucking allergy," says Ronan. "It's my magic. We're fine. Everyone out except Sylvie. *Now.*"

I've never heard his tone so severe. It does the trick though— despite their concerns, everyone leaves us alone in the antechamber.

The moment they're gone, it hits again. Gods, it's like he's actively kissing me even though we're across the room from each other. My entire body is pulsing with heat and energy. And primal, desperate need.

I rush over to him, but he holds his hands up to stop me. "Wait. Wait," he says, catching his breath. "Give it a second. It'll pass. I can do this."

"What's going on?" I ask once my head finally clears. "Are you doing this somehow?"

"I think so," he admits. "I'm sorry. I don't know how it's happening, not exactly. But I think it's to do with you being able to feel me. Whether I'm projecting my power or it's something in yours, I don't know. But I think—"

He stops and looks around the room. "No mirrors or looking glasses in here. There's one in my chambers—"

Fuck, this is the worst wave yet. I don't merely feel like I'm kissing him, I feel like I'm in bed with him. My body is *aching*. I'm so wet, I'm glad I'm standing. It would have pooled beneath my dress if I was still sitting down.

"Not there," he says, forcefully shaking something out of his head. "Have you ever held up a mirror to another mirror?"

"Sure," I say. My servants do it to show me the back of my hair sometimes.

"Do you know how it looks like it goes on forever? Repeating over and over again, into infinity?"

"Yes…"

"It's like that, I think, only when we're feeling the same thing at the same time. You feel it, and I feel you feeling it. And you feel me feeling you feeling it. And I feel you feeling me feeling you feeling it. And so on."

"Oh, gods," I say. "I was just thinking about yesterday, when we were in here—"

And there it is again. I reach for him this time, and he comes extremely close to taking me in his arms—

"No," he says, taking a step back from me. "As much as I want to, and gods, *I want to*, no. I felt you this morning. Your uncertainty, your indecision. I don't want you to do something you'll regret."

I close my eyes, trying to focus on his words and not the pull of his body. "I know I want this too. It's just…everything else…"

"I know," he says.

"Perhaps we should spend a bit of time apart. Just to keep things…clearer."

His face falls, and I can feel the pain of his disappointment, his longing—our joint disappointment, our joint longing—reverberate between us. It's sudden and poignant and heartbreakingly sad.

"Fuck," I say.

"Fuck," he agrees.

I don't want to leave, and he doesn't want me to go. But the echoing desire to stay is exactly why I must leave him.

I can never work out what I need to do with our feelings consuming my every thought, even if they weren't being heightened by each other.

"Sylvie?" he asks when I'm at the door.

"Yes?"

He doesn't say anything else, but I feel something deep pass between us. Something I don't dare name.

I nod once, and I open the door.

Chapter Twenty-Eight

Quinn packs my days and nights with festival events and parties, carefully avoiding anywhere Ronan is meant to be.

We take in galleries of vibrant paintings and impressive sculptures inspired by the gods, concerts by grand orchestras and small folk bands and everything in between, plays and street acts and dancing troupes, and, my favorite of all, sky-high performances by acrobats in the arena, where wind-born use their powers to send the ropes and ribbons flying in death-defying feats that make me long to be back on the griffin, soaring through the air.

That make me long to be back with Ronan.

I see him only once in days after the griffin ride, when he approaches me in the dining hall to let me know that the city guard has searched the Alchemists' Guild and nearby areas in search of our missing alchemist (and the missing shadow-born, although he doesn't mention that due to prying ears) without success. The disappearance of Hermes goes largely unnoticed by the rest of the court, just as the disappearance of the shadow-born has gone unnoticed in Faros.

We make it through the conversation without any unwanted re-verberations of feeling, but I don't make it through the rest of the day that follows without thinking about him endlessly. Without wondering what he's doing, what he's seeing, what he's thinking of.

And then, that night, I dream of him. We're back on the griffin, this time flying over Nithyria. We sail on a cold breeze over Pyka, over the home I once knew. The beaches of black sand. The waves crashing on moss-covered stone, icy spray nipping at our heels as we dive low. It's freezing, but Ronan is warm behind me.

The griffin soars into dusky skies as the sliver of a moon rises over the mountains. Ronan kisses my neck. The heat of his lips on my frozen skin ignites me. I turn to give him my lips, to taste him, but I see movement far below on the castle walls.

By the time I hear the shot, it's too late. An enormous arrow strikes the griffin in its side. In her panic, she nearly throws us from her back, my shadows the only thing keeping us anchored there. I scream as another arrow hits its target. The griffin dives for the tree line, but one of her wings is too injured to open. She tumbles from the sky, crashing through the branches, sending Ronan and me falling as I try desperately to stop us, to grab at something with my shadow, to keep us from splattering against the frozen ground—

I wake from the jolt of impact. My head is spinning, and my body feels as tense as if I had really just fallen to my death. My eyes snap open, scanning around the room, trying to find something to anchor me back to reality.

There's a soft tapping at the door.

I glance over at Adria. She's passed out, mouth hanging open. I envy her ability to sleep anywhere through anything.

Another knock, this one a little louder. I rise from the bed, wrapping my nightgown around my shaking body, the memory of the dream clinging to my muscles as I cross the room.

I feel him on the other side. Ronan. He felt my dream. I feel his concern, deep and heavy, with a longing to hold me, to comfort me, to take my pain away. I hear his body shift, hear the fabric of his robe brush the wood. He's pressed himself to the door, listening inside.

I know he feels me here. I lean a bit closer, reaching for the knob.

But I stop. It would be so easy to open it and to fall back into his arms. So easy to let him whisper soothing words into my ears, to kiss the fear from my aching neck. To hold me until the tension fades and I drift back into a warm, dreamless sleep.

I lean back against the door instead. It's cold and hard through the thin fabric of my nightgown, but I stand against it anyway, unmoving, for a long time. I stand there until my breathing returns to normal, until the nightmare releases me, and I forget the spinning of the world, the sensation of falling, eternally, through the darkened air.

From the other side of the door, there's a long, weary sigh, and then the retreating sound of footsteps through the empty hall.

I stay by the door for a minute longer, and then I climb back into bed, feeling its emptiness more acutely than ever before.

The moment I realize what I must do comes unexpectedly.

It's been almost two weeks since the griffin ride. Larus has been delayed, and although I sent him a letter telling him I needed help and for him to return as soon as possible, I wasn't able to mention more than that out of fear of the letter being intercepted. I visit the docks each day to see if there's any news or correspondence, but no luck so far. After my daily check with the postmaster, I meet Quinn in the throne room, where she's watching the competition she mentioned, the one she thought I should enter with my flute. Unlike most of the events, this one is open to all, no audition required.

Which means it's been highly entertaining. We've listened to more botched renditions of "Selara, Vayla's Favored Land" than I can count, which makes the woman on the stage all the more surprising.

"Holy shit," says Quinn. "She's actually good."

She's Orsan, though her tattoos are different from Taran's, so I imagine she isn't water-born. Her voice is deep and soulful, and although I can't understand the words of the song, I can read some of its feeling.

Loss, probably because of something my people did to her or whoever wrote it.

I swallow, my throat feeling tight.

"I forgot you hate the Orsa," says Quinn, reading my expression.

"I don't hate them. Not anymore. I just…"

"I get it. It's how I felt about you."

The woman is from Pyka, the place I grew up. I wonder if she has ever been inside the castle there. I wonder if she performs at the inn where Father took us from time to time.

We left them hungry. We left them to fend for themselves in the elements, in the mountains and the frozen north during our harsh winters. All King Aurelian offered them was food and shelter. It's all it took to win them to his side.

The harvest is coming. There's something we can do to undermine Adria and Seth's plan, I realize.

"Do you know where I can find him?" I ask Quinn during the applause.

"Him? Whomever do you mean?" She bounces her eyebrows at me in the most ridiculous way I've ever seen.

I push on her shoulder, or rather, I attempt to. She's like a wall of stone. "It's not like that. It's important."

She shakes her head, absolutely not believing me. "He'll be in the palace market square. They've got it closed down for some street theatre today."

I slip away before the next performer starts, but not before Quinn grabs my arm. "I'm rooting for you."

I shrug her off, but I can't help but smile a little. I'm excited to see him again, to talk to him, even if it isn't about what I really want to talk to him about.

I can't manage that. Not yet. But as soon as Larus is back, as soon as I'm certain we'll be able to stop what's coming without anyone getting hurt or hanged, I'll return to him.

I find him in the market square in a special tent with royal banners. The play is a comedy about Kerensa and Sai interfering in the love lives of mortals, and the part I see of it as I pass through the crowd is actually really funny. So it surprises me to see him looking so glum. He's usually better at masking his true feelings.

When he sees me approach, he lights up, quite literally. His skin takes on that faint glow it has from time to time, that radiating warmth that I'm drawn to. He exits the tent, coming to meet me in one of the side alleys with Taran trailing behind at a short distance.

He's cut his hair since I saw him last. It takes everything in me not to touch it. Not to touch him. "Would you do something for me?" I ask, straining to keep my voice level.

He mirrors my neutral expression, and for a moment, I feel our lie—the lie that we can keep things neutral between us at all—echoed in our feelings. "Of course," he says. "Name it."

"Would you double the grain shipments to Kalla? Whatever extra you were planning to send, would you send twice that? And some extra guards with it as well. Say it's in celebration of the harvest festival or something."

I don't know what Seth and Adria do to sabotage the grain, but I figure there's only so much they can manage while they're organizing everything else. If Ronan can overwhelm them with shipments, some of them have to make it there. And if the people are full on the king's bread, maybe they'll find it harder to lift a sword against him.

"I'm sure we can find a way to do that, especially with the harvest coming so soon. Do you think they're being attacked on the road?"

"Sometimes. We were, on the way here."

Barely contained rage flashes in his eyes. "Did they hurt you?"

"Not badly," I say. "Just a scratch on my throat."

He looks at my neck then. It's been weeks since the fight on the road, and he and Zara have both healed me since then, but he can't stop himself from checking anyway. His fingers hover above my skin, but he doesn't press down. I can feel how badly he wants to touch me, and I want him to so badly the desire echoes between us. When we regain our composure, he withdraws his hand, and he asks, "Why didn't you tell me?"

"I didn't trust you then." There's something implicit underneath that—*I do trust you now.* I hope he hears it.

"If that's all you need, I'll go ask Cyrus—"

"Can you do it, Ronan?" His name on my lips fills us both with desire. *Fuck,* I can't take this much longer. "Can you see to it yourself?"

He nods, understanding my meaning. "I will."

As I leave him, the last feeling that's shared between us is the desire for me to stay.

Larus finally arrives a week later, more than two weeks after we were expecting him. I meet him in the palace dining hall the afternoon he returns, thankfully without Felix.

There are deep shadows beneath Larus's eyes now—either his trip or his return voyage must have taken a lot out of him. But he looks a bit softer around the belly than he did when he left us a few weeks ago. I hope his mother fed him well at least.

"Sylvie," he says, pulling me into a hug. Gods, it's such a relief to have him back. With Larus back, it feels like everything will be alright. "I leave for a month, and I come back to find you're a hero. Both of you champions. Your parents would have been proud."

Maybe the people they were before the war would have been proud. The people they became though? They were probably rolling in their graves seeing us on the stage with Ronan.

But somehow it doesn't matter as much to me now. I loved my parents, but they aren't the ones who raised me. They chose their war over me time and time again. Larus is the one who stayed. He's the only one whose opinion I care about.

I ask him about his mother while we're in earshot of the court, and he tells me some made-up story about a nature-born healer who was able to cure her nonexistent illness. Then I tell him about a gallery I heard about, one made by shadow-born artists that's meant to be viewed by other shadow-born in the dark. He suggests we go so that I can describe the art to him, and I agree.

My assumption that the gallery would be quiet proves to be correct. There's no one else there when we arrive, which is a pity, because the paintings are like nothing I've ever seen before. The gallery runner draws back a heavy curtain so that we can see how the paintings appear completely ordinary in daylight. A landscape of the Palador Mountains. An orchard of some kind. A portrait of Ronan's father. But in the darkness, I can see other images layered on top in swirls of reddish color: a wildfire in the mountains, pomegranates growing on the trees, a golden glow around King Aurelian that's not unlike the way I perceive Ronan in real life.

I describe the paintings to Larus until the gallery runner finally leaves, giving us an opportunity to speak freely.

"Larus, so much has happened. I wish you had been here. I didn't know what to do."

"It seems like you did a pretty good job on your own, from what Adria told me. Tell me about the night you saved Ronan."

I blush at just the mention of his name. Thank Vahlo it's dark in here. "There wasn't much to it. I saw the man in the darkness, and I did what we practiced a thousand times."

"I wish I could have seen it. I imagine it helped you get closer to him?"

"For a time," I say, choosing my words carefully. "I've taken a step back from him lately."

"So Adria tells me. She says you told her it's to prevent things burning out before we're ready."

"That's what I told her, yes." My chest begins to tighten. "But there's more to it than that."

"You like him. The real him." It's not a question. He can hear it in my voice.

"Yes," I admit. "I thought maybe with some distance—but yes. I do."

"You like him too much to do what we've asked of you?" Larus cocks his head to the side as if he could read my reaction, but he can't in the dark.

"Maybe," I say. "I don't know." I do know, but I'm afraid that even Larus won't understand. "But he's not the reason I'm having doubts."

"Then what is?"

"It's Adria that's the problem. Adria and Seth." I know this is going to come as a shock to him. "The food shipments. It's them, not Ronan. They've been sabotaging them for months. Everything you and Typhon have been doing to fix it, they've been countering in secret. I don't know if they always meant to keep it from you or if they did so because they thought you and Typhon are friends—"

"Hmm," he grunts. It's the hollow, laugh-like sound he makes when he's been fooled. "I'd be impressed if it wasn't so terrible."

"What do you mean?"

"If they've done what you're saying, it's a massive undertaking. I could believe it from Adria. But Seth? Never would have thought he had it in him. I thought she was a fool to trust him to gather the forces on his own, but it seems she knew something I didn't."

"Larus, she admitted it to me. I told her that I figured it out, acting like I was helping her, and she admitted it. They starved our own people. They kept them hungry and desperate on purpose, so they could get their revenge. This war has been built on a lie. We have to find a way to stop them. I need your help."

"I wish I'd known two weeks ago…" he says. "What I agreed to in order to get my mother's ships. And for nothing. Worse than nothing." He makes a gesture like he's going to spit but thinks better of it in the gallery.

"What did you agree to?"

"To marry. I'm to take a bride from the Islands when the war ends. At least I won't have to do that now, I suppose."

When I was younger, I asked Larus why he hadn't married, and he'd told me that a Guardian's duty was to their House first and foremost. And that if he married, it would only be in service to the House.

I wonder for the first time what it had cost him to keep that vow, and I wonder what it will cost him now to turn his back on his promise to his mother. "You could still marry, even if we don't go to war," I say. "You ought to be happy, Larus."

He laughs. "It's because I want to be happy that I don't marry." He turns to look at me and shakes his head again in the dark. "Tell them to bring back that damn candle so I can have a look at you. I want to see this clever young woman that I'm going to stop a war for."

"Then you'll help me? You'll help me find a way to stop them?"

"Of course, Sylvie. How could I ever deny you? Just give me a bit of time to think."

Chapter Twenty-Nine

I feel lighter than I have in weeks when I return to the palace with Larus.

We're going to stop this somehow. He won't be able to call off Felix's ships, but he can cause a rift with his mother easily enough. I tell him not to do so on our behalf—she's an old woman, and who knows how much time they have left together? But he assures me that it'll be easier to cause a rift with her than keep the peace, and that she'll welcome him back with open arms in the end, like she always does.

Then there's the matter of Seth's army. I explain to Larus what I've asked of Ronan regarding the grain, and he thinks it's a good start, although he worries that it will give Seth additional resources and it won't prevent our more loyal or aggressive subjects from joining the fight. He believes that organizing the troops will be relatively easy to sabotage, considering it's the last thing we're waiting on to be ready. Coordinating just the forward armies involves a large number of people who aren't given the full information on what's happening or why they're arriving in Selara prepared for war, and Larus thinks there are plenty of opportunities to ruin

Seth's plans without exposing him to the king and provoking his justice.

Which leaves Adria to me. Larus believes my best chance of stopping her from taking out Ronan is to act as his personal protector. She's a lot of things, but she isn't reckless. Once she sees the plan has fallen apart, she'll be angry, but she'll likely withdraw to regroup and try again later. But just in case she decides to go for revenge anyway, consequences be damned, I can be there to keep him safe.

Which means, after three agonizing weeks apart, I can finally see him again. I can finally be with him, knowing that I'm doing everything I can to protect him and all of our people. I can't tell him the truth about the plans we had, but it won't matter once they're ruined.

I meet Quinn at our usual palace exit for the day's events. It's the last week of the Festival of Arts, and the final competitions are taking place, which means that some of the very best shows are about to happen. But Quinn is distracted—she met a dancer at a tavern last night.

"Blonde hair down to here," she says, gesturing to her ass. "Like spun silk. And her mouth. Sylvie, *her mouth.*"

"I'm jealous," I admit. "I wanted to talk to you about that."

Her eyes light up. "Coming over to the fun side at last? I've got so many great options for you. There's that musician from the Redwoods Band. The one with the stringed thing. Harp? Lyre? Something. Or the sculptor from a couple of weeks ago. He was looking at you like he wanted to study your curves." She mimes running her hands down my body. "Or the painter from House Juni. The one who also throws the javelin—"

"None of those," I say, though I have to admit her encyclopedic knowledge of fuckable people is impressive. "I'm thinking of someone a bit more...regal."

Her mouth drops open. Then she bursts into a broad smile. "Really? I thought you were for sure over it after nothing happened last week. Oh man, he's going to be thrilled. He's been *pining.* It's so pathetic."

"Has he?"

"Gods, yes. I didn't want to say anything—I thought it would be weird if I did. But he is *bereft.* A shell of a man. Shit, he's going to come on so strong when you see him again. Give me a chance to warn him so he doesn't scare you off."

"No," I say quickly. "I—that is—don't do that."

"Oh *nooooo,*" she says, putting her arm around me. "You're a better liar than he is. I thought you were over it, but you were pining this whole time too, weren't you?"

"I don't know about pining…" I say.

"Oh gods. You were *made* for each other. Can I be there? Can I be there when you tell him? I just want to see him be happy. And you too, Sylvie."

"Well, I was hoping you would help me find him."

Her eyes flash with an idea. "He's going to the opera tonight. Father is joining him in the royal box. But what if you show up instead?"

"Just show up? Don't you think I should tell him first?" What if he doesn't want me there? What if he's changed his mind in the three weeks it's taken me to decide?

"Surprise him. Trust me. He loves a surprise. It'll be so sweet and romantic. I almost want to vomit, it makes me so happy. Come on, let's skip the day and go get you ready. There's so much to do. You need a killer dress; you need jewelry. Oh, we need to remove every single hair from your body—"

"Quinn!"

"Just trust me on that one too, alright? I don't know his prefer-ences, but I do know a bit about getting things tangled in your teeth—"

"Gross."

"Exactly! Which is why we're going to remove it all, starting with this unibrow—"

"I do not have a unibrow!"

"Not yet, but it's on its way…"

After an excruciating day of plucking, waxing, shaving, and cram-ming myself into a thin and silky black dress that leaves exactly nothing to the imagination, Quinn declares me ready to seduce the God-King himself.

"If he turns you down, I'll take pity on you."

"Quinn!"

"I'm kidding. You're gorgeous. He's going to explode when he sees you. Hopefully not literally, but don't be surprised."

"You're absolutely disgusting," I say to her with affection.

"You know it, and you love it."

And she's right. I never would have thought it was possible when I met her, but she's basically my best friend now.

We share a carriage from the palace to a theatre north of the palace market. It's an older building, but the inside has been re-cently redone. The seats and balconies are made from Nithyrian wood, with cushions and accents in the rich reds and blues Ronan seems to prefer.

If the walls weren't trimmed with gold, I would have suspected he oversaw the renovations himself.

Quinn leads me up a series of staircases to the royal box at the top. She has the guards get her father first.

"Come on, old man," she says to him, looping her arm with his. "We need your seat."

He takes a moment to look at me before realizing what she's saying. "Oh. I suppose you do," he says in his usual tone of boredom and disdain.

Quinn shoots me an approving look. "Go get him, girl."

I take a deep, steadying breath before I turn the doorknob and enter the royal box.

It's a small balcony at the top of the theatre, covered on top with a canopy of red velvet curtains and rich golden tassels. Though it looks like it could seat about eight comfortably, only two seats have been placed within it.

Ronan is sitting in one of them with his back to me. One leg is crossed over his lap, resting on his opposite knee. He's leaning back, his head tilted to the side as if whatever he's about to see holds no interest for him. As if his mind is somewhere else entirely.

I watch the tap of his fingers on the arm of his chair cease when he senses me. He doesn't move. He doesn't turn or get up.

I walk around the side of the other chair. He's so…*beautiful.* Gods, he's just beautiful. Honestly, this entire festival is pointless. The best tribute to Kerensa is sitting right here.

Though, like the time I saw him at the arena after we'd been apart for a while, he looks a bit rough around the edges.

I hope that isn't because of me. But if it is, at least it'll be over soon.

"Is this seat taken?" I say. I'm so nervous he'll say no that I'm shaking.

"I—" He stares at me for a long while, drinking me in. Then he looks back at the door and shakes his head. Sorry, Cyrus. "Not anymore."

I smile lightly as I sit down beside him, my heart fluttering in my chest.

Damn, it feels good to be here. I can smell that spicy scent coming off of him, and it's like coming home again.

"Is this real?" he whispers. He's so close to me I can feel his breath on me.

"Yes," I say. "I've made my choice." I reach into his lap and take his hand, and a powerful reverberation of feeling pulses through me. Pulses through us.

Want, need, longing. Desire.

"And everything I told you? Everything I did?" He pushes his words through the overwhelming feelings.

I wait for it to pass before I turn in my seat to face him. "It doesn't change the way I feel about you." He reaches for me, taking my face in his hand, and I thrill at his touch. "It doesn't make me want you any less." I kiss his palm, and he shivers.

"*Gods*, Sylvie," he whispers. He gestures to the stage. "Are you sure you want to see this?"

"You can't let them down," I say. This might be the highlight of their lives, performing for the king. "And besides." I point to the sides of the box. No one in the room can see below about chest height. "No one needs to know what we do in the shadows."

He groans, and it sends another incredible pulse between us. "We have a few minutes before they start. Can I show you this beautiful doorknob?" He stands and points to the darkened back of the box where the door is.

If we go back there now, it'll look like we've just stepped outside for a minute.

"Please do," I say.

We don't even make it to the door before his hands are on me. I drop the shadows around us even lower.

"Gods, I missed you," he says into the back of my neck before turning me to kiss him.

I moan as his lips make contact with mine. Everything feels heightened, and it's not just the power that connects us. It's the absence, the weeks lying in bed, dreaming of him. All of the agonizing distance between us finally closing.

"I need you," he says, his hands ruining the hair that took us hours to do. And I don't even care. "I *ache* for you."

"Ronan," I murmur as his hand grazes my breast.

"Fuck," he says, turning his head to the side in pleasure. "Say it again. Say my name."

"Ronan, they're lowering the lights."

"Fuck!"

I laugh and smooth my dress and my hair. "Come on," I tell him, taking his hand and leading him to the seat.

We wait until they've made the announcement that includes acknowledging the king before continuing.

"You're lucky that they made the railing this high," he says when he sits back down after waving to the crowd. "Or I would've given everyone more of a show than they bargained for."

His silken Selaran pants, like my dress, leave nothing to the imagination. The bulge of his cock is incredibly obvious as he takes his seat.

"I'm lucky that the men around here seem to want everyone to take a look. These pants are driving me crazy. They're obscene."

I watch his cock rise with my words, and it's immensely satisfying to see.

He drops his voice low and leans to speak directly into my ear even though no one is near to hear us. "Says the woman whose entire breasts are on display. I can see the exact shape of them. I can even see your little brown nipples. Look, they can hear me."

They tighten under the thin fabric at his attention.

"Fuck you," I whisper.

He chuckles, looking free and happy for the first time in ages.

Then, just as suddenly as it arrived, the smile fades from his face. His hand tenses on the armrest. He doesn't want to ask me this, but he can't help himself. "Are you staying?"

"For tonight? Or—"

"I don't know," he says, taking my hand. "I don't need you to decide right now."

It's a lie. I can feel it. I can feel how much he wants me to stay with him, how terrified he is that I'll just walk away from him again after tonight.

And I am terrified too. Terrified of being with him and what it will mean, but far more terrified of losing him.

I can't lose him.

I lean over the handle of his chair to whisper in his ear. "I'll stay as long as you'll have me."

I don't lean back yet. There's something else I need to say to him. I swallow, pushing my heart back down out of my throat. I can do this. I need to do this. After what I've put him through, he deserves to hear this.

The truth is, he's too good for me. I don't know if I'll ever deserve him.

But I want him. Only him.

I belong to him.

"I'm yours, Ronan," I say to him, forcing myself to say the words despite my fear. I don't want to leave it as a feeling for him to interpret. I want him to know it, to be certain of it. To know that there's no one else for me but him.

"Darken the shadows," he replies.

"What?"

"Just for a moment. The show has begun. No one will notice."

"Alright, but—"

I darken the shadows over us. It would be incredibly obvious to anyone not shadow-born, and the shadow-born would be able to see, but I don't think Ronan cares.

He places his hand on my cheek and pulls me to his lips, softly and slowly. "Sylvie, I've been yours since the day you arrived."

Then he kisses me deeply, and it's like nothing I've ever felt before, not even with him. It's the beginning and ending of everything, of everything I am, of everything I came here to do. I'm being reborn on Ronan's lips. I'll never be the same again, and it doesn't matter.

All that matters is us.

When I finally pull away, I take a long moment to look at him before I let go of the shadows. I asked Larus once what being in love felt like. He told me he'd only ever really been in love once, long before he came into our service, but that he knew it when he looked at her and he believed, truly believed, that she was the most wonderful person in the world. That no one else could ever compare to her, and that he felt sorry for every person who didn't get to know her because they were missing out on the best that the world had to offer.

He said it was pure delusion. He knew it couldn't be true because everyone must feel that way, and only one person in the world can be the most wonderful, by definition.

And yet, he told me, when you're in love, you believe it anyway. Even when they annoy you. Even when you hate them. There's a part of you that keeps on believing that the most wonderful person is still in there, waiting for you to find them again.

That's what love is.

Looking at him here, looking at Ronan. *My Ronan.*

I can't imagine anyone, anything, in the world more wonderful than him.

I force myself to look at the stage when the torchlight of the theatre reaches my eyes again. There are about a dozen people down there in costumes, some ancient warriors, some tree spirits or something else vaguely floral. They sing in the Selaran common language, but their voices are so exaggerated that it's difficult for me to understand the words. I'm sure it's beautiful, or I would think so if I'd paid attention to any of it so far.

"Are you regretting saying you wanted to watch the show?" Ronan mutters without turning.

"Maybe."

"Would you like to regret it even more?"

He slips his hand over the arm of my chair and grazes his fingertips on my thigh. The dress I've borrowed from Quinn has a slit that he's dangerously close to reaching.

I say a silent thank you to her for making me shave. "Yes," I whisper back.

His fingers glide over the thin, silky fabric. It's soft and impossibly smooth on my skin. I feel a prick of realization from him when he finds the overlap in the layers. He spreads the slit in the dress with his thumb and forefinger, and it's impossible for me not to think of him spreading something else.

That desire is mirrored between us. I press my teeth to my bottom lip to keep from sighing as his hand touches the bare skin of my leg. He rubs little circles there, and then his hand drifts lower.

I shift in my chair to give him better access. I'm wearing nothing under the dress; any of the undergarments that I own would have been visible. The space between my thighs slickens as he moves closer to it. He'll feel it any moment. All he has to do is drift his hand a little bit lower…

"This part is funny," he says, moving his hand to my other thigh and skipping the good part altogether. "Pretend to laugh when they laugh."

"They" being the audience. Thank the gods for the box. No one can see where Ronan's hand is, but they can certainly see the look on my face in response to it.

I laugh when they laugh, and Ronan tugs my thighs open, forcing me to gasp.

"Good," he says. "Convincing."

Gods, I love to hear it.

Then he trails his fingers up once more. I feel the moment his fingers touch the growing wet patch between my legs. The feeling runs from his fingers, up his arm, down his body, and right into his cock, which twitches in his pants. "Sylvie," he says. "Is this for me?"

"All of it," I say. I'm spread open obscenely in the chair, the fabric of the dress pushed aside for him. I take his hand and shove it back to the other slit. The one on my body.

He moans at my forwardness. "Take what you want from me. I love it."

He strokes my lower lips teasingly, his fingers gliding over my folds with such tenderness that it makes me shiver. I want him in me, want him to press the heel of his hand against me as his fingers work in me. I want him to make me come.

But not yet.

"There is something else I want," I say.

"Name it."

I don't. Instead, I reach over the arm of his chair and stroke him through his trousers. Those slutty Selaran trousers. So thin, so silky soft. He shifts and rolls his head back, then he covers the action with a stretch.

"Gods," he says, his voice dark and husky.

He looks at me in disbelief as I stroke him through the fabric. I trace the outline of his length, feeling it grow in my hand as I wrap my fingers around it. Damn, it feels amazing to touch him like this. "Is this for me?" I ask.

"Only for you," he says, pressing a quick kiss to my bare shoulder. "Whenever you want it."

"How about now?"

"Done with the show?"

I am, but there's a part of me that's enjoying this too much to leave.

"Hang on," he says at my hesitation. "I have another idea."

He removes his hand from me, and I feel the lack almost immediately. And then the strangest thing I've ever seen happens.

Ronan slides down in his chair until he's kneeling on the floor in front of it. But he's still there in the chair too. The image of him is, at least.

"What the fuck," I whisper.

He presses a finger to his lips to quiet me. It's the same finger he was stroking me with. He licks my juices off of it, and I feel his primal pleasure deep in my core. "You're delicious," he murmurs, crawling until he's in front of me. "I need more."

The image of Ronan beside me smiles uncannily, watching the show.

The Ronan between my legs is cloaked in shadow and hidden by the railing, but there are people just on the other side of the walls of the box. It's terrifying and yet deeply erotic to know that I'm spread open with people just a few feet away.

He must sense my fear because he kisses the inside of my thigh near my knee. "Unless you don't want me to."

Fuck, I want him to.

I put my hand in his perfect hair and tug him to me.

"Fuck yes," he rasps, skimming the inside of my thigh with his tongue before pushing my legs open further.

Then he reaches back and grabs me by my ass, pulling me forward a few inches.

My mouth falls open, but I clench it shut as quickly as I can. Beside me, the image of Ronan sinks a few inches in the chair to hide my movement.

"You're so beautiful. Every part of you. I've been thinking about this since that day at the baths."

"You saw me?" I blush at the memory of me naked, scrambling for my towel with him across the room.

"Not nearly enough," he says. "But enough for a fantasy or two. Now do your best to stay quiet. We're nearly to the sad part. When I'm done with you, you're going to look as if you've been deeply moved by the music. Very deeply."

I moan as he parts my lower lips just as he parted the dress.

He places a soft kiss right on my clit. It's so light, so gentle that it drives me wild with need. "Ronan," I beg.

He tilts his head up as he teases me with his tongue. I look down and meet his eyes. They're dark and full of longing. A need to taste me, to please me. I have to blink a dozen times to get myself to look up again.

I wait, my hands clutching the arms of the chair as he kisses me softly inside and outside my lips. "Beautiful," he murmurs.

"*Ronan,*" I beg again.

And the need for it reverberates between us. It sears into my mind, his burning desire to taste me, to feel me explode on his tongue, mingling with my desire to lose myself to him, to let him claim the darkest places in me.

He can't hold back anymore, not when the feeling of our shared desire consumes him just as it does me. "I need you," he says into my thigh. "I need to feel you come."

Then he dives into my folds, devouring me with his tongue. He licks every inch of me, sucking and pulling on me with his lips. He presses his tongue at my entrance, and I shift my hips to invite him in.

The feeling is so warm, so wet and light. It's everything and nothing, wonderful but nowhere near enough. "More. *Please*, Ronan."

He grips me with one hand, kneading my thigh, as he strokes his other hand over my soaking folds. Then he slips one finger inside me as he takes my swollen clit into his mouth, sucking it hard.

"Yes," I say, bending my head back in pleasure before I catch myself and neutralize my expression once more.

It's a rush, trying not to let anyone know what's happening. Imagining what they'd think if they knew the God-King of Selara had his finger inside me while he eats me out in a crowded theatre. It's filthy. It's shameful.

And it's the hottest thing I've ever done.

I'm so soaking wet that he slides a second finger into me with almost no resistance. He's really working my clit now, and I can feel the heat rising up my spine. My back arches. I clench around him as he pumps me with his fingers.

A wave of his desire hits me. His need to push down his pants and push himself in me, to take me even with everyone watching. It's so hot that I echo it the moment it reaches my mind, so hot that I thread my fingers in his hair again, fighting the urge to pull him up to my mouth so he can fill me with his cock.

He moans at my desire, and I feel the vibrations from his mouth on my clit. I clench around him, feeling the waves building within me. I'm close and getting closer by the second.

He tilts his head back to look at me again. "Come for me, beautiful. I want to feel it while I'm inside of you."

I whimper as he thrusts his fingers in me deep. The pressure on my clit is intoxicating; the heat in my back has reached my neck and flushed my face.

I want to lean back and cry out, but I can't. Instead, I look down into Ronan's eyes. They're so filled with lust that it sends me over the edge.

My Ronan. My king.

But I'm the one on the throne. I'm the one being worshipped.

I bite my lip, hard, as the waves of pleasure wash over me. My lower body spasms, squeezing against Ronan's fingers. He keeps the pressure on my clit until the waves reside, lightening his touch in perfect synchronization with my feelings, drawing out every last drop of my pleasure.

"Beautiful," he says again, looking up at me. "And delicious," he says as he cleans his fingers with his mouth. "Everything I dreamt of and more."

The praise, the pleasure, the man between my legs. It's all too much. I'm so completely and utterly undone, I can't form words.

He kisses my thighs gently as he nudges my legs back together and replaces my gown, smoothing the fabric until it looks like nothing has happened. Then he crouches back into his seat and leans the image of Ronan forward until they merge. When he sits back, it's like he only leaned forward for a second.

Except that his hair is a mess, his face is red, and his lips are swollen and glistening with me.

He's gorgeous.

"Bravo," he says, applauding at the end of a song. I clap too, in a daze. "Wonderful," he says loudly enough for others to hear him.

On stage, the performer's faces light up from the king's admiration.

But he leans over to me and whispers, "I mean you."

A jolt of excitement pulses through me, already ready and desperate for more of him.

"Now, are you ready to leave?"

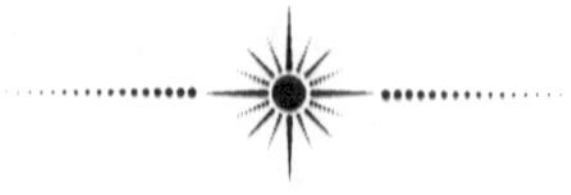

I'm aching with need again by the time we make it outside during intermission.

The cool night air blows my dress around me and freezes my nipples into hard points as we wait for the carriage to arrive. Ronan wraps his arm around me, rubbing warmth into my shoulders.

"When the carriage gets here, I'll warm them as well. They look cold," he says, brushing one of my breasts with his fingertip quickly before one of the guards can see.

"With your mouth?" I ask hopefully.

He laughs. "What do you think?"

"Ronan, a quick word before you leave?"

I recognize the voice before we turn to look. It's Cyrus. He must have spotted us leaving the theatre.

Ronan looks at me regretfully, then removes his arm from my shoulder. "What is it?"

"It's a question Lord Junta had about the farm taxes."

"Fuck the damn taxes," he says. "Can't it wait until the morning?"

"Well…" needles Cyrus. "It would really be better if—"

Ronan sighs. "Give me a moment," he says to me. "Just one moment," he says to Cyrus. "Make it quick."

I miss him the moment he walks away.

Two of his guards follow him, but Taran stays with me, no doubt at Ronan's instruction. He stands several feet back out of the torchlight of the streetlamp, but I can see him clearly in the darkness.

I haven't spoken to Taran since Ronan told me what happened with my father. I haven't dared say anything. But something about tonight's activities has left me feeling bolder than usual.

"He told me, you know," I say to him. "About what happened."

"What?" Taran asks as he approaches.

"He told me what happened. With my father. About what you did."

His blue eyes widen. Ronan didn't tell him he told me. "I—I don't—"

"I know why you did what you did. What I don't know is whether to hate you for it or thank you for it. Because you took my father from me. But you gave me Ronan in return."

Taran looks down at me and then looks at his feet in shame. "I'm sorry. Whether you hate me or not, I'm sorry. I couldn't let him die."

"I know," I say.

We stand for a while in silence, but the carriage doesn't come, and Ronan doesn't return. I'm about to go back inside where it's warm when I see a flash of light in a nearby alley. "Did you see that?" I ask Taran.

But he doesn't answer.

My eyes detect movement in the night. There's something out there, and it isn't the carriage.

"Taran, your sword," I say, but when I look back at him, I see he's doubled over on the ground.

"Taran!" I scream. "Ronan!"

I have no weapons on me tonight. No sword, no dagger to save me.

Nothing but my magic, if I can figure out how to use it.

"Come out!" I shout. "I know you're there."

"Do you?" asks a woman's voice from nearby. It's familiar, so familiar, but I can't place it.

The voice is close, close enough that anyone should be able to see it, but I see nothing but the emptiness of the city street at night.

"Good night, Sylvie," the woman says.

I feel movement behind me. I lash out with my shadows, but it's too late.

A cloth covers my face, and my legs collapse beneath me as my vision fades to black.

Chapter Thirty

I awake in a darkened room.

I'm lying down on something hard, maybe a table, judging by the height of the ceiling overhead. The air is damp and cool with a vague scent of rot. It's a familiar scent, one that transports me immediately to the dripping, dreary cellars beneath Pyka.

I lift my head to look around, but it doesn't move. Am I restrained somehow? I don't feel anything. My eyes are able to dart around the room though, taking in walls lined with shelves of books and strange bottles of liquid, peculiar implements of metal and glass. There's a single candle burning somewhere behind me, but my head won't budge to see it.

There's a pain in my left arm. I reach my right arm up to see what's hurting, but it won't move either.

Fuck. I can't move. I'm still breathing, and my heart is still beating, but my body won't move at all.

"Help," I call out, but it comes out as a quiet creak, barely audible though the room is silent.

"Sylvie," says a comforting voice. It's a woman's voice, but she's behind me, back in a place my eyes can't reach. "Relax. You're alright."

"Where am I?" My lips can barely form the words, but the woman seems to understand.

"You're back in the palace," she says. "Someone poisoned you. We're giving the elixir time to work. Don't worry. You'll feel better soon."

She moves around the table, but I can't see her face. All I can see is the brown robe of the Alchemists' Guild.

The Alchemists' Guild.

That sends alarm bells ringing through me, but I can't quite recall why.

"Ronan?" I ask. I was with Ronan before I came here, I'm pretty sure.

"He'll be back soon," she says. "Just get some rest."

The voice is familiar. There's an accent, something foreign. Not Selaran or Nithyrian. Not the Enez Islands. It's different. It's warm and comforting, though, and it's saying nice things.

So why does it feel wrong?

"My arm." I try to lift my left arm to see what's wrong with it, and that works, a little. There's something sticking out of it. A tube of some kind, strange and soft like a noodle, emerging from the inside of my elbow.

"It's the medicine," says the voice. She moves around the table to check on it. I can't see what she reaches for near the ground, but there's something down there on the end of the tube. I feel it move when she pulls, just barely.

I've never seen medicine given like this. But then again, I've never been poisoned.

The woman looks up, and I recognize her.

"Zara," I say, relaxing. She should have just said. Maybe she did say before I woke; I'm having trouble remembering much from tonight. "How did I—?"

"We found you, like I said. You'd been poisoned."

Found me. Where? Where had they found me?

And who were they?

"You might need a different medicine," she says, reaching into a shelf for a jar. "It's a delicate balance, curing this poison. I don't want you to move, but I also don't want to stop your heart."

An image comes back to me. Taran, collapsed on the ground. He had been poisoned too. I look around, but I don't see another table in the room. "Taran?" I ask her.

"He's fine," she says. "They found him first. He's with the king."

At least there was that. Taran and Ronan must be trying to do something about the poisoner.

"Here," says Zara. She lifts a spoon of something to my mouth. It smells foul and musty, like the inside of a barn.

I clamp my lips shut. It's possible for me to do so, I realize. Whatever was keeping me from moving must be wearing off a little.

"I know, it smells awful. But it will help."

There's another image. This time, I'm being carried through a darkened hallway. I'm fighting with my captor, someone wearing brown robes.

My heart races. Something is wrong here.

I shake my head at Zara. I begin to push myself up, and she shoves the spoon in my mouth.

"I guess we're doing this the hard way," she says. Then she calls out behind her. "Hermes, get in here."

I spit out the spoon and try to pull myself upright, reaching for whatever is in my arm. But I'm too weak. She forces me back down onto the table and holds me there, trapped under her arm.

"What are you doing?"

My muscles are seizing under me. Whatever fight I had drains out of my body as however much of the elixir that I ingested reaches me.

"That's better," she says as I freeze. She releases me, and though I try with all my might to move, I can't. "Truly, I am sorry about this. It's not how this was supposed to go."

My eyes dart with fear.

Hermes enters the room. "Problem?"

"Not anymore. She should be finished draining soon. Start the boilers, would you?"

I look down in horror at my arm. The tube is dark inside. Dark red.

She's draining the blood from my body.

All of it.

Chapter Thirty-One

"Why?" I croak.

Why is Zara, the head of the Alchemists' Guild, the person who helped me during the Festival of Sport, a close confidante of Ronan and one of his most trusted advisors, trying to kill me?

Not trying. Actively killing me. She's killing me, and there's nothing I can do about it.

"Don't look at me like that," she says.

I couldn't stop if I tried.

"I didn't want to do this. You gave me no choice. Don't worry; I won't be killing you today. I need you alive to use the blood, so it'll be a day or two. Honestly, it's a shame to have to kill you at all. A shadow-born as powerful as you? I have such high hopes for your blood. But Ronan has been enough of a nuisance with just those spies of his missing. I'd never have taken them, of course, but they were getting too close as well. But you? You're going to need to turn up dead so we can finish what we started."

"What?" It's all I can manage to say. I have no idea what she's talking about.

Zara sighs. "I'm just trying to do what he asked me to. You understand that, right?"

I manage a single blink at her. She shifts, stroking her dark braid. "I guess we have some time."

She opens a door across from the table and returns a moment later with a wooden chair, placing it so that she's facing me. Then she tilts my head down so that I'm looking at her. It's strange, the effort she takes to make this seem like an ordinary conversation, given what she's told me she's planning to do. Perhaps she truly is as lonely as Larus says. "Ronan asked us to find an alternative to the phoenix cypress ash. A couple of years ago, when I became the Guild Mistress. And I told him I'd do it, only he wouldn't let me try the one thing that might work. Blood. So I had no choice."

The forbidden magic she spoke about in the bathing caves.

"Blood's not exactly something easy to come by, at least not the quantity we needed. We had a source for it, but then you shut that down too."

I struggle to understand her meaning.

Then it hits me: Marcella. The imports in the warehouse. She must have been smuggling things that the Guild wasn't allowed to use. Things like human blood.

"We still don't have an answer for the ash, but it turns out shadow-born blood does have a use. It suppresses light magic, after a delicate refinement process, of course. The process is not unlike the gold alchemy, actually. But we do have to keep them alive. The blood of the dead holds no magic."

The missing shadow-born. If what she's saying is true, they must be alive here somewhere.

Or some of them must be.

I look around the room while she's speaking, as much as I can under the effects of the elixir. I'm not in the palace, of that much I'm certain. If Ronan were nearby, he would come for me. My thoughts of a cellar were probably accurate. A hidden room, con-nected to the Alchemists' Guild somehow, maybe accessed from that door in the alleyway. Tunnels underground.

If I escape—which is a big "if" at the moment, considering she has me paralyzed—could I find my way to the other shadow-born? Maybe she'll keep me with them once I'm done for the day.

"Why?" I croak again. Why suppress light magic?

"The problem, like every problem in this place, is Ronan. He's right about freeing Selara from its dependence on the ash. The ash isn't sustainable, not the way we use it. The forest can't regenerate itself in time. We have five years, maybe ten at this rate, before it runs out. But to find an alternative, we need Ronan gone. He won't let us do what we need to do."

I imagine Ronan would take issue with harvesting mass quanti-ties of blood for any reason, even if the donors weren't killed. It would be trading one exploitation for another.

"Kill—?" I try to ask. They're trying to kill Ronan?

"Yes, and we've explored a lot of avenues to do it. And then you and Adria showed up, and I thought we had a real chance. Adria came to me, looking for an alliance of sorts. She was careful not to give herself away, but I understood her meaning."

Of course she did. *Of course* she did.

Zara shifts back a bit so I can see her better, and then she puts on Adria's face.

Fuck.

The illusion is weak, but it's passable. How many times did she pose as Adria?

"I had better ideas where she was involved," she says, her voice rasping. That time in the tunnel when she was waiting for Quinn and her voice sounded strange.

It was Zara.

She drops the illusion, looking as though it had strained her somewhat. "I declined to help her. You never can be sure of the outcome of a war in advance, and I didn't want to jeopardize my position within Ronan's confidence in case things didn't turn out the way we both wanted."

Well, at least there's that. At least there's one thing Adria isn't involved with, although not for lack of trying.

"But you? I thought you were amazing at the beginning. I couldn't have made someone better for the task if I tried. You were mysterious, beguiling. Beautiful and deadly, the perfect temptation. I thought you would succeed in your plans, and then we'd have someone on the throne who would understand our needs. Who would be more than happy to sacrifice a few Selaran shadow-born for the sake of Nithyrian workers."

She sighs deeply, shaking her head. "But I was wrong. Oh, how you disappointed me, Sylvie. When I saw you with him, looking for the shadow-born, I thought it was simply part of the plan. Simply a way to keep him close. But then you spared him at the festival. I told Calliope her plan was flawed, but I never thought it would be *you* to end it."

She had worked with Calliope. She had probably worked with the man in the throne room from the first day of the festival too. She was the mole Ronan had been looking for, the one who had undermined his plans, the one who had leaked his secrets. She'd been working against him all along.

"Hermes nearly convinced me that it was just because you wanted to get the timing right on Ronan's death to give your precious war the best chance of succeeding. But I could see the truth that night when they brought you to his chambers. You loved him, or you were growing to love him. I knew then that you'd never kill him. And so, I had to change the plans a bit."

She gestures around her. "He'll come here on his own because he doesn't trust anyone but you. I left the path less concealed this time; he'll find it eventually. And when he does, we'll be ready for him. Maybe if he hurries, I'll be able to keep you alive for a bit longer. The blood replenishes, you know. We won't need the light magic suppression anymore, but I'm convinced that the answer is there for the gold process. It's not my best work, as far as plans go, but it'll have to do for now."

My blood—what's left of it in my body; how much has she taken from me?—runs cold. I have to find a way to stop Ronan from coming here. Can he feel me? He'll be able to when he gets close.

Don't come here. It's a trap. Don't come. Don't come. Don't come. I think it over and over again, trying to feel the words with every ounce of my being. Can he feel them? Will he understand?

Zara looks at whatever on the floor is holding my blood. "I think that's about enough for now. I'm sorry for this, but I'm going to have to put you out to move you. Don't worry; I promise I won't kill you until the wax has been made. Sleep well."

I thrash against the table, but my legs and arms barely flex at all. I strain, trying my best to move my head to the side, but I can't do it.

Zara approaches me and holds a handkerchief over my face again.

And in a moment, I'm back under.

Chapter Thirty-Two

Ronan

Lord Cyrus, I can tell by the timing of his interruption, is well and truly sick of my shit.

We've been going back and forth over this farm tax and subsidy issue for weeks. It's the typical story: we need food to live. The kingdom needs taxes to support itself. Someone is going to win, and someone is going to lose because this system is fucked beyond repair. And somehow, as always, doing the right thing is the one thing guaranteed to make everyone unhappy.

"I'm sorry to ruin your evening, your majesty," he says, sounding anything but, "but the heads of House Grana and Modesto are here tonight, and if I can just get your thoughts on—"

"Do whatever you think is best."

There's a woman standing out in the cold who is practically *screaming* the most beautifully lurid feelings at me, and I fully intend to spend the better part of the evening inside of her, farm taxes be damned.

"Sir? But there's the issue of the fishing rights as well. House Nauta demands to speak with you—"

"Are you telling me that what you want to do is the wrong idea?"

Cyrus raises his silver eyebrows so high I think they might reach his hair. "No, sir. Not at all. It's just that—"

I sigh. The man is exhausting, but he has a better sense for these things than I do. Every time he's told me I need to speak with someone, he's been right. If House Nauta needs to hear whatever bullshit Cyrus has come up with from my lips, I might as well get it over with or pay for it later.

"Very well," I say, following him inside with a regretful glance back at Sylvie.

Gods, Sylvie. I can still feel her longing for me, even though I must be a hundred feet away by now. I've been waiting for so long for this. For her. I never thought I'd be able to share myself with someone in this way. Never thought anyone would see me the way I see them, would know me the way I have no choice but to know them. To be able to share my feelings with her. It's the greatest thing that's ever happened to me.

And it's *her*.

Of course it's her. It had to be her. I've never met anyone so incredible. So *good*. So smart. So capable of seeing through the lies she was raised with. I'm so fucking proud of her. I knew I was right about her. I knew she could do it.

And she did.

I'm yours, Ronan, she said.

I can't believe it. I probably shouldn't believe it, in spite of what I feel. She came here to kill me, I'm certain of it, and I ought to assume that everything I've felt from her has been an act. She's probably *still* trying to kill me.

And fuck me, I'd let her. I'd let her kill me just to feel her touch.

She *is* killing me. It has been killing me, watching her from a distance. Watching the way the freckles on her cheeks dance when she laughs at one of Quinn's stupid jokes in the dining hall. Watching her twirl the ring she wears on her finger when she's nervous, when she feels my eyes on her. Feeling her fear from across the palace and not being able to comfort her, to hold her. Trying desperately not to think of her, not to think about touching her, not to let the unrelenting desire echo between us. Trying to give her the space and time she needs. Trying to trust that she'd come back to me.

She came back to me.

I can still taste her on my lips, sweet like honey. I want to be back there, between her legs. I want to lie on the bed and let her straddle my face, let her smother me to death with her dripping wet—

Fuck, I need to calm down. My throbbing hard erection is just about the last thing I need during these tax negotiations.

I suppose I also ought to visit a washbasin before letting Thaddeus kiss the ring, considering where that finger has been.

Sylvie's feelings shift a bit as I wash my hands. Sadness and anger. Talking to someone? Taran, probably. I know I've complicated things between them by telling her, but they're both reasonable people. They'll work through it eventually.

I'm drying my hands when I feel a sudden, stomach-dropping flash of fear and panic from her.

Then terror.

FUCK.

I throw open the washroom door, nearly knocking over a young boy from House Faber. "Guards! With me!" I shout, shoving aside anyone who gets in my way.

"Ronan?" calls Cyrus.

"It's Sylvie. Get Quinn."

I slam through the exterior door, and I'm running down the stairs when her feelings vanish.

They're gone.

They're just gone, as suddenly as when she falls into a deep sleep. I choke, my heart in my throat, as I consider what it could mean.

"Sylvie!" I shout.

Someone is there under the streetlamp on the ground.

My blood turns to ice. *No.* It can't be her.

It can't be.

It isn't.

Gods, the relief is…short-lived. It's Taran, and that's also terrible. I can't feel him either, and Sylvie is nowhere to be seen.

"Find her," I shout to the guards clambering directionless behind me. I'll head for her myself just as soon as I know if Taran's alright.

I reach down for him. He's only a couple of years younger than me, but he looks like a boy down on the ground, slumped on his side. There's no blood visible, and when I touch his forehead, I can't feel any wounds or bruises.

His blood is still flowing. I sigh in relief.

He must have been ambushed somehow. Taran's a skilled fighter. If there had been combat, he would have fought back, but his sword is still at his side. Maybe it was a sleeping elixir like the one I took to the warehouse.

If so, it has an easy fix, and I need him with me if someone has taken Sylvie. "Healer!" I shout. "Bring the smelling salts."

There's some commotion on the steps now as some of the theatre goers come out to see where the guards rushed off to. I'm fortunate that an alchemist is among them. I don't recognize the white-haired woman who approaches, but I'm grateful to see her brown robes.

She kneels and holds a vial up to Taran's nose. He jolts awake, thrashing out and pulling himself upright suddenly. "Sylvie," he says to me, reaching for his sword.

It's not Taran's first time being woken this way.

The alchemist still crouches on the ground, looking shocked. "He really ought to—"

"Thank you," I tell her.

"Your majesty!" she exclaims, just then realizing who she was speaking to.

But Taran and I are already running for the nearest alley.

"Ronan!" yells Quinn from far behind.

"This way." I have no idea if I'm heading in the right direction, but my legs don't care. They need me to run to her.

"Sir, over here!" It's Stella from an alley to the south.

Taran and I turn on our heels, and Quinn manages to catch us as we race for Stella's voice.

Stella is gasping for breath when we reach her. "I saw a figure in the alley. I can't find them."

"With us," I tell her, and she falls in behind me.

I'm losing my goddamn mind with worry as we race down the darkened street, dodging under a line of washing. There are people in the homes nearby, but none of them is Sylvie. None of them feel as though they're hiding or running or doing anything out of the ordinary.

Where the fuck is she?

She's alive, I tell myself, willing myself to keep calm long enough to find her. To help her. *She's alive she's alive she's alive she's alive...*

We follow the alley as it turns in another direction, and I realize where we're going just as Stella does. "The doorway Sylvie led me to, sir?"

"I think so," I say, breathing hard from the run.

"Where?" asks Quinn.

"I'll explain once we get there."

The doorway where Mery told us he saw Vesper, the doorway Sylvie's alchemist went through, isn't far from here. It's very close, I realize with a sinking feeling in my stomach.

The door is unlocked, and the interior looks as empty and un-touched as Sylvie described it. "There must be something here," I say. "Some way in."

"Some way where, Ronan? What's going on?"

"Look for anything out of the ordinary," I say, and then I explain to Quinn and Taran what we've been up to and what we think is going on.

Both of them are furious at me for not telling them. Well, Quinn is furious. Taran is quietly disapproving, bordering on betrayed.

"I can't *believe* you didn't trust me," says Quinn as she knocks a dusty picture frame from the wall. "You trusted her even back then?"

Quinn had been deeply critical of my trust in Sylvie back in the beginning, back before the archery tournament changed everything. "She's definitely trying to kill you, Ronan," she had said. "Her and that sister of hers. They are 100% here to murder you, and you're *flirting* with her! I can't believe you even invited them. I've always known you were an idiot, but this is a new low, even for you. If you were that desperate for a woman, I have a dozen I could recommend—"

I'd cut her off there.

"Always," I say. I don't blame Quinn for not being able to understand. She doesn't—and can never—understand people the way that I do. And she's not wrong that feelings matter little compared to actions, but she also doesn't live with other people's feelings in her head all day, every day. She doesn't know what it's like to know someone inside and out the minute I meet them. She doesn't know how rare it is to find someone who not only doesn't disappoint you, but someone who fascinates you and challenges you and humbles you. Someone who reminds you not just that it's worthwhile to care, but that there are things in this world worth caring for.

Taran pushes a cobweb-covered desk back to check behind it, and I come over to help. "You could have told me," he says.

I nod and say, "I know."

This is all I need to say to him.

"What are we even looking for? Are you sure she was here?" asks Quinn.

I'm not, but I am. "I think if they let Stella see them, it's because they wanted her to see them. Especially if they managed to ambush Sylvie and Taran. I don't think it's a coincidence that they led us this way."

Quinn grumbles and complains more about my distrust, but I don't hear her.

"Sylvie," I say. She's waking up. *She's alive. Thank the gods, she's alive. Thank you, Vayla. Thank you. I'll never doubt you again.* She's frightened, but it's mixed with some degree of comfort. Someone must be with her. Hermes, her alchemist?

"She's in this direction," I say, pointing to the floor at the back corner. "Look at these floorboards."

The others come over, and we tug at each of the floorboards. Nothing. Not even a hint of movement.

"Fuck," says Quinn, sitting back against the wall.

There's a soft *clink* of metal behind her.

"Was that your dagger?" I ask.

"No," she says, tapping it at her side. She moves away from the wall.

I shine the light from my hands there. It's incredibly small, but there's a little piece of metal jutting out from the wall. I push on it harder.

The stones move back, swinging into a passage.

A hidden door. It's just like the ones at the palace. I'm not sure how they could have missed it.

"Wait, Ronan," says Quinn as I pass the threshold. "It could be a trap."

"Of course it's a trap," I say. "Why else would they let us find it?" I'm convinced this metal wasn't here before. They must have removed it to keep us from finding the door until now. And if this door works similarly to the ones in the palace, they have a way to secure it from the other side. Which they didn't do.

"Ronan, stop. Let's think about this," says Quinn.

"There's nothing to think about. She's through here, and she's alive. If I wait, she may not be. Stella, go get the other guards and bring them here. There may be others with Sylvie."

"Yes, sir," says Stella.

I know once again that Quinn isn't wrong. But what am I meant to do about a trap set by an alchemist? What would that even look like? Some kind of elixir or poison? Do they intend to dip me into a great big vat of molten gold?

"Let me go first at least, sir," says Taran, nudging me to the side.

I nod to him. That placates them both.

The passage is pitch black beyond. I send a light floating down the hall where it slopes downwards into a cellar of some kind.

"Let's go," says Taran, following my light.

We keep a brisk pace, but we don't run. Taran uses my light to check for traps, but the passage is perfectly clear.

"They wanted us to keep going," says Taran. "I don't like that."

I don't either. The cellar we saw from above is really just a wider passage. There aren't any junctions or rooms. Just a set of connected corridors carved from stone and earth, leading further down beneath the city.

"How did they even dig a tunnel like this? How long do you think this has been here?" asks Quinn.

"A while," I say, looking at the way the stone crumbles on the walls. There are many cellars and basement passages in the city, some of which even lead into the palace, but they tend to be short, connected only to the next building or so. This tunnel leads across several blocks.

This tunnel leads to the Alchemists' Guild. I can feel it.

"Still feel her?" asks Taran as we wind around another junction-less bend.

"She's frightened but no longer terrified. She's maybe a little confused?"

"Confused?" says Quinn. "I swear to Vayla, if we find her and she's just having tea with Hermes at the guild…"

There's an edge to Quinn's voice despite her words. They've become friends these past few weeks, and I can feel Quinn's worry for her. I was glad to see them grow closer, not that I could have prevented it even if I wasn't. But I was also immensely jealous, feeling her joy and excitement from a distance and not being part of it. I wanted to share the things they shared with her, with them both. I still can, I tell myself as the fear begins to seize me. All we have to do is find her.

"She's close now," I say finally. I can't believe I felt her through all this distance. I don't understand how or why my connection to her seems to keep growing, but I'm grateful for it, especially right now.

"Should we do this together?" asks Quinn. "Or one by one, in case they have something that can take us out?"

"I still have the smelling salts," says Taran. "I'll go first, but one of you should carry them."

"No," I say. He's right—I know he's right—but I have to let her see me first. "I'll go alone. Let them think there's no one else here. You wait in the hall."

"But we can't feel you like you can feel us," says Quinn. "It doesn't make sense. Come on, Ronan. I know you love her, but think rationally."

My pulse picks up when I hear those words. Of course Quinn can tell. Hell, I think the entire court can tell.

As much as I'm grateful for Quinn and Taran, I wish I had a shadow-born here to help me. We've been trying to hire a shadow-born guard after Sylvie's rescue pointed out the holes in our security, but they're in short supply. Maybe we'll find one in whatever room they have Sylvie in.

"Fine," I say. "Taran, go around that bend. There's no one in the hall, but I expect there's a door nearby. Look, listen, and make no sound. Then we can decide. I'll keep the light here around the corner. Signal if it isn't enough for you to tell."

He creeps in the darkness, his footsteps almost completely silent in spite of his armor. It's something the Orsa must have taught him because I have no other guards who can keep as quiet.

"There's a single door on the left. Then the passage continues, but the light didn't reach far. I see no one around and no obvious traps."

"Should we knock?" asks Quinn.

I chuckle in spite of myself, and I'm glad she's here to help lighten the mood. "I'm going."

They both start to protest, and I silence them. "I know. But she's there, and she needs me. Wait around the corner. If you hear anything—anything—that sounds like a struggle, come in."

"Yes, sir," says Taran.

"Go get her, you idiot," says Quinn.

I walk to the door, and I reach for the handle, but then—

Sylvie is gone again. Her feelings vanish, and I'm filled with the sudden terror that I'll find her dead on the other side. That I won't find her at all, and that *this* is the trap. They've somehow impersonated her, or she's tricked me somehow. That Quinn was right, and this was all part of her plan to kill me.

No. I don't believe it. I could never believe it.

She's here, and she needs me.

I fling the door open, traps be damned.

Chapter Thirty-Three

Ronan

The room is silent and still when I enter it, with only the flicker of a candle in the corner to let me know someone has been in here recently.

And then I see her on the table.

"Sylvie! She's here!"

I hear Quinn and Taran rush in behind me. "What's that?" asks Quinn, pointing to something on the floor as I rush to Sylvie. "Cracked door," says Taran. "Footsteps. Looks like someone left in a hurry—"

I don't know what they're talking about, and I don't care. Sylvie is here. I touch her—she's alive; thank the gods, she's alive—but she's hurt. Some light bruises on her hands and wrists, and gods, what's that? There's blood flowing from her arm. Now I see what Quinn meant. There's some kind of tube coming out. Quinn picks up a bag from the floor. I can't tell what either thing is made of. I've never seen anything like it in my life.

Quinn moves to detach whatever it is from Sylvie's arm, but I stop her. "She needs that," I say about the blood in the bag. There's so much of it. "She's weak."

"Can it just…go back in?" she asks, giving the bag a gentle squeeze.

"I don't know. Maybe," I say, holding the bag up. "Yes," I say, feeling Sylvie's pulse. I squeeze the bag again. "I think that's working."

"Where's the trap, Ronan?" asks Quinn. "There was meant to be a trap."

"I don't know, but I'm getting her out of here. Find Taran. The other shadow-born may be here somewhere."

Quinn takes off down the hall. I lift Sylvie into my arms, carefully holding the bag above her.

Once Quinn's footsteps are gone, I feel the slice of steel at my left ankle.

What the fuck?

The wound burns and then fades suddenly, strangely. It's deep. My left leg collapses beneath me, and I nearly lose my grip on Sylvie.

There's someone under the table where I found her. How? There was no one there when I came into the room.

"Quinn!" I shout, but there's commotion at the end of the hall.

I fire out light from my hands to see what I'm doing. I can probably heal it myself, though if it's deep enough, I may need a nature-born to walk again.

Fuck. We've got to get out of here. "Taran!" I yell.

He doesn't respond, but I have another problem. The wound on my heel isn't closing all the way. The light I'm using to heal myself barely shines. My magic has been weakened again somehow, even though it was working just fine moments ago.

"Problem?" says a voice. The person under the table, the person who cut me, is a woman.

The person under the table is Zara.

For a moment, I think I had it wrong, and that she was kidnapped too. But then I see the blade in her hand.

I shouldn't be surprised. This is hardly my first betrayal, and yet this one still hurts because not only did I trust Zara, I liked her. She was like me.

Or at least she let me believe she was.

"Poisoned blade?" I ask her. If there's one thing I've never liked about Zara, it's that she has a tendency to gloat. Without the full use of my magic, my only option is my sword, and I can't both reach for my sword to take her out and keep hold of Sylvie. So what I need to do is buy some time until help arrives.

"Hardly," she says. She crawls out from under the table and glances down the hall. "They're busy down there, but I don't think we have long enough for me to explain." She sighs, rolling her dagger's handle in her hand. "I thought you'd come alone. I didn't want to have to be the one to do this."

She's going to try to fight me directly. Gods, she's arrogant. She has no combat experience that I know of. She thinks she can beat me because I'm down a leg?

"How did you hide yourself? At least tell me that."

I can see where she concealed herself beneath the table and why I didn't notice her, but I should have been able to feel her there.

"In Eki, there's a form of meditation that lets you enter into a state without thoughts or feelings. It's like a conscious sleep state. It's nearly impossible to do while moving, but it's fairly easily managed sitting still. The real trick is not reacting when someone shows up. But I've had lots of practice over the past few years."

"The candle," I say as she brings the dagger closer. "It's the candle, isn't it?" It's a wild guess, but there isn't much else in the room that could be affecting my magic.

"Not bad, Ronan. Not bad at all. Yes, it's the candle that suppresses your power. One of my best ideas, I think. It only affects the magic of the light-born, and only when you burn it, but there are so many candles in the palace. In the arena. It wasn't hard to replace enough of them to make you vulnerable."

I feel Sylvie stirring. Not her body, but her feelings. They're faint, but I can't tell if it's because she's weak or because I am. *Don't move,* I tell her. I have no idea if she can feel me right now, but I beg her not to move nonetheless.

"Doesn't it affect you?" I ask.

Zara smiles. "Yes, but a bit less than you. Oh, it really is interesting why."

Now I've got her.

"Tell me."

"I would love to, but…well, it's complicated." She leans out into the hall to check on what's happening down there. To check if she has time to patronize me. "Have you noticed something unusual about Sylvie?"

"My magic is different around her. Do you know why I feel her so strongly?" I don't admit the rest to Zara, the way that I'm able to share some of my power with her, the way my light shines even in her darkness. I can't risk that Zara can do something with that knowledge if I don't make it and Sylvie does.

"It's more than just you. It's her magic, too. The two of you together, affecting each other. You're shadowbound. The texts on the phenomenon are difficult to come by, most of them destroyed in one of the purges. But I managed to locate a copy some time ago…such a pity I don't have time to show you. I do think you'd find it fascinating. Now, I really am going to have to just do it." She raises the dagger to strike at my throat, giving me no time to consider what she said.

I can't let her kill me. Not while Sylvie still needs me. "It's harder than you thought it would be, isn't it?" I ask. Even with my magic weakened, I can feel her hesitation. She's been responsible for some terrible things here, but she's never directly taken a life before. "You don't have to do this. You can heal me, and you can let us go."

"It's a touching idea, Ronan, but no. I don't love killing you, but it's for the greater good. You understand that, don't you? I know everything you've tried to do has been for the same reason. We really do have a lot in common. It's a pity you could never understand that some ends justify all means. We could have done so much together."

Sylvie reaches out beneath me. She's paralyzed, her body paralyzed somehow though her mind has awoken, but her magic is there.

And I can feel what she's going to do the moment before she does it.

Sylvie reaches out with her shadows, invisible in the darkness until they reach the candle, and she snuffs it out.

The candle's effects don't vanish immediately, but they don't need to. I can't see what's happening, but I can feel it as Sylvie turns the shadows with alarming speed. I hear Zara fly back through the open door as she screams.

I lower Sylvie to the ground, fumbling to place the blood bag on the table. Sylvie is trying to hold Zara, but she can't see her from her position. I draw my sword just as Zara feels an opening in the shadows that bind her. She bursts free, dagger in hand, lunging forward…

But she can't see what she's aiming for. She stabs blindly, striking Sylvie as my sword, guided by feel, plunges into Zara's gut.

I toss Zara back, hobbling to the ground to help Sylvie. I feel the blood rush out of her leg when I touch her skin, but the candle's effects linger. I can't heal her. The wound won't close.

"Quinn!" I shout. "Quinn, get back here!"

"Just a minute," she calls from down the hall. There are muffled cries coming from behind a door. I can't sense how many people are there from this distance and with my magic as weak as it is, but it's a lot.

"NOW!"

"Fuck!" she yells. "Taran!"

And then I hear her footsteps tearing down the hall. I smell the smoke and sweat on her as she steps over Zara and into the room, a flame in her palm.

"Is that the Guild Mistress?"

"Heal Sylvie," I demand. In the flickering light of Quinn's flame, I see just how much blood is pouring from her, and it flips my stomach upside down.

"What? Oh, shit." Quinn kneels down to Sylvie and presses the flame to the wound in the leg.

Sylvie doesn't cry out. I don't think she can feel much of the pain, at least.

"I'm sorry," I murmur to her, rocking her motionless body. "I'll fix it as soon as I can."

Quinn's flame stops the bleeding, thank the gods, but it leaves a terrible mark of burnt flesh on Sylvie's thigh. She's so weak, and I have no fucking idea what to do about whatever is keeping her from moving.

It chills me to the bone. It reminds me of losing my mother, how her body went before her mind. It was just after my magic settled, just after I'd begun to feel her and others. I felt her trapped in there for days, unable to move or speak. And then I felt her mind slip away too.

It was horrible. I can't bear it again.

"I'm going to fix this," I promise Sylvie. "I don't know how, but I'm going to."

"What the fuck happened? Where's your magic?" asks Quinn.

"Don't light the candle," I say as she gets near it. "It's poison. That's what has been affecting my magic. Did you find the shadow-born?"

"Yeah, and about twenty alchemists guarding them. More than half of them fled once the fighting really got going. Are you alright here? I should make sure more of them haven't shown up."

Quinn's fire won't be able to heal my ankle; I'm going to need to wait until I can heal myself to be able to walk, if that even works. Sylvie needs help, but not the kind that fire can provide. "If any of the alchemists are alive, send them here to heal her. A nature-born, if they have one."

"You got it," she says. "What about her?" she asks as she nudges Zara's stilling body with her foot.

Her feelings are fading. Maybe there was a chance for her, but it passed long ago.

If I'm honest with myself, it passed the moment she touched Sylvie.

"It's too late for her," I say. "Go."

Chapter Thirty-Four

Ronan

I cradle Sylvie to me as I wait for Quinn to return. I feel the slightest stir of her shoulder against my body. *Please, Sylvie. Please be alright.*

My beautiful, darling Sylvie. I'm not going to lose her. I'm not. Not again. I can't lose her.

The panic shifts to anger. What was Zara doing to her? What was she doing to the shadow-born, and why?

Was it all to get to me? Is Sylvie in this state because of me?

Sylvie knows something, I realize. She's trying to tell me something with her feelings, but I can't understand it.

"Just rest," I tell her. "We'll figure it out when you're better."

The pain in my ankle makes itself known as my heart rate returns to normal. I reach out and touch it, trying my magic once more.

It's working, a little. It's slower than ordinary, but something is happening at last.

"Finally." I stop what I'm doing and focus on Sylvie, sending a light into the room so I can see her clearly. I do what I can for the wound on her leg; she'll need a nature-born to prevent it from scarring, but it shouldn't cause her much pain. Then I remove the tube from her arm—at least most of the blood from the bag went back in—and I heal the small hole it leaves behind.

Only then do I return to my own ankle. Thankfully, the flesh there is thin, so although the wound is deep, it's accessible to my light. I'd feel better if I had an elixir, though.

Zara would have made one for me. Fuck, I'd been so blind. She had done so much of my care the past couple of years, refusing to let the other alchemists do it. And I'd let her. I'd appreciated the personal attention of the Guild Mistress. I'd appreciated the presence of someone light-born, the only one I'd met after my father died. It blinded me to her true intentions.

But it does validate what I've long suspected about the nature of light magic.

I feel multiple people coming through the halls we traveled to get here before I can hear them. Stella and my guards.

"In here," I call. I stand up, lifting Sylvie into my arms once more.

"Sir?" Stella freezes inside the door at the bloody scene, torch in hand.

"Help Quinn and Taran down the hall."

They rush through the room, pushing Zara's body to the side as they vanish into the darkened corridor. They return only minutes later, trailing behind Quinn, who shoves an alchemist into the room. "Heal her, and maybe I won't kill you."

The alchemist examines Sylvie as others trail into the small room. He lifts her limbs and examines the movement of her eyes as I hold her. "Tincture of hemlock," he says, his voice trembling. "One of the Guild Mistress's. There's no antidote, but from her movements, the Guild Mistress didn't use enough to kill her. It will wear off on its own in a few hours."

She could have died. Gods, she could have died.

Why didn't she die? What was the purpose of keeping her alive? "Why didn't Zara kill her?"

"We need them alive for the alchemy, sir. Forgive me, your majesty," he says, cowering before me. "I didn't know—"

"Enough," I say. They were using the blood of the shadow-born for the fucking alchemy. I should have known. The rage rises in me as he sputters, trying to justify himself. If he doesn't get away from me this moment, I'm going to kill him. And I might need him alive to help Sylvie and the shadow-born. "Get him out of my sight."

Stella rushes forward and takes the man away into the hallway. It's a sorry scene in the little room and the hallway beyond. My guards are either restraining alchemists or holding up one of a group of people in decaying rags that looks like they haven't had a proper meal in weeks.

I look over the shadow-born, trying to find Vesper, but I don't see her there among them.

Damn. Sylvie nearly died tonight, *and* I was too late to save Vesper.

This is my fault. They were in this mess because of me. I did this.

And then I notice a woman with reddish brown hair.

"Vesper?" I ask. Her hair is so filthy I can barely tell, but it looks like it might have been Vesper's vibrant red once. And there are holes in her ears that once held earrings. She's unrecognizable otherwise. Her face is gaunt, and her skin is sallow. She looks days away from death.

Fucking hell, what did they do to her? She's only nineteen. She was just meant to track Cyrus when he left the palace. It's my fault she ended up here.

It's my fault Sylvie ended up here.

"Your majesty?" she asks weakly. Of course. She doesn't know who I am without Soren's mask.

"Someone has been looking for you," I say. I feel Sylvie urge me to let her see. "We found her," I whisper as I hold her up.

There are eight shadow-born in all. The three we knew were missing, and another five that we didn't. And gods know what else we'll find here and in the Guild when we return.

"Let's get the fuck out of here," I say as Taran hobbles in, clutching at his side. I heal him quickly; the wound is shallow. He tries to carry Sylvie for me, but I won't let him.

We make our way back through the narrow halls and into an awaiting carriage in the alley. Sylvie lifts her head slightly as we approach it, and I sigh in immense relief at her movement.

"I've got you," I tell her. "I'll never let anything happen to you."

But I don't know if I can really promise her that. I'm the reason she was here tonight. Zara came after her to get to me. She must have been watching, waiting for this opportunity to strike.

And she's far from my only enemy.

"Ronan," she groans out, her voice barely more than a whisper. I feel her fear. She must have sensed my feelings about endangering her. She's worried that I'm going to leave her.

I should. I should at least consider it, consider what's best for her.

She is screaming at me with her feelings. The feeling is so strong, I can almost hear her voice in my mind. "Don't you dare," she's saying. "Don't you dare leave me."

"I'm here, Sylvie. I'm here. I'm not going anywhere."

Gods, I don't think I could if I tried. And I hate myself for it. I hate how selfish it is. I hate the way that it strengthens my magic to admit it to myself, to her. To admit that I'm going to keep her as close to me as I can, no matter the consequences for us both.

I can't let her go.

I hold her in my arms and press my light into her skin through my hands, gripping her as tightly as I can. I don't think she's in pain, but I hope the light soothes her. I hope it comforts her.

I whisper soothing words to her, my lips on her forehead, in her hair. My hands stroking her back. "I've got you. You're safe. I'm here. I won't let you go." I whisper them over and over as the carriage takes us home.

As I carry Sylvie into the palace, she croaks out another word at me. "Bath."

I can't say I blame her for asking. Her dress is soaked in her blood, and her hair and body are filthy from the cellar floor.

But I'm ashamed to admit that my own body responds to her request. I know I shouldn't want to see her naked in this state, but it's hard to forget what we were doing before all of this happened.

And it's even harder when she starts feeling things at me again. Wicked, wonderful things.

"Should I get a servant?" I ask. They're busy replacing all the candles in the entire palace, but it's the polite thing to do, to offer to let a servant bathe her. The gentlemanly thing to do.

I don't want to be polite.

"No," she says, shaking her head to the side a tiny bit. "You."

With fucking pleasure.

I carry her down the stairs into my private bathing chambers. There's a large copper basin that I use when I'm too dirty to enter the natural pools, and I ask the servants to fill it while I tend to her.

I place her on a bench with a towel beneath her. Her feelings are begging me to undress her, to hold her, to kiss her again, and fuck, I want to. "You have no idea how fucking badly I want to."

But I can't do it, not while she can't respond to me.

"I promise I'll give you everything you want," I say to her. "But not until you can move on your own. Not until you can feel it with your body as well as your mind."

Her mouth pouts a little at the corners. I want to kiss the smile back onto her face.

But I resist. I pull her toward me, feeling her warm breath on my neck as I slip the fabric off her shoulders. She's straining, trying to get her lips to move.

"Just relax," I say. "Let me take care of you."

I step back to ease the fabric from her waist, and gods, the sight of her naked drives me wild with desire.

I've wanted this so badly. I've pictured her body so many times; I've touched myself to the fantasy of her. I've come in my hand with her name on my lips. But to see her, to finally see all of her, it's beyond my wildest dreams.

"Touch me," she begs, her voice just a tiny bit stronger. Gods, I want to. I want to hold those beautiful breasts in my hands, to circle her perfect little nipples with my tongue, to feel her arch under me—

"No," I say. There won't be any arching, not for a while yet. And there won't be much feeling either, not on her part. I shimmy the fabric from beneath her, trying very hard not to look at the space between her legs, the space where my tongue was only hours earlier.

I pick her up before I can get a better look, but it doesn't help. If anything, it's worse with her naked body pressed against me. Her desperate attempts to push herself against me, fruitless though they are, are driving me mad.

"I'm getting you clean, and then you're getting some rest. And then we can talk about whatever you're trying to do down there."

"Talk now," she whines.

I hold her head up and look her in the eyes. "I can't. If I talk about it…"

I swallow. Fuck, I can barely stop myself from touching her as it is.

I lower her into the steaming bath. Her fingertips grip the fabric of my shirt, begging me to remove it and join her.

I want to. I'm filthy too. Would it be so bad to bathe with her?

The throbbing erection in my pants tells me that yes, yes, it would be.

"You're going to be the death of me," I tell her. She wanted to be the death of me, once. And now she's succeeded. At this rate, I'm going to die from wanting her.

I take a washcloth from a tray and soak it in the warm water. Then I lather it with soap until it's covered in delicate bubbles.

I take a deep breath before running it over her body.

I can do this.

I swipe the cloth across her skin, focusing first on her arms and shoulders. "It would be easier if you'd stop that." I feel her begging for me to rub the cloth on her breasts, to dip it under the surface of the water and rub it between her legs.

Fuck. *Fuck*, I want that too, and so the feeling reverberates between us, and it's like I'm already doing it even though my hands are nowhere near any of the forbidden places. I lean forward, gripping the side of the tub for balance.

Her lips part, and her eyes are soft and inviting. She looks so lovely and erotic there against the walls of the bath.

"Nope," I say, and I drop the cloth into the water. I grab a pitcher from the stand and fill it, then I pour it gently over her hair. I stand and move behind her so that I can work her hair into a lather.

It's safer back here. If I kneel down, I can't see her body. I can almost forget that she's naked and begging for me, and all I have to do is—

Stop it, I tell myself. Well, less myself and more my dick. It's straining within the silk fabric of my pants, rubbing a droplet of my need for her around. Thank the gods that one of my great-great-grandparents changed the house color to black.

Although there's only one person here to see if I make a mess of my pants, and I have a feeling she would enjoy it.

I lather the soap into her hair, washing out the sweat and grime and blood. I massage her scalp as I work her hair clean, and she moans softly.

I feel the sound directly in my cock.

Gently, slowly, I dip my hands beneath the surface and push her body forward, trying to ignore the way her ass feels under my hands, trying to forget the memory of pulling her towards me and tasting her. I keep one hand on her neck as I dip her head back into the water, rinsing the suds from her hair.

She looks up at me, her face full of bliss. "Kiss me," she begs, her voice clearer now than earlier.

I tilt my head down and plant a soft kiss on her forehead.

"No," she groans. "More." She tries to lift her arm up to pull me to her, and it nearly breaks the surface.

"Not long now," I tell her.

She splashes the water with her fingertips in frustration.

"Believe me, I know how you feel."

I turn my attention back to bathing her. I push her back by her hips until she's sitting against the wall of the tub once more, and then I draw her dark, wet hair over her chest like a curtain.

She makes a pouty sound, but I ignore her. I retrieve the cloth from the surface and wipe it over her arms, her legs, and finally her stomach. As I clean the inside of her bellybutton, she thrusts her hips upwards to force my hand down, and I feel the motion echo in my own hips.

"Mm," I grunt as it nearly doubles me over the tub. She's *begging* me with her feelings to clean her.

"Please," she says.

It would be unfair to her to get her in the bath and leave her dirty. It's for this reason that I allow myself two quick swipes of the cloth over her breasts, pinching the interior of my thigh with my other hand to keep myself from losing control.

Then, before I can think about it, I part her legs and clean between them. I turn my head to the side so I can't see it. I know if I see it, I'm going to give in. The sounds she makes as I touch her are nearly enough on their own.

"You too," she says. Her hand breaks the surface—finally—but she can't lift it beyond it. But I can feel what she wants. She wants me to join her, and I'm powerless to fight it any longer.

I set the cloth aside and stand next to the tub. Her eyes track my movement, and she manages to tilt her head towards me. She watches, breathless, as I pull my shirt from my body. Her hands twitch beneath the surface as I untie the laces of my breeches.

The look she gives me when she sees me, naked and throbbing hard for her, makes my mouth water.

I don't join her in the tub. The water is tinged red with her blood. Instead, I lift her out of it, holding her sideways against my chest so that none of our sensitive places are touching. Then I carry her to the natural bath. I place her seated upright on a smooth shelf of rock while I bathe myself.

She watches hungrily as I wash my hair and body, straining to touch me. "Ronan, get over here," she pleads. She's almost able to push herself up now.

I sink beneath the surface, needing a moment without her eyes on me to calm me down. It doesn't help. When I reemerge, she's pushed herself away from the rock wall.

Fuck it, I can't wait any longer.

"Close enough," I say, and I splash through the water, pulling her into my arms.

Her mouth responds to my hungry, claiming kiss, but that's about all that does.

She moans and weakly thrashes her little fist where it's pressed against my chest in frustration.

"That's better than it was," I say to her encouragingly, lifting her fist to my mouth and kissing it. "By the time we're upstairs, you'll be ready. Wait and see."

I carry her from the pool and set her down on a chair. Her legs still can't support their own weight, but she can mostly sit up now as I dry her off. I dry myself as well, but I don't bother to put the clothes the servants have left us on us, which makes her happy.

I pick her up again, but this time to hold her facing me, letting her rest the soft folds between her legs on my belly. I feel the skin there slicken as I kiss her again, carrying her up the private staircase to my bed chambers.

She doesn't regain her motion by the time I set her on the bed, but she's close. She writhes against the dark, velvety fabric of the comforter as I peel it back to help her into the sheets. The fire crackles in the fireplace, but the sheets are cool, and by the time I climb into bed with her, she's shivering.

I pull her onto me, rubbing her arms to warm her. Her hand drifts up my chest, reaching for my jaw, and I bend down and kiss her the way she wants. The way she's been begging me to.

Her body responds now, her legs spreading to rub herself against me. I moan as I pull her up, taking her mouth with my hands in her damp hair. She breaks the kiss, panting and kissing my jaw.

She's really moving now, and it's driving me even wilder than the anticipation of it did.

She lowers herself to my neck and then my chest, and I tug on her to stop her. If she takes me in her mouth now, I'll finish there, and I don't want to finish yet. "You don't need to—" I start, but she presses a kiss off-center to the left side of my chest.

"I do need to," she says. Her voice is clear and warm now, but there's a tinge of sadness to it, and I can feel something like sadness coming from her.

"Sylvie?" I ask, but she nudges my arm aside so she can reach the side of my body.

My scar. The scar her father gave me.

My heart hammers in my chest as she approaches it. She runs her fingertips along the shining white length of it, and then—with painstaking slowness—she presses a kiss to it.

I choke. Heat rises up my back into my neck and into my face, springing tears to my eyes. I fight them back, swallowing hard, trying to hide the feeling. I jerk my head to the side and squeeze my eyes shut.

Gods, I'm ashamed. I have this beautiful woman, this woman that I'm absolutely insane about, in my bed, and I'm about to fucking cry—

She reaches for me, taking my face in her hands. Then she presses kisses to my eyelashes, to the corner of my eyes, and fuck, I can't hold on—

I collapse into her, the tears wrenching themselves from me. The loneliness, the guilt, the regret. All of the terrible things I've done, all of the lives I've taken, all of the times I've felt sick with the shame, the times I've hated myself, the times I've wished I wasn't here. Standing on the cliff, feeling the blade coming for me, wanting it to come. The selfishness of wanting her, the fear of losing her. All of it comes pouring out, dissolving into her, melting away into her perfect comfort and understanding, her kindness and forgiveness, the balm my soul needs to rest.

I love her. I've known it for a while, but I haven't been able to fully say the words, even to myself. But now, here, the feeling unleashes itself from within me. I'm coming undone, and I don't even care.

I'm in love with her.

I let the feeling consume me, let it drive away the darkness, let it shine its incandescent glow into the recesses of my mind, the shadowy, secret places I've kept for myself alone.

And then, with her beautiful face hovering above me, with the flickering firelight dancing in her eyes, kissing her skin with warmth and heat, I feel the echo of it.

I feel my love echoed in her heart.

I kiss her, sighing my confession onto her lips.

Then I lose myself completely.

Chapter Thirty-Five

I taste Ronan's tears on my lips, salty and sweet, as I hover over him.

There's a feeling between us that's more than the raw desire and lust I felt while he bathed me. While he tortured me. Damn his respect. I didn't care that I wouldn't have been able to feel it all. Just seeing him touching me would have been enough.

Seeing him naked for the first time. Seeing the length of him, the hardness of his cock and his body, and not being able to touch him?

Agony.

I didn't think I'd be able to feel anything but the all-consuming desire he built up in me over those long, excruciating hours of denial ever again.

But here it is. A feeling I can't name. I'm not ready to say it, to give it form in my mind, but I know what it is.

And instead of holding it back, I let the wall that holds the feeling back fall. It crumbles somewhere deep within me, and I feel the sweet release of letting go, letting the floodgates open.

The reverberation of the feeling is all-consuming. It's the most intense thing I've ever felt, an endless echo not only of the passion and desire between us but of the care we have for each other, the intense need to see the other happy, the compulsion to give ourselves completely.

It echoes on my skin as I touch him, as I feel him pressing himself to me, as he kisses my mouth and then my neck. As he clutches me to him, pulling us upright until I'm facing him, my hips straining to meet his.

He grabs my ass and pulls me to him as he lowers his mouth to my breasts. He greedily kisses and licks them, sucking each nipple into his mouth until I'm moaning and grinding myself wet against him, begging him to enter me.

He takes my face in his hands and kisses me deeply. I feel the tingle of his light on my skin. I'm not sure if he means to do it or if he can even control it, but it feels wonderful. I beg him in my feelings not to stop.

Then he pulls back and looks me in the eyes.

"I'm yours," he says. I kiss him fiercely, and he responds, lifting me and throwing me down onto the soft bed. His strength, his power. It turns me on even more. I'm melting, molten under his touch. "Only yours, Sylvie."

He kisses my neck, reaching low and rubbing my clit as his cock presses against my entrance. I moan and wrap my legs around him, inviting him in. "Please, Ronan," I beg. "Please take me."

He groans, low and deep, his eyes rolling with his arousal.

"Silphium?" he asks.

"Yes," I say. I took my contraceptive elixir in the morning, like every morning.

I press my foot into his back. I'm so wet, the head of his cock slips into me, and I feel the reverberation of our desires for him to slam into me to the hilt echo between us.

He doesn't slam in though, not at first.

He moves achingly slowly, taking me a little at a time, letting me relax around his length, in and out, just a bit more each time, until he finally slides all the way in, his body pressed against mine as close as it can be.

He holds me there for a long moment, stroking my hair and kissing my lips. "You feel so fucking good." He groans and leans off to the side, straining to control himself. "The way you feel inside. The way you take me. Fuck, Sylvie. It's incredible. You're incredible."

I sigh at the praise, desperate for him to fuck me. To claim me. To make me his. He waits until I push against him, begging for him with my body and mind, before he moves.

"*Ronan*," I gasp as he relinquishes control. The feelings echo between us, longing and the nameless other thing, the pleasure of his body and mine, endlessly repeating in my body and my mind. My body clenches around him as I squeeze my legs—finally fully free, finally fully moving—around his back, as I claw at his shoulders, as I ruin his damp hair with my tugging grasp.

Finally.

Finally he slams into me, guided by my desire for it, plunging in deep and working in me there, pressing himself against the center of my pleasure, building me to a place of exquisite release. The heat flows into my back, my hips, my thighs. I drive him into me with my heels, raising my hips to him, begging him to get closer, to lose himself in me, to find his release with mine.

He groans in my ear, holding me down to his bed, gripping the back of my neck like he's holding on for dear life. I gasp as he lifts my right hip to bury himself even further, his movements becoming erratic, pulling out and plunging back in with wild abandon. He's gasping in my ear, moaning my name, and it sends me over the edge, my body tightening and then releasing in waves of starlight behind my closed eyes, waves that send spasms into my muscles until I'm shaking, trembling beneath him. Until I feel the pleasure echoed in his body, his frantic thrusts culminating into a deep, gasping plunge as his release fills me with warmth and light, the aftershocks of his climax shaking and jolting us until he finally, breathlessly, collapses on top of me.

I stroke his hair—almost dry and mussed beyond his worst imaginings—as he kisses my breast; soft kisses tinged with yearning that tell me this night has only just begun.

I press a kiss to his forehead.

This is the man I was sent here to kill.

I hear my own words in my memory, the Sylvie from months ago swearing she'd never take him into her bed. I don't know her. I don't recognize her anymore.

But I remember her loneliness.

I wish I could go back and talk to her. To tell her that the thing she fears, the worst thing she could ever imagine, is exactly what she needs. To tell her she isn't alone. There's someone like her, someone who will see her in ways she's never been seen, if only she'll just let him.

Ronan lifts himself above me and brushes a soft kiss to my lips, a question in his eyes. What am I thinking?

I tell him. Not the thing I can't name for myself, not yet, but I tell him the only thing I can think of right now, the only thought I'm capable of having when I'm near him.

"I'm yours, Ronan," I say, and he takes me in his arms again.

Chapter Thirty-Six

I wake in the morning on my side with Ronan's arms wrapped around me, his body pressed against mine.

There's a chill in the room where the fire has gone out, though I can only feel it on my cheek, the rest of my body shielded from it by his embrace. The morning light is streaming through airy white curtains, casting soft shadows through the room.

Ronan's bedchambers. A place I'd thought about so many times, and I'm finally here, waking up with him.

The space is smaller than I had imagined. The four-post bed takes up most of it, leaving only enough room for a velvet chair and a small table near the fireplace. The furniture in here, as I expected, is all Nithyrian wood. The sheets against my body are smooth white silk, and the comforter over us is soft and wine-colored, with golden threads running through it.

Ronan stirs against me, and I feel the length of him as he shifts my hips back to him. We woke each other twice more in the night, and I thought that after the last time had left me so satiated I couldn't see straight that we'd taken care of our desires at least until the evening came again. But feeling him against me, my body responds, sending warmth between my legs once more.

He kisses my shoulder as I pull him into me again. We're both so exhausted, our bodies so spent, that we stay exactly where we are. We take turns, him thrusting into me, me shoving my hips back and taking him in, until we find our release again in moaning gasps, our bodies slick with sweat and each other.

By the time I wake again a little while later, the windows have been opened, allowing a warm, late morning breeze into the room. The bed beside me is empty, but Ronan hasn't gone far. He's wrapped in a loose robe, sitting at the small table eating breakfast.

When he hears me sit up, he comes over to me, kissing me on the cheek. "Good morning," he says. It wasn't a dream, then. Thank Kerensa for that. "I hope you don't mind that I started without you. You looked too peaceful to disturb."

Another chair has been brought into the room. Ronan shows me to his washroom through an absurdly large chamber dedicated entirely to his clothes—which do exist in colors other than black, although black predominates—and I take the opportunity to freshen up, donning a silk robe of my own in a sage green color.

I notice that he's already fixed his hair. I muss it up as I join him at the table, eliciting a very adorable, "Hey!" and a lot of frantic smoothing.

I devour my breakfast—eggs, sausage, roasted vegetables, and a chewy honeyed pastry that I've grown particularly fond of and that has appeared more and more frequently on the palace menu in recent weeks, purely coincidentally, I'm sure.

As I'm eating, Ronan explains that he'll need to spend the day, possibly the next few days, dealing with the Alchemists' Guild situation. He invites me to join him, but I decline, at least for today. I need to let Larus know what happened to me before they hear it from someone else. (And Adria too, I suppose.)

And I need to find out if Larus has managed to derail the invasion. Because there is one last thing between us—the reason that we came here. I want to tell him the truth even more now after he saved me. After what happened between us last night.

But I can't betray my family. Not unless I have no other choice.

After breakfast and one final morning tumble in the sheets, Ronan shows me a passage that leads from his chambers to the hall that contains the chambers Adria and I share.

"I'd like to introduce you to the court," he says, suddenly shy, as I'm about to leave. "At the closing ball. If it would be alright with you."

He doesn't say it, but I understand his meaning. He'd like to introduce me to the court as his consort. His partner.

It's a serious move. From what I know of courtly politics, only official relationships receive such an introduction typically, and only when the monarch or other royal intends to marry, although the marriage could still be far off.

It's a lot to grasp. As much as I feel for him, I don't know how I feel about letting everyone else know. There's a part of me that wants to shout it from the palace rooftops, but there's also a part of me that wants to keep it entirely to ourselves. To keep it our secret, something that we share with only each other, for as long as possible.

Maybe it's the shadow-born in me.

"Oh," he says, feeling my panic. There's a twinge of pain, and then he smiles mischievously. "Of course. I'm getting ahead of myself. Our secret for now, then."

And then he fucking winks at me.

"I swear to the gods—"

"You love it," he says, winking wildly so that it looks like his face is spasming and pulling me into his arms.

He kisses me while laughing. The kiss deepens, as all of our kisses seem to do now, but he breaks from it, spanking me as he sends me into the passage.

"Get out of here before I take you back to bed," he says, and I sigh as I return to my chambers, missing him already.

I find Adria and Larus together in a palace courtyard, watching the winning comedy street performance. It's a bawdy, silly affair about fishmongers going on an epic quest; Quinn and I saw it a couple of weeks ago before the competition came to a close.

"And where have you been?" Adria whispers to me.

Damn. I was hoping she would have found someone to keep her entertained last night, but it seems like she noticed I was gone.

"Kidnapped," I say simply. Larus's eyes open wide. "Nearly killed."

"Very funny," she says.

"Sylvie?" asks Larus, realizing I'm serious.

"I found the missing shadow-born I told you about a few weeks ago," I say to Adria. "The Guild Mistress decided I needed to join their number. Apparently Hermes was helping her. He's dead."

That finally gets her attention. "Are you saying that the Mistress of the Alchemists' Guild kidnapped shadow-born?"

"Kidnapped you?" asks Larus.

This is the part I know they'll both like. They know he's still alive, so it doesn't jeopardize their plans. "It was a trap for the king."

They shoot an approving look between them. "Did it work?" asks Adria. She guides me by the shoulder, and the three of us leave the courtyard and head onto a path out of the palace.

The streets are busy once again, this time with carts full of the incoming harvest. The harvest festival next week, which I'd once thought to be a dangerous waste of limited resources, is now something I'm really looking forward to. Even Adria forgets to mime her discontent as a cart of wonderfully fragrant plums passes.

We find a bench overlooking an empty plaza, tucked out of the way of the main thoroughfare. There, I explain to them how the king rescued me and healed me, killing Zara in the process.

"And you stayed with him last night?"

I smile but shake my head. "I was paralyzed. I stayed under the supervision of a healer until I could move again this morning."

Mostly true.

Adria exchanges a look with Larus, something from an earlier conversation of theirs that I can't interpret. I find myself wishing I could feel them just as I can feel Ronan when I'm near him.

"Do you think…is there a chance he'd ask you to stay longer? After the festival is over?"

"Why?" Has Larus come through for me? Is something wrong with the plan?

She smiles weakly, her annoyance underneath apparent. "Our brother is giving me grief. I gave him one task—"

"Adria," Larus warns as her voice rises.

She composes herself. "We may need a bit longer than we imagined. The festival ends in ten days, and we aren't ready. And not only Seth, but the ships aren't willing to risk the storm—"

"There's a storm coming?" There hasn't been a drop of rain since we left Nithyria.

"It's far from here, out on the southern reaches of the Blue Sea," says Larus. "Some of the ships coming in warned my mother, and she won't send her ships out of harbor until it passes. I doubt it will even come here, but there's no arguing with her once she's made up her mind."

I could hug him. Larus did it. I don't know how, but he's managed to delay the plan at least. It's not the end of it, but it gives me enough time to think of something to make Adria change her mind.

But I need to suppress my joy if I want to keep Ronan alive. "So you're saying I need to…keep doing what I'm doing?" I feign disgust. "I don't know how much longer I can keep him from…" I shudder. I hope it's convincing.

"You can do it," says Adria. "I've seen what you're capable of. Now that you have him, push him away again. He'll come back."

Larus nods in agreement. "She's right. I don't think there's much you can do now to dissuade him if what you said happened last night is true. He killed for you, Sylvie."

He had. I hadn't truly thought about what that must have cost him.

"It won't be much longer," promises Larus. Adria looks at him skeptically, but she doesn't argue with him. "Tell him you need to spend some time with us, if you need an excuse to get away. We've missed you."

Adria does her best "I've missed you" face, which is closer to "If you fuck this up for me, I'll murder you in my sleep," but that's about what I expected.

I do end up spending the day with them. Having been entertained nearly to death by the previous weeks of the Festival of Arts, we go for a walk along the River Mara instead, following a paved path down to the sea.

"Just…there," says Larus, pointing to the southeast. "If you keep going, you'll reach Port Limin."

Adria looks out over the waves as if willing the storm away. Her eyes are filled with determination, even with this setback. I can't imagine how to convince her to change her course.

What would I do to stop her? How far would I go for the sake of Ronan? For the sake of Selara and Nithyria both?

How far would I go for the greater good?

Wherever my limits lie, I suspect I'll find out soon enough.

One way or another.

Chapter Thirty-Seven

The next day, I run into Quinn as she's leaving the dungeons. Her hair is matted to her head, and she looks as though she hasn't slept in a couple of days.

"They're lucky," she says, thumbing over her shoulder towards the stairs to the incarcerated alchemists, the same stairs she carried me up after I'd been wrongfully imprisoned. "The guards that took care of you were put in a cell themselves for a couple of weeks, and then they were given a chance to improve the conditions down there. They must have been pretty motivated because it's as clean as I've ever seen it."

"Are they talking?" I ask her.

"Endlessly," she says with a smile. "I wouldn't have been pulled in—not really my area; I'm more of a court jester than anything of-ficial—but so many of them were involved, they really had no choice. It's a mess. The Alchemists' Guild, foreign merchants. Even some of the nobility. You helped him uncover the biggest fucking scheme to take control of the crown in the history of Selara."

Well, one of the biggest schemes. I'm still working on taking down the other one. I'll be forever grateful to Larus for whatever he did to delay things. The Alchemists' Guild crisis would have made for the perfect opportunity to strike amid the chaos.

"I do what I can," I say.

"I hear that's true," she says, her brows bouncing. "He won't tell me anything, but I could see it on his face. *Everyone* is talking about how he went there to save you and what must have happened after."

My cheeks turn red. "Everyone?"

"I won't make you tell me what he's like. Although I have always wondered; who hasn't? But tell me at least if you're together. I won't tell anyone. Maybe Taran, but he probably already knows, although he'd never tell me. Which is really quite unfair, now that I'm saying it out loud. I think I'll go and start a fight with him about it later."

"I bet you will."

"Well?" She nudges me with her elbow.

I think about last night after we returned from my walk with Adria and Larus to the sea. About how I felt his need when he passed me in the dining hall. How I'd waited until Adria was asleep to creep back into the corridor and through the passage into his chambers. About the many wonderful hours I'd spent there, and how I'll do it again tonight, the second that I'm able.

"Yes," I say. "There's…something there. *Don't* tell anyone."

"Your secret is safe with me," she says. "Are you free later? I need help with my mask for the ball."

The masked ball. It's in two days, on my *birthday*, of all days, and I'd forgotten all about it. "Shit. You don't have two masks by any chance?"

"Meet me after lunch," she says. "We'll go shopping."

Quinn takes me to the vendor in the market that hates Nithyrians over my repeated protests.

"There is no one in this city who doesn't know who you are. You are going to be the consort of the king. The queen, one day. No one will dare defy you."

The world spins wildly beneath me when she says it. I'd forgotten that bit too. It had felt fun to imagine back on stage when Ronan had crowned me at the end of the Festival of Sport. But it feels different now that I'm spending my nights in his bed.

It feels real.

Queen Sylvie of Selara.

It's a long way away if it ever happens. But it's difficult to imagine my life without Ronan in it now. It's difficult imagining any sort of future that *doesn't* involve binding myself to him in some way.

It's scary, but a future without him feels scarier.

Quinn was right about at least one thing: between all the events of the Festival of Sport and the Alchemists' Guild crisis, people do recognize me in the street now. The rumors reach beyond the palace walls, making it difficult to walk through crowded places without being stopped. Ronan had offered to send a couple of his guards with me—well, he'd insisted, really—but I had thought that would just draw even more attention.

Of course, he'd sent them anyway, trailing behind Quinn and me at a reasonable distance.

The mask-seller is a handsome man with curly dark hair and sculpted features that he contorts into haughty expressions as the stragglers from court, ourselves included, fight over the last remaining masks. He's an asshole through and through, but he doesn't say anything about my Nithyrian heritage, although admittedly I'm passing for Selaran these days in my attire. But he also doesn't make any remark when I greet a pair of distant cousins in their Nithyrian leathers.

"See? He's a changed man."

I sincerely doubt that's the case, but if my presence here means other Nithyrians were welcome, I suppose it can't have been all bad. Though I still didn't know if I should be supporting his business.

But Ronan had been right about the masks: even the limited supply he has remaining is lovely. Quinn chooses a fox for herself made from delicate filigreed gold. It's expensive; the Alchemists' Guild shake-up has people worried about gold scarcity. With only a few days remaining, Ronan has dialed back the harvest festival celebrations to prepare for shortfalls.

I'm concerned about it myself, having seen the effects of hunger firsthand. But I know Ronan would strip the palace of all the gold it has before letting the people go hungry.

He may just do that anyway.

I'm ready to take the last remaining silver mask, which was intended for a man and covers more than half of my face, when Quinn finds a golden eagle mask. I can't resist it. It looks just like the griffin.

She grins, concealing some private joke, but I'm in too good a mood to care.

On the day of the ball, Adria embarrasses me at lunch by having the chef bake me a plum pie and doing the Nithyrian birthday chant, which causes a lot of other people to join in, although they don't know all the words.

There's no one like a sister to mortify you in front of a crowd.

Still, I'm grateful to her. Displays like this, laced with humiliation though they may be, are rare from her. Maybe they're a sign that she has affection for me deep down. That she still has a heart, and that heart might be changed.

I receive further proof that evening as we're getting ready. I'm dressing with Quinn in her chambers after a long day of plucking and preening when a knock comes at the door.

"Come in," says Quinn. Her servant is drawing sharp lines of eyeliner over her eyelids as Quinn holds up the fox mask to preview the effect in the mirror.

"Lady Adria of House Verran to see Miss Sylvara," says Quinn's servant.

"Sylvie," Quinn and I both correct automatically.

I catch Quinn's eye in the mirror. She's as surprised as I am that Adria has come here. And then I catch something pass between them as we turn to face Adria that's apparent in spite of the masks. Something…*charged.*

I really can't tell if they want to kill each other or fuck each other. *Gods, please tell me Quinn isn't fucking my sister.*

"I brought you something," says Adria. She hands me a little box covered in a fraying blue fabric. "It was Mother's."

I open it to find a golden necklace set with a large piece of amber. "It's beautiful," I say. "I didn't know you had this."

"There's never much occasion to wear it. I thought it would go better with your outfit than mine."

Adria's gown is one of our mother's as well, a silver and black dress made from a heavy, structured fabric that creates curves where she has few. Her mask itself is black—a wolf.

She's right that the necklace goes better with my outfit. My dress has been made from a shiny silk in a deep golden brown, with a low-slung belt of golden medallions. "It looks like Ronan's hair," Quinn said when she pulled it from her wardrobe for me to try, and I knew immediately that I had to wear it.

"Here, let me put it on you," says Adria. She takes the necklace from the box and unclasps it. Then she drapes it around my neck, admiring it in the mirror. "You look so much like her, you know. More than I do."

"Thank you," I say, my voice wavering.

There's more she wants to say, but she looks at Quinn and changes her posture and tone. "You'd better hurry up before they finish the good wine," she says to me sharply. "They had to bring out the Selaran trash at the last ball."

"Selaran trash for Nithyrian trash. Truly the peaceful future Ronan hoped for," says Quinn. Her hand, which had been gently resting on the dressing table, tightens around it.

"Enough," I say to them both. "Thank you, Adria. We'll see you there."

Despite Adria's warning, Quinn and I arrive at the ballroom quite late. I can see quickly why Ronan enjoys masked balls so much. The court has really gone all out on their costumes, with some people going as far as having their entire outfits made to match the mask. The most impressive by far is a peacock gown worn by a cousin of House Nauta decorated with real feathers that shimmer and shake as she moves.

This party is far larger than the last one. It extends from the ballroom onto a balcony—the larger balcony, not the small one where Ronan kissed me the first time—and then out into the courtyard beyond, where the palace gates have been opened to allow the commoners to join the festivities.

It takes me a long time to find Ronan. Not just because many of the masks effectively conceal the wearer's identity, but also because

Ronan isn't with the court at all. He's out in the courtyard among the people.

The costumes of the commoners make up for a lack of quality materials with extraordinary creativity. A young boy sports a unicorn mask crafted from a spiraled seashell, which glitters in the lantern light as he darts through the crowd. Nearby, a slim man dances in armor transformed into an impressive imitation of snakeskin. Then a woman glides past, butterfly wings fashioned from a gauzy material stretched delicately across a frame made of picture wire trailing behind.

At the center of it all is Ronan. The people don't recognize him; his golden lion mask covers most of his face, but I can feel him, even from a bit of distance now. *This* is why he loves masked balls, I realize. He doesn't have to be the God-King here. Out in this courtyard, he's just Ronan.

I dance my way into the crowd to join him. I don't know the dance they're doing, but it's easy enough to pick up. And it's far more fun than the courtly dances with their complicated patterns and rules that keep you at a distance from each other.

"I see we had the same idea," he says as I finally make it to him.

"We did," I say, touching his mask and then mine. Eagle and lion. The two halves of the griffin. "I'm the head, and you're the ass."

"And what a fine ass I am." He laughs and kisses me right on the lips in front of everyone.

"What are you doing?"

"No one knows who we are! It's the best night of the year. Come on, enjoy yourself. I insist."

Ronan takes me by the arm and leads me into the crowd to join the dance. We dance for hours in a dizzying whirl of costumes and color, the heat of our bodies keeping away the growing cold, until finally, wordlessly, he leads me up the stairs and back into the ballroom.

"I have a surprise for you," he says.

He leads me past some guards and out onto the small balcony where we kissed. Sitting there grazing on some kind of fish is the griffin.

"She stayed," I say. I walk to her cautiously, but she recognizes me. She headbutts me, nearly taking off my mask. I pull the mask the rest of the way off, and Ronan does the same.

"I named her Kira. In honor of Kerensa."

"I thought you weren't a believer."

"I have a soft spot for the goddess of beauty."

"And love," I say without thinking. Then my heart begins to race as I realize what I've said. "Are those straps?" I say, quickly changing the subject.

They're anchored around her neck and waist. It looks like we'd fit on her back between her wings, which seems like a much more comfortable place to ride than her neck had been.

"I want to have a saddle made, but there hasn't been time. The stablemaster did a couple of test flights with the straps. I'm not sure if he was more excited or terrified, but he said they work well to keep you strapped on. What do you say?"

"Are we going somewhere?"

"You'll see."

I climb up onto her back with Ronan's help, sitting at the front. He takes a seat behind me and then tightens the straps around us both. Then he takes a thin strap connected to a collar around her neck. Reins.

"I'm thinking of going back after the festival to see if I can find more of them. Imagine it: griffins for everyone. We could cross the desert safely. You could return to Nithyria to visit when you wanted to. It would be wonderful."

To return to Nithyria to visit. I hadn't thought of that. If I stay with Ronan, I'll have to move here. I won't be going back home. Not that there are many people there I'd miss, to be honest. But would Larus stay with me here? Or would he return with my siblings, assuming I can get Adria to go home and stay there?

I don't have time to give it much thought before Kira flaps her great wings, and we're off into the night sky over the ball.

The view is as spectacular as I remembered, more so without the fear of falling. The straps keep us firmly attached to her as she soars and dives, flying at Ronan's direction up the River Mara.

Kira climbs sharply as we round a bend in the river, and I can finally see her target: the Ivory Spire, home of the Great Library of Faros.

"Is it open?" I ask.

Ronan laughs. "For us, it is."

Kira lands on a very narrow balcony that circles the top of the tower. The ledge is decorated with marble statues of the gods, each of them facing outwards to overlook the city. Vayla, a torch in her hand; Vahlo, a sickle in his; Arnan with his trident; Kerensa with her bow and arrow; and Sai with his sword and shield. Ronan helps me down and moves a waiting bucket to Kira: more fish.

"I know you wanted to see the Five Wonders, but this place is a wonder to me. My favorite place in the city."

Here at night, we're the only ones inside. Ronan leads me through an arched doorway into a small observation room. There are strange golden instruments on wooden stands near the windows, the kind they use to chart the stars. "Are we interrupting their work?"

"Not for long." He leads me to a staircase that spirals down into the tower proper.

"Good *gods*," I say as we step onto the landing. The floor we're standing on spirals down at least a dozen stories, with bookshelves lining every wall. Thousands of books. Tens of thousands.

"That's just the third floor," says Ronan, leaning over a wooden railing. "There are two more floors below it."

"Are you serious?"

I'm jogging down the ramp now, scanning the books as I go by. Histories, biographies, dictionaries of languages I've never heard of, books of poetry and music. The ceiling is painted with men and women in ancient robes frolicking in nature and recording observations on scrolls.

I understand their joy. It's beautiful here. It's everything everyone knows about the entire world, all of it in one miraculous place.

I pick a book at random off the shelf. "*A Complete Study of Brakkari Architecture, 3rd Century to 5th.*" I don't know the first thing about Brakkari architecture.

Looking around here, I realize I know so little about *anything*. It's overwhelming. "There's an entire world out there I know nothing about."

"That's why I brought you here," says Ronan, taking my hands after I put the book back. "You said you wanted to see the world. I thought we could make a list of places to go. There's a section—where are we?" He leans out to read the nearest sign. "There's a section a couple of floors down with maps and travel accounts. It should be much more up-to-date than the books you had back at home. That is, if you want to. If you wanted to do that with me tonight. I wouldn't have to come on the trip with you, if you didn't want me to. We could just plan it."

His eyes dart away, suddenly shy. I understand why he's worried: this was the trip I'd told him about in honor of my father, and he still doesn't know if I'd want to take it with him.

But just the fact that he remembered what I told him, that he arranged all of this so he could help me, that's enough for me to know what I want.

"This is the nicest thing anyone has ever done for me," I say, tears in my eyes. I lean forward and kiss him softly on the lips. "I only want to go if it's with you."

He smiles so brightly he's glowing. "Come on," he says, leading down the ramp.

We spend hours sorting through the volumes, unfurling great scrolls of maps onto a wide table exclusively for that purpose until late into the night. Ronan takes notes in an elegant script, filling a blank book with ideas, references, and even rough sketches of some of the things I wish to see.

"It says there's a statue of an octopus covering a woman's breasts. And it's thirty feet high," I say, holding out a book to show him.

"Well, *that* I have to see. Should we add Larunia back then?"

"We better."

I love the "we." I'm not sure where we were in the world—somewhere past Brakkar but not yet to Velmora—when we started saying it, but *we* haven't been able to stop since.

He looks up and gives me a shy smile when he sees me watching him. And it's such a small thing, just a tiny, fleeting moment, one of thousands since we've met, but something about it breaks me in half.

I love him, I realize suddenly. I've known it, I've felt it, but looking at him, the sleep in his eyes, the barely suppressed yawn on his lips as he keeps going, unable to stop himself from giving me what I want, I can't deny it any longer. I let the thoughts take form, let them take shape in my mind, wrapping myself around them. Rebuilding myself with them into something better than I was.

I love him. I want nothing but him.

But there are other thoughts taking shape as well. Guilty thoughts full of shame and regret.

I love him, but I don't deserve him. How can I wash away the stain of what we came here to do? What my family is still trying to do to him, to his people? Even if I can stop it, how could I ever look at him and think I'm worthy of him? Worthy to be his queen?

A queen that conspired to wage a war against her people.

He has stopped writing, sensing my feelings.

When he gets a look at my face, he stands immediately and rushes to where I stand against the map table, holding my head in his hands. Tears spring into my eyes at his touch. I clamp my mouth shut and try not to cry.

"Hey," he says softly, pulling me to him. "What's wrong?"

"I don't deserve you," I choke out through sobs. The gentleness of his hands, the warmth of his voice. It makes me sob even harder, clinging to his chest, my body shaking.

"Hey," he says again. "It's okay. Look at me, Sylvie."

I can't. I can't look at him. I'm not good enough for him.

"Sylvie," he says, gently but firmly. He lifts my chin until I'm looking into his eyes. "Do you have any idea how rare you are? How few people there in the world like you? Do you know how many people deny what they see with their own eyes? Do you know how many of them refuse to see the truth even when it's right in front of them?

"You were raised to believe one thing, and your parents weren't wrong to teach it to you. They were survivors. They were fighters. Though I disagree with their methods, I can't fault them for what they did for the sake of your people. But for you to be able to come here with an open mind and an open heart, to find it in yourself to get to know me, to trust me, to find another path forward for us? That's rare, Sylvie. That's remarkable.

"You are remarkable. You are everything I've ever wanted, more than I ever even thought to dream of. It has been the greatest privilege of my life getting to know you. Sharing everything with you, sharing my gift. Showing you myself in a way no one ever has ever known me before. I never thought I would get to experience that.

"Every day since you've been here, you've surprised me. You've shocked me. You've humbled me. You've made me feel like life is worth living. You've made me feel like the vision I have of the world is achievable. It's possible. I see it reflected in your beauty. I see it in your giving heart."

He wipes the tears from my eyes as I look at him. I want to believe him, but I know the truth about myself.

"Do you know what my version of this would be?" He gestures around the room. "The thing I want the most in the world, what you could do to make it happen for me?"

I shake my head.

"It's this. It's exactly this. It's giving you what you want. It's making you happy. If you asked me what I would do if I had one day left to live, my answer would be whatever *you* want to do. There are many things that I want in this world, that I want *for* this world. But there is *nothing* that I want more than that."

I can't hold myself together. I fall apart, collapsing against his chest as he holds me. I let the guilt and the grief of deceiving him out. I let his comfort, his light, in.

"Thank you," I say finally, weakly. "Thank you for bringing me to this place. It's a wonderful gift."

He places a hand on each of my cheeks and draws me to him for a kiss.

It's soft and slow, gentler than our kisses usually are.

When he pulls back, he looks me deep in the eye, his gaze piercing. Consuming. "I'm in love with you, Sylvie. I knew I would love you before I opened that door the first time. I've been waiting all my life for you."

The feeling reflects between us again, but how I can say it back? How can I when I know what I am? When I know what I deserve, despite his beautiful words to the contrary?

But then again, how can I let it go unsaid? How can I keep it from him when I know in my heart that I love him as much as he loves me?

"Don't say it now," he says, sensing the conflict in me. "Say it when you're ready. I'll wait for you, as long as you need. I just needed to say it to you. I couldn't hold it in any longer."

I kiss it onto his lips instead. I pull him back to me, pull him down on me as he shoves aside the books, the maps, the quill. It crashes to the floor, and I don't care. I need him on me, in me, everywhere.

"Oh, and Sylvie?" he says as he kisses down my neck, lifting my dress. "Happy Birthday."

I return to the chambers I share with Adria before dawn. As much as I'd love to stay with Ronan, I need to speak with Adria.

I can't imagine how I can convince her not to start this war, but I'm just going to have to try. Delaying it isn't good enough. I can't keep lying to Ronan, and I can't let the war happen. If I come out and tell her that directly, I'll risk forcing her into action, but I can't go on like this any longer, knowing that he loves me and trusts me.

I don't know what I'm going to do, but I have to give my sister this one final opportunity to make things right before I give her up.

Adria stumbles down the hall, heeled shoes in hand. She's just getting back herself. "I'll give it to the Selarans. They know how to throw a party," she says.

Her mask is off, and her knuckles look a bit bloody. "Good night?" I ask.

"Not bad at all."

We undress quickly inside, freeing ourselves from the tight fabrics and getting comfortable in our nightgowns. As I remove the necklace, Adria joins me at my dresser.

"I wanted to say this when I gave it to you, but Quinn was there. You remind me of her. Mother, not Quinn."

"I hope not Quinn." I laugh, but my heart rate is increasing. Adria never talks about Mother.

This is my chance.

"She was kind, like you," she says. "Too kind. It cost her her life. I hope the same won't happen to you, Sylvie."

This is the nicest thing she's ever said to me.

Maybe there is hope. Maybe she could see reason.

But I don't understand part of what she said, and it bothers me. "What do you mean, it cost her her life?" Mother was a spy. She was killed in her sleep by King Aurelian when they discovered her. I don't see what that has to do with kindness.

"She infiltrated Ronan's forces. She could have killed him. But instead of doing what she should have done and taking him out to give Father an easier road to victory, she gave Aurelian a chance to surrender before killing his son. She knew how much Ronan meant to him, his only child. She thought it would spare more bloodshed. Instead, Aurelian murdered her in her sleep."

"I didn't know that." I knew she'd been killed for spying, but not for threatening Ronan, and I also didn't know she had given Aurelian a chance to stop it.

And he had chosen the war over Ronan, just as my parents had chosen the war over me. And I know that they all felt like they were doing the right thing, that they made those sacrifices for the greater good, but I'm sure that offered little comfort to Ronan, just as it offered little comfort to me on the sleepless nights when I wondered if they'd ever come home.

Adria nods. "Of course, her spies were instructed to kill Ronan if they didn't hear from her after a certain amount of time. And they very nearly succeeded. They killed all of his guards but one. That Orsan of his. Both of them nearly died before the spies had to flee. It was so close. Can you imagine if they'd succeeded? How different things would have been?"

I can't bear to hear her talk about him dying that way. "I do think things would have been different. But I'm not sure they would have been any better." I say it as diplomatically as I can, trying not to let venom enter my voice, trying not to let the rage I'm feeling rise to the surface. "If we had won, we might be here defending Father against people like us."

"No, we wouldn't have been. Because we're not fool enough to let them try."

I do believe she's right about that, but I'm not sure that it's a good thing. "Do you think Mother was a fool?"

"I think she was naïve. I think she believed in the best in people. But some people have no best. Father understood that even if Mother never did."

Maybe I'm a fool to believe in the best in Adria.

"You understand that, right, Sylvie? You understand Father was right. There can be no mercy for our enemies. What our mother did, she thought she was doing for love. But it was weakness. You know that, don't you? You understand?" She looks me in the eye. The eyes we both share, our mother's eyes.

And I see her, really see her. I don't need Ronan's gift to know her. This is who she is. This is who she has always been. And I don't think there's a way to ever, *ever* change her mind.

"I understand," I tell her. "I'm no fool."

Not anymore.

Chapter Thirty-Eight

The days between the Festival of Arts and the beginning of the Great Feast are best described by their sound: the scraping of wood on stone.

From my window in the palace, it seems like every chair, table, stool, bench, barrel, crate, and cart in the kingdom is groaning along the floor and in the streets outside, arranging themselves in preparation for a meal that will somehow last for three days. If this is the pared-down version of the Feast, I hate to imagine what the original intent had been.

I don't know how we're going to handle any more partying at this point. I'm surprised that anyone has the appetite for it after nearly three months of celebrations.

But I seem to be in the minority with that opinion. No one can talk about anything but the meals that will be served, the delicacies from distant kingdoms and comfort dishes of home. The freshly harvested produce and cured and aged meats, cheeses, vinegars, and wines. The salty, the sweet, the fatty, the spicy. It seems that every single person in court, from the servants to the king himself, has *something* they're looking forward to.

For Ronan, it's a seafood stew that Queen Claudia made for him once when he stayed with her on a visit to her home of Minar as a boy. She had servants of her own and a talented cook, but she insisted on making the dish herself because she swore no one could get the broth quite right. She rarely makes it these days, but Ronan has convinced her to honor Arnan with it for the Great Feast.

I'm looking forward to trying it, but it's Typhon's favored dish that sounds the most exciting to me. It's a noodle dish from far away in Velmora with a spicy pepper that leaves your mouth numb when you eat it. Ronan thinks it sounds insane, but I'm so curious to find out what it's like.

I get my wish and more when the Feast begins.

I've never seen so much food in my damn life.

Starting at dawn, the court files outside into the same courtyard where the ball had been held a few days before. The endless scraping of chairs and tables has culminated in an unending sea of culinary delights. After the court has their first meal, the palace gates are opened to allow the commoners to take part. Ronan tells me the city's plazas are filled with buffets like this one. While the palace provides much of the food and most of the ingredients, everyone around the city contributes to the Feast. I ask Ronan if we can visit each neighborhood and try something from each table, and he loves the idea. But he tells me he has something he needs to do first.

"Meet me by the northern entrance in an hour," he says. "Come in disguise."

I arrive at the gates just when he says, having changed into some of the trousers I bought at the market and tucked my hair into a flat cap. But Ronan isn't there.

Soren is.

"Are we going to see Vesper?" I ask. Ronan-as-Soren is carrying a wooden box of some kind.

"There are some who can't make it to the Feast," he explains, shifting the box in his hands. "The old, the infirm. Vesper's grandfather is bedbound."

"Is there enough for all of them? Can we bring it to them instead of trying something at every table?"

"We can do both," he says. He sighs, a deep, soul-affirming sigh that relaxes his entire body. "Today, we can do both. I can't tell you what a relief it is. What this Feast means to me. It means more than any of the other Festivals. I think I lost my faith in Arnan before any of the other gods, ridiculous as that sounds. Why would a god let people starve?"

I look around reflexively, still nervous about the way he talks about the gods. "They say it's a test of faith. *You* said that in your speech to begin the Feast."

"I said it because I had to. What kind of petty god needs to test us with starving children?"

I don't have an answer for him, but I also don't want anyone to report a man with Soren's description to the priests, so I lead us to the shop where we met Vesper's mother, asking about the food he's bringing them along the way.

Vesper greets us at the door. She's looking better already after bathing and putting her earrings back in. But the hollows of her cheeks are still too hollow, and I'm glad we have something with us to help remedy that.

I worry that when she sees Soren that she'll blame him for what happened to her, but she hugs him instead. "I didn't tell them anything. They asked again and again what I was doing, but I made up something different every time. It was like a game. They believed the first few stories, but eventually they figured me out."

"Did they treat you well otherwise?" asks Ronan.

"No, they damn well didn't," says Vesper's mother, coming to the door. "I have a mind to throw you into the street for what she went through because of you. But I won't. And only because you brought her back to me. She said you were the one who told them where to go. The king himself went. Can you imagine?"

"He's so handsome," says Vesper, her eyelids fluttering in a way that sends a jolt of jealousy through me. "I begged the guards who took us out of there to let me thank him myself, but they wouldn't. I'm going to the palace for the feast later to try to find him, but first, there's Grandpapa—"

"I have something for you for that," says Ronan, trying to hide his blush by distracting them with the box. "For your Grandpapa."

"Oh!" says Vesper's mother, clapping her hands together. "Let's see what you have there."

She lets us come inside then, leading us up the stairs from the shop into a small set of private rooms. Only once we've entered does Vesper notice that I look familiar. "Aren't you…weren't you there too? Were you one of the shadow-born?"

"Me?" I ask, looking to Ronan. I'm not sure if I should tell them.

"I didn't see many of their faces until the night God-King Ronan saved us. They kept us in separate cells so we wouldn't work to-gether to escape. Although we did manage it once anyway—Mery told me he talked to you, Soren."

"He led us to the place. And then I convinced the guards to keep an eye on it. They finally saw someone go in there that night. It just so happened that Ronan was in the neighborhood, on the way back from the play."

"Gods, can you imagine how it felt to see those guards of his show up? And then there he was himself, in all his finery, all covered in blood. I'll never forget that. Not for as long as I live."

Ronan shoots me a look that says he's going to be insufferable about this later.

"Can I help you with that?" I ask Vesper's mother as she removes something large and heavy from the box. A pot of stew with a lid that screws on to keep it from spilling.

"Not unless you're fire-born," she says, gesturing to the cold fireplace.

"Soren is," says Vesper.

He must have told her that to explain his magic, just as I'd assumed he was nature-born when I met him.

I distract them with questions about the jewelry their shop sells while Ronan ignites some firewood with his light.

Vesper's mother heats the stew on the fire, and then she insists we join them for a bowl after she feeds her father. Ronan offers to chop some vegetables to go in it, and to my surprise, he knows his way around a kitchen knife, far better than I do.

"From the battlefield," he explains as I watch him. "Come here." He waits until Vesper and her mother are distracted by the fire and pops a bite of radish into my mouth. It's deliciously fresh, tangy with just a bit of heat. And the act of his putting it into my mouth, well…

"How are those radishes coming? We're about at a boil over here."

I bring them the chopped radishes as Ronan starts on some carrots, thinking that it's a pity I can't play suggestively with the carrots in front of him, and to my surprise and delight, that feeling is reverberated between us. We both laugh, which I'm sure looks insane considering nothing has been said or done and we're nowhere near each other, but Vesper and her mother are too polite to say anything about it.

I sit with Vesper while we wait for the vegetables to cook, listening to her tell the story of her rescue at least three times, with the king becoming magically more handsome in each retelling. Ronan's ears are so red by the end of it, I'm sure she must have figured him out.

But if she does, she never lets on. "That's the shadow-born for you," I tell Ronan as we're leaving the house. "We're so good at keeping secrets, sometimes you can't even tell whether we are or not."

"That's certainly true," he says.

Then he pulls me into an alley and pins me against the wall, covering my mouth.

My chest tightens in alarm. My hand is reaching for my sword when he winks. "Remember this?"

"Fuck!" I push him, but he grabs me and pulls me to him.

He pins me against the wall again, an echo of the encounter from the first night we met, but there are no bells to stop us. He kisses me, and I melt instantly, my knees buckling. I brace myself against him for support, running my hands into his hair and onto his smooth, unscarred cheeks.

I break from the kiss, and he pulls back. "What's wrong? Soren not doing it for you anymore?"

I trace the lines on his face, the deep scars that exist in appearance only. The skin beneath them bears no mark, but these scars are real.

These are the scars my mother's people gave him.

These are the scars my mother gave him. Her actions. Her death.

I know it before asking. "When did this happen to you?"

He looks away. "A year or so into the war."

"When my mother died?"

"Yes," he says softly.

I turn his face to look at me. "Because my mother died?"

"Yes," he says.

"Why didn't you tell me?" He had told me what happened with my father. Why conceal this? Why leave a secret between us?

"I thought you knew," he says. "Or that you would have guessed."

I should have guessed. "Adria said all of your guards died. All except Taran."

Ronan leads us to a stone bench at the end of the alley. He takes off his hat but keeps Soren's face.

"There were many terrible days during the war. Some of them…some are hard to even think about, even now. But that was one of the worst."

"You don't have to tell me," I say. But I can sense there's a part of him that wants to talk about this. That wants to remember it, given that he still wears Soren's face.

Ronan sits for a long moment before he speaks. "My guards aren't just my guards, as I'm sure you've seen by now. They're my friends. They were my father's friends, people I had known all my life. They all died that day. Not on the battlefield, not in a blaze of glory. But defending me. It's what they were sworn to do. It's what they trained their whole lives for. But to hear it happen to them one by one? To watch my light flicker into nothing in the shadows, leaving me blind to what was happening, the only sound their dying screams? That was the worst day of my life. The worst day until the day my father died. Until the day your father died."

Shadow nullifying light. Or light nullifying shadow. That's how it's supposed to work.

But not mine. Not ours. Ours seem to strengthen each other somehow.

My mother's shadows could have stopped his light, though. The shadows of her men did.

Gods, we'd taken so much from him. We'd taken so much from each other.

No more.

"After everything, I can't believe you didn't hate us all. How could you even think of giving me a chance?"

"I did hate you. For years, I hated every last one of you. But it's like I told you. I'm trying to change things. And having you around makes it all the easier. You're different, Sylvie. You're not to blame for any of what happened."

"I'm not different," I tell Ronan. I can't lie to him any longer. Whatever it costs me, whatever it costs my family, I can't let this continue. I can't let Adria and Seth have their war, and I can't count on myself and Larus to be able to stop them. Not when they're my parents' children. I know now what my parents were capable of, and I know Adria and Seth are just the same.

I will not let this kingdom go to war for the sake of the love I have for my brother and sister. For the love I have for Larus and all of the rest of our House.

I will not let this kingdom go to war for my sake.

I'm so sorry, Ronan. I love you, and that's why I have to break your heart.

"I've been lying to you. I've lied to you since we got here. We did come to kill you. I know you know that. And I know you know it changed for me, but it didn't change for Adria. I thought I could stop her, but I can't. And it's worse than that. We weren't just trying to kill you. Adria and Seth are planning a war. An invasion. An infiltration and siege, by land and sea. I've delayed it; I'm trying to stop it—"

"What?" Ronan sits upright, dropping Soren's face. "Sylvie, if this is some kind of a joke—"

"Why would I joke about this? I'm sorry I didn't tell you sooner. I thought I could stop it. I tried. I didn't want them to die." I wipe away guilty tears, furious with myself for crying when this is my fault. "I didn't want to lose anyone else. But I already lost them. I don't want anyone else to die for my family. I don't want to see

Adria on the throne. I don't want another war, even if they lose. I'll tell you everything. Everything I know. Ronan, please. Please believe me. I need you to believe me."

He isn't looking at me. He's staring at the ground, completely frozen. And I can't feel him. I can't feel a single thing coming from him. It's like we're nowhere near each other.

It's like he's walked away from me.

"Ronan?"

"Let's go," he says. He doesn't reach for me. "I'll convene the war council. I need you to tell them exactly what you've told me. And anything you can think of that could be useful. That could stop this."

"I will," I say.

And though it tears me apart, I don't reach for him. I don't deserve his comfort. I don't deserve his pity, and I certainly don't deserve his love.

But I'll do this anyway, even if he never looks at me the same way again. Not just because I love him, although I do. But because it's right. Because if there's one thing I've learned from him, it's to do the right thing no matter the personal cost. It was a hard lesson, a painful lesson, but it's one I've finally learned.

I only hope it isn't too late.

Chapter Thirty-Nine

I spend the rest of the Great Feast in Ronan's living chamber recounting everything I know to Ronan's most trusted advisors. Grand Vizier Cyrus, Typhon, and Queen Claudia, and also Quinn and Taran, who were both elevated to general in the last war and who will serve Ronan again in that capacity if this war can't be stopped.

The reactions to my news are about as I expected. Cyrus generally seems unsurprised by my revelations, choosing to focus on the solutions to the problems I raise rather than the fact that I concealed the plans. Typhon is heartbroken by Larus's betrayal most of all, although he does his best to conceal that fact. Queen Claudia is impressed with me for speaking up. She glowers at Ronan for his coolness towards me, but I take the entirety of the blame. This impresses her even further.

Quinn is furious, not just because I didn't trust Ronan, but because I didn't trust her. "After everything we've done together, everything I've done for you, and this is the way you repay me. Lies on lies on lies. That's what I get for trusting a shadow-born. That's what I get for trusting a Nithyrian."

But it's Taran who is the most upset, even though he carries it as quietly as ever. There are many betrayals between us personally and between our peoples, but the real reason he's upset is because Ronan is upset. Because I've hurt Ronan, because through my inaction, I may have doomed us all to another war. Because Taran knows better than anyone what the last war cost Ronan. I don't know if we'll ever come back from this, even if Ronan finds it in his heart to forgive me.

Ronan, for his part, says little to me beyond what we need to discuss. I don't blame him. His focus is on preserving his kingdom, and it's my focus too. There are moments when I feel glimpses of his feelings: sadness, mostly, but some anger and even some of the love he felt for me before. But I don't let it get my hopes up.

Love seldom fades quickly, even when you want it to.

I spend hours telling them every last detail, every person involved, every aspect of the plan that I know about. Ronan lays down the map, and I move the pieces into place, feeling sick as I watch it fill up once more. I don't withhold anything, not even about Larus, as much as it hurts me to give him up. The fact that he's been trying to help me stop it all wins him some support, especially from Typhon. I hope it's enough to save him from whatever consequences are coming.

Quinn wants to send me away while they discuss what to do with us, but Ronan refuses her. "She's here to help. Let her help."

In the end, three possibilities are floated. The first is the military option. It involves accepting that war is inevitable and doing everything possible to gain the best advantage going into it. It would mean sailing the ships out of the harbor to flank Felix's invading navy, declaring an end to the festival to get as many civilians out of the capital and away from the battlefields as possible before the siege, rounding up any Nithyrians that remain within Faros, calling the houses to arms, and focusing on the defense of the Gap, a strategic chokepoint where the city walls meet the River Mara.

Cyrus and Quinn support this option, Quinn mostly because it also entails immediately imprisoning Adria, and possibly me, and using us as leverage to try to get Seth to surrender quickly.

Then there's the diplomatic option. That would involve bringing in Adria and Larus and attempting to negotiate with them, explaining that the war is unlikely to succeed without them, and possibly using them as leverage in a negotiation with Seth. Ronan suggests this option, mostly because he refuses to consider the military option.

"I will not declare war on my own people preemptively. No one is getting rounded up in the streets."

"If you don't do it, your people will *die*, Ronan," says Quinn. "You can't have it all. There's no reason for them to come to the table yet. They have a very good chance of winning, no matter what we do. Someone is going to die here, and I don't want it to be us."

Ronan looks around the room for other support. "Taran?"

Taran shakes his head slowly. "Quinn is right. They won't negotiate. Why would they? They have everything where they want it." He looks at me with his last sentence, and I can tell he doesn't trust me, even after all that I've told them.

He's probably the smartest person in this room.

Cyrus and Queen Claudia are also against Ronan's solution. Even Typhon can't bring himself to believe it's a good idea, despite wanting to give Larus a chance. Then he turns to me. "What do you think? Would they negotiate? What would *you* do? You know them better than any of us. What would you do to stop this, if you had all of our resources at your disposal?"

I've given it a lot of thought, both before this meeting and during it. "I agree with the others that they won't negotiate, not while they have a chance at victory." I give him an apologetic look, but I don't know if he feels anything from it because I can't feel him anymore to know. I miss knowing what he was feeling so badly. "I'd prepare for war as quietly as possible without provoking Adria. I'd keep her imprisoned under false pretenses, anything to keep her from communicating without arousing her suspicions that she's been found out, which could make her act out of desperation or cause some contingency to play out like the one my mother had."

"Do you think that's likely?" asks Cyrus. "She doesn't seem much like your mother."

"She isn't, but she mentioned my mother's plan to me the other day. I wouldn't be surprised if she has one, although I can't imagine who could be involved." My eyes flash to Ronan. If she has any sort of contingency plan for the war, it almost certainly involves making sure he dies.

"What else?" Ronan asks, his voice strained.

I try to ignore how much it hurts to hear him hurting. I have to keep going. For him. "I'd send out some of the ships to try to flank the Third Navy, but I'd keep some around to defend the harbor and the Gap. I'd prepare for a siege by stockpiling whatever food is left from the festival and recruiting more guards under the cover of needing increased security for the Festivals of Night and Day. And then I'd send Larus out on a ship to negotiate with Felix. Felix has no particular loyalty to us. I believe, based on what I've been told about him, that he could be bought. You have more to offer him than we did. We gave him the promise of future wealth. You could offer him current wealth. Without his navy, my brother's siege will fail in the desert, and he'll be forced to surrender."

They debate the details of my plan—who should go with Larus or whether he could be trusted to go at all, what they should offer Felix, whether it's better to go ahead and call people to arms now or to wait until after the negotiations—but almost everyone appreciates the broad strokes of my idea, even Quinn and Taran.

In the end, we go with a modified version of my plan. They decide to confine Adria to her quarters along with me, under the pretense that threats have been made against our lives by someone at court with a grudge against Nithyrians. Quinn suggests working with one of the cooperating alchemists to try to find a way to suppress her magic, which Ronan reluctantly agrees to. Worse comes to worst, they can throw her in a fire-born cell in the dungeon. Those cells are isolated from the others to prevent the fire-born from burning the entire damn palace down.

When, at last, we seem to have exhausted everything I know and planned for every eventuality, I prepare to return to my quarters for confinement with my sister.

"Sylvie? Can I speak with you for a moment?" Ronan asks before I leave. He leads me from the common room of his chambers into the receiving room where we spoke the night of the raid on the warehouse.

My chest tightens so much it leaves me breathless as I wait for him to speak. He looks absolutely drained, more exhausted than I've ever seen him. I want nothing more than to reach for him, but I don't. I can't, and it kills me.

"I know I've been distant since you told me, and I'm sorry about that—"

"Ronan, please. You don't need to apologize to me." For fuck's sake. This is my mess.

"I do," he says. He gestures for me to sit, and I take the seat across from his preferred spot. But rather than facing me, he sits next to me on the same bench. There's a bit of cautious distance between us, but far less than there has been for the last two days.

"I wanted to say that I know what it cost you to come clean. I know what it meant to betray your family. I know how much trust you put in me. And I'm grateful for it. I'll forever be grateful for it."

It sounds like a goodbye. He's letting me go, then. And I get it, of course I get it, but *fuck*. It hurts so much.

I want to beg him not to. I want to scream and cry and tell him how sorry I am, that I'll never keep anything from him again as long as I live if he'll just give me a chance to earn back his trust.

But I don't.

"But?" I ask, knowing the word is coming, feeling it shake in my mouth as I say it.

"But—and it doesn't seem fair of me to ask this of you—I have to know if any of it was real. I know you were faking it in the beginning. And I know you changed your mind about killing me, and I'm so glad you're helping us, but—godsdammit, this is selfish of me. Is it just because you've realized that this is the right thing to do? Or is there any part of you, however small, that truly feels something for me? That ever felt something for me?"

I'm shocked. He isn't angry with me? He's upset not because of what I kept from him, but because he isn't sure if my feelings were real? Can't he feel me anymore? Doesn't he know that I did this not just because it's right, but because I love him? I did it because I love him, and I want him to survive this. I want that more than anything else. I should have seen the truth earlier, I should have turned on my family earlier, but I didn't. And the only reason I did in the end, regardless of what I've been telling myself, was because I love him. And that makes me a coward, and it makes me selfish. But about this one thing, I did not lie. "Ronan, I know you believe all of these wonderful things about me, but the truth is, I didn't do this just because it's right. I did it because I love you. I'm in love with you." Each word wrenches itself painfully from me. An agonizing confession, and all because it came too late. "I love you *so much*," I say, my words barely a whisper. "I thought you knew that. Couldn't you feel it?"

He freezes, his expression unreadable. He's still for so long, I begin to worry about him. Then his eyebrows furrow, and he shakes his head, leaning forward and clutching it with his hands.

Fuck, I hurt him so badly. He looks up at me, and the war that plays out on his face is the worst one yet. He wants to believe me, desperately, but he knows he shouldn't. And that damn near breaks my heart. "I could feel your guilt and your determination to make things right, but…you love me? It wasn't just part of the plan?"

"It wasn't part of the plan *at all*. Getting close to you was. But developing real feelings? If Adria knew, she would have killed me for that already." I'd thought it before, but saying it out loud now, I know it to be true. My own sister would kill me for loving Ronan, even if I had never told him what we were planning.

He looks so fragile in front of me. I did this to him. I thought I was doing the right thing, I thought I was protecting my family, but this is what I did, and I hate it so much.

I need him. I need to touch him, need to hold him and to comfort him. I need to take this pain away from him, this pain I caused him.

I can't stop myself from trying. Gently, cautiously, I reach for him. Painstakingly slowly, I take Ronan's hands and pull them to me, holding them in my lap.

He inhales sharply but doesn't fight me, doesn't move.

I hold his hands there for a long moment, stroking his strong fingers, feeling his smooth skin. There are no cuts here, none of the marks my mother's people made, but there are callouses. I can feel where he holds his sword from the layers of rough skin, and I hate more than anything that he's going to have to raise it again on the battlefield.

He doesn't deserve this.

"You love me?" he asks me again. There's a bit of hope in his voice this time.

I lift one of his hands to my cheek and kiss his palm. It's so warm and soft, so comforting. "I love you, Ronan. I don't deserve you. I don't blame you if you hate me. But I love you."

I close my eyes.

He could do anything to me right now. He could kill me as easily as kiss me, and I'm not certain which he'll do. I'm completely vulnerable, completely at his mercy.

I wait for him to react, holding my breath. Not daring to move.

And then, he strokes my cheek with his thumb. I let his hand go as he grazes his fingertips over my freckles, tapping them, counting them. Memorizing them.

And then, so suddenly it feels as though a dam has burst, I feel him again—the love and longing he's been holding back from me. It pours out from him, white hot and as radiant as the sun. "I love you," I whisper to him as I bathe in the glow of it. "I love you. I love you. I love you…"

"*Sylvie.*" He pulls me into his lap and kisses me as I repeat it over and over, the words becoming a chant, an oath.

The unspoken words have finally been spoken between us, the secrets and lies all revealed, my magic be damned. I don't care about the shadows, not when his light is here for me to claim as my own. I claim it and him, taking charge, kissing him with the same passion he gives to me. He lets me take what I want from him, lets me kiss his neck, lets me push myself against him, rocking my body against his until I feel his desire beneath me. "I love you," he whispers against my neck, nuzzling into me, wrapping his arms around my back, holding me tight to him.

"I need you," I say because it's true. "I need you right now."

"Fuck," he moans. "Can you keep quiet?"

"I don't know." As hot as it is to think of him taking me just on the other side of the door from everyone else, I don't want to keep quiet. "I don't think so."

"Quinn's gonna have my ass for this," he says as he lifts me off of him and sets me down. He leads me back into the living room. "Everyone out. I'll escort Sylvie to her quarters myself."

Quinn gives Ronan the most scathing look I've ever seen as she does what he says. "When she kills you in your sleep, you'll have no one to blame but yourself. I can't believe I serve a fucking moron."

Everyone else leaves without question, but Queen Claudia winks at me as she goes.

I guess that's where he got it from.

Ronan misses the moment, but I'll have to tell him about it later. There are more pressing matters at hand.

The moment the door closes, Ronan picks me up, his hands digging into my hips as he shoves me against him, kissing me ferociously.

The last thread of his control snaps.

In all the times we've been together since the first, it's never been like this. It's feral, animal, the need for each other almost violent. Almost like we know it could be the last time, with a war on the horizon. I cry out a "yes!" as he flings me against the living room wall, his magic healing me before I can feel any pain. The paintings in their frames rattle around us as he kisses me within an inch of my life, his hands roaming savagely over my chest, my waist, my hips, tearing at the fabric there.

This is what I need. I don't want gentle. I don't want sweet. I need him to let go and give me the full force of his power, knowing that he would never, ever hurt me. Knowing that I'm safe with him, that he will keep me safe.

I take one of his wild hands and grab it, pulling it to my mouth and holding it over it.

"Fuck," he says as he realizes what I'm doing. I want him to cover my mouth like Soren did in the alley.

He gives me what I want. He takes his starving kisses away from my covered mouth and moves them to my neck and then my breasts, ripping my shirt open with his other hand.

I moan against his hand as his lips lock around my nipple, sucking so hard it nearly hurts, and then he presses a bite into the sensitive flesh that makes me cry out.

He heals me again, the familiar light from his fingertips so welcome amidst all the new sensations. It feels so good, the pain and then the pleasure. It pulses in my core, soaking me as I grab him with my leg, hitching it around his and yanking him to me so hard he nearly hits his head on the wall behind me.

He grunts as I press against him. He lets go of my mouth and grabs my arms, pinning them over my head to the wall.

"*Yes*," I say as he shoves a hand down my pants, the other one still holding my arms in place. He wrenches a kiss from my mouth as he pushes a finger inside my folds.

"You're so fucking wet for me," he moans. "You said you couldn't be quiet. I want to hear you scream."

"Please, Ronan," I beg. "Fill me. Fill me, and I'll scream for you."

Ronan shudders at my words, and then he gives me what I asked for. He plunges two of his fingers into me with no resistance, my body so wet and desperate for him that I open to him immediately. He forces his fingers in and out of me wildly, the butt of his wrist against my clit, pressing hard. I tighten my leg around him and grind into him, demanding he take me deeper and harder.

Heat floods my core as he works within me, stroking my walls rhythmically, building me towards my release. "I want you to come on my hand," he says, his voice strained with desire. "I want you to come on my hand and my face and my tongue and my cock."

Just the mention of his cock undoes me. My climax shakes my body as I yell out his name, my core tightening so much that I nearly force him from me, but he pushes against me and keeps working inside me until my shaking subsides. I flop against the wall, barely able to stay upright, as he uses his legs and the hold he has on my arms to keep me in place.

"Not loud enough," he says. "Tell me what you want. What will make you scream?"

I know he can feel it because it reverberates between us. "I need more. I need you inside me. Take me like this, then turn me against the wall and take me from behind."

And fuck me, he does.

He lets go of my arms to undress himself. I help him yank the tunic over his head, then I fumble with the laces of his breeches until he rips them off. When I see his perfect cock fall out of his pants—rock hard, so red it's purple, glistening with his arousal—I can't stop myself from bending forward to take it into my mouth.

I swallow as much of him as I can, which isn't much because he's far bigger than my mouth can handle, but he doesn't seem to mind. "Fuck yes," he moans as he puts his hands in my hair, knotting them there, pulling me to him. "Fuck, you're so good at that."

I use my mouth and tongue and hands to please him, feeling his desire for it, slipping a hand down to stroke his balls, which makes him shudder and forces him to lean against the wall to stay upright.

It feels so good, both in my own feelings and in his, which are practically vibrating with ecstasy at my touch. It makes me feel powerful, primal, to hear the moans and gasps I pull from his lips through his cock. He's a God-King, and I'm a goddess on her knees, giving him what he needs.

"That's good, but that's not what I need," he says, pulling me up from him. He tastes himself on my mouth when he kisses me, feels the heat of himself on my lips.

It drives him wild with desire. He shoves my pants the rest of the way down and I step out of them, then he lifts me by the hips and lowers me until he's against my entrance, pushing me so my back is against the wall.

And then, finally, he slams into me all the way to the hilt.

"Fuck!" I scream, giving him what he wanted, my eyes rolling back as I feel the entire length of him take me. "Yes, Ronan! Fuck me like that. *Ruin* me."

He grabs my face and holds it still, looking me in the eye. "I could never ruin you. You are perfect."

Then he kisses me, claiming my mouth as he thrusts so hard and deep within my body, I think I might die from the pleasure.

I can't stop my climax from happening again with him slamming into me like that, with his feelings echoing infinitely in my mind. The waves build up within me quickly and then crash over and over, unrelenting.

He catches my head in his hand, holding my body against the wall, his cock still slamming inside me. He pushes his head to mine, our foreheads touching, the distance between our eyes too close to focus as he rams himself into me, a low groan in his throat. He watches me come and come for him, over and over without a break, until my vision is blurry and my legs can't hold themselves against him.

But he isn't finished yet. When I finally come down in shuddering gasps, he lowers me to the ground and turns me against the wall like I asked for. I press my hands and bare breasts against it as he shoves open my legs. "Is this what you wanted?" he asks.

"Yes," I breathe. I can barely speak, but I don't want him to stop. I need him to fill me, need to feel his release in me. He grabs my face and turns it to him, pulling me upright so my back is against his chest, kissing me as he enters me once more.

Gods, it's good from this angle. He's hitting a spot right on my inner walls that feels so good, I see stars behind my eyes. He lets out a guttural groan as I back my ass up into him, spreading open for him, inviting him even deeper.

"I want to feel you come again," he says. "I need it. Come with me." He squeezes a nipple with one hand as the other works my clit. He kisses my neck, all the while never stopping the relentless rhythm of his thrusting, which is growing more and more erratic the closer he gets.

It's so many sensations all at once, I can't handle it. I arch my back against him, tilting my head back to look at him, to kiss his lips, to see the hot, feral look on his face as he can't take it anymore, as he bucks wildly into me, finding his release.

His shuddering, gasping final thrusts send me over the edge one last time, and I tighten around him in explosive waves, my body so spent with pleasure that I collapse under him before I finish, forcing him to hold me to keep me upright.

He presses himself against me, still inside of me, stroking my neck and my hair, tilting my face to him to kiss gentle kisses on my lips. The power, the passion between us, melts into something softer, deeper. It fills my heart as well as my body.

"I love you," he says, his voice a caress. He turns me back to him and takes me into his arms, burying his face in my neck, wrapping his arms around me so tight I can barely breathe, his chest heaving from the exertion and the emotion and everything that we are and will be together.

"I love you, Ronan," I whisper into his shoulder, feeling his hands tighten and relax at my words. "I'm yours."

"I'm yours," he says, stroking my face, sending a healing touch through my body that fills me with warmth.

I let him hold me for a long time, until I feel the rhythm of his heart return to normal, until it matches mine, our hearts echoing their beats and their love for each other.

Then, reluctantly, we part, dressing once more and joining the guards where they're waiting in the hall to escort me to my chambers.

I hear Ronan's words in my mind as I prepare for Adria to join me. They give me the strength I need to give the performance of my life. I need her to believe that I'm just as angry as she is. I'll no longer be trying to convince her to give up on her plans. Instead, I need to keep her believing that I support them.

I'm pacing the area in front of the window when the door opens.

"This is fucking ridiculous," she shouts to poor Stella, who has apparently been tasked with being her escort. "*Credible threat.* There are credible threats every day! We've been persecuted for years. I won't be made a prisoner."

"The king assures me it's only a temporary measure—"

"It better damn well be. Go on then. Guard us. *Protect* us." Adria slams the door in Stella's face.

Then she turns to me. "What did you fucking do?"

"Me? They told me someone sent a letter threatening to kill us. How is that my fault?"

"A fucking letter. There's no way. You did something. Did you make him angry?" She moves to the end of the bed and gestures forcefully for me to join her. "Did you give him reason to suspect you? Where were you during the feast?"

"We delivered food to those shadow-born that were found with me," I say. It's one of those partial truths that fuels my magic, which is important right now. I can feel the impact all my truth-telling has had on it. I'm weaker now than I've been since we arrived. "No one saw us."

"Someone must have seen you."

"They didn't." I sigh. There would be no convincing her, even if I were being fully honest. "Don't worry. They won't keep us here for long."

"How do you know?"

"Because he won't stay away from me for long." I let that sink in for her. Let her remember what I'm sacrificing for her plan. What she thinks I'm sacrificing.

"Did you ever find the servants' passages? There's a meeting I can't miss."

I want to ask her with whom, but I know I can't without arousing her suspicions. "There isn't one directly into this room. The nearest is in the hall just outside. You'll need to get past the guards. I could distract them, or you could take them out, but then they'd know what you were doing."

"Fuck," she says, shaking her head.

"What about a note? One of the servants, maybe?" They know to intercept anything she tries to send. It should be safe to let her try.

She rubs her face, thinking. "Maybe. It seems reasonable that we would want to communicate with someone while we're locked up. We have our code, but if I could find a way to get it to Larus or someone where I wouldn't need to explain who it's meant for…"

Felix, maybe, although I didn't think he'd returned from the Islands yet. Perhaps there's someone else she's working with. And from the sounds of it, Larus knows. I need to encourage her to write the letter, but I won't do it immediately. The plan is to keep us here until they're able to find Larus and arrange the meeting with Felix, which could take a few days.

So I have a few days trapped in this room with her to convince her. A few days to build up her boredom and paranoia. A few days to let her believe her precious plan might get derailed once more.

And I plan to enjoy them.

The next day, I give a note to the guards to ask Ronan to check on me. Adria believes he's obsessed with me, so I need him to act the part, or she'll get suspicious. He arrives shortly after, and I greet him at the door, not inviting him in.

I pretend to pretend to enjoy his company, my lies layers deep, now that I'm lying for Adria's benefit alone. I let her think that I'm deceiving him, that I'm acting as if I want him, but I'm not.

Sleeping alone last night after the evening we spent together was terrible. I don't know how I can bear being apart from him for days.

I tell him that. I tell him because Adria thinks it's me looking for a way out of our confinement. And it is, but not for the reason that she thinks.

I spend the rest of the day thumbing through books he brought me, several more travel guides that we didn't have time to review the night at the library. I alternate my reading with poking at Adria, asking her questions about the state of things and how much this impacts them until she finally writes the damn note.

Dear Larus,

I won't be able to have dinner with you tonight. In case you haven't heard, I've been delayed. Please accept my apologies. I'll need to reschedule to the end of next week.

Yours,
Lady Adria of House Verran

It's not her best work.

But perhaps there is something useful in it. The only time she references is the end of next week. That's earlier than we'd been anticipating for the attack based on what she and Larus told me last.

Of course, she may not be referencing the actual date of the siege. It could truly be a meeting, as she said. But it's something to go on.

Stella, who is back on shift outside our door, agrees to have the note delivered to Larus, once they find him.

Which they haven't yet. That little piece of news concerns me. He didn't mention going away when I saw him last, and if he somehow caught wind of us being confined in the palace, it seems like he would come to us to try to secure our safety rather than flee.

Maybe he's meeting with whoever Adria was planning to meet.

Either way, I've done what I can. I spend the rest of the evening thinking about whether there's anything I can do to change her mind before they throw her in jail for sedition. Anything I could say to her without making her realize where my allegiance now lies.

But there's nothing. If I want to live, I need to keep my secret.

I wake the next day to movement on my bed.

"Make a sound, and I'll kill you," says Adria.

My muscles turn to ice as I realize she's hovering over me, a flame in her hand. She lowers it to my face until I can feel its heat.

"What are you doing?" I cry out. "What the fuck, Adria?"

"I *know* you did something. I don't know what, but I know you did it. You're going to tell me right now, or I'm burning this bed to the ground with you in it."

Fuck this. She's insane. I'm not doing this anymore. I'm getting the fuck out of here before she kills me. She can rot in the dungeons.

I lower the shadows and reach for the ones I can shape to throw her off of me. With my life threatened yet again, they should be easy to find, but I can't seem to grasp them.

"You've still got some fight in you at least," she says in the darkness. The shadow I drop over us is strong, strengthened by the lies of the last few days. It nearly extinguishes her flame. "Tell me what you did, and I'll let you live. As long as you didn't fuck up the plan, I'll let you live."

"I didn't do anything!" I shove her, trying to push her off of me, but she's stronger than me. She overpowers me, grabbing my wrist cruelly and twisting, hurting me.

"Tell. Me. What. You. Did." She lowers the flame to my cheek again until I smell the delicate hairs there burning, until I feel the heat licking my flesh.

"Stop! You're hurting me!"

"You told him something, didn't you? That's why we're in here. You betrayed us. You lied to us. Didn't you, Sylvie? You think I couldn't tell?"

"No," I whimper, lying to her. I can't fight her without my shadows. I try to force them out again, but they just won't come. *Fuck!* "I didn't. I *didn't*." I screw my face up, pretending to cry.

"Pathetic," she says. "You're pathetic. You're *nothing—*"

The door bursts open. "Get the fuck away from her," says Ronan, crossing the room in an instant. He throws Adria off of me as she tries to ignite him, sending a piercing flame into his shoulder.

The guards—five of them, including Taran—sweep in behind him, cornering her.

Ronan takes me from the bed, holding me to him. "Are you alright? I felt your pain." He touches my cheek, healing the burn there.

"Your shoulder," I tell him. His robes are smoldering where she pierced him.

He pats out the flame and winces as he heals himself. "That one went deep."

"But you're okay?" I ask, my voice shaking.

"I'm okay. I'm here."

"I knew it," says Adria, watching us. "You lying whore! I knew it."

"Sir?" asks Taran. "What should we do with her?"

Ronan sits me down on the ground beside the bed. Then he steps towards Adria, to the corner of the room near the window where the guards have her surrounded.

"I want to kill you for hurting her. For all of the other things you've done as well, but for hurting her most of all. I want to watch the light dim from your eyes. I want to hear you take your last gasping breath, knowing I'm the one that killed you."

"Do it," says Adria, defiant to the end. "Just fucking do it and stop wasting my time talking about it."

My heart leaps from across the room. I hate her, I hate everything she's done, I hate everything she's made me do, but underneath it all, I love her still.

She's my family. She's my blood.

I hate her, but I don't want her to die. I don't want him to kill her.

I can't look.

"But I won't," says Ronan, shocking us both. "Because *I'm not like you*. Because she's not like you. She's better than you. She still sees a chance for you, even now."

Adria laughs bitterly, shaking her head. "Then she's a fool."

"Maybe," says Ronan. "But she's my fool. And I'm hers."

He turns to the guards. "Take her to the dungeons."

Chapter Forty

With Adria under the watch of no less than twelve guards in the dungeons, I'm more terrified than ever.

"She has to have a backup plan. There's no way she'll let this fail," I tell Ronan when we're safely back in his chambers. "She's going to try to kill you. I don't know how she'll do it, but she's going to try. You can't go out there."

The Festival of Night is tonight, and I know the chances of convincing Ronan not to participate are nonexistent, but I have to try to get him to see reason.

"Listen to her," says Taran. They're the same words he used when we were trying to convince Ronan to leave the griffin alone. I can picture him saying the same words under similar circumstances fifty years from now, assuming any of us survive that long.

"You both know what I'm going to say. Let's just spare ourselves the argument, and you can both stay right next to me all night."

I look at Taran. He doesn't seem thrilled to have to stay with *me* all night, but he'll do it, for Ronan's sake.

"Fine," I say. "But *don't you dare* leave my sight."

"I promise," he says.

The pounding of the drums begins right at sunset. The rituals of Vahlo, the God of the Moon, Shadow, and Death, are steeped in violence, the drumbeats meant to echo the heartbeats of the slain. Animal sacrifices are made in hopes of appeasing the god and keeping him from coming for us early. Flaming effigies are cast down the river, emulating the River of Fire on which souls are transported to Vahlo's gates. The people gather on the bridges and the riverside, dancing and chanting, begging Vahlo to have mercy on them. To come for them late in life. To let them pass his judgment and be reborn.

My mother loved Vahlo's worship. She had a morbid curiosity about the darker things in life, something I'd never quite understood in spite of the shadow-born nature I shared with her. I had found comfort in the hidden spaces of the forest, the darkened coves where ancient secrets were kept. She preferred the pitch black of the crypt, the burial grounds near our Temple of Vahlo, places where most feared to tread. Where shadowy dealings could be done.

She would have loved this festival.

I, on the other hand, am ready for it to be over. By the time Ronan and I are escorted from his rooms, the court has gathered along a grand balcony overlooking the river. The mood is still somber, but as the beer and wine start flowing and the sacrifices begin, it will rise to a fever pitch.

I shudder at the thought.

I hate this, and not just because of the festival. I hate being exposed here with so many people around. So many people wearing the black robes of Vahlo, blending together, nearly all of them armed, and the rest of them dangerous.

All I can think of is Ronan. How to protect him. How to keep him safe.

"It's okay," he says, wrapping his arm around me, rubbing the tension from my shoulders. "It'll be over soon."

I let him keep his arm around me. I don't care who sees. I don't care what they say. Let them see who stands between them and Ronan. Let them know that he's protected.

When the bells ring midnight, the servants bring up a goat for the slaughter.

I don't want to be near the sacrifice. I know it's silly to be squeamish when I eat meat all the time, but I hate to hear the scream of the animal. I hate to watch its blood spill on the altar, to smell the burning of its flesh until only ash and bone remain for the ritual. It makes me sick.

Ronan lets go of my hand. He won't make the sacrifice himself—a priest will do that—but, as the God-King, he must bless it.

I can't back away from the altar. I can't leave him there alone, but I can't look either. The bells chime again. The beginning of the ritual.

I close my eyes and brace for the scream.

But it doesn't come.

"What's that?" someone yells.

"What's going on?"

Cries are coming from the distance. The cries of the animals, I think at first. There are a hundred altars like this one on the banks of the river, a hundred goats being slaughtered at once.

But there are more than one hundred cries in the air. And they aren't the cries of the goats.

They're the cries of the people.

"Fire!" someone shouts. The bells begin to chime in alarm, a continuous ringing.

Something is wrong.

I meet Ronan's eyes. It can't be. It's too soon.

But there's no other explanation.

It's the siege.

The crowd on the balcony is panicking. There's fire down on the water, but it's far bigger than any ritual altar.

It's a ship. A ferry. And it's burning down the river. Then another comes. And off to the east, there are more in the harbor.

Darkness falls around us, darker than the night.

The darkness of a shadow-born.

"Ronan!" I scream.

But I'm far from the only one screaming. There's a clash of steel down in the courtyard.

I can still see him, but I can't get to him. The balcony crowd is crushing blindly. It's surging to the palace doors, carrying me off my feet with it.

I can't breathe. I can't turn around to see the doors behind me. I make room with my shadows, which thankfully come to me, shoving just enough space around me to take a breath.

Ronan's light cuts through the shadow-born's darkness, stronger than it. Taran is beside him, thank the gods. "Sylvie!" he shouts. "Go inside. I'll find you!"

A door opens somewhere behind me, and the crowd rushes forward. I have no choice but to move with them or be trampled to the ground.

"Inside!" Cyrus yells. "Everyone inside!"

All that waits inside the palace hallways is more panic. There's shouting from the stairs, doors swinging open and slamming shut as the smell of smoke fills the air. It's happening all around us. Nowhere seems to be safe.

Someone in a black robe rushes to my side. "Sylvie," he says. It's Titus. I haven't seen much of him since we danced at the ball. "You need to come quickly. It's your Guardian. He told me to find you. Adria has escaped."

Ice fills my veins. "What?"

"They were fighting in the throne room. I tried to stop her, but she wouldn't listen to me. She's in there with a dozen guards. You have to stop her. I'm sorry. I told her not to do this, I told her there had to be another way…"

Larus. She has Larus.

"What did you do?" I remember Titus walking with Adria once. I remember thinking I should have warned him about her.

The backup plan.

"I helped her escape. She told me to, if something happened to her. She told me Ronan was trying to have her killed. But we ran into your Guardian, and he told me she did this. All of this. I didn't want any of this to happen. Please, you have to help me. Help us."

I can't leave Larus to her, but I can't leave Ronan either.

And Adria would know that.

She would count on it.

Titus is part of the plan. "I'm not going anywhere with you," I say, drawing my dagger.

Titus lunges forward. I strike out at him, but my dagger hits chainmail. He came in armor.

He grabs my wrist and squeezes it hard, forcing the dagger from it.

"She told me you might say that," he says as he grabs me, throwing me over his shoulders and carrying me kicking and screaming down the hall, towards the throne room.

Chapter Forty-One

My shadows won't come to me, even with Titus carrying me to my doom, and I suddenly realize why.

Ronan isn't here. Every time my shadows have taken form, Ronan has been nearby.

That has to mean something, but I don't have time to contemplate what. I have to find another way out of this situation.

And I have to stop Ronan from following me. If he follows me to Adria, she'll kill him.

I have to let him think I'm okay.

I let my body relax against Titus's back. I force my heart back down my throat. I breathe deeply, trying to think of anything other than everything that's happening right now.

I think of Ronan. I think of him in the library, recording all my dreams into a book. Making a list of them, making a promise to me to fulfill them.

"I didn't think you'd give up so easily," says Titus. "Adria said he'd poisoned your mind. You should have stayed with me that night. None of this had to happen."

I don't react. I don't hear his words. I'm with Ronan, on the back of the griffin. I'm with Ronan, leaning against him, my head on his shoulder. I'm with Ronan, feeling him kiss my hair when I say something cute.

I can't warn him not to come here. He'll never listen.

But maybe, if he thinks I'm safe, he'll stay in the fight outside.

Which terrifies me too, but his chances are better out there than with Adria.

Titus carries me into the throne room, and I do my best not to react to the smell of smoke and blood, to the bodies on the ground.

"What's wrong with her?" says Adria as he puts me down. I don't move from the spot on the dais where he drops me, taking my sword from my belt. I look at her, my sister, her blonde hair slicked back, her armor covered in blood and soot, and I feel nothing.

"I don't know. I didn't do anything to her. She just went like this."

"What are you doing? Why aren't you fighting?" She slaps my face, and it stings, but I don't react.

I'm with Ronan, in the bath as he washes me. I'm with Ronan, beside him in the theatre. I'm with Ronan, watching him from across the carriage, watching him smile when I catch him looking at me.

"I see what this is," says Adria. "You think he won't come for you if you're like this. Well, there's something we can do about that."

I don't react as Adria summons a flame in her hand.

"Tie her up," she says to Titus. She grabs my wrist, holding the flame near my face as he pulls a rope from a bag they have hidden near the throne.

I keep my mind as clear as I can as I lower my shadows. I can't make them take form, not now, not without Ronan, but I can make it harder for them.

Or so I thought.

"That won't work on me," says Titus.

He's shadow-born.

He walks over to me, seeing me perfectly in the darkness. I breathe deeply, trying to stop my pulse from racing. I can't let them tie me up, but I can't run either. And I can't fight them. I have no weapons. I have no shadows.

I let Titus bind my wrists. I can't see another option. The longer I can make it without reacting, the longer I can keep Ronan alive.

"I know you think I enjoy this, but I don't," says Adria. "I didn't want it to be this way. I wanted to believe you. I thought you had finally grown up. But I know what you've been doing. You thought I wouldn't find out?"

"What I've been doing?" I ask, my voice as bored and detached as I can make it. "What about what you've been doing? The grain shipments, Adria."

She laughs humorlessly. "Are you kidding me? You betrayed your family, you spat on the graves of our parents, over some fucking grain?"

I don't react. I keep my face straight and my voice steady. "You killed our people for your revenge. You let them die so you could have something you'll never deserve. You don't deserve the throne."

"And he does?"

"More than you. More than anyone."

"You're a child, Sylvie. He slaughtered us. He humiliated us. He robbed us of our home. And you got into his bed. You're nothing. You're worse than nothing. You're the shit stuck to my shoe. You always have been."

I let the words wash over me. I've known this is what she thinks of me for a long time. I don't need to react to her saying what I already know.

"Very well," she says. "I told you I didn't want to do this, but I will."

She presses the flame to my arm, just above where my hands are bound.

I scream.

I can't help it. It's agony, even just a small flame. It scorches my skin but doesn't ignite, doesn't tear a hole through me like she tore through Ronan.

And still, I can't suppress the pain.

"I'm sure that will work, but just in case…"

I scream as she does it again, pressing another flame just above the first.

Don't come, Ronan. Don't come here. Please.

But it's no good. I know he's coming. I try to find a way to use my feelings to let him know what he's facing. He knows Adria is here, but I picture Titus in the arena, Titus on the dance floor, Ronan's jealousy. I try to capture the feelings, to communicate them with him.

I picture the shadow-born. Marcella, fighting us by the warehouse. Nico and Vesper and the others in the cellar beneath the Alchemists' Guild.

I have no idea if he can feel it. *Please, Ronan.*

"Get by the door. He should be coming from that way."

Adria points to the door we came from. They're going to ambush him. She's not brave enough to face him.

I have to do something. My sword is just there on the ground. My arm aches terribly from the burns, and I can't get it now, but when Ronan arrives—

The door bursts open.

Ronan's light fills the room as he enters behind Quinn, with Stella trailing behind him.

"It's a trap! Shadow-born!" I shout as I reach for my shadows, which take form the second he arrives, pulling Titus away from them.

He throws something, and it shatters at their feet, spreading some kind of smoking liquid near them.

Stella charges forward, impaling Titus with her sword while I hold him with my shadows.

But then Adria's flame, a tiny candle of it no larger than an arrowhead, burns a hole through Stella's forehead. She goes limp and falls to the ground, dead instantly.

"No!" I shout.

Ronan fires off light at Adria as he collapses to the ground a few feet from where Stella has fallen.

Poison. Titus poisoned them.

Adria jumps behind the throne to avoid Ronan's light, wildly flinging fire in his direction.

She misses, but it ignites the fuming liquid behind him, causing it to explode. The explosion sends Quinn flying forward, her head smacking on stone.

I grab my sword with my shadows and free my hands, trying to avoid the terrible burn on my left arm. It screams in agony, but I have to ignore it if I want to live.

Then I run to them, run to Ronan and the others. I race down from the dais, my heart screaming so hard in my chest that I feel like I might collapse.

I come upon Quinn first. She's unmoving, a trickle of blood trailing down her forehead from the impact.

And behind her, just a few feet back.

Ronan.

He's there on the ground, unmoving.

I can't feel him. I can't feel anything. I'm going to vomit—

I bend down to him. I can't feel him, but his body is still warm. And it's moving, just a little.

He's still breathing.

"Get out of my way, Sylvie," says Adria. She's standing on the dais, standing in front of the throne that can never be hers. Will never be hers.

She points her sword at Ronan, and I stand in front of him, holding my sword out in front of me.

"You will not hurt him."

"Hurt him?" laughs Adria. "He's already dead. I'm going to put him out of his misery, something you never learned to do. I've always had to clean up after you. Always had to clean up your messes. You're useless. You've never been anything but useless."

"And you've never been anything but cruel," I say, holding my ground as she approaches. "You've never cared about anyone but yourself. I thought it was my fault. I spent my whole life thinking I'd done something wrong to make you hate me. But that's who you are. You're poison. Larus knew it. He believed me the second I told him."

She laughs again, but this time, she's delighted. "Is that what you think? That Larus helped you? Oh you poor, stupid little girl. Larus betrayed you, Sylvie. How do you think this happened?" She gestures around her to the chaos outside.

No. Larus couldn't have betrayed me. He's on my side. He's always been on my side.

"Larus came to me with some bullshit story about storms. I knew you'd gotten to him. I knew you'd fed him some of your lies—"

"They weren't lies—"

"—your pathetic little stories to make him hate me. Just like you've always done. He's sworn to me, Sylvie. Not you. To me, the Lady of House Verran. It took a bit of reminding, but he remembered his oath in the end."

"What did you do to him, Adria?" If she'd hurt him…

"I did what I always do. I did what needed to be done. He lied to you. We cut you out of the plans. I wanted to kill you, but he wouldn't let me. I needed those ships. I still need them. And so here we are. If I could prove to him that you were lost, he swore he'd let you go."

My heart sinks. I had just proven it with my actions to save Ronan. He's still not moving on the ground.

"Larus? Are you awake yet? Come out, Larus."

No.

From behind one of the great columns, Larus crawls out. He's nursing a wound to his head.

"What did you do, Adria?" he says, his voice small.

"I knew you wouldn't like some of what had to happen tonight, so I knocked you out. See, Sylvie? I do what I have to."

I want to go to him, to help him, but the second I leave Ronan, Adria will kill him.

"Larus," I beg him. "Larus, I'm here. It's Sylvie. I can help you. You know I'm right. You know this war is wrong. You know that thousands of people will die if we don't stop this. I'm not lost. I'm your Sylvie. The same Sylvie I've always been. I didn't turn my back on my family. They turned their back on me."

"Then come with us," he says as he gets on his knees and then his feet.

"What?" asks Adria.

"What?" I ask.

"Come with us now. There doesn't have to be any bloodshed between you."

"I can't," I say. "Innocent people are dying in the streets—"

"Larus, what the *fuck* are you doing? You *swore* to me that you'd support me if she turned her back on us—"

"I lied. Sylvie, I told you how I felt about the Orsa. How I felt about the war. And you haven't changed my mind about it. You've had your fun. It's time to come home. Adria, I'm not willing to stand by while you harm your own people in the name of vengeance. You got your war. Save your vengeance for the battlefield."

Larus didn't betray me. He betrayed us both, and he did it for our own sakes. He did it to keep us both alive. He did it to bring us home, something he couldn't do for our parents.

But I'm not going home. I have no home. No home except here, with Ronan.

Please wake up, Ronan.

"Larus, you've disappointed me for the last time," says Adria. She spins the flame in her hand.

"At least stand and fight me," says Larus, drawing his sword.

"No, I don't think I will," she says, and she throws the flame right between his eyes.

"No!" I scream. I reach out with my shadows. They're faster than her flame. They're as fast as light.

They don't put it out. But they do shield Larus's face just enough to let him dodge the worst of it. It catches on his long hair, but my shadow quickly snuffs it out.

"Look who finally learned to fight," says Adria, and she throws another flame at him, this time aimed at his chest.

I'm not ready for it. My shadows don't make it in time. Larus cries out as the fire cuts through him.

"Larus!"

He staggers over, clutching at where the flame tore through him. Did it get his heart? Did it get his lungs?

I don't have time to find out. Adria turns, and I plunge the entire dais into darkness before she can throw a flame at me.

Her flame is weak in my darkness, but it's enough to let her see. She launches her dagger at me instead, and I have to let the darkness go to give my shadows enough form to stop it.

I turn my shadows to her, to bind her, to stop her, to choke the life out of her if I have to, when she holds up her hand.

"Fine. You want to fight fair? Let's fight."

She extinguishes the flame and holds out her sword in front of her.

I take my guard.

Behind me, on the ground, a figure stirs.

I turn to face him as he rises to his knees, slowly, and then he pushes himself to his feet.

He lifts his sword in front of him and points it at Adria.

"You want a fight?" Ronan asks, his voice weak but unwavering. "Here it is."

Chapter Forty-Two

"**R**onan!"

I rush to his side. He's alive.

He's alive.

He's alive, and he's an idiot. There's no way he can fight her in this state. He's barely able to stand.

Adria laughs and laughs. I want to rip her tongue right out of her mouth. "How moronically noble. Sure. Let's go."

"Help them," I tell him. His eyes are still glazed from the poison. "You can heal them. Help Quinn. Help Stella. Help Larus. Let me fight for you."

"Your arm," he says, pressing his fingertips to it.

Sweet, wonderful relief. The throbbing ache of Adria's burn is gone in an instant.

At least whatever she poisoned him with didn't affect his magic.

"Quinn," he says weakly. I protect him from Adria's fire as he stumbles over to her. I don't think he'll be able to help her—he couldn't heal me from poison. And I don't think he can help Stella, judging by the way she fell. But at least he can try.

At least he can help Larus.

"A fair fight?" I ask Adria as I face her. I take my guard, my body turned to the side as it should be for this weapon.

This is my real blade. Its edges are deadly sharp. It's not made for sport. I'm not here to score the most points.

I'm here to kill.

Adria, the greatest sword fighter in Selara, the Champion of Sai, nods her head and raises her sword at me. "A fair fight."

I remember what Ronan told me. Fighting to the death is different from fighting for sport. In a fight for sport, you take chances. You make mistakes to learn how your opponent moves. You find their weaknesses through trial and error, hopefully before they find yours.

But in a fight to the death, there is no room for error. One wrong move means your death. You can't leave yourself unguarded, even for a second. You can't hesitate. You can't let an opportunity pass you by.

Most duels last mere seconds. Few go longer than two, maybe three, exchanges.

One of us will die today.

One of us will be dead, seconds from now.

I can't—I won't—let it be me.

Adria makes the first move, a quick lunge forward, testing my defenses.

Is that hesitation I see? Could it be that there's a part of her, somewhere deep down, that doesn't really want to do this?

"Say goodbye to your lover," she taunts. "It's your last chance."

Ronan has quietly moved away from Quinn to Larus. My heart aches for Quinn, but maybe there's hope for Larus. Maybe if he gets there in time…

Adria takes advantage of my distraction to strike. I parry her just in time, binding our blades. I push forward until I'm close enough to kick her. She grabs at my hair with her free hand, and both of us lose control of our points.

I fling myself out of her grasp, tearing a chunk of hair from the back of my head. She stumbles and then regains her balance in time to try another thrust at me, but she just grazes my arm.

The wound stings, but it's not deep enough for me to drop my sword. She's moving behind me now. I spin to face her, bringing my sword down. She blocks it with the basket of her hilt, but my point slashes her chest as she tries to jump out of the way.

I go in for another thrust, but she parries it hard to the side, sending me off balance. I parry her next cut from the ground, just stopping her sword from taking half of my arm with it.

I spring up and forward while she's recovering, putting distance between us and getting back on guard.

Then she feints to the left.

I see it coming. I know what's coming next. Her right thrust, quick and aimed at my heart.

I parry it with the strong part of my sword, finally avoiding her trap. There's a chance here. I can go for a riposte. One quick thrust into her neck, and she's dead.

I lunge forward—

"Enough!" yells Larus. It is enough. Enough to throw me off my balance. Enough to make Adria turn her head. Just enough for my thrust to miss the mark. "Adria, let's go. They're coming."

There are boots in the hallway beyond. The main doors burst open with a rush of magic.

I lower my sword as Larus runs over, healed by Ronan. He takes Adria by the arm, and with one last, regretful look in my direction, he runs with her into the antechamber as the guards close in.

We're running through the courtyard. Taran, Ronan, and I. Ronan is still weak, but he refuses to wait while his kingdom is falling around him.

Stella is gone. Stella, who never wanted to be a guard. Stella, who never failed to help me, to help Ronan. She's gone.

The healers are with Quinn. The best nature-born and the last of the loyal alchemists. Ronan healed her head wound, but she took the worst of the poison, and she still hasn't woken. I say a silent prayer to Vayla to save her as we run.

The streets are filled with blood and death and chaos. We move to the sound of fighting, the sound of steel, the smell of smoke. It takes us a moment to find our rhythm, to learn how to work together. How to help each other with blade and magic.

This isn't like the fight where Ronan, dressed as Soren, defeated Marcella's guards nearly single-handedly. As weak as he is, he fights like a normal man. He can take one, maybe two people at a time. He can't cut his way through a dozen in moments.

That's where Taran and I come in. Taran flings not water, but ice at our enemies. Sometimes, it stops them in their tracks. Other times, it cuts through them like a knife through butter. I've never seen a water-born fight like this. It's a terrifying thing.

I don't think about anything that has happened between us. I throw my shadows out to defend him when he needs it, just as he uses his ice to defend me. None of it matters now. We're a team.

The fights are quick and bloody. We take no time to ensure the defeated are fallen. I take no time to grieve for my fallen compatriots. Not even when I recognize them, as I do from time to time.

They made their choice.

And I have made mine.

It feels like hours, but it's over before dawn. The guards are in the streets with us. The fighting thins until we go minutes hearing nothing. This isn't the main battle. This is only a distraction from the real war that wages in the harbor. That marches in across the desert beyond the city walls, in companies of green soldiers my brother is leading.

This is a distraction that lets Adria escape. They pursue her, but she loses them. Larus shifts the earth to let them get away.

Larus chooses her. Larus saves her.

I can't think about it now.

I'm bleeding from where she cut me. I'm bleeding from a lucky stab with a dagger. Ronan heals me, and then I'm bleeding again moments later. My clothes are burnt. My leathers are destroyed.

I'm exhausted, physically and emotionally. I'm terrified of what's to come.

But I'm alive. And Ronan is alive.

Side by side, we take on the fight my family started.

Side by side, we'll finish it.

Chapter Forty-Three

We collapse into the gates just as the sun begins to rise.

The Festival of Night is over.

There will be no Festival of Day. The dawn itself is as much of a celebration as Faros will get. Vayla will have to take comfort in the fact that there's still a city for her dawn to touch.

The guards and healers help us in. Ronan is too spent to heal us any further, so we have to rely on the nature-born to do their work. The nature-born magic is slow. It relies on the body's own processes. Given the right guidance, it can heal without a trace, like Ronan's light can. But unlike his light, it's painful.

We make it back inside. The palace looks as though it's been sacked, although there was little fighting within its walls. The destruction of magic is near limitless. As wild as it looks, it could have been done by only a handful of people.

At least the walls are still standing.

People in black Vahlo robes limp through the halls. The elixirs have run out. So many of them were destroyed in the purge of the Guild. They weren't safe. They couldn't be trusted.

Quinn has been taken back to her chambers. She hasn't woken yet, although the healers have hope that the poison may yet wear off. They believe Titus failed to get enough poison into her to kill her, based on Ronan's recovery. They've managed to keep her breathing, to keep her heart beating with their magic.

They've given her a chance.

I tell her I'm sorry as I stand by her side. I'm sorry I failed her. I'm sorry I couldn't stop Adria. I'm sorry I let it happen at all.

I don't know if she understands or if she would forgive me even if she could, but I tell her anyway.

Ronan takes my hand and leads me back to his chambers. We fall into his bed without removing our clothes. We sink into each other's arms, and I sob against him. He strokes my back. He whispers to me that he loves me. He whispers that we're alive, that we're together. That we'll make it through this.

He holds me, giving me comfort I don't deserve, until my tears finally subside.

Then, we collapse into a dreamless sleep.

When I wake again, it's night. Ronan is beside me, still sleeping. I brush his ruined hair from his forehead. I kiss his soot-stained cheek.

He's alive. He's right. Nothing else matters.

We'll find a way to stop Adria. We'll find a way to stop Seth, and Felix, and even Larus if we have to.

We'll find a way to stop this war. *I* will stop it.

Even if it kills me. I will stop it.

I pull my aching body from the bed. I'm thirsty. I haven't had a sip of water since last night.

I creep through Ronan's chambers in the dark. There's no fire in the fireplace, but I don't need it to see.

I wrap my robe around me to keep out the chill. I open the door to his common room. There's usually a pitcher in here.

Silence. The room is still, untouched by last night's events. It will be full soon, packed with friends and family made soldiers and generals. The tiny markers on the map will move. They'll move across the board like a game, only every time a piece is captured and taken away, a thousand people will die. Five thousand. Ten.

I know this because I've seen it. I know this because I lived it, for five years, I lived it within the walls of Pyka.

And here it is again. This time, I will fight.

I will fight for the right side.

I find the pitcher near a shelf. As I lift it, I hear a soft clicking sound. The opening of a lock.

I spin around but see nothing. Was the pitcher sitting on something?

I bend over to look.

I feel the presence behind me, but I have no weapon. I reach out with my shadows, but I'm too late.

I smell something like sweet mint and spoiled wine.

And then, there's only darkness.

Epilogue

Ronan

When I wake, I feel her absence immediately.

She was just here with me, in my bed. And now I can't feel her anywhere at all.

I try not to panic, but I'm already screaming inside by the time I reach for the hidden button on the wall that calls the guards to me. I know she isn't in my chambers, but I check anyway. I check the living room, the washroom, the closet. I look under the damn bed in case she fell in the night and couldn't get back up.

Taran arrives when I'm checking the balconies. "Has anyone seen her?" I ask.

"Sylvie?"

I give Taran a deadly look. Now is not the moment to play dumb.

"No. Not since last night. We thought she was with you."

"She was. And now she isn't. I can't feel her. I can't feel her at all, not anywhere."

It's the night at the theatre all over again. Only I don't know how I'm going to get to her, even if I can find out where they've taken her.

Not with a war raging.

"Do you think—" Taran stops himself.

"Say it." I already know what he's thinking from his feelings.

"Do you think there's a chance she left on her own? That she waited until you fell asleep, and she left? Maybe she changed her mind. Maybe it was too much for her."

I know he's angry with her, and he's angry with me for forgiving her, so I'll forgive him this lapse. "Never speak of her that way again. Don't even think it, Taran."

"I'm sorry, sir." Taran looks at me as if I'm a crazed animal preparing to bite, and I might as well be with the way I'm feeling.

They took her. Her own people. They broke in here, and they took her from right underneath me somehow. They have her, and she's hurt, and she's unconscious.

I refuse to consider any alternatives. I can't let myself think of them. Not if I'm going to find her.

I march from the room, not bothering to dress in anything other than my robe.

"Are you coming with me?" I ask Taran. It's an actual question, not an order. I know how he feels about her.

"You can't mean to leave at the beginning of the war. The people need you."

"Fuck the people," I say, but I don't mean it. And then: "Of course I'm not leaving. Not for long."

He follows me from the room as I head to the stables. We pass the other guards on the way in, and I give them the instruction to scour the room and the grounds for signs of her as I get Kira ready.

I work with Marta, the stablemaster, to get her fed and into the straps. Kira's so patient. She's frightened after everything she heard last night, but she lets me comfort her, stroking her neck. I'm leading her out into the courtyard when Paul, one of my guards, returns.

"We found this," he says, giving me a ring made of silver.

Sylvie's ring. She must have dropped it for me when they were taking her. I don't see how it could have come off otherwise. "Where?" I ask.

"Near the western gate, sir. One of the passages out."

Damn, they'd found some of the secret ways in and out of the palace. But I'd stationed guards there since the fighting began. "Any casualties?"

"Two, sir. Lucia and Arun. Both dead. No one else saw anything."

Someone else saw something. Someone whose feelings are awakening, miles away to the west.

"She's alive," I say, my relief immense. "I feel her." I begin to climb onto Kira's back.

"Do you think that's wise?" asks Taran. "They know you'll come for her. They have their entire army behind them. They're not just going to let her go willingly."

"I never said I was wise. Are you coming, or not?"

Taran sighs as he climbs on in front of me, strapping himself in.

"Hold on, my love," I say as Kira flaps her wings and takes to the skies. "We're coming."

About the Author

Amy Yorke is an author of cozy and romantic fantasy and lover of all things magical. She is half English, half American, and she offers her sincere apology to readers of both languages for her idiosyncrasies in word choice. In her spare time, she enjoys gardening, playing video and tabletop games, and chasing after her cats.

Join her mailing list to receive news, updates, and promotions, including free advanced reader copies prior to new releases: https://www.amyyorke.com.